DON BERRY

considered himself a native Oregonian, despite the fact that he was born in Minnesota, with a lineage from Fox Indians. After attending Reed College, where his housemates included poet Gary Snyder, who shared his interest in Eastern metaphysics, Berry began a lifetime of pursuing his many passions: playing down-home blues and composing synthesizer music, sumi drawing and painting, sculpting in bronze, exploring theoretical mathematics, and writing for prize-winning films.

In addition to his three novels about the Oregon Territory (*Trask*, *Moontrap*, and *To Build a Ship*), published in the early 1960s, Berry wrote *A Majority of Scoundrels*, a history of the Rocky Mountain fur trade. An early Internet pioneer, he also created a remarkable body of literature that exists now only in cyberspace.

Married with three children, Don Berry died at age seventy in 2001.

Trask

DON BERRY

introduction by Jeff Baker

Oregon State University Press

Corvallis

Library of Congress Cataloging-in-Publication Data
Berry, Don.
 Trask / by Don Berry ; introduction by Jeff Baker.— 1st OSU
Press ed.
  p. cm.
 ISBN 0-87071-023-0 (alk. paper)
 1. Oregon—Fiction. I. Title.
 PS3552.E7463T73 2004
 813'.54—dc22

                          2003028120

Oregon State University
OSU Press

Oregon State University Press
121 The Valley Library
Corvallis OR 97331
541-737-3166 • fax 541-737-3170
www.osupress.oregonstate.edu

Introduction

Jeff Baker

A few years ago, I was standing on the bank of the Clackamas River with Robin Cody, author of *Ricochet River*, a novel set on the same river we were skipping rocks across. We were talking about other novels set in Oregon and how there are only a few really good ones.

H. L. Davis' *Honey in the Horn* is the only novel by an Oregonian to win the Pulitzer Prize, and that was in 1936. Bernard Malamud wrote *A New Life* in Corvallis and based it on a fictionalized Oregon State University, then moved to Vermont before the locals figured out they were being teased.

Cody said he thought the Great Oregon Novel was *Sometimes a Great Notion* by Ken Kesey. No doubt about it, Cody said—*Sometimes a Great Notion* is big, it's raw, it's stylistically inventive, it gets right what it's like to live in this rugged, beautiful land.

True enough, I said. I love that book, and I think it shows Kesey's brilliance way more than *One Flew Over the Cuckoo's Nest*. There's one novel that's better, though, one that has more to do with who we are as Oregonians and how we came so far in such a short time and lost so much along the way. It's *Trask* by Don Berry, and it changed my life when I read it as a teenager.

Cody's next rock whizzed suspiciously close to my ear. He liked *Trask* just fine but thought *Notion* was more ambitious and more successful on more levels. Kesey was aiming higher, he said, and he pulled it off. He wrote about a family, a town, an industry, a way of life. Nobody's come close to getting so much about Oregon into one book and doing it in such an intense, exciting way.

I still like *Trask* better, I said. We agreed to disagree and went back to skipping rocks over the green surface of the river. Three years later, Berry and Kesey were dead. They were Oregon's best fiction writers of the post-World War II generation and, despite obvious differences in temperament and style, had much in common. Both were born elsewhere but considered Oregon their home. Both did their best work before they were thirty in marathon sessions of intense creative concentration they were unable or unwilling to repeat in later years. Both turned away from writing novels in favor of other, more personal artistic pursuits that included living their lives as art, and both spent their last years experimenting with technology that didn't exist when they were ambitious young writers.

There's a statue of Kesey in downtown Eugene. His life is celebrated by his many friends and his novels have never been out of print. His influence on twentieth-century American culture is immense—as a link between the Beat Generation of the 1950s and the counterculture of the 1960s, as a proponent of drug use to expand consciousness, and as a rebel who took every opportunity to cheerfully challenge authority.

Berry's life and accomplishments are less well-known but no less interesting. He was a key figure—along with Gary Snyder, Philip Whalen, and Lew Welch—in the small group of writers who attended Reed College in the late 1940s. A self-taught researcher who never took a history class, he wrote an influential history of the Rocky Mountain fur trade called *A Majority of Scoundrels*. A musician, a painter and sculptor, a filmmaker, a poet, an essayist, and a spiritual seeker, toward the end of his life he put his restless energies into an amazing Web site (www.donberry.com) and became one of the first writers to fully explore the possibilities of the Internet.

His most important artistic achievement is the three novels (*Trask, Moontrap*, and *To Build a Ship*) published between 1960 and 1963 and written in a spasm of sustained creativity unequaled in Oregon literature. All three are set in the Oregon Territory in the decade before statehood and form a loose trilogy that tells the story of our state's origins better than any history book. They are set firmly on Oregon soil and mix historical figures such as Elbridge Trask, Joe Meek, John McLoughlin, and the Tillamook chief Kilchis with fictional characters. Berry believed fiction could tell larger truths as effectively as history and shared the opinion of Ben Thaler, the narrator of *To Build a Ship*, who thought "literal truth is not the important consideration ... history tells us only what we have already made our minds up to believe."

More than forty years after they were first published, Berry's novels speak for themselves and need no detailed explication. (It is interesting but not necessary, for example, to know that unlike Berry's childless Trask, the real Elbridge Trask—after whom the Trask River is named—and his wife Hannah had eight children before leaving the Clatsop Plains for Tillamook Bay.) A brief examination of who Berry was, how he wrote these remarkable books, and what he did with the rest of his life can provide a more complete context in which to appreciate a true Northwest treasure.

Berry was born January 23, 1932, in Redwood Falls, Minnesota. His parents were touring musicians; his father played the banjo and guitar, his mother was a singer. His father left the family when Berry was two and did not see his son again until Berry was eighteen, although they enjoyed a friendly relationship in later years. His mother moved frequently around the Midwest and Berry said he attended six schools in five states one year. Berry was small for his age and extremely intelligent, the kind of kid who had to get adults to check out books for him from the library. In grade school, he was given the nickname "China" for his interest in the far east.

By the time he was fifteen, Berry and his mother were living in Vanport, the city that was destroyed by a flood of the Columbia River in 1948. Berry took the newspaper notice of his death in the flood as an opportunity to leave home and disappear. He attended high school in Portland and was offered scholarships in mathematics by both Harvard and Reed.

In 1949, Berry was attending Reed, working in the bookstore and sleeping on top of a boiler he tended on campus. He was invited to live in a house on Southeast Lambert Street with several other students, including Snyder, already a serious student of Eastern philosophy and on the way to becoming one of the finest American poets of the twentieth century; Whalen, a Portland native who became a prominent Beat poet and later a Buddhist monk; and Welch, another poet whose *Ring of Bone: Collected Poems 1950-71* is one of the best books from the Beat era. The young men formed what they called the Adelaide Crapsey-Oswald Spengler Mutual Admiration Poetasters Society and drank wine, wrote poetry, and goofed off for the better part of two years.

"It was probably the birth canal for the Beat Generation," said Berry, who was more interested in painting than poetry at the time. "It was classic post-war Bohemianism, and also one of the richest experiences of my life. The quality of minds involved was extraordinary, and it was also hugely funny."

As a freshman, Berry was one of the editors of the Reed literary magazine. "I once rejected a poem as being too derivative of Lew Welch," he remembered. "Lew gave me hell later, because he had written it."

Berry, Snyder, and Whalen studied with the legendary calligrapher Lloyd Reynolds, an inspiration to generations of Reedies. Reynolds would tell his students, "You've got a million bad letters in your fist, and the only way to get rid of them is to write them down."

"Lloyd was one of the four great teachers of my life," Berry said. "Not necessarily in any specific detail, but in the sense that he was the first teacher who ignited me, as a candle is ignited from a flame already burning. He showed the most astonishing confidence in my ability. When I was a freshman, Lloyd had me deliver the lectures on Chinese art to his art history classes. Those were the only lectures they received on the subject, and Lloyd seemed content. At the time, it seemed perfectly reasonable to me … The clichés of a young artist. Lordy, lordy."

Berry left Reed in 1951 to earn a living. He had met his future wife by this time and was beginning to write science fiction, a genre that appealed to him because he could sell stories, learn to write, and let his imagination wander freely. His goal was to write a short story every week and he sold about a dozen between 1956 and 1958. But he wanted to write something different, a commercial novel set in the present day on the Oregon coast, and wanted, he said, "to include some folk stories, or Indian legends, or something to give some local depth and flavor."

Wyn Berry brought home a study by Reed historian Dorothy Johansen of coastal Indian cultures around 1850. Berry's reaction to it, as described in a 1997 email, deserves to be quoted at some length:

> This was not academic history, it was a complilation of
> very personal anecdotes and records of ordinary people—not
> "history-makers."

At one point Dorothy Jo was describing a trip made by Elbridge Trask from the northern coast down to Tillamook Bay (where he later settled) to scout out land. She commented that nobody ever could figure out why he made some particular decision.

Well, I knew why, because it was exactly the decision I would have made under the circumstances. And at that instant, I had a small epiphany about the nature of history. History was actually made by people. People like me, even. This had never occurred to me before, as I had no sense of history myself, and no particular interest in it.

That night I climbed up on the roof of the Red House and sat on the peak to watch the sunset over the fields and the Willamette River. I had demonstrated that I could write commercial magazine fiction. But I increasingly felt that if I wanted this career to last for twenty or thirty years I would have to write something that was deeper, that used more of me than commercial writing, or I would eventually become bored. I have always preferred doing things I don't know how to do.

Watching that sunset, I decided to change direction completely. I decided to write a serious novel of history, and Elbridge Trask's exploratory trip to Tillamook Bay would be the story, and Trask the main character. The next morning I drove down to the Oregon coast, and eventually found the Tillamook County Historical Museum.

The museum was a treasure trove for Berry, who said that the material he found there served as the basis for all three novels. He spent several weeks reading and copying everything in sight, then moved on to the Oregon Historical Society in Portland. He said he wrote *Trask* at the same time he was doing his research, "and by the time I had finished the research, I had also finished the novel."

Maybe so, but there is much that it is in the novel that can't be found in a museum. A bare-bones summary of the plot doesn't begin to do it justice: In 1848, Elbridge Trask, once a trapper and mountain man, has settled on the Clatsop Plains but feels restless. He decides to take a trip to Tillamook Bay and is accompanied by Wakila, a young Clatsop Indian, and Charley Kehwa, a *tamanawis* man or spiritual leader of the tribe, who acts as a guide. The party travels from present-day Gearhart south along the coast across Tillamook Head, Cape Falcon, and Neahkanie Mountain. After a shocking, unexpected tragedy, they reach the bay and are greeted by Kilchis, the chief of the Killamook tribe (Berry notes in *A Majority of Scoundrels* that Tillamook was usually spelled with a "k" sound until 1852). As a result of a power struggle within the tribe and to prove his worthiness, Trask volunteers to go on a vision quest called the Searching, a purification ritual involving fasting and prayer. He survives it, at great cost, and is free.

What is initially most striking about *Trask* is its clear, sure sense of place. Glen Love, professor emeritus of English at the University of Oregon and a great champion of Berry's work, wrote in a short study of his novels that "a regional work of literature may be defined as one in which landscape is character, perhaps the central character, so much so that a change in setting would completely alter and destroy the essential quality of the work."

By that standard, *Trask* is a regional work. With love and precision, Berry describes everything from Short Sands Beach ("the white lines of breakers were tiny as they marched slowly in, and along their humped green backs ran the quicksilver reflections of the sun") to a rainstorm in the Coast Range ("The rain came like whiplashes, driven out of the low clouds with a startling viciousness. It drummed and whacked against the waxy leaves of the salal with such force it seemed certain to tear them from their stems.")

Everyone in *Trask* is unsettled and unsure of where they fit. Trask has traveled the world as a sailor and a mountain man before settling on the Clatsop Plains but now is itching to strike out for somewhere new. Wakila has come of age in a tribe that has been decimated by smallpox and is now succumbing to gambling and alcohol. Charley Kehwa is a spiritual leader who has lived among whites and knows the inevitability of their push for land and power. He sees in Trask a rare white man who respects Indian culture and perhaps can prevent what happened to the Clatsop from happening to the Killamooks.

Trask's restlessness is much more than a mountain man's independence and love of freedom. In an unsure, inarticulate way, he is on a quest to find a deeper meaning to his life long before he goes on the Searching. He explicitly rejects Christianity and Western society but is unsettled by Charley's dreams and premonitions. He looks to nature and looks within himself in a way that reflects a traditional Eastern path toward enlightenment without ever explicitly stating it.

That this takes place in a novel set in the Oregon Territory in 1848, within the context of an adventure story about first contact between white settlers and Indians, is remarkable. It's as if Berry gutted a Louis L'Amour novel and replaced it with Somerset Maugham's *The Razor's Edge*. The Searching scenes are the soul of the novel and the final chapter (added, according to Wyn Berry, when the novel was in galleys) is stunningly powerful, a coda that gives fresh meaning to all that has come before.

"All his senses shared the same bright clarity; the intensity of any simple act of perception was almost unbearable," Berry writes. "The sheer brilliance of color was blinding; the sweet, clear tone of every sound came to him almost as a physical shock, making him catch his breath. The swinging glide of a gull came to have an almost-grasped significance that kept his mind hovering on the edge of joy."

Trask had a troubled publishing history. Berry said his first agent told him "there was no possible way he could submit such a book to publishers, and thought it better if we parted ways. Which we did." A different agent sold the book to Doubleday, where it was turned over to an editor who Berry thought "confused himself with an author." Unwilling to make the requested changes, Berry returned his advance and withdrew the book at Christmas of 1958. Viking Press eventually bought it and published it in 1960, to strong reviews. (The *Saturday Review* called it great. The *Northwest Review* said it was the best first novel by an Oregonian since *Honey in the Horn*.)

Berry already had moved on. *A Majority of Scoundrels: An Informal History of the Rocky Mountain Fur Company* was published in 1961. It is an amazing work, a combination of scholarship and narrative that proves true the cliché about history coming alive and shows why many of those closest to Berry considered him a genius. He did much of his research through microfilms from the Missouri Historical Society and was able to go where some of the finest western historians of the century—men such as Hiram M. Chittenden, Dale Morgan, and Bernard DeVoto—had gone before and break new ground.

Moontrap (1962) and *To Build a Ship* (1963) were mostly written while Berry was traveling, first in France and then around the world. He carried copies of some of the material he had found in the Tillamook museum with him, including a typed copy of pioneer Warren Vaughn's diary that is the backbone of *To Build a Ship*. Wyn Berry, who read and edited all of her husband's manuscripts, said there was something in what the pioneers did and thought that moved Berry.

"He identified with their values," she said. "He thought the kind of quiet, everyday heroism they had was undervalued in the present day, and he felt many of the agriculture people had sold their birthright. The mountain men, the guys who had to adjust to society—he loved them the most."

There are references to Elbridge Trask in both *Moontrap* and *To Build a Ship* and the books make sense when read in succession. There are plenty of discrepancies and departures from the historical record, all of them falling under the large umbrella of artistic license. Berry said 90 percent of *To Build a Ship* comes from Vaughn's diary but the novel is narrated by Thaler, not Vaughn, and has a sensibility that is wholly Berry's.

Like *Trask*, *Moontrap* has a lead character who is a mountain man struggling to find a place in settled society. In this case, the setting is Oregon City in 1850 and the character is Johnson Monday, a trapper who wants to make a home with his Indian wife but has "never really been willing to accept this new world he was living in. He had never committed himself fully, and now he had to pay for it."

Monday pays for his independence early and often, and so do others who live outside the boundaries drawn by the newcomers. Monday's old trapper friend, an unrepentant, uncivilized mountain man named Webster T. Webster, is the comic relief, the moral center, and the scene-stealer of *Moontrap*. Monday wrestles with his dilemmas; Webb curses at his and clings hard to the life he loves. Webb is Berry's most memorable character, one the author said jumped up during the novel's creation and demanded a larger role.

A brilliantly rendered centerpiece of the novel is the trial and hanging of a group of Cayuse Indians for the Whitman massacre six months earlier. The Indians who were hanged almost certainly were not directly involved in the massacre at the Walla Walla mission, a fact that didn't give pause to those who executed them.

After the hanging, Monday and Webb visit John McLoughlin. Berry's sketch of the eagle in his roost at Oregon City, retired from the Hudson's Bay Company and fighting futilely against the Americans who were biting the hand that had so generously fed them, is a poignant snapshot of McLoughlin's final years:

> "I heard there was some trouble about the land,"
> Monday said, embarrassed. The trouble was simply that the Americans, Thurston most prominently, were methodically stripping McLoughlin of all his holdings in the Oregon country, their only legal weapon a campaign of hate against the "damned Jesuitical rascal of a Hudson's Bay man."
> "Yes, yes, quite. But it has all been turned over to intermediaries for settlement now, and I am a bit hopeful. I am expecting them momentarily with the papers. But now—" McLoughlin suddenly swept his arms up in a great despairing gesture to heaven. "*Now*, Mr. Monday."

When civilization comes crashing down on Monday, it is Webb who takes frontier revenge for his friend and flees to Saddle Mountain, where he holds off the pursuing mob and builds a moontrap, a more explicitly Eastern practice than anything in *Trask*. Berry said that despite his immersion in Chinese literature and friendship with Snyder and Whalen, he did not study Zen Buddhism until a good ten years after he wrote his novels.

To Build a Ship is different in tone and style than the novels that preceded it. It is narrated in the first person, by someone who is not a skilled mountain man and not a fair-minded friend to the Indians.

History tells us that the kind of me-first moral relativism that consumes Thaler was more typical of the white settlers to the Oregon Territory than the open-minded, live-and-let-live attitude of Trask and Monday. Indians in Oregon were wiped out by disease, killed by settlers or local militia, and moved to reservations, in a very short time after first contact.

"The cumulative death rate for Oregon Indians is estimated by 1850 to have ranged between 50 and 90 percent in some originally heavily populated areas," notes the *Atlas of Oregon*. "… What disease began, warfare completed."

It is to Berry's credit that he wrote honestly and sympathetically about Indians during a time (the late 1950s and early 1960s) when attitudes toward them had not noticeably begun to change. Thaler, a rationalist who puts the construction of the ship above anything his conscience might be trying to tell him, is still sensitive enough to recognize that he "has never known a more intelligent man of any color" than Kilchis. When Kilchis asks Thaler why Trask did not come back and tells him Thaler must keep the peace in Tillamook Bay, he knows he is asking the impossible from someone not capable of giving it. The settlers came, and the Indians soon disappeared.

So did Berry. After four books in four years, a National Book Award nomination (for *Moontrap*) and a stack of great reviews, nothing. He wrote a children's book called *The Mountain Men* in 1966, but published no more novels for the rest of his life. Why?

When I made contact with Berry in 1997, via email, that was the first question I asked him. This is his reply:

> At different times I've been interested in different explorations. Some of these explorations involved writing (my primary medium), but many did not. Writing is not my "career." I have no idea what a "career" is. Basically, I have wandered the world physically and mentally, most of the time fascinated and astounded by what I discover, and sometimes putting that astonishment into words, or music, or film, or bronze, or design, or teaching, or philosophy.
>
> The trilogy of Oregon novels and historical works were all done before I was thirty. *Moontrap* and *To Build a Ship*

were written in France while I was travelling around the
world with a packsack, a guitar and a typewriter.

I am also hopelessly inept at the business side of art, and
don't have the patience to deal with it. I am not a dependable
source of a predictable product. The vast majority of my
life work—in all forms of art and thought—doesn't fit into
market categories. And I don't think a marketing committee
ought to determine whether what I write gets read or not.

Berry did not make much money from his novels. Wyn Berry
estimated he never made more than about a thousand dollars per
year from his writing, excluding movie options, and Berry guessed he
averaged about a hundred dollars per year in royalties for twenty years.
(There was some movie interest—Jack Nicholson briefly held the rights
to *Moontrap* just before he won the Oscar for *Cuckoo's Nest*.) Berry was
frustrated that he made money more easily from science fiction than
historical novels. At that time, he thought of himself more as a painter
than a writer, he wanted to travel and follow his interests wherever they
led, so why spend all that time writing novels?

"He never valued his own work very highly until much later in his
life," said Wyn Berry, who always was the primary supporter of the
family. "He didn't expect great things, but he was annoyed that he
wasn't making a living."

However, there was more writing that never got published. Wyn
Berry said her husband wrote a sequel to *Trask* that he burned because
he felt it didn't work as a story and put another finished novel called
Eye of the Bear "into the fire." Love writes that Berry destroyed these
books "because he realized he had not been changed by the experience
of writing [them]." Wyn Berry said he was "a very accurate critic, but
fierce in all ways."

Berry did have a regular job for a while, as a writer on the film unit
at KGW in Portland. There he met a gifted producer and director
named Laszlo Pal and began a collaboration that lasted more than
thirty years. Berry worked as a writer on many of Pal's award-winning
documentaries and on industrial and institutional films, which he
enjoyed because he could immerse himself in a subject and learn all

about it. Pal accepted Berry's wandering ways and Berry said that "if I disappear for five or six years, he accepts that, and when I return we can resume work together again as though no time has passed."

Berry wrote some commissioned books, such as *The Eddie Bauer Guide to Flyfishing* and *Understanding Your Finances*, and taught creative writing at the University of Washington and other colleges. He built a bronze foundry on Vashon Island for his sculpture and played in a band called Vashimba that performed the music of the Shona tribe of Zimbabwe. He spent several years living in a boat in Eagle Harbor, off Bainbridge Island.

And he discovered the World Wide Web. His Web site, Berryworks, contains a historical novel set in the goddess culture of Minoan Crete called "Sketches from the Palace at Knossos," eight different short stories, a children's book, some essays (including "On the Submissiveness of Women in Tango" and the beautiful "Snapshots of My Daughter, Turning"), twenty-one chapters about living on Eagle Harbor called "Magic Harbor," a large amount of poetry, art, and philosophy. Some of the writing is excellent and all of it is original and wholly Berry.

He was passionate about the possibilities of the Internet and a strong believer in it as a creative medium. "Long before I set up my studio in cyberspace, I had been exploring in a different literary form—a mosiac of individual pieces, rather than linear narrative," he said. "Each individual piece ... can be read separately, in any order. In Berryworks, you can move from any place to any other place, with a single hyperlink. Everything is available simultaneously."

Everything is available simultaneously, and for nothing.

"I am invariably asked why someone who has been nominated for the National Book Award would simply give their work away," he said. "But I have never been part of that world. It has always been my dream to write exactly what I want to write and give it away to anybody who wants it. Cyberspace makes that possible. And I didn't get paid for probably 90 percent of the other work I've done, so it's not all that different. Economically I'm marginal and always have been, even when the books were new."

Berry was cautious but curious when I contacted him in 1997. He wanted to have Berryworks reviewed as a whole, the way a book is reviewed, and wanted to do everything by email. Six months of electronic exchanges led to phone calls and finally a meeting in a coffee shop on Vashon Island. Berry suffered from chronic pulmonary obstructive disease, the result, he said, of "forty-five years of rolling cigarettes out of pipe tobacco." He needed oxygen for any exertion and carried a portable tank when he left his house. He spent up to ten hours every day on-line but did confess to a weakness for "Xena, the Warrior Princess."

Berry died in Seattle on February 20, 2001. At the end of his life, he knew he would be remembered for *Trask* and *Moontrap* and *To Build a Ship* and *A Majority of Scoundrels* and was pleased and proud that people still read them.

"When I wrote *Trask* I didn't even have any idea anyone would read it," he said. "As to the durability of these works, it is much like watching your children grow up. After twenty years or so you think 'good lord, how did that ever happen?'

"A writer can plan to make a book entertaining, or plan to make a book interesting, and many other things. But a writer cannot plan to make a book last. That is not in our hands."

Trask

For Pappy:

after the long journey finding what pleased him behind a
ring of mountains

Yam Hill District

Oregon   April 29 [1848]

This day Stormy again and does not look like it will ever Stop,
Mud almost to the Knees now. . . .

I hear today from a Clackamas Indian there is some "Dam Fool"
of a white man has got himself into trouble with the Killamooks
down at the coast, which have a prety hard reputation. And who shd
it turn out to be but my old Comrade Elbridge Trask that I free-
trapped with out of Fort Hall. Well I am not surprised any but hope
he does not get himself killd which wd be just like him. He was the
most restless man I ever knew. . . .

—From the later journals of Osbourne Russell, 1845–1857

Chapter One

It had been fair. The sky all day was endlessly wide, and so pale it was without color; a veil of almost-blue stretched taut between the earth and sun. Toward evening the first clouds appeared at sea, rising tentatively above the edge of the world as though appraising the land ahead. Soon the soft mass stretched across the line of sea and sky as far as a man could see in either direction.

The pale gold sun slipped down behind the clouds, silhouetting the tumbled forms against a sudden hot sky, pink and orange with angry red streamers. The edges of the great bank glowed for minutes, then slowly dimmed until all that remained were the giant shadows black and distinct on the sea, and moving toward the land.

Storm, thought Elbridge Trask, and the growing tension in the air pleased him.

He squatted on his heels on the first ridge of dunes and watched until the world at sea turned to shades of gray and black, broken only by the gentle white rollers coming up the long beach slope. Then he stood, stretching his arms wide against the sky, enjoying in the center of him this ending of the day. His body made a long angular shape as he yawned against the vastness of sea and sky and cloud.

He turned his back to the ocean and half slid, half walked down the inland slope of the ridge. As he descended into the first depression behind the dunes the steady rumble of the surf became a higher-pitched whisper, the deep tones smothered by the bulwark of land.

In the dusk the weather-stained skin of his face and hands was almost black; only slightly lighter than the jet darkness of his curly, close-trimmed beard. His eyes had a startling clarity in the half-darkness of his face, clear whites and pupils the gray of the sea in a storm.

He walked with long, quick strides across the valley toward the next dune ridge, half an hour away. His head moved slightly from side to side as he walked, with the habitual watchfulness of a mountain man;

a constant alertness of which he was not even aware, and which five years as a stable settler had not dulled.

It was dark when he reached home, and the warm light from lamps inside threw yellow shafts out into the night; which the night swallowed without disturbance. The moon was behind the eastern range of mountains now, not yet visible but lighting the sky behind the twisted peaks with a faint glow like the ocean's phosphorescence. It would be full tonight, thought Trask, and that ought to be worth seeing. If the storm at sea didn't come in too fast.

In some vague, internal way, two parts of him debated which would reach the center of the sky first, the great full moon or the storm. He had reached the point of betting with himself on it, when he laughed suddenly; at himself, and at all the foolish dialogues men have had with themselves since time began. He was still chuckling when he pushed open the cedar-plank door to his cabin.

Hannah was there, at the small loom, patiently weaving the yarn she had spun in the afternoon; trying almost hopelessly to satisfy the endless clothing-appetite of a husband who didn't have the good sense to stay out of the brush. She looked up when Trask came in, and smiled. The flickering light from the fire softened her face, smoothing the harsh sharpness of her chin and high cheekbones, casting an aura of softness around the straight severity of her pulled-back hair.

"What are you so happy about, Bridge?" she asked.

"Arguin' with myself out there," Trask said, tolerantly amused at his own foolishness. "Which gets first to the top of the sky; moon or storm."

"Storm coming in?"

"Yes, it comes," Trask said. "Rain tonight."

He folded his long body into a chair before the fire and watched the flames in silence. Hannah went back to her weaving, and the only sound in the cabin was the soft susurration of the shuttle and the crackling of the fire. After a while he took a pouch of tobacco from the mantel and filled his pipe. He contemplated it with pleasure before lighting it, because it was the single possession he was proud of. A Norwegian pipe, a meerschaum long since stained rich red-brown. It gave him pleasure to think of the different lands his pipe had seen before it came to his hands from the ill-tempered captain who owned it. Norway, where it was made, and England certainly, and all the coastal countries of South America, going around the Horn. And the last stop before Trask himself had gotten it had been Oahu, in the Sandwich Islands.

Many countries, many peoples all speaking different languages, many ports, and rivers and mountains of a different shape . . . There were things to see in the world, he thought, if a man could but get to them. The sailors manning the trading ships got to them, but it wasn't right somehow. Trask had tried that when the world first opened up for him; had gone to sea for two years from his birthplace in New England. But it wasn't right.

You dropped your anchor and—barring bad weather—were gone again in weeks. You never got to know anything beyond the trading ports, and only the surface of them. It was not enough to satisfy a man in his belly.

Trask sighed, and picked a coal from the fire with tongs; lit the pipe; and soon the cabin smelled of the harsh fragrance of his tobacco.

The only way you could know was to live in a land, and walk it, and plant it and harvest it and see it in storm and calm until you got the rhythm of it into your belly. And then you looked up and there were another five years gone: where? But it was better, he thought, than not knowing.

He stood and went to the door and stepped out. The moon had risen above the mountains and lost the reddish cast that made it seem the mirror image of the setting sun. It was rising high and fast, as if intentionally to beat the storm to the sky's peak.

"I believe the moon's going to win," Trask said, watching.

Hannah smiled at her loom. "You're as bad as Wakila and his all the time *mamook itlokum*." Wakila was the Clatsop youth who occasionally cut Trask's firewood. He used every earned cent gambling on the itlokum game, and usually lost; but cheerfully.

Trask laughed at the comparison. "No," he said thoughtfully after a moment. "Itlokum is gambling with men; this is gambling with gods."

"Well," Hannah said dryly, "best to get good odds, in that case."

Trask looked around sharply, but Hannah's face was turned away and he could not see her expression. She went about weaving impassively.

"All right," he said, "poke fun. Man can't even get a little poetic with some *cultus klootchman* have to bring him down."

He stepped outside the door. Even as the moon approached its zenith, the storm began to make itself felt in the air. The soft wind from the ocean brought an almost invisible mist and the smell of salt. The grasses of the Plains flattened themselves and pointed toward the mountains in the east, silver in the light of the moon. They whispered softly among themselves, and near the beach their trailing tips drew tiny tracks on the sand, like the marks of a forgotten language.

Soon there came from the ocean side the outriders of the storm; lean gray shapes spearing inland silently through the sky.

There was a restless tautness in Trask's chest as he watched them come like the spare hunting dogs of the storm, smelling out the land ahead. A wedge of mist sliced across the moon and turned black in silhouette. Suddenly the moon seemed smaller. Gradually, as more of the low-sliding shapes attacked, her light grew dim. The surf, always heard faintly over the seaward ridge, seemed quieter now, waiting.

Trask watched the combat joined between moon and storm, and the inevitable defeat of the peaceful moon, with excitement. He knew—and would not try to deceive himself otherwise—that the thing existed in his own mind alone. Sometimes it angered him to become entangled with the impersonal forces of the world in this way, in this imagined way, but it was not a thing he could control. He was a part of it and his participation in the moon and storm excited him; and he could feel the pulse of it in his neck.

And he wished to tell Hannah about it, but there were no words for it that he knew of; and it embarrassed him to try.

When the moon had become no more than a diffuse glow through the mist, he went back inside the cabin, relit his pipe and sat before the fire again.

"Well, we'll get the rain all right tonight," he said.

"You've got the fog in your beard," Hannah said, and watched the firelight sparkle from the tiny drops caught in the beard's curly darkness.

2

The main body of the storm broke against the Oregon coast shortly before midnight. The whispering of the wind in the grasses increased in pitch until it was a keening wail; and the sound lay flat and tense across Clatsop Plains. At the mouth of the Columbia the probing fingers of the wind lashed the water into white froth over the bar, flicking the tops of waves and casting white nets of mist toward the land.

Clatsop Plains lay at the northerly end of the storm, a coastal prairie stretching twenty miles south of the mouth of the river. It was made of three parallel ridges, as though the god Kahnie himself had taken three fingers and drawn grooves along the coast from just south of Astoria to the base of the mountain called Neahseu'su. Several miles inland from the whipping gray water of the Pacific, the coast range began abruptly; sweeping up and away from the Plains as the combers swept up from the surface of the sea.

A gray wall of rain stalked across the beach slope and slammed against the first ridge and moved down into the depression beyond. At the south end of the Plains the wind and water drove against the double-peaked massiveness of Neahseu'su and ran from the seaward face in heavy rivulets back into the breakers below. The sea churned and rolled at the base of the cliffs; withdrew; surged up and crashed against the rock again.

The top of the mountain was gone in cloud. The base, rising out of the sea, made its own white shroud in the destruction of waves. On the mountain's bulky body trees swayed back to make room for the wind; and deer wakened wet and frightened and snorted gently in the night. Does moved to windward of their fawns and lay back down again, eyes open and wary, and bucks lifted their muzzles into the wind and shook their antlers and pawed at the wet ground.

As the first rain splatted against the seaward side of his cabin Elbridge Trask wakened in the night and lay still. A glow from the dying fire still cast a redness on the beams above his head, and he watched this and listened to the rain around him. There was a faint sense of victory in him, that he was warm and dry; the notion of a minor skirmish won with an unnamed enemy, the contest gone unnoticed except by him. He smiled slightly in his satisfaction.

Hannah too had half wakened, and watched the face of her husband through almost closed eyes. It was not a handsome face, even in Hannah's eyes, and it had never occurred to her that it would be good to have a handsome husband. Elbridge Trask's face, like his body, had been scored and carved by so many forces in his thirty-three years that it was essentially without age, as human faces go. The great hawk nose had not changed in the six years of their marriage, nor the heavy ridge of eyebrows, nor the myriads of wrinkles around the clear gray eyes. The only thing that changed was his beard, and it was sometimes longer, sometimes shorter, depending on how long it took to talk him into letting her trim it. She saw no reason he should ever change at all; he was now as he had been and would be until he died. The gentle erosion of time would have no more effect on him than the rain had on the rocky face of Neahseu'su; it would take the earthquake of death to change him.

Elbridge Trask shifted slightly in bed, watching the beams glow red and listening to the cold, flat sound of the rain. He felt, as he shifted, the sudden hot length of his wife's body along his side, and he smiled again. That, too, was a part of his victory in the world. He closed his eyes and let the rain's tattoo drum him back to sleep again.

3

The storm had spent itself by morning and the day dawned clear. Trask wakened to the smell of bacon and coffee, and painfully forced himself to squeeze his eyes open. The sun was not yet over the skyline of the coast range, and the light in the cabin was gray and cool. It was not later than five o'clock. Hannah stood at the stove, turning bacon slowly in the pan.

Trask muttered something indistinguishable, cleared his throat and blinked sleepily.

"Morning," Hannah said, smiling.

Trask sat up in bed and tried to fight his way to wakefulness. "What're you doing up so early?" he asked.

"Thought you would maybe want some breakfast," Hannah said.

Trask nodded.

"You've been going out so early lately . . ."

"I just go down to the beach for a while," Trask said.

"That's what I thought."

Trask stood out of bed and stretched himself. He fumbled into his heavy muslin shirt and grabbed a pair of pants from the foot of the bed.

Hannah brought him coffee and he sat sipping it, watching the wisps of steam curl up from the cup.

"This is real coffee," he said finally.

"Yes."

"Where'd you get it?"

"Oh, places," Hannah said. "Had it hid from you."

"You got more than this?"

"None of your business," Hannah said firmly. "You let me run this house. You'll be back on barley coffee tomorrow."

Trask shrugged. Coffee this morning, barley tomorrow. If that's how it is, that's how it is.

"You get your bacon now," Hannah told him.

The two sat down at the table Trask had made when they first moved into the cabin. Made of the same material as the house itself, split cedar planks, the top was scarred and pitted from the years' hard use.

Trask finished his bacon and leaned back, savoring the flavor of the coffee. Hannah leaned forward across the table, her face serious.

"Bridge," she said quietly, "I want to talk to you."

"*Kwonesum mamook wawa*," Trask said. "Always talking." Hannah did not laugh, or fend off the comment, and Trask brought the front legs of the chair back to the floor, his face sobering. "All. right," he said.

"Bridge, what's troublin' you?"

"Nothing," he said. "There's nothing."

"There is," Hannah said.

"Not if I say not."

"Bridge, every day for the past week you've gone down to the beach at dawn and then again at sunset."

"Like to watch," Trask said.

"That's what you do when you got something in your mind, Bridge, don't you know that?"

Trask shook his head.

"Every time you get something in your head to do, you start going down to the beach like that."

Trask sniffed and turned the cup around in his hands, watching the faint tendrils of steam. "Maybe so," he admitted finally. Hannah leaned back in her chair. "What is it, Bridge?"

Absently the man tucked the ends of his beard under his chin.

After a moment he said, "I don't know, Hannah."

"You sure? Or just don't want to tell me?"

He shook his head. "I don't know," he repeated. "Something. Something about—the land, maybe. I don't know."

"It's good land here."

"Not for wheat. You can't grow wheat in this soil."

"About the only thing. Everything else grows."

"Wheat's important," Trask insisted. "We got to pay too much for flour."

Hannah did not answer, and after a moment Trask raised his head to meet her eyes.

"Hannah," he said, "you're making me argue something I'm not ready to argue. Suppose it isn't the wheat. You're making me make up reasons where I don't have any reasons yet. I got to think this out more."

"All right, Bridge. But you tell me, will you? When you know?"

"If I can, Hannah. There's lots of things I can't say . . ." He lowered his eyes to his cup again.

Hannah leaned forward across the table and put her hand on his arm. "You don't have to tell me anything about why, Bridge. You know that. All I want is for you to tell me what you want me to do, all right?"

Trask nodded slowly.

"Because I can't do the right thing if I don't know what you want, Bridge." Hannah stood suddenly and busied herself at the stove. "You see Wakila, you better get him to come up and cut us some more wood," she said.

"All right." Trask stood and drained the last of the coffee, throwing his head back to let the still warm liquid trail down his throat. He wiped his mouth and mustache on the back of his sleeve, with the oddly precise gesture of a bearded man, and put the cup back on the table.

He turned at the door and said, "I should be back around noon."

"All right. You aren't working today."

"No."

Hannah nodded. "All right."

"I'm going to the beach for a while. Then I'm going over and talk to Solomon, maybe."

Hannah looked up in surprise, then nodded slowly. "That might be a good idea, Bridge."

"It might." He closed the door behind him and set off in the direction of the steady murmur of the breakers on the beach.

4

In this spring of 1848 the twenty-mile stretch of Clatsop Plains held over forty families. Trask had seen most of them come. He had been among the first to settle on the fertile prairie, in the fall of 1843.

Almost five years, he thought. Henry Hunt and Tom Owens and Tibbets and me, we were about the first.

Solomon had been there first, of course. But somehow Solomon was different. You couldn't imagine that Clatsop Plains had ever been without Solomon Smith and Celiast; they were like a core, a symbol of the meeting of white and Indian.

Trask had seen a lot of mixed marriages in his time; trapping out of Fort Hall—sometimes wintering in the mountains—he had been tempted more than once by the easy availability of a squaw to keep his fire and make his meals and warm his body at night with her own. Most of them you could have for a pint of whisky that was half water; and they'd spread their legs for less than that. The "marriages" dissolved as fluidly as they were made. Sometimes they ended in passion—as they were made—and then there was anger, and trouble with the tribes. He admitted to himself his temptation had not been particularly great; for he learned soon enough the available squaws were the tramps of the tribe, and he had a strangely fastidious bent for a mountain man. Drunks and whores and witless profiteers stealing scraps and living on tidbits snatched from under white noses. And these were all the hungry trappers ever got to see, at least by the time he got to the mountains. It was not, after all, so very different from the white way. Except that most of the men he'd run with would have been shocked at the idea of marrying with a white woman of the same level. Somehow the difference in skin seemed to make it all right. For some.

Solomon and Celiast, now—that was different. Celiast was the daughter of the Clatsop *tyee*, Coboway. In the Clatsop tribe she was a strong and respected figure, and her marriage to Solomon Smith had not diminished that respect. It was a new relation to Trask, one he had not seen before; the meeting of the races on a basis of respect and equality. He flushed as he recalled his first assumptions concerning the marriage, before he had gotten to know Celiast for what she was.

Trask shook his head ruefully. It was bad when a man made assumptions. It had always been bad for him, anyway. The assumptions he made, as far as he could remember, had invariably been wrong. Not just some of the time; but always. One of those things; it was the way he was. He had always to look at things carefully and with his head clear, or he did it wrong. There was no reason for it that he could see, it was a difference of people. Some were quick and instinctive—Hannah was like that—and others had to work things out and reason them through carefully and that was how he was. It was all right, as long as you knew it.

From where he sat on the dunes, Trask could see two of the cabins on the Plains. Several miles south of him, beyond Little Beach and the mouth of Neahcoxie creek, was the great headland Neahseu'su, humped like a buffalo at the edge of the sea. The ocean was still turbulent from the night's storm; the only trace of it that remained, other than the still wet dune grass flattened by the wind. The sound of the surf was steady and loud in his ears. It would be several days before it quieted, and he would be reminded of the storm's fury each time he heard it.

He looked back at the fertile Plains, with its squares of cultivation and fenced pasturage for the dairy cattle.

It's good land, he thought. It seemed good to me five years ago. What's wrong?

Land, land, good land. And yet that had been the thing that came to his mind when talking to Hannah. He had not been able to think it out before, but he had told Hannah the trouble in him was about the land, something about it. Why was that?

Something about the land that was not satisfying him, something that made him uneasy. Yet all the settlers expected a great growth of population in the Plains. Look at the resources, they said. Look at the timber in the hills, look at the size of those potatoes. Look at transportation, right on the artery of the whole Northwest, the Columbia. Look at this, look at that.

He had looked at it all, and something still seemed wrong. There was something deceptive in the reasoning, and he was not good enough with words to draw it out.

The coasters stopped at Astoria, it was true. And there was no doubt Astoria would grow, but . . . The real growth was inland, it always had been. In the Willamette Valley, the rich valley. Oregon City, a hundred miles from the mouth of the Columbia. He had the strange conviction it would make little difference to anyone but the Plainers if the coasters simply quit docking at the mouth and went straight up to Oregon City. There were even a half-dozen houses at Portland, now. "Little Stumptown" they called it in Oregon City; still, there were those who thought it would grow.

He could not make sense of his own feelings. He had a sureness about it, but when he tried to explain the idea that Clatsop Plains was somehow blocked, he could not put it in the right words to make sense. There was always somebody with arguments that sounded so much more reasonable.

And it would have made little difference, since he was not particularly interested in arguing about it, if it weren't for his own uneasiness. And arguments or no, he could not deny that he was troubled. That made it something that had to be worked out, just to settle his own mind.

Well, he would have a talk with Solomon and Celiast. When he talked to them, he didn't always have to make everything make sense. Those things he could not say accurately, they could guess, and understand what he was thinking. Hannah could do that, but she was too closely bound up in his own life; it was her life, too. He needed a new view, a clear view.

He stood up on the dunes and walked down to the beach, turned south and followed the long sweeping curve around the small bay that formed the mouth of the Neahcoxie.

Chapter Two

The white settlers had given the name Neahcoxie to the sluggish stream that wound languidly across Clatsop Plains to the sea. The name was taken from the Clatsop village of Neahcoxie, located near the mouth of the stream; it had never occurred to the Clatsops themselves to name moving water. It was like air; everywhere, and in every place the same. There was no need to distinguish between the parts of it in different places. All was chuck, though the universal Jargon made a grudging distinction in favor of the Pacific Ocean by calling it salt chuck.

Six Clatsop villages were strung down the Plains, from Konape in the north to Necotat, almost in the shadow of Neahseu'su. The village of Neahcoxie was several miles north of the headland and it was near this village that Solomon Smith had first built his cabin. In time he had replaced his own relatively crude log hut with an Indian cedar-plank house, as most of the sensible settlers eventually did. The Clatsops still retained some of their age-old carpentry skills, though with the coming of the white settlers the craft was rapidly dying.

Trask's path took him through Neahcoxie, and he saw the village was already preparing for the summer run of salmon. Several new canoes were in the first stages of construction; cedar logs being hollowed with mallet and chisel. They were netting canoes; not as impressive as the great ocean-going craft of the past, but still beautiful. The Clatsops no longer went to sea.

Many of the workmen Trask knew, and they greeted him as he passed, stopping now and then to inspect a canoe out of courtesy.

"Klahowya, Tlask!"

"Klahowya." Trask stopped and appraised a long dugout, making a show of meticulous inspection, running his finger along the inside rim. The workmen stopped; stood back to give him space to examine the work. They watched him seriously as he moved along the length of the log, which as yet was only begun.

Trask stepped back a few paces and regarded the log, pulling absently at his nose. Then he turned to the carpenter in charge the building and nodded slowly.

"*Hyas kloshe canim,*" he said emphatically. "Very good canoe.

The Clatsop grinned broadly and nodded his head eagerly, his eyes shining with pleasure. "*Ahha, ahha, hyas kloshe canim!*"

Trask moved down the village, watching the people work. Women, young and old, sat tying seines of wild flax in front of their houses. Those he knew gave him klahowya, and also many he had only seen at a distance. All the village seemed to recognize the tall, bony man with the eagle's nose.

Just away from the village, three men worked hollowing out half a dozen smaller canoes. These were only seven feet or so in length, and made of logs of much smaller diameter. The men worked quickly, and without the usual bantering humor that accompanied Clatsop efforts. Their faces were morose, unpleasant to see.

Trask stopped, startled.

Then he moved on again, but in that moment the feeling of pleasant camaraderie he had had in the main village disappeared. The contrast depressed him, the main village happily preparing for the summer run of salmon, busied with the things of life; and behind, just out of sight, men busied with the things of death. The burial canoes.

What had startled him was the number of the death canoes. So many, so many . . . And the death rate increasing all the time. Births could not keep pace, and the numbers of each village slowly dwindled, year after year, in a relentless slide toward extinction.

Trask shook his head. The "Boston sick" was taking more and more each year, even years when there was nothing that could be called an epidemic. And there seemed to be nothing either Indian or white could do about it.

He was gloomy by the time he reached Solomon's house; and tried to pull himself out of it before entering. There was no need to depress Solomon; he had watched the relentless thinning of the villages with the same—or a greater—frustration and anguish.

One of Solomon's slaves, the old man, met Trask outside the door. He had been captured and enslaved by different tribes so many times in his long life he had forgotten his original band. All the coastal tribes were slavers, and the Chinook—of which the Clatsops were one band—had once been middlemen in the trade for the whole coast; go-betweens for the vigorous northern raiders, the Nootka and Makah and even Tlingit, and the tribes of the interior who wished to buy. But the white man had put a stop to that; though not through any moral influence. The white-carried epidemic of ten years past had wiped out nine-tenths of the Chinook.

The old man gave him klahowya, wrinkling his eyes and showing toothless gums. He swung the door open for the white man to enter. The inside was dark and cool.

"Hello, Bridge," Solomon said, extending his hand.

"How are you, Solomon." Trask paused for a moment, letting his eyes become accustomed to the darkness inside the house.

"A good storm last night," Solomon said. "Have a smoke."

"Thanks."

Solomon Smith was a little shorter than Trask, a little heavier. His face had the same dark permanence as the other man's, but was not as heavily creased and lined by wind and sun. His eyes were dark brown, almost black, and he was clean-shaven, his chin as bare as any Indian's.

Trask lit his pipe and leaned back in the chair Solomon indicated. For the first few moments neither man spoke. Sat quietly pulling on the pipes, exhaling clouds of blue smoke that gathered around the beams above them, savoring the pleasure of tobacco.

Trask tried to marshal his thoughts in logical fashion, but they were too tenuous. He was almost surprised to hear himself say, "Solomon, what do you know about Murderer's Harbor?"

Solomon leaned forward, interested. "Not much," he admitted. "I was through there once. Celiast could probably tell you more."

"Mm." Trask puffed thoughtfully.

"Thinking of going down there?"

"Hadn't thought much about it, to tell you the truth. Just popped out of my head."

"That's the Killamook country."

"I know," Trask said.

Solomon was silent for a moment. Then he stood, crossed to the door, and called the old slave. "*Mika klatawa klap Celiast*," he said. The old man nodded quickly and started off at an awkward lope.

Solomon returned and sat down. "Celiast could tell you more," he repeated. "Old Man'll get her."

Trask nodded. "Thanks. What's she up to?"

"Berrypicking. Her and the two women."

"What's left?"

"Not much. A few late strawberries is all. They just went out for the walk mostly. We don't really need three slaves around here anyway, but Celiast has to have 'em for the sake of appearances."

Trask was slightly surprised. "Celiast worried about appearances?"

"Well—" Solomon was apologetic, a little embarrassed. "It wouldn't be too good if the people got the notion Coboway's daughter was chako Boston."

"No, I guess not," Trask agreed. If the tyee's daughter became too Americanized, the Clatsops would suffer for it. It occurred to Trask that Solomon and Celiast had to face this kind of problem every day; had to think carefully what effect each action of their own would have on the tribe. "No, that wouldn't be too good."

"Matter of fact," Solomon said, returning to the previous subject, "I had a Killamook slave a while back, but I gave her to Coboway. She was from right around in there, Murderer's Harbor."

"How serious is this thing between the Clatsops and Killamooks?" Trask asked.

Solomon shrugged. "How serious is anything? Depends on the individuals involved. They skirmish sometimes. It just depends."

"You have any trouble while you were going through?"

"No." Solomon shook his head. "But—you know I walk pretty soft in a situation like that."

Trask nodded.

The old man poked his head in the door and piped, "Celiast, *yaka chako*." He giggled toothlessly in the general direction of Trask, then disappeared.

Celiast came in a few seconds later, carrying a woven cedar-bark basket half full of strawberries. Outside, Trask could hear the faint voices of the two slave women arguing about something. Celiast walked quickly across the room, motioning Trask to keep his seat.

"Klahowya, Bridge. Good to see you here."

She was a woman in her middle forties—older than her husband by five years—but she carried herself like a girl. Her eyes were clear and large, her features fine. There was an almost Oriental cast to her face, as was true of most of the coastal peoples. Her forehead sloped sharply back from her brow, showing the effect of the weighted boards with which a high-born child's head was shaped. Trask, while not finding the head-flattening of the Clatsops particularly beautiful, did not find it offensive, either. She had a finely shaped body, except for the legs, which were too short; but this was true of most canoe Indians. Trask found he had gradually accepted a different standard of appearance and now found the sloping forehead and short legs normal.

"Charley Kehwa said you might be coming," Celiast continued.

"Charley? How would he know?" Trask asked.

Solomon laughed. "I didn't tell Bridge he was expected."

"Charley's a *tamanawis* man, Bridge," Celiast explained.

"Well—sure, I know, but—"

"You don't believe the tamanawis," Solomon finished for him.

"Do you, Solomon?" Trask asked. "You believe the things Charley and the others claim they can do?"

"I've been around the people quite a while," Solomon said, his eyes amused.

"Is that an answer?"

"It might be."

Trask shook his head mutely.

"Well," Celiast said, "it isn't important whether you do or not. What's on your mind, Bridge?"

"Not much," Trask said, wishing to make the thing that troubled him as inconsequential as possible. "I was asking Solomon what he knew about the country around Murderer's Harbor. He said you could probably tell me more."

"Well—" Celiast hesitated. "You know the Killamooks haven't ever had any whites on their land, not settlers. It's hard to say what they'd think about it."

"Who said anything about settling?"

"Charley Kehwa said you had it in your mind to go some place," Celiast said.

"Charley knows more about my mind than I do, then," Trask said sharply.

"He might at that," Solomon said, and laughed. "Don't get mad, Bridge. Charley doesn't mean you any harm."

"All right, I know it," Trask said sheepishly. "Sorry."

"It was just a dream he had about you, anyway," Celiast said, sorry to see their guest made uncomfortable.

"All right," Trask said. "But about the Killamooks—what do they say about the murder?"

"One that gave the harbor its name?"

"Yes."

Celiast shrugged. "Not much different from the white version. They say that in their fathers' time a big boat came across the bar and the crew came ashore. They traded, and everything went fine. One of the crew had stuck a big knife up in the sand. A Killamook picked it up, and the crewman attacked him, thinking he was trying to steal it. Maybe he was. The Killamooks killed the sailor and drove the rest of the crew back aboard the ship. Then it sailed away."

Trask nodded. "Pretty much the way I heard it."

"That was Gray's ship," Solomon said. "I read the log, when I was teaching school for McLoughlin at Vancouver."

"But they will trade peaceably," Trask said.

"As long as they aren't offended, or don't get angry."

"Sounds reasonable."

"Maybe," Solomon said. "They get offended pretty easy."

"One other thing you ought to take into account," Celiast said. "There's talk that their tyee isn't very strong on having whites around."

"Who's tyee there?" Trask said.

"Name of Kilchis," Solomon said. "Something of a legend, even up here. They say he's strong as three men and shrewd as ten. He rules the band jointly with a man called Illga. Illga, far as I can make out, is the lineal chief, whatever that may mean. Kilchis came from nowhere."

"He's the one you'd have to deal with, though," said Celiast. "The stories are pretty fantastic."

"Like what?"

Celiast shook her head. "They don't bear repeating. He sounds like Kahnie himself."

"Mm."

"He may be a nigger," Solomon said.

"He *what?*"

Solomon shrugged. "That's the story. I don't know, myself."

"Well," Trask said, after a pause, "I guess I'll have to go down and see for myself."

"That would be the thing, if you really want to know," Solomon said.

"Bridge," Celiast said, "it isn't any of our business, but—where's your quarrel with Clatsop Plains?"

"No quarrel," said Trask dubiously. He frowned. "I don't know. Sometimes I think I get an idea of what's wrong, but when I try to put it into words it goes away. I don't know."

"Try it."

Briefly, Trask tried to phrase his feeling that Clatsop Plains was blocked; that in spite of the present appearances, there was an end ahead, and not too far in the future. When he had finished, Solomon nodded thoughtfully. He tapped out his pipe in the fireplace, and remained there, leaning back against the mantel, when he finally spoke.

"Much of what you say is true, Bridge," Solomon said quietly, "The Plains may die out after all. Economically we haven't anything in back of us. Just the mountains. But—I'll say something I haven't any right to say, if you'll let me."

"Go ahead."

"I think what's bothering you isn't in the Plains at all. I think it's in your own belly. I think the other thing is just a kind of excuse, to tell you the truth."

"What do you mean?"

"I don't really know. Just a notion." Solomon shrugged, then grinned at Trask, whose face was impassive. "More in Charley Kehwa's line than mine."

Trask considered it. "I don't know," he said at last. "You may be right. I'd hate to think it. I never had much use for a drifter."

"There's other men that move besides drifters, Bridge."

"Like who?"

Solomon studied the other man's face with his eyes half closed, leaning back against the mantel. He cleared his throat. "Well, I don't know. I'm not one of them. Maybe that's something else you have to find out for yourself."

Trask shook his head impatiently, as if to say there were more immediate and tangible worries.

"How is the trail down there, Solomon?"

Solomon laughed. "It doesn't exist."

"Bad, is it?"

"Worse than that." Solomon leaned forward seriously. "I tell you true, Bridge, parts of it are impossible. Neahkahnie is the worst. Once you're over the mountain, it's better. Couple of rivers a good-sized bay to cross, but you can get Killamooks to ferry you over, or make a raft. It's Neahkahnie that'll kill you."

"Maybe a canoe . . ." Trask said.

Solomon shook his head. "Not a chance, Bridge. The Clatsops haven't gone to sea since the epidemic. I hear the Killamooks still do, but—not us. Just the rivers and bays."

Trask frowned, pulled at his beaked nose thoughtfully.

"Also," Celiast added quietly, "the people are afraid of it. No one lives on Neahkahnie. No one lives for several miles on either side. They say it isn't only Neah-Kahnie—the place of Kahnie—but the mountain itself is Kahnie's body turned to stone."

"Do you believe that, Celiast?"

"I'm telling you what the people say. I'm telling you you'll have trouble with that mountain."

"You crossed it, Solomon."

"I crossed it."

"And you had trouble."

"It damn near killed us all," Solomon said flatly. "Bridge, there are places you have to cross on that mountain where the trail is no wider than a man's two hands. Tilted like a roof, sliding shale—and if you slip it's five hundred damn feet straight down into sea."

Trask was silent for a long while. Finally he said, "Can I get guide?"

Solomon sighed. "I'll ask around the tribe. They won't like it. On top of everything else, Neahkahnie is more or less the official line between us and the Killamooks. Soon as a Clatsop is over the mountain, he's in trouble."

"Thought you said there were just occasional skirmishes."

"You get dead enough in a skirmish."

"What makes you so cheerful?" Trask said.

"Natural high spirits," Solomon said. "But I mean it about the mountain, Bridge. It's hard."

"It's just a damn mountain," Trask said impatiently.

Celiast smiled gently, glanced at her husband. "But it is Neah-kahnie, Bridge," she said finally.

2

Trask trudged slowly along the beach in the bright morning sun, swinging around the curve of the bay. The tide was out now, and the sun high. Within the half-moon inlet was a sea of low fog, high as a man's knees, with tendrils that reached upward gropingly and dissipated in the sun's heat. Trask found himself listening carefully to the squeak of sand beneath his boots; as though the shrill voice of the beach could tell him something he needed to know.

When he went to Solomon, he had not known what he wanted to talk about. The question about Murderer's Harbor had come to his lips almost without volition. It was an uneasy sensation. He must have been thinking about it and not known the contents of his own mind.

"God damn it," he said aloud.

In the unexplored reaches of his own thinking, Trask found himself as witless and confused as any *cheechako* in the mountains. Too many things, thoughts and ideas as many as trees, and as confusing. To pick out the important things required a trained eye, as it took the eye of a mountain man to pick out the faint trail signs of game. An eye like Charley Kehwa's? Maybe. Maybe that was what he wanted, a tamanawis man to tell him what he was thinking.

Trask snorted. You worry too much, he told himself. God damn Charley Kehwa anyway.

Celiast's parting words had been no more comforting than the conversation about Neahkahnie.

"Bridge," she had said hesitantly, "one other thing. It won't make any difference to you, but I think you ought to know."

"What?"

"Charley dreamed about death."

Trask cleared his throat. "Mine?"

"He didn't know. It was in the same dream."

"Charley isn't always right."

"No, he isn't. Tamanawis men have ordinary dreams, too."

Trask neither believed nor disbelieved in the tamanawis power. And further, he did not want to be forced into a position regarding it, and that was what all this talk seemed to be leading toward.

Some of it he knew to be ridiculous. He had watched Charley and others examining sick people, listened to the diagnosis. Bugs, always bugs inside. Bugs or worms or something. And the more potent the tamanawis man the more exactly he could tell you what kind of bugs, and where.

"Spider in the liver, small spider, black spider, this long." The tamanawis man would measure an exact and careful length for the spider and the watchers would be silent, impressed by his exactitude.

"Orange spots on the back. *Hyas tenas* spots, very small."

Surely the tamanawis man must be *hyas skookum* to be able to see orange spots that small on such a tiny spider!

And what to Trask was the most uncomfortable treatment of all; when the tamanawis man fasted and went into a trance, lying beside the patient. "Following the Spirit," they called it, and the tamanawis man's spirit chased the patient's into the netherworld and brought it back again.

Foolishness. But it had always made Trask acutely uneasy, and even a little frightened.

"Hell with it," he muttered, kicking a spurt of sand out in front of him. "I got other things to worry about than Charley Kehwa."

He turned right through a low depression in the dune ridge and began to walk inland toward his cabin.

Chapter Three

Hannah expressed no surprise when he told her. Her sole comment was a dry, "Awful name, Murderer's Harbor."

"We'll change it," Trask assured her.

"What's Solomon think about the notion?"

Trask shrugged. "Hard to tell, with him. Why?"

"Solomon knows more than a lot of people, that's all."

"He's only been through there once."

"Think he can get you a good guide?" Hannah asked.

"Said he'd try. I didn't see Wakila about the wood."

"He came by a little after you left. He still had a two-bits he wanted to spend before he went to work again."

Trask took his Norwegian pipe from the mantelpiece and stuffed it with tobacco. He sat down at the table and blew a long plume of blue smoke that flattened out on the scarred cedar like the mist he'd seen rising from the wet tidelands. Hannah, without his asking, brought him a steaming cup.

"Barley coffee," Trask said.

"I told you."

Trask nodded. He took a sip of the coffee, and put it down quickly. "Hot," he said. Then he frowned; shook his head slightly in a puzzled way. "Why's he have to spend every cent before he'll go to work?"

"Who, Wakila? He thinks it's sinful. He told me all about it one time, very serious. Said it was very, very bad for a man to work when he already had money. Said if everybody did that, pretty soon there wouldn't be any more money, because it would all be paid out in wages."

"That doesn't make any sense," Trask objected.

"What's wrong with it?" Hannah asked seriously. "I think he's right."

"Money isn't like that," Trask began patiently; then suddenly broke off. "You're pokin' at me again," he objected.

Hannah laughed at him; a happy laugh, full of affection. "You need pokin' now and again, Bridge. You take everything so serious."

Trask pulled mournfully at his nose. "I suppose," he admitted grudgingly. "Anyhow, Wakila's wrong about the money."

"I'll tell him," Hannah said. "He'll be disappointed."

"Woman, will you quit pullin' at my leg!"

"As God's my judge, Bridge, you're so stubborn and serious it's more temptation than a saint could stand!"

Trask grumbled something and jammed the bit of his pipe between his teeth. He stared defiantly at the fireplace opposite, and the pipe bowl glowed furiously as he puffed. After a few moments he took the bit gingerly from his mouth and looked at it with an expression of resignation. "Now you made me smoke so hard my pipe's too hot," he complained mournfully.

"Oh, Lord," Hannah whispered, looking up at the ceiling. "Another day in the Trask house." She sighed loudly.

Trask put his pipe back in its carved rack, secretly pleased. Hannah's poking satisfied something deep in him; gave him the sense of having said something to her he could not ordinarily say. Satisfied him, and he knew there had been a closeness, and he knew it was now over. Finished, a complete thing between them, so tangible he might almost put it up on the mantel next to his pipe. A real thing.

There was a long silence in the house. Hannah took a piece of soft, dressed buckskin from a shelf in the back and spread it out on the plank floor. She surveyed it critically, trying to guess whether she could get a whole shirt from the one skin. Without looking up, she said, "Bridge, you thinking about settling that country down there?"

"Haven't seen it yet."

Hannah lifted the skin and held it up to the light. "If it was good, would you?"

"I haven't seen it yet," Trask repeated.

"I was just wondering," Hannah said. She put the skin back on the floor and knelt over it. "This is a good skin you got."

"He was a good big buck, that one," Trask said complacently. "Anyhow, it takes more than thinking about it to settle someplace like that. Takes work. Takes money."

"Yes." Hannah began to mark the skin around a stiff paper pattern she kept for Trask's shirts.

"Could do the work, all right," the man mused softly. "Money's something else again."

"There's some money in Clatsop Plains," Hannah said.

"Man'd have to buy provision for the first year at least, till he could get a crop, maybe take some cattle."

"Yes. And tools. What about the Indians?"

"Killamooks down there. I don't know."

"Supposed to be pretty wild, those Killamooks."

Trask shrugged, rubbed the back of his neck. "Maybe. Not like up here, anyway, with whites around off and on for forty years."

"Hand me my scissors, Bridge," Hannah said. "Killamooks trade with white ships, don't they?"

"Some," Trask admitted. "Not as much as the Clatsops. They keep pretty much to themselves. You making me a shirt?"

"Yes. Well, suppose you liked the land and you didn't have any trouble with the Killamooks."

"That's supposing quite a bit."

"All right, suppose anyway. What then?"

Trask shook his head and looked down at the table. "I don't know, Hannah. Have to see about money, I guess. Money and men. I don't believe a man would be smart to try to open up rough country like that by himself."

Hannah nodded. "Solomon has some money," she said after a moment. She laid the sleeve pattern down on the buckskin and began to trace around it. "You got the longest arms this side of one of those African monkeys."

"I got a notion Solomon has his own plans for what money he has," Trask said thoughtfully.

"Might talk to him about it anyway," Hannah said.

"Maybe." Trask nodded, thinking about it.

"Only other money I can think of at the moment is in Loveman Anders' pocket," Hannah said.

Trask grimaced ruefully. "That's a fact," he said. "But I sure do hate to think about that."

"Well," Hannah said, "depends on how bad you want the money, I guess."

"Haven't even seen the country yet, and already worryin' about borrowing money from Anders." Trask shook his head. "Man's imagination sure can run away with him if he don't watch it."

Hannah laughed and Trask looked up sharply. "What're you laughin' at now?"

"I don't know," she said. "Just you."

"Now what's so funny about me?" he demanded, not understanding. But she wouldn't tell him. She almost never did.

2

The sun came up and away from the eastern mountains and floated into the pale blue sky. As it rose the tide began to ebb, as though the sea itself retreated from the advancing eastern heat. The storm-gray water curled back upon itself, and by noon the sand ran several hundred yards from the dunes to first water. A flight of sandpipers whirred low across the beach, coming from somewhere behind the dunes. They swept over the ridge like leaves in a gust of wind, making the air flutter with the sound of their coming. In unison they wheeled just short of the water itself; landed; and became a scattered group of individuals walking stilt-legged by the small pools. Like puppets worked by an idiot, their heads jerked this way and that, up and down as they inspected the sand at their feet with the awful, quick intensity of hunger. Now and again one would pause, watching its own reflection in a pool with a cocked eye, hoping vacantly it would turn out to be good to eat after all. It never did, and the bird pattered jerkily along to a much more likely spot a few feet away.

Far out, barely within sight of the land, two whales cruised slowly south, ponderously intent on some huge business of their own. Sometimes as many as six of the living islands could be seen from the Clatsop dunes, spouting and sounding, and at those times the Indians had great and feverish concourse with one god and another. Kahnie was courteously invoked; gently chided; reminded he had not beached a whale for a good long while now. Talipas the Coyote was highly praised for his shrewdness and ingenuity, and the suggestion advanced that he might demonstrate these admirable qualities by beaching a whale for the great good of the Clatsop people.

Even the night-roving demon Tsiatko was occasionally invoked—though Tsiatko had little or nothing to do with whales—on the theory that it did no harm and might possibly do some good. If none of the white preachers were around, the Saghalie Tyee and His son Jesus would be asked to bear a hand. Jehovah's earthly representatives, however, seemed to resent the notion that He would do anything so practically helpful as beaching a whale, and the Clatsops were too courteous to request it in their presence. (The Saghalie Tyee, it seemed to the Clatsops, was a very busy god indeed, but they accepted gracefully the fact that He could spare them only Sunday mornings, preferably at Loveman Anders' Presbyterian services. When there were whales to be beached, He was always elsewhere, doubtless busied with affairs of greater importance . . .)

The light wind flicked its tail at the land and sea, switching and fluttering across dunes and rollers alike. The salt sea-tang misted inland and mingled with the smell of sweet lupin and the wild strawberries on the dunes; from the foothills came the coolness of the needle-smells; fir and cedar, tentative as a virgin's wish.

The tidelands of Neahcoxie bay dried out in the sun, leaving flat and glittering pools staring blankly upwards; the earth's own pale blue eyes. At the south end of the flat, Neahseu'su's bulk humped up, as massively indifferent to the sun as it had been to the storm.

From the village of Necotat across the tidelands, came a small figure, moving unsteadily north. In one hand was a bottle, occasionally held out as a counterweight for balance, more often tilted up. Wakila walked with careful precision on this morning, for the tidelands—usually so flat and stable—were shifty and unreliable. More than once the plane of the earth tilted up as abruptly as the bottle, and slammed him heavily on his side. He found that if he lay quietly for a moment, and thought carefully about it, and consulted the bottle with respect, the ground would steady after a while, and he could make another hundred feet or so. For certain he knew he did not want to be there, lying betrayed on his back, when the tide returned.

"*Alta chuck klatawa*," he reasoned, "*pe alki chuck chako.*" He nodded emphatically and blinked. The water was gone now, but it would come back.

He peered to seaward, and could see the white line of breakers. He waved the bottle and shouted. "*Hya, hya! Killapi, killapi!*" The sand sprang up and hit him beside the face, and he laughed. Could hit him all it wanted, but he knew the sea would obey his command in the end, and turn around. His voice sounded tiny beneath the endless sky.

He made it to his feet again, and trudged on. In time he reached the northern end of the Neahcoxie inlet, and sat down to rest.

It was necessary to get some money, for he had none. All he had was the bottle, and he knew with a wisdom beyond his years that the bottle was not going to last forever. It was necessary to have some money.

It had been a good morning for Wakila; he had changed games. He had been unable to find anyone to play itlokum for his last two-bitser, but he had raised a lahal game in Necotat. Lahal was simpler anyway, he thought. And sometimes it was a good thing to have a simple game; when you were a little blurry was a good time for a simple game. Lahal was played with ten sticks, one of which was marked. The game was simply to guess which hand held the marked stick; the Man. Old game, too. Older than itlokum, even. Old ways were best, Wakila thought, tilting the bottle and letting the watered *wiskey* run down his throat.

He stood up and started around the beach. He wanted to get to Trask's house, to cut some wood. He was taking the long way; it would have been faster to take the inland route, but he was afraid of meeting Anders or Gray or one of the other Jesus-men. Anders made seal-eyes at him behind his little spectacles; made "tchik-tchik" at him with his tongue.

Wakila spat on the sand. One man give you wiskey, another one take it away from you. You couldn't trust the Boston men. King Chautsh men either, he thought, remembering the English traders from Hudson's Bay Company. Except Trask. You could trust Trask all right.

It wasn't even the loss of the wiskey so much, but Anders always made so much talk at him. Wakila nodded again. *Mamook hiyu wawa*, Anders. Much, much talk. And all the time with the little round seal-eyes blinking behind the glass.

"How old are you, boy? *Kunsih cole?*"

"*Tahtlum pe taghum.*"

"Sixteen . . . dear me, dear me. Tchik-tchik." Seal-eyes.

"Won't you come to services next Sunday . . ."

Wakila spat again on the sand.

Then he laughed, as he saw he had dropped to his knees, and the spittle dribbled on his jeans. He got to his feet again. He had better get to Trask's soon. He knew he wouldn't be able to cut wood right away, but Han-ha, *klootchman* Trask, always gave him the hot coffee and let him sleep a little first.

He started inland across the first ridge of dunes, floundering in the sand, heading toward the faint plume of smoke that marked Trask's cabin.

3

Trask looked down at the huddled figure that lay on his doorstep. With the toe of his boot he rolled the heap over, saw Wakila's almost cherubic face, slack and pale. Without expression he grabbed the boy under the armpits and dragged him into the house, and plunked him into a chair.

Over his shoulder he called to Hannah, "Wakila's here."

Hannah came in from the back, where she had been working on the new shirt in the sunlight. "So I see," she said.

"Was he drunk when he came by?" Trask asked.

"No. He's gotten it since. Must've won at *itlokum*." Hannah hung the coffee pot on the fireplace hook, swung the hook in and stirred up the coals.

"*Halo itlokum*," Wakila muttered vaguely. "*Halo itlokum. Mamook lahal alta.*" His eyes remained closed.

"Changed games," Hannah commented.

"Wake up," Trask said. He began to slap the boy's face in a steady rhythm, back and forth, back and forth. The head swung loosely on his neck, following the impact of Trask's hand. After a moment Wakila's eyes opened slowly, one at a time. Painfully he focused, and a ghost of a smile flickered across his mouth.

"*Klahowy*a, Tlask. *Ticky wiskey.*" The smile faded and the eyes shut again.

"Wake up, siwash." Trask started to slap him again.

"Leave him alone for a while," Hannah said. "Coffee."

Trask stood straight again, and shrugged, still looking down at the boy. "He can't cut wood like that, sure as hell."

"He'll be all right after while," Hannah said. "We don't need but a little kindling right away."

"He been coming drunk like this?"

"Most all the time, lately," Hannah said.

Trask grunted, and sat in the chair opposite Wakila. After a moment he said, "He's going to have to give up one of the two, drinking or gambling. He can't make enough money to do both."

"Unless he wins pretty regular."

"Does he?"

"Not that I know of. Nobody wins regular at anything, that I know of." Hannah swung the coffee pot out of the fireplace and poured two cups of the hot barley brew.

"This barley won't wake him up," Trask said.

"I been saving the real coffee for treats," Hannah protested.

"Well—"

"You want to use your real coffee to wake up Mr. Siwash?"

Trask looked at her. "He's got a name, Hannah," he said quietly.

Hannah looked at the floor, caught suddenly in a rare embarrassment. "Sorry," she said, almost inaudibly. Then she raised her head again and met Trask's eyes squarely. "What about the coffee?" she said calmly.

Trask's glance moved from the unconscious Wakila to the coffee pot to Hannah. Finally he shook his head. "No, I guess not. Make sure the barley's hot, though."

"It is." Hannah hesitated. "Bridge," she said, "what I said, calling him Mr. Siwash—"

"Forget it, Hannah."

"All right." After a moment Hannah said softly, "It's funny, though. When I see Wakila like that, I think of him as just another Mr. Indian."

Trask nodded slowly. "Pour me a cup, too," he said. "Thing is, who made the wiskey, Mr. Siwash or Mr. Boston?"

"Who has to drink it all the time?"

"Why the hell does it have to be like this?" There was an unaccustomed edge to Trask's voice.

"I don't know, Bridge. I really don't know." Hannah shook her head.

Trask leaned forward and slapped Wakila's face again, harder this time, and almost in anger. "Come on, wake up. Wake-up, wake-up, wake-up." Whack-whack-whack-whack-whack . . .

4

Wakila finally roused enough to be helped up the ladder into the sleeping loft, and was put to bed, assuring them solemnly that just as soon as he could stand again, he would work hard as any three men cutting wood.

"You lay off that wiskey or you can't work at all," Trask said.

"*Skookum! Hyas skookum!*" Wakila said. "Very strong."

"Not with a whisky-head you aren't," Trask told him. "You sleep it off."

As Trask started back down the ladder, Wakila's voice came again, in a different tone. The white man turned, his head just above the loft floor, and saw the boy raised on one elbow. His eyes had a strange, dull pleading, confused by the liquor. "*Halo cultus siwash,*" he said plaintively. "Tlask? *Halo cultus siwash* . . ." The voice was more that of a sleepy and frightened eight-year-old than of a young man.

"No," Trask said, when he could find words. "No, Wakila."

The boy lay back down, staring at the rafters above him. "*Halo cultus siwash,*" he repeated softly to himself.

Trask went down into the main room, shaken. Seeing the bleakness on his face, Hannah asked, "What's wrong, Bridge?"

He shook his head. The Chinook—*cultus siwash*—meant literally "worthless Indian," but the actual meaning went beyond translation. It was the final word, and one seldom used . . .

"He wanted to tell me he was no *cultus siwash,*" Trask said bitterly. "He wanted to tell me that."

"I—I don't think I ever heard an Indian use that," Hannah said.

"No." Trask rubbed his close-cropped beard with his knuckles. "No, I don't think so. I wonder if these damn churchmen been at him again."

The thought was broken off by the clack of the latch as someone outside tugged the lanyard. Solomon Smith came in, a half-smile on his face. He stopped just inside to adjust to the lesser light. It was well past noon, now, and the afternoon sun was bright.

"Hello, Solomon," Hannah said.

"Hannah." Solomon inclined his head. To Trask he said, "Trouble, Bridge? You look angry."

Trask grunted. "No. Nothing. Wakila's *pahtlum* again." He jerked a thumb at the planks above without looking up. "He's up there sleeping it off."

"Oh?" Solomon said casually. "You paying him in wiskey these days?"

Trask just scowled at him and pushed the fireplace hook with the coffee pot back over the coals.

"Sorry," Solomon said. "It's getting so I'm suspicious of everybody. No offense, but a lot of people don't know what they're doing."

"I do," Trask said.

"Sorry," Solomon repeated. He sat down at the central table and looked up at the loft where Wakila slept. "That boy is getting to be a problem," he said. "The people are beginning to worry about him."

"He's beginning to worry a little himself," Trask said.

Solomon shook his head thoughtfully. "I've seen it all before, Bridge. When I was teaching at Fort Vancouver I had kids about his age, some of them. Some made it through all right. But most of 'em just went to hell in a basket. Discouraging."

"Why's it have to be this way?"

"I wish I knew," Solomon said morosely. "Nobody wants it this way. Coboway's trying, I'm trying, all the *tillicums* and most of the whites are trying. It still happens."

"Doesn't Wakila have any parents?"

"Sure. They can't interfere. They're old stock, they do things the old way. He's past the age of discipline, by the old reckoning. They'd no more discipline him than they would you."

Trask snorted. "A little discipline at the right time and we wouldn't have this." He gestured upwards. "How can they let their kids run free like that?"

"Listen," Solomon said. "In the old way the young kids had a discipline you never dreamed of. But by God when they passed the age, they were free. It's the way they've always done it, Bridge. It worked all right till we came."

While the two men had been talking, Hannah had quietly taken the empty pot out of the fireplace where Trask had put it, smiling a little to herself at his automatic action. She dipped into the dwindling store of real coffee and ground up enough beans for one pot, if boiled long enough. She just caught the last words of something her husband had said.

". . . you and Celiast?"

There was a long pause before Solomon answered. Hannah watched him, and saw a sadness settle over his shoulders like a cloak. He almost bent under it, and his voice was low when he finally replied.

"We stand right in the middle, Celiast and me," he said. "It isn't always the best place to be. We're neither one thing nor the other and yet we're both. We do what we can." He seemed almost to be talking to himself. When he had finished he sat silent for a long moment, then shook himself, as though to clear his head. He looked up at Trask again, and his eyes regained the more familiar sparkle of good humor. "But we get the best of both worlds, too. Sometimes."

"Never give up, the man says," Trask said ruefully.

"Can't," Solomon told him. "If I gave up easy, you never would've gotten yourself a guide down to Murderer's Harbor."

"You get one already?" Trask looked up in surprise.

"Well," Solomon said slowly, "I told you the people wouldn't care much for the idea, what with Neahkahnie in the way and Killamooks on the other side . . ."

"But you got one."

"Had a pretty good idea where to look. Matter of fact, I got a volunteer for the job come by my house." Solomon had a strange look in his eyes that made Trask uneasy.

"All right," Trask said. "Where is he?"

"He wants *kwinnum tolar* a day, five dollars," Solomon said.

Trask winced, but said, "All right, I knew he'd be expensive. Where is he?"

"Now, Bridge," Solomon said slowly, "you got to remember this is something most people wouldn't take for any amount—"

"What are you getting at, Solomon?" Trask was beginning to feel the same sense of battling pillows he had when Hannah was "pokin' at him." Solomon's familiar grin was now all over his face.

"You won't get mad, now," Solomon cautioned.

"Hell, no! You got a guide, I'm satisfied. Now cough it up what's in your head." Trask was getting confused, and Solomon laughed aloud at the scrambled phrase.

"Matter of fact, I think you've met," he said.

"All right, all right—"

"It's Charley Kehwa."

Chapter Four

"C harley Kehwa!" Trask exploded.

"You said you weren't going to get mad, Bridge," Solomon reminded him. He seemed to consider it the very best kind of joke.

"But—a tamanawis man!—for Christ's sake, Solomon, you're grinning like an ugly bride's mother! What's so funny about it?"

"Calm down, Bridge," Hannah said. "What's got into you all of a sudden about Charley Kehwa? He's a good man, Charley."

"Who knows?" Solomon asked mildly. "Maybe you'll need a good tamanawis man to get you over Neahkahnie."

"If I can't get there on my own legs I won't get there," Trask growled.

"Well, I don't guess Charley's figuring on giving you wings," Hannah said.

"That ain't the point—"

"Just what *is* the point, then? Charley's one of the best guides in the tribe. His mother was a Killamook slave. Hell, Charley's got people down there."

"Bullshit," said Trask, unable to think of any better argument. He sat down heavily.

There was a rustling overhead and Wakila's fuzzy voice said, "*Ikta okoke?*"

"Nothing!" Trask shouted. "Go back to sleep. *Mamook moosum!*"

"*Nowitka, nowitka,*" was the mumbled reply, and there was a thump as Wakila misjudged the distance of his head from the floor.

"What's the matter with him about Charley?" Hannah asked Solomon, genuinely puzzled.

Solomon shrugged. "I don't know. I think he's got it in his fool head that Charley means him bad or something."

"No, not that—" Trask said.

"Then what?" Hannah asked reasonably.

"I just don't like the idea of a tamanawis man for a guide. Not dependable. Something."

"Ah, Bridge, you're just making that up," Hannah said.

"How do you know?"

"I can tell about you."

"Charley makes him nervous," Solomon offered.

Hannah: "Why?"

Solomon shrugged.

"The hell with the whole thing," Trask muttered obscurely.

"*Ikta okoke?*" from up in the loft.

"Shut up."

"*Nowitka.*" Thump.

They sat in silence for a few moments, Trask brooding, trying to collect his thoughts; Solomon still amused; Hannah waiting patiently to find out what it was all about.

"Solomon, you carry a joke too far," Trask said finally.

"Any far's too far for you," Hannah said. "What is this with Charley?" Her tone was that of one who had asked the same question many times.

Solomon said carefully, looking at the table, "I think Bridge is afraid of Charley."

"Not Charley or anybody else," Trask said.

"Tamanawis, then."

"That kind of foolish superstition never hurt anybody."

"Well, that's not true," Solomon said, "but it doesn't matter. Look, Bridge, why don't you admit the only reason you don't like Charley for a guide is that he knew ahead of time what you were figuring on."

"Is that right?" Hannah asked.

Trask nodded. "That's what Solomon says, anyway."

"He came to my place and offered to guide you down," Solomon said. "Before I'd even talked it around the village."

"He could have seen me go to your place and guessed what I was doing," Trask said.

Solomon shrugged again.

"I don't see it makes a mite of difference," Hannah said flatly. "You want a guide, you got a guide; what difference is it how he knew?"

"None," Solomon said.

"Nobody else?" Trask asked, knowing the answer.

"Don't think there's another man in the tribe with guts enough."

Trask sighed. "*Kloshe kahkwa*," he said finally. "So be it. But I don't like it."

"All right." Solomon stood and crossed to the door in two long strides. "I'll tell Charley it's all right. Who else is going?"

"Hadn't thought about it," Trask admitted. "Didn't even know I was until I started talking."

"Well, you better take one more man," Solomon said. "If you can get one. I can let you have Doctor McLoughlin to carry your gear."

"Doctor's pretty old," Trask said dubiously.

"I know," Solomon said calmly. "He's the only horse I can afford to lose."

Trask looked up and saw from Solomon's eyes he was not joking. "Oh."

Solomon left, leaving Trask to consider the prospect of a trip on which the pack horse had to be one Solomon felt he could afford to lose.

2

In the western end of the sleeping loft was a tiny oiled-paper window. The late-afternoon sun floated gently down from above and framed itself in the translucent square, casting a bright shaft of gold across the loft.

Wakila rolled over on the blanket and came to rest with his face in the light. Gradually he stirred; blinked against the brightness. Somewhere at a distance he could hear a rhythmic "chik! chik! chik!" It took him a few moments to sort out the sound in his mind as an ax, and wood.

He cleared his throat and sat up, cringing a little at the sudden dart of pain that ran behind his eyes, bright and sharp as the sun's light across the floor. After the first surge, he ignored it. His eyes were heavy and there was a burned taste in his mouth.

He stretched his shoulder and grunted; then sat quietly, listening to the sound of the ax. He had come to chop wood. Someone else was chopping it instead of him. It meant he had not done what he should.

He was embarrassed by this, and tentative about going downstairs because of it. He stood up cautiously and found he was still dizzy from the wiskey. He had sobered just enough to have the hurt in his head.

Well, it could be all right. An hour with the ax would work the dizziness and the hurt out of him, and maybe give him a two-bitser besides. He was still embarrassed, and he didn't know what he was going to say. It made him feel small inside that someone else was doing the work he had come to do. He hoped Trask had not gotten someone else; he hoped Trask was just chopping a *little* wood, maybe. To light the fire again.

Then he could go down and chop up *hiyu* stick, much wood, and everything would be all right again. But if Trask had gotten somebody else to do the job . . . *halo kloshe, halo kloshe.*

Wakila shook his head sadly, and refused to recognize the new surge of pain. He would have to walk down—steadily—and speak to Trask in a dignified way; walk away from the house without shame. It would be hard.

Shame was a new thing for Wakila. It was a thing that came inside him when he could not work because of the wiskey. It was when the Mister Anders made the seal-eyes rolling behind the little spectacles and made the "tchik-tchik" at him.

The smallness inside; the Mister Anders did that to him, and also several of the other Boston men on the Plains. Trask did not do that, and Wakila wondered what the difference was. He knew he could not understand the Boston men. He did not usually try. Their minds were like a big box, full of many, many things, and sometimes the Mister Anders would reach into his box and pull out one of the things and hold it up in front of him and shake it angrily. Then Wakila would have the smallness, because the Mister Anders was angry with him, and he did not know why. The Mister Anders did not explain. He pulled the thing out of his mind and called it Savior or Redemption or Heathen, and Wakila could not even recognize what kind of thing it was. It meant something to the Boston men, maybe, but how was Wakila to know about that? How could he know all the things in their minds? When Trask was angry with him, Wakila knew why. There was not enough wood. The wood was too long, or too short. But something you could understand. The others did not do that.

The only thing that would help the smallness inside was either the wiskey or good hard work. He worked well, and was very strong, and when he swung the ax he could feel his muscles swell and the sweat run down his back, and it washed away the smallness because he knew his strength. But when he could not even work—because of the wiskey— then he felt small again.

Now the steady "chik-chik-chik" outside meant he had not been able to do what he should, and he would have to set it right.

Wakila stood up and crossed to the ladder leading down. His blue cloth pants, his very best, were dirty. He must have fallen down somewhere on the beach. He started down the ladder.

He still did not know what he would say to Trask. He would have to stand straight and work hard, and in an hour the dizziness and pain would be gone and he would feel the strength of his body again.

Han-ha, *klootchman* Trask, was already trimming the fat off a couple of elk steaks, getting them ready for dinner. Wakila realized he must have slept for a number of hours. He had a vague recollection of hearing voices, but nothing he could remember exactly. He had been very sleepy.

"Klahowya, Wakila," Hannah said pleasantly.

"Klahowya." Wakila smiled broadly.

"*Elip kloshe tum-tum?*" she said. "Feeling better?"

Wakila nodded and smiled again. He pointed toward the sound of the ax. "*Nika mamook cut stick alta.*"

Hannah nodded. "Good."

Wakila went out. Trask was splitting cedar logs. Wakila watched as the ax blade made a great shining crescent, ending in a heavy chunk! as the bit buried itself in the wood. Trask was stripped to the waist, and his body was wet. The ax swung again, catching the light of the sun and flicking it across the ground as reflections are flicked along the surface of a breaker.

Chunk!

The log split, two halves sliding almost slowly apart. Trask looked up and saw Wakila standing beside the door. He nodded and hefted the ax again, returning his attention to work. Wakila took his shirt off and folded it carefully on the ground.

The white man's body was thin, and very hard. Wakila noted with approval how the muscles of his belly stood out at the moment of impact, like sand ripples on the beach when the tide has gone. Trask, he decided, was a good, hard animal. If he had been a horse Wakila would have bought him.

Trask leaned the ax against the block. He picked up his shirt and wiped his forehead. He looked again at Wakila, without expression, and walked over.

"Klahowya, Tlask."

"Klahowya. Can you work now?"

Wakila nodded.

"Then work." Trask turned and went into the house, and Wakila heard his flat voice speaking to Han-ha. He smiled, and walked over to the ax. He hefted it and the long smooth arc shone like a silver rainbow.

"Hya!" he shouted as the bit sank. The log split evenly.

So there had been no shame in this at all. He should have known there would not be with Trask.

He smiled again, to himself. "Hya!"

And in an hour there was much wood, and the clean blood was flowing in him again and his eyes were clear.

3

Hannah fried the elk steaks and there were potatoes. Trask called Wakila into the house, and they were eating when the sun went down.

Hannah lit the lamps, and when she came back to the table brought Trask's Norwegian pipe from the mantel, and one of common clay with a wooden stem for Wakila. They lit, and smoked in silence.

Wakila felt very good. The sour taste was gone from his mouth and the tobacco smoke rolled warm and sweet before he let it out in a long stream toward the beams above.

Trask was preoccupied, brooding long over his pipe and staring at the hot fireplace coals. His beard was shiny, and caught red glints from the fire like tiny copper wires. The heavy ridge of his nose was pronounced, receding into blackness beneath his brows. His eyes were set deep, giving his forehead the look of a granite ledge overhanging two caves, within which burned the tiny, precise reflections of the fire. It was not a sympathetic face; too hard, too bleak.

Like Kahnie himself, Wakila thought, preparing some great thing.

Hannah, too, watched her husband's dispassionate pondering, in silence. There were occasional times when she wondered very deeply about this hard man she had married, this lean animal with a hawk's face. Times when she knew with a certainty there were parts of him she could not touch, or know. Times when he stared out at the ocean, or at the mountains, or into the fire, with his face showing no more of human concern than the gray cliffs of Neahkahnie that face the sea. She wondered what he thought then; wondered if what he thought might be understandable to her, if he could have set his thinking into words. Sometimes she questioned painfully whether this was love, that held so much back.

It sometimes seemed to her they shared little in their life; and still it was more than she could have found with any other man. It seemed to her that his angers, and confusions, and foolishnesses were like masks dropped over his face, to give it the semblance of humanity as lesser men wore masks to give them the semblance of gods.

And when the masks were torn away at the end of the ritual, the gods became men again, skinny or fat, strong or weak. And Trask became—simply Trask.

Neither kind nor cruel, loving nor hating; not concerning himself with the flickering emotions by which men know and label one another. Concerned and involved in the world as the mountain is concerned, as the sea is involved. Solitary as the moon, familied as the grasses, and without knowledge of good and evil as if the Tree had never been. She wondered how he moved through life, what passions shook him in that somber region no other being could reach or share. She wondered to what gods he prayed in the lost reaches of the night when he walked the sea-ridges like some restless, prowling cat.

Hannah shook her head sharply, as if to clear it, aware of her great uneasiness. What gods are Trask's? This was the thing; a thing she did not know and, not knowing, feared.

Her motion seemed to shake the stillness, as a mother gently shakes a child to waken it. Wakila coughed, noticed that his pipe had gone out. Trask stirred slightly in his chair; stood and replaced his pipe in the mantel rack.

"Wakila," he said suddenly, "I'm going down the coast soon."

"Ah. *Siah?*"

"No. Not far. Over Neahkahnie, into the Killamook country."

Wakila frowned, but was silent.

"I have a guide. Charley Kehwa"—Wakila looked up in surprise—"and a pack horse. I need another man."

"I am a very strong carrier," Wakila said. It was without pride; a simple fact.

"No wiskey," Trask said. "None."

"No wiskey," Wakila repeated.

"It will be very hard," Trask cautioned.

"Yes. I will go with you."

"We will go over Neahkahnie. Are you afraid of Neahkahnie?"

"Yes," Wakila said simply. "Also of the Killamook people."

"All right," Trask said. "I will get Charley Kehwa and the horse in the morning. We will leave the day after, early. You may stay here with us until then."

Wakila nodded happily. It was very good to be asked by Trask, and he would go. There would be a great honor in this thing, and when they came back he would know more of his own strength, and the smallness in him would have a very hard time of it.

He smiled again and nodded his head slowly. It seemed to him possible that even the Mister Anders could not make him ashamed any more, if he should do his work well for Trask. None of the Boston men on the Plains would have belly enough to call him *cultus siwash*—not ever again—if he went into the Killamook country and over Neahkahnie with Trask, standing straight and working hard.

That he would do.

He could feel the smallness in him shrivel and die even in that moment, sitting quiet before the fire and smiling to himself.

4

It clouded in the night and the dawn was gray. Trask walked out to discover the morning, and in the cool light, saw a figure coming from the south, trudging steadily up the depression just behind the seaward ridge. Without haste, but without hesitation, moving smoothly behind the dunes like a loping wolf, and Trask found himself watching the figure move with pleasure, as he would watch a gull wheel over the beach. At this distance he could not make out the face, but he knew he saw Charley Kehwa come walking.

He turned and went back into the house, met by the smells of frying bacon and coffee. Wakila was curled beneath a blanket in front of the fire, oblivious to the activity around him. He shifted and rustled a little, and his nose twitched in acknowledgment of the good smells that came to it. He would wake up soon.

Trask sat at the scarred table with an air of resignation. "He's coming."

"Charley?" Hannah said, without turning from the stove.

"Mm."

"He's spookin' you, that Charley," she chided.

"Some."

Hannah came over and leaned deliberately on the table, looking squarely at Trask. "Listen," she said. "Solomon went back through the village to get home. He'd stop and talk to Charley Kehwa because he *always* stops and talks to Charley Kehwa. He'd tell Charley it was all right, and Charley would come up to see what had to be done before you left. It's all very simple and natural. Will you get it out of your bone head that Charley's readin' your mind?"

"I suppose," Trask said dubiously.

"Bridge, you're making up trouble where you don't need it. You *like* Charley, remember? I like Charley, we all do. Only thing wrong with Charley Kehwa is he's smarter than most of us. You're going to need all the smarts you can get."

Trask nodded reluctantly. Hannah turned back to the stove.

"You get a good fast horse, you don't hobble him so he'll go slow as the rest. Now don't you go hobbling Charley Kehwa just because you don't understand him, you hear me?"

"All right, Hannah. I got nothing against him."

"No. You're scared he knows more about you than you want him to know, is all."

"Now, Hannah—"

Trask was interrupted by a quiet knock at the door. Wakila's head came up from the floor, and he looked around him with sleepy eyes, finally fixing on Hannah's back as the probable source of the good food smells. Trask crossed to the door and opened it.

"Klahowya, Bridge."

"Klahowya, Charley. Come on in." He stepped back from the door, holding it open.

Charley Kehwa was a young man, perhaps in his late twenties. His face was broad and flat, with wide nostrils and almond-shaped eyes set wide apart. His eyes were so dark they were almost black; they seemed to have no visible whites, like those of a deer. His shoulders and arms were massively muscled; he had grown to manhood stroking the swift canoes. The tribe still talked of the time Charley, aged ten, took his small hunting canoe through the breakers by Neahseu'su and up the coast to Astoria, seriously intent on doing a little trading. A thirty-mile trip in a heavy sea, with the treacherous Columbia Bar to cross at the end of it . . .

When he came into the house, Charley's dark eyes flicked quickly all around. There was about him an almost tangible aura of awareness, as much a part of him as his arms. Trask had never seen even a lessening of this preternatural alertness; even in relaxation Charley Kehwa's body had the slight, tense set of a man listening for a faint sound.

And perhaps he was. As a tamanawis man, Charley doubtless heard many voices too slight for the ears of other men.

"Breakfast is about ready, Charley," Hannah said. "How are you?"

"Very well. Klahowya, Wakila."

"Klahowya, Cholly." Wakila had scrambled to his feet on seeing Charley and stood in front of the fireplace holding his blanket in one hand. Still sleepy, he was swaying slightly. He looked faintly confused at being caught sleeping while others were already busy.

"Will you be going to the Killamook country?" Charley asked, using the Chinook.

"Yes," Wakila told him, with a trace of pride.

"*Hyas kloshe*," Charley said. He grinned broadly at the boy. Turning to Trask, he repeated, "Very good." His dark, animal eyes searched Trask's face and he nodded slowly. "Yes," he said. "Very, very good."

Trask was unaccountably embarrassed, and fumbled at a chair. "Sit down, Charley."

"Thank you. Can I help with something?" he asked Hannah.

"You might make tamanawis on the coffee," Hannah said. "I'm trying a new way."

Trask scowled at her, and Charley laughed. "The one who makes the best tamanawis is the one who knows most about the object," he said. "For coffee I could make a drinking tamanawis, maybe, but not a brewing tamanawis."

In an effort to steer the conversation away from what was—to him—an uncomfortable subject, Trask said, "Charley, have you ever been to Murderer's Harbor?"

"Once," Charley said, "but I don't remember it. My mother was a Killamook slave."

Trask nodded. In this country a guide was not so much a man who knew his way to a particular place, as one who could find his way there. The best woodsmen were the best guides.

"What's their language?" Trask asked.

"The tribal language is Salishan," Charley said. "But they speak the Chinook, of course."

Trask nodded. Jargon was pretty universal; it had been used as the trading language long before white men came, and had adopted French and English words with as little difficulty as the Chinook and Nootka it began with.

"Here's coffee," Hannah said, putting down three cups. Wakila joined the other two at the table. "You speak the Salish, Charley?"

Charley shook his head regretfully. "No," he admitted. "Not much. Chinook and English is all."

Hannah laughed. "I'd think that's enough."

"Nothing is ever enough," Charley said seriously.

"You may be right," Hannah said dryly. "Try your coffee."

Wakila had been following the conversation with his eyes, smiling at everybody. Since they had been speaking in English, he did not understand, but he was interested and courteous. When Trask raised his cup, Wakila did the same.

"Not bad," Trask said. "What'd you do? Tastes like coffee."

"Good, good," Hannah said. "We do move along. Boiled a little real coffee till it was mud, then mixed it up with mostly barley coffee. It's all right?"

"Got a good flavor to it. More or less."

Hannah smiled happily and nodded to herself with pleasure. The discovery would eke out their waning supply of coffee greatly; she hadn't used but four or five beans of real coffee to make it. It gave her great satisfaction to solve the small problems of living effectively. Now if she could figure some way to make Bridge up some good tobacco, that would really be something . . .

Well, that's for another day, she thought.

"I best start making up your pack," she said. "How long you gone for?"

Trask glanced at Charley Kehwa. His flat face was impassive, but Trask thought the almond eyes narrowed slightly with some unreadable emotion when he answered.

"Ten days, maybe," Charley said.

"*Ten days!* It's only about fifty miles down."

Charley nodded, without taking his eyes from Trask. He seemed to be studying the white man. "Many places there is no trail at all. It is"—he shrugged—"*halo kloshe illahee*. Not good country."

Wakila, catching the Chinook, muttered, "*Mesachie illahee.*"

"No," Charley said quietly. "No land is evil. Men alone can call it evil. But—very strong."

Trask laced his fingers together on the table. He stared at them, tightly clasped so the knuckles were beginning to show white. He shook his head sharply twice, looking miserable.

"Charley," he started hesitantly, "it isn't that—well, I figured on closer to four or five. What I mean—"

Hannah's quiet voice interrupted. "What he means, Charley, is that we don't have the money. *Halo chickamin.*" She raised her palms in an empty gesture, let them fall. "Just that."

"See," Trask said. "Five dollars a day for you is fifty dollars and Wakila should get a dollar a day . . . I just don't have sixty dollars, is all. I don't even have fifty, far as that goes."

Wakila stood straight up at the table, very dignified. He looked over the top of Trask's head at the opposite wall. His face was expressionless, almost grim as he announced, "Tlask, *yaka sikhs. Nika halo iskum chickamin.*" Having delivered his speech, he sat down again abruptly and looked into his coffee cup, without meeting anyone's eyes. It was the first time he had ever called a Boston man by the intimate *sikhs.* He almost expected Trask to be angry with him.

After a moment he heard Trask's soft voice say, "*Mahsie, sikhs.*"

Wakila bit his lower lip, and swallowed heavily. Something had gotten into his eyes, dust perhaps. He stood again and said, "I will cut more wood now." He left the house, walking straight.

When he had gone, Trask turned his eyes back to Charley Kehwa, to find the disquieting gaze of the Indian already fixed thoughtfully on him.

"Ah," said Charley quietly. "So you are *sikhs* to that boy. The people are worried for him."

Trask cleared his throat and scowled irritably. "All right," he said. "Even if Wakila works for nothing, I still don't have fifty dollars."

Charley did not answer. Instead he turned to Hannah and said, "Please make the packs ready. Bacon, jerky elk, maybe salmon. A little bit of flour, but make it mostly into bread, for carrying. Not too much meat, we will get clams and crabs from the beach maybe. Sugar, no coffee."

Trask coughed.

"Bridge couldn't walk a mile without his coffee in the morning," Hannah said.

"I did in the mountains," Trask said defensively. "Had to."

"Well, you can't now, and you know it," Hannah said.

Charley smiled faintly. "I will bring the coffee all right," he said. "Also for the house."

"I said I didn't have the fifty dollars."

Charley stood at the table. "I will be paid," he said confidently. "And Wakila will be paid, and maybe even you will be paid. Also Hannah will be paid for the provisions we take."

"Charley, you—"

The Indian waved off Trask's objection. "It will be arranged. It is necessary that a man be paid," he said seriously. "A man must be paid in order to live."

"Who's doing the paying?"

"A man. We will have to take him with us."

"Who is he?"

"There are five rivers flowing into the bay called Murderer's Harbor," Charley said evasively. "That is very much water. If a man wished to make a sawmill, he must look where there is much fast water."

"Charley, you're crazy. You couldn't put a mill down there. There's not a settler any closer than us. How'd you get the logging done? How'd you get millhands? How—"

Charley spread his hands in bewilderment. "I know nothing of all this," he said blandly. "I am Siwash, ignorant savage of the Oregon country. If a man wishes to be taken to fast-running water, this can be done. But of these other things, Mr. Siwash knows nothing. He lacks education in practical matters, spending his time in drinking wiskey and worshiping heathen gods."

Hannah began to chuckle. "I think it's a lovely idea."

"I take it there's a ship in from the East," Trask said.

"There is. I am on my way to Astoria now. I stopped here to see if this thing would be necessary. A man must be paid."

"All right," Trask said. "How much trouble will he be on the trip?"

"Endless," Charley said. "While he lasts."

"Can he make it?"

"No farther than that." Charley pointed out the window to the bulk of Neahseu'su. "I will get our money in advance. For provisions."

"It's a lot like stealing," Trask mused, a little reluctant.

"Yes," Charley said. "*Delate kahkwa*. Exactly like."

Trask frowned dubiously.

Hannah leaned stiffly over the table, her fists suddenly clenched.

"Bridge," she said, and her voice was tense. "These people come out here thinking it's a paradise for a smart man. Women in fancy clothes, everything store-bought on 'em. We make 'em welcome and they eat our best food and never even think of payin' a penny for it.

I don't begrudge it. But *we* had to scratch it out of the dirt with our
fingernails. *We* had to fight for it and work for it. They can come now,
and they can buy what they want. There was no buyin' when we came,
all there was was *work*. Everything you got, you made or built or dug.

"First ax you ever had in this country Coboway give you. No bunch
of settlers to feed you and dance you. All *we* had was Coboway and
Solomon and Celiast. Mr. Siwash, Bridge. We'da starved and froze to
death a dozen times that first winter if it wasn't for Mr. Siwash."

Hannah's voice had begun to shake, and she broke off. She put her
hands to her face for a moment, and when she took them down she
was calm again.

"I'm sorry," she said, more quietly. "We get women come here off
the boats with their silk petticoats and pretty dresses and all the nice
things they got. 'N they walk in *my house*, 'n say how lovely it must be
to have all the salmon we want. Salmon, my God! All we ate for two
years was salmon and potatoes! Till it came out our ears. And the men
never tasted barley coffee in their life and for the first two years all the
dress I ever *had* was what Celiast give me and what I made myself outa
the flour sacks.

"I'm not sayin' it right, Bridge. I can't say it right, I get too wrought
up. But any man comes out here to make a million dollars is figuring
on makin' it off our backs and off Mr. Siwash, you can count on it. We
don't owe them nothing. It ain't right they should be able to buy what
we had to break our backs for. I say it's more important for you to go
down there and look at that country you want to look at than some fat
cheechako pork-eater should keep his hundred dollars. We got to do it
the hard way, Bridge, because it's the only way we know and the only
way there is around here. But if you can get somebody else to pay for
it because he's greedy, don't you go worryin' about your immortal soul.

"What it amounts to is we belong here, you and me. And it didn't
come easy for us. And belonging to this country isn't ever going to
come easy, because it's hard country and it takes hard people.

"And while I'm makin' a big speech, let me tell you something else,
when you start worrying. We got a lot of good settlers here on the
Plains. But you count up the people we can trust, and see how many
of 'em are white."

Trask was stunned by her vehemence, and her bitterness. It had not been an easy life for Hannah, and he knew it well. But he had never guessed there was such a violent sense of injustice, or such a bitterness toward those who had had it easier. And yet, in a way, it was not that. It was a kind of anger toward those who had not earned the right to ask anything of this country, and yet who demanded with confidence and—perhaps—scorn.

Charley Kehwa had stood silent beside the door, listening to Hannah, his eyes flickering back and forth between husband and wife, appraising, absorbing. Finally he spoke, breaking the tense silence that soaked the room.

"Make the pack for the horse so it can be divided among the men."

Hannah nodded. Charley turned and went out the door, closing it softly behind him. Through the window Trask could see him heading toward the beach; easier walking on the way north to Astoria.

"Well," he said. "Guess we'd better start getting things together."

"Yes," Hannah said. "Sorry I got so het up."

"It's all right," Trask said. "I didn't know it bothered you so much. I—I like to know these things."

"Bridge," she said awkwardly. "Does it ever—do you ever wish I was . . ."

"Was what?"

"Oh, I don't know," Hannah said, exaggeratedly casual. "Pretty or something. Like some of these young girls that come on the boats. You know. Pretty." She was examining her hands, folded in her lap.

For the second time, Trask was startled. "Is *that* what—Why you damn fool Hannah! You know well as I do there's not a one of 'em could ever make four-bean coffee!"

She looked up at him, a very plain woman with a too-sharp chin and too-prominent cheekbones and her hair pulled too severely back. When she spoke, her voice had regained its usual faintly ironic tinge. "Well," she said, standing from the table, "guess that's why I married you. You're so romantic."

"Go to hell," Trask grumbled at her.

"But sometimes I like to know, too," she said, almost to herself.

Chapter Five

I

Trask carried in more firewood to heat the oven for the bread making. From her storeroom Hannah had brought out the last precious hundred-pound bag of flour, and had begun to mix up the dough. She stirred the stiffening batter in the great pan until the sweat stood out on her forehead in tiny beads. Wisps of hair loosened with the rhythmic motion of her body and she pushed them away from her eyes with automatic and ineffective brushes of her wrist.

"I'm going down to Solomon's and get Doctor," Trask said.

"All right." Hannah put the pan down and wiped her forehead with the hem of her apron. "I'll get the packs started as soon as I get a batch of this bread in the oven. How many?"

"Four for the men, one for the horse, I guess. Besides the panniers."

"You going to give our sawmill man a pack to carry?"

"Hell yes. Why not?"

Hannah shrugged. "No reason. Might make him mad, have to pay and carry a pack, too."

"Let him," Trask said shortly. "Far as he goes, he'll have to pull his weight."

"Don't be so belligerent," Hannah chided gently.

"I'm not belligerent." Trask scowled. "What's wrong with asking a man to carry a pack? What's he want?"

"Now look at you," Hannah said. "Mad at him already and you haven't even seen him. You always get mad when you think you may be wrong."

Trask grunted. "Give him a pack anyway."

Hannah sighed. "All right, Bridge."

She put a batch of the stiff dough above the stove to rise before she worked it, and began to mix up another batch. She figured it would take three ovenloads to make up the full amount they would want for ten

days. That would give them about a half a loaf per man per day, if the
sawmill man didn't get any farther than Charley figured. She nodded
to herself. That would be all right.

"I'm going to take Wakila down to Solomon's with me. He's cuttin'
wood so hard I'm scared he'll start on the house when he runs out of
logs."

Hannah laughed. "He's pretty happy to be going along."

"He's a good carrier," Trask said, in explanation of something.

Trask left the house, and Hannah could hear him talking to Wakila.
After a moment, Wakila put down the ax, but with reluctance. He looked
at the stack of wood beside the block, as though estimating whether it
would last while he was gone. Trask said something, then turned on his
heel and began to walk south toward Neahcoxie and Solomon's house.
Wakila cast one almost apologetic glance at the house, shrugged, and
trotted to catch up with the long-striding mountain man.

Watching through the window as her hands worked automatically,
Hannah smiled. When a man wanted to chop wood, he wanted to chop
wood. But—she could almost visualize Wakila's mental shrug—if Trask
wanted something else, something else it would be.

Wakila was a nice boy, she thought. If he'd been a little older when
the white men came to settle, he wouldn't have this endless trouble
with the whisky and gambling games. She shook her head sadly, and
brushed away the lock of hair that swung in front of her eyes, leaving
it white with flour.

Wakila was happiest when he was working, she thought. But he
couldn't find anything to work at. To a boy of sixteen—his learning
years spent in a time when the old ways were beginning to weaken,
and the new not yet strongly rooted—the world must be a confusing
place. No place firm to stand and look around you; no way to judge
and pick from the confusion. Wakila needed someplace to stand in his
own mind. Some Greek said "Give me a place to stand and I'll move
the earth," something like that. Wakila didn't want to move the world.
But he needed to find one he could live in. He needed that bad.

She turned out a wad of partly risen dough on the flour-covered
breadboard and began to knead it. The rich, malty smell rose sweet
to her nostrils.

Briefly Hannah wondered what she'd do if she had to face the same thing. How would it look to you if half the things you saw told you how ignorant you were, and all your people?

How could you take a beavertooth chisel and gnaw your way painstakingly into a cedar log, when you could walk up to Skipanon Landing and watch the white men's ships sweeping up the coast like white-winged gulls. Sails pregnant with the wind and their bellies laden with strange things from tribes you'd never see, tribes so far away you couldn't believe the world was that wide.

How could you split out the beautiful cedar planks with an elk-horn wedge, when in his mill at Cathlamet Henry Hunt could do it so much faster? And the river itself ran the saw. The planks that had been of so much worth to the people were suddenly worth—nothing. Ten dollars for a thousand board feet.

The dough was growing cooler beneath her fingers now, and she pounded and worked it smooth with a steady, hypnotic rhythm.

He has a choice, Hannah thought suddenly. And no choice at all. Two worlds, and he can't have either of them. He knows too much of us to find pride in his own people any more, and not enough to become a white man.

Where was the place for Wakila? Where he could find the dignity of being a man? Who could say to him—ever—"You are a man, and this is your world and life; and it is good that it should belong to you."

No one.

Hannah swallowed heavily and slammed the lump of dough down hard on the board.

2

It was nearly an hour's walk from Trask's house to the village of Neahcoxie. Most of the way Wakila chattered like a ground squirrel.

He could carry the biggest pack. He would find it, and carry it. He carried very well. Tireless. He liked to walk; he was a very good man on the trail because he liked to walk and he never got tired. He remembered this trip he had taken, and that trip. This trip was twelve days to here; that one eight days to there. You could believe it: nobody outwalked Wakila.

Elk he shot with great skill, if it could be arranged that he might have a gun . . .

. . . a sideward glance at Trask . . .

Deer he also shot very well, but if he didn't have a gun, that was all right, so much the less to carry. Not that he minded carrying. It would be hard for a man to starve with Wakila on a trip. He knew how the clams thought, he knew what they were thinking all the time. Good eating, clams. The thoughts of crabs he also knew. It was a kind of tamanawis he himself had. Charley Kehwa was a very strong tamanawis man, the strongest—so said the people—in many years. Charley Kehwa could become any of the things in the world, so said the people. This was Charley's greatness, that he understood and was one with all the powers: the wind and the seas and mountains and spirits and the minds of men. Animals, also. Doubtless, We were very lucky to have Charley going with Us . . .

But as they neared the village, Wakila quieted. When they came within hearing of the first canoe-builders, his voice gradually slowed and dwindled until it stopped entirely. Glancing at him, Trask noticed a slight increase in Wakila's height, as he walked a little straighter. Within the distance of a few paces, the sparkling dark face had assumed an expression of grave solemnity; from a jabbering youth, Wakila had been magically transformed into a man concerned with matters of some seriousness.

Trask frowned, slightly puzzled at first.

"Klahowya, Tlask!" They passed the first of the workmen.

"Klahowya," Trask answered.

Wakila returned the greeting with a dignified nod. He preferred to walk directly to Solomon's, looking to neither left nor right. Trask turned to the side and smiled, but when he faced forward again, he too had taken on an air of impassive dignity.

The women were still out near the center of the village, plaiting the flax strands for salmon nets. Before the hut of a toothless crone he knew to be an incorrigible gossip, Trask stopped. The woman bobbed her head several times and demonstrated her gums by way of greeting.

Trask nodded perfunctorily; talking to her was not his present business at all. He turned to Wakila with an attitude of extreme seriousness.

"It might be well," he said, speaking the Chinook clearly and slowly, "if you should inform your parents of the trip we have planned together."

Wakila's eyes widened slightly.

"The dangerous trip," Trask continued, "over the sacred and fearful mountain Neahkahnie and into the country of the fierce Killamooks."

The old woman sat dumfounded at this unparalleled opportunity to eavesdrop on matters of importance, her fingers moving idly on the net. Her mouth was slightly open, and she blinked rapidly.

"I am pleased," Trask continued methodically, "that you have consented to accompany me; to carry the heaviest pack; and to be responsible for the welfare-of-the-entire-party."

Wakila found he was able to nod his agreement. His eyes darted to the woman a few feet away and back to Trask's eagle-face, which regarded him unsmilingly.

"Very well," Trask said gravely. "Until we meet then at Solomon's: *klahowya, sikhs.*"

The old woman put her net on the ground, blinked twice at Wakila, and skittered around the corner with a rapid, crablike gait. In a moment her shrill, reedy voice was heard behind the hut. "Have you heard? Have you heard about Wakila?"

Trask watched the woman disappear, then turned to Wakila, his face as expressionless as the cliffs of Neahseu'su. He nodded briefly and walked off in the direction of Solomon's house.

Wakila stood transfixed for a moment, watching Trask's retreating back, unable to grasp the magnitude of this thing that had so suddenly happened. From behind the hut he vaguely heard patches of a high-pitched narrative: "Dangerous . . . Killamook . . . heaviest pack . . . whole party . . ."

Dazedly he turned to his left and began to walk toward his parents' cabin, just south of the main village. Gradually his head came up and his shoulders moved almost imperceptibly back and his stride lengthened. He walked tall and straight past people who turned to watch, unaccustomed to see Wakila so.

He might well have flown; but flying is frivolous. It has not the dignity of a sixteen-year-old walking to give his parents pride in him; a gift like a silver fish with its sides flashing in the sun.

Nothing has quite the dignity of that.

3

"Well, he's got ribs," Trask said dubiously, staring at Doctor McLoughlin.

"Count 'em if you want to," Solomon offered helpfully.

"Sure his hipbones aren't going to come out through the hide?"

Solomon laughed. "No, he's all right, Doctor is. Short on pretty, maybe, but he can carry a pack farther than you'll ever go."

"How do you move him? Sails? Paddles?"

"Wakila knows how," Solomon said. "Doctor'll be all right for you. You'll see."

Trask turned to him. "How'd you know Wakila was going? Wait a minute—" He finished his sentence and Solomon answered at the same time, their voices in unison: "Charley said so."

Trask shook his head and turned back to the sad contemplation of Doctor McLoughlin. The horse returned his gaze with neither curiosity nor malice.

"I'm going to give up," Trask said with discouragement.

"You might as well," Solomon agreed. "Fact that's the first smart thing you've said about Charley in quite a spell."

"You know I like Charley as a man," Trask said.

"What else is there? How else can you look at him?"

"You know damn well—as a tamanawis man."

"He's still just a man. Everybody's got tamanawis some way or other. Some have it stronger than others, and they eventually get to be official, that's all. Ask Charley."

"Hell I will," Trask said.

"Might not hurt you a goddam bit, Bridge. Might just do you some good to listen to Charley for a while." Solomon's voice was edged with impatience, and Trask immediately felt foolish.

"Sorry," he said. "Sometimes I sound more bonehead about things than I really am."

"Ah. I know it," Solomon said. "Thing is, Bridge, tamanawis makes everybody a little nervous till you get settled in your mind about it. One way or the other, you don't worry about it after a while. You either accept it as something that's there, whether you can explain it or not—like me—or you figure it's just *hiyu wawa*, a lot of talk. Like Anders and the rest of the churchmen. Me and the Clatsops figure one way, they figure another. It doesn't matter."

"Does to Anders."

Solomon shrugged. "Can't help that."

"I'll get used to it," Trask said. "Seems like it keeps comin' up lately is all."

"Now wait a minute," Solomon said. "You been here on the Plains five years and around the country for ten or more. You can't tell me it just started coming up about the tamanawis."

Trask frowned slightly. "Didn't seem like I ever thought about it much. Funny."

"Well, you don't think about *anything* till you're damn good and ready to."

"What do you mean by that?" Trask said suspiciously.

"Nothing. I'm just sayin', is all. That's how you are." Solomon shrugged. He wasn't at all sure in himself what he had meant. But Solomon's brand of logic was simple and direct, and it had answered well for most of his life: When something happens, there's a reason. You may not always see it right away, but—there's a reason. And if Bridge can live happily with the notion of tamanawis for a long time; and he suddenly gets spooked by Charley Kehwa just because he's tamanawis—there's a reason for that, too. If you can find it. But you don't get as touchy about a thing as Bridge had gotten unless it's some way important; something tucked away in the back of your head that says, "You got to watch out for this."

Well, you can listen to it or not. Solomon had learned to trust that little something back there. More than once he'd got the sudden notion to walk easy—just before he heard the deer snort. Or something say, "Gone wrong," and a couple minutes later he'd discover he'd wandered onto an aimless elk trail instead of the one he was supposed to be following.

Just hunches; and you had to listen careful as hell to hear them at all. Pretty faint, compared to all the noise going around in a man's head most of the time. But you learned. He wondered if Bridge trusted his own hunches. They were the only thing you had to go on, a lot of the time. Particularly in the mountains. Eventually most mountain men came to rely pretty heavy on that still little voice inside, and he supposed Bridge probably did, too.

"Here comes Wakila," Trask said.

"Good." Solomon clipped short his musings. "He can handle Doctor fine. He's done it before."

Doctor submitted to the minor indignities of bridle and blanket with indifference; an attitude with which he viewed the world and its crazy demands generally. Wakila, familiar with Doctor's eccentricities, carefully pointed him in the proper general direction before mounting.

"Doctor begin very fast," he told Trask seriously. "Then slow down." He nodded his head emphatically to emphasize the statement.

Wakila mounted and leaned far over Doctor's neck. He spoke softly and pleasantly in the horse's ear, simultaneously beginning a thunderous tattoo with his heels on the bony sides. After a moment, this combination of opposites seemed to excite Doctor McLoughlin greatly. He rolled his eyes, jerked once, and began to run immediately, rolling from side to side like a ship whose ballast has shifted in heavy seas.

Trask watched this awe-inspiring departure with outright disbelief mirrored on his face. "Oh my God," he whispered. "Oh my God."

"That's a wonderful horse," Solomon assured him. "He's a little nervous right now."

"So am I," Trask said. Doctor McLoughlin and Wakila were still flailing somewhat northerly. Gradually, Wakila seemed to exert some control over the animal—beyond stop-and-go, which didn't seem a problem—and Doctor began a wide turn to the right, slowing as he turned.

"I used to race him," Solomon reflected. "He won me a lot of money at one time, racing with the Clatsop horses."

"That's fine," Trask said. "That's the craziest horse I ever had the misfortune to see in my life."

"Oh, he's not crazy," Solomon said negligently. "He just don't give a damn."

Trask glanced sharply at the other, to be met with an expression of bland innocence. He scowled, and turned back to watch the approach of Wakila and Doctor, who had slowed to a steady walk. Wakila waved.

Trask couldn't find it in himself to wave back.

4

Doctor, however, after recovering from his initial "nervousness," plodded methodically along and gave promise of being an adequate horse for the trip. Trask's apprehensions gradually faded as they trudged around the crescent of the small bay. Wakila, mounted, rode on the inland side and Trask walked the hard-packed sand near the water. Doctor McLoughlin occasionally rolled his head sideways to peer at Trask, his eye showing an unnatural amount of white. He seemed to regard this as simply the latest in a long series of betrayals—of which, in fact, his life had been composed—and to be satisfying himself that it was indeed the hawkfaced man who was responsible for the outrage. Possibly he had similarly regarded his previous masters, memorizing their ugly people-faces against a day in some distant horse heaven when he would be called on to dispense justice to all featherless bipeds.

When they reached home, Hannah had the equipment and provisions divided for packing, with the exception of the bread. At Trask's insistence they made up a trial pack for Doctor McLoughlin, and Wakila walked him over dunes and rock and through brush until Trask was satisfied the horse would actually carry a pack. Wakila patiently ran Doctor through his paces, considering it a waste of effort, but probably necessary. In spite of the fact that he knew Doctor's capabilities perfectly well, he also knew no amount of talking would make any impression on Trask; he would have to see for himself. It was too bad; but it was Trask.

It was after dark when Charley Kehwa arrived from Astoria with George Roode.

Roode was jowly and jovial; a big man, well over two hundred pounds. His eyebrows were thick and black and met in the middle, so that he looked like a man with a mustache on upside down. He was clean-shaven, except for sideburns, which were thick and woolly and as black as his eyebrows. After meeting him, you would remember him as a man who laughed much, talked much, and whose jowls vibrated like the wattles of a turkey when he did either. They did not, in actuality, but they gave the impression they should. His eyes were a startling blue, alert and quick. He might have been anywhere between thirty and forty years old. He habitually stood rigidly erect, a posture which projected his ample stomach well ahead of the rest of his body like a wall of fortifications.

When they entered, he sailed slowly and majestically across the room to Hannah, taking one of her hands in both his own and bending attentively to her.

"Mrs. Trask," he said seriously. "Mrs. Trask, I don't mind telling you what a pleasure it is to be here."

Flustered, Hannah mumbled something in reply. Roode nodded; held her eyes for a moment, and turned to Trask.

"Elbridge Trask," he said, extending his hand. "It's an honor to meet you, sir." Roode's grip was surprisingly strong for a man who appeared fat.

"Mr. Roode," Charley said, not having had the chance to identify their guest before.

"Pleased to meet you," Trask said.

Roode's presence filled the room; aside from his physical bulk, he had an air of confidence and permanence that was almost tangible.

"If you'd like a bite to eat, Mr. Roode . . . ?" Hannah said.

"No, no," Roode protested. "Wouldn't think of it. Mr. Kehwa and I had dinner at the hotel. Thanks. Thanks very much. I don't mind telling you I appreciate your hospitality."

Trask glanced at Charley, who shrugged slightly and sat down at the table silently. He had a faintly dazed air, which Trask could understand. The trip from Astoria with the overwhelming Mr. Roode must have been something.

"Well, we'll have coffee, then," Hannah said.

"That would be fine, very fine," Roode said. "Mr. Kehwa?"

Charley stood again, as though stung, and started for the door as Roode said, "We brought a bit of provision with us, Mr. Kehwa and me. Little coffee, few things we thought we might need. Eh?"

Charley came in with the pack they had left at the door.

"Here, here, give that to me." Roode placed the pack in the center of the table and opened it carefully. He leaned far over and peered in, hiding the contents from the others with his body. He straightened and smiled broadly, a gesture which lifted his eyebrows.

"Now, now," he said. "What do we have here? Eh? Well." His hand came out of the pack with a folded square of bright material. He let it unfold with a theatrical sweep.

"Well," he said. "I believe it's a dress." It was; a remarkably colorful gingham dress. He held it at arm's length to Hannah. "Here," he said, and immediately thrust his hand back in the pack.

"Mr. Roode—" Hannah faltered. "I—well, I can't—"

Roode withdrew his hand, empty; turned to Hannah with astonishment.

"But Mrs. Trask," he said. "Mrs. Trask, ho ho ho." His tone was very serious.

"Ho ho ho?" Hannah repeated weakly.

"Ho ho ho," Roode assured her. "I am jolly Santa Claus." He nodded emphatically, and absently repeated, "Ho ho ho." He plunged his hand into the pack again and winked ostentatiously at Trask.

"Now," said Roode. "Now, here we have—Mr. Trask?"

Trask had been watching with numb surprise, and he was startled out of it by Roode's voice. "What—yes. Yes."

"Mr. Trask, I am given to understand by certain sources"—here he favored Charley with his enormous wink—"that you are a lover of tobaccos. Now this here is a bit of fire-cured Virginia. I would like your opinion." He thrust a large, paper-wrapped package at Trask, who accepted it automatically, stumbling out his thanks.

Roode gave them no chance to regain their balance. Keeping up a rapid and virtually meaningless monologue, he continued to hand out small gifts. All had a slight element of surprise about them; all were enough more elaborate than normal to startle them a little, but they were without exception useful items.

Ribbons for Hannah—a rainbow cascade as Roode swept them from the pack—and cloth; gaily patterned, but durable. Fine needles of all sizes; an apron; a Sunday hat—of excellent quality, but not too gaudy for a settler's wife.

Trask was presented with the tobacco; a powder horn with finely worked and unobtrusive silver ornamentation; a knife; a bullet mold; a superb meerschaum, for which Roode apologized.

"You will note this pipe is raw, and white. It will require a good deal of handling to mellow."

The pack was seemingly bottomless. Roode presented each gift with the ease of a showman and invested each unveiling with an aura of suspense, maintained perfectly until the presentation.

"I don't mind telling you folks I admire your courage in settling a country like this, but a few civilized amenities make a hard life so much the better. Eh? Hold this."

The heavy man worked rapidly and intensely. Beads of sweat stood out on his broad forehead like dew on the beach grass. Nothing was put down on the table; when one of the Trasks could hold no more in his arms, part of the burden was transferred to Charley Kehwa or Wakila, and soon the two Indians were heavily laden, too. Everything that could be unfolded was spread to its full dimensions and remained that way. Subtly Roode arranged and ordered and placed each object without seeming to take care, and the eventual impression was one of disordered luxury, a cornucopia gone wild.

The sweat on his forehead began to run in little rivulets down the bridge of his nose. Without pausing, he wiped it impatiently away with an immaculate linen handkerchief that appeared from nowhere, and disappeared as rapidly. His eyes flickered rapidly from one to the other of the people in the room. All except Charley Kehwa were dazed, stunned by the performance as by the act of a skilled magician. Charley had recovered himself as Roode's focus had shifted to the Trasks, and was watching the heavy man alertly, his face impassive. He glanced sharply at Trask, then back to Roode. The big man caught Charley's eye, and smiled slightly.

Abruptly Roode stopped and stood bolt upright; a sudden and massive gesture that thrust his belly forward and pinned all eyes to him. Trask and the others stood, loaded with presents they had to balance in their arms.

Without a break in his patter, without changing the tone of his voice, Roode said, "Ho ho ho. Santa Claus' pack is empty. Now, boys, it's time for business."

He sat heavily and took a small notebook from his pocket. "Mrs. Trask. If you will be so kind—I don't mind telling you I haven't met a more charming woman in years—if you will be so kind as to make out an itemized inventory of the provisions in these packs"—he gestured to the row of packs against the wall—"I will make payment immediately."

He handed Hannah the notebook. "Please sign the account, and I will require a receipt for payment." He turned to Trask. "Mr. Trask. My partners and I are much interested in establishing a sawmill in this country. Now tell me. At this Murderer's Harbor, there is good water?"

"Well, ah—yes. Yes, very good," Trask said. "Five rivers flow into the bay."

"Overland transportation is naturally very difficult," Roode said.

"Yes—well, there hasn't been much—"

"Of course. And the country rough."

"Yes—"

"And by sea? That would be more the thing, eh? Come in by sea?"

"Well, the Indians do, of course, but I don't know. The bar—" Trask frowned, dubious. He was not accustomed to the speed with which this thing was going.

"Is the bar bad? What vessels can cross? Sloop? Brigantine? What?" Roode was snapping questions like whiplashes now.

"I don't know for sure. Gray took the *Lady Washington* across, but I don't remember—"

"Sloop," Roode informed him. "August fourteenth, seventeen eighty-eight. But on July fifth of the same year, Captain Gray reported the entrance to this bay as completely closed by a sandy bar. Is it that unreliable?"

"I don't know."

"Haven't you heard from the other settlers?"

"Well, you see, there aren't—I mean—"

"None there at all. Eh? No whites?"

"I don't think so," Trask said.

"Don't you know?"

"There aren't any."

Roode nodded thoughtfully. He glanced quickly at Charley Kehwa, then back to Trask. "And are the natives—ah, sympathetic to whites?"

"It's hard to say," Trask said. "A lot depends on the people involved."

"Naturally. But you wouldn't say the murder of Gray's man Lopeus would be a typical response to whites?"

"Not exactly."

"Exactly what, then?" Roode said.

"I think probably he asked for it," Trask said.

"But you don't know."

"I'm just going by what they say—"

"I've read the mate's report and the log of the *Washington*. Do you know any more than that?"

"No."

"All right. What's all this talk about a territorial conference amount to?"

"I think they're talking about late this summer," Trask said.

"You think this country'll become a territory of the United States?"

"Sure," Trask said. "It's just a matter of time—"

"But the boundary question with Britain was settled two years ago."

"Well, yes, that's true."

"Isn't it also true you've been expecting to be made a territory ever since then?"

"Yes, but there've been delays. Joe Meek's on his way to Washington right now to see about—"

"I thought a man named Thurston was going," Roode snapped.

"Well, Thurston's representing Governor Abernethy—"

"You mean you people are so divided that one man represents the settlers and another man has to represent the provisional governor?"

"Well, it's kind of complicated . . ."

Roode laughed shortly, and leaned back. He nodded to himself. Trask had pretty much confirmed his previous impressions. In spite of the settlers' optimism, there seemed to Roode to be some doubt whether territoriality for Oregon was so self-evident after all. President Polk, certainly, was all for the move, but was meeting incredibly obstinate opposition. The bloc of Southern Senators had repeatedly killed action on the Oregon question, hoping they could keep the country open for slavery. And Polk, after all, would be leaving office in under a year . . .

Not good, not good. An unstable situation; not enough good solid information. Well, you always have to make your decisions on the basis of what you can get hold of, even if it isn't enough. He wasn't a gambling man, Roode, and it was all a gamble. Still, he liked it well enough sometimes.

He sighed and leaned back in the chair, wholly absorbed in trying to organize the information he had. He tented his fingertips beneath his chin and his bushy black eyebrows drew together in a brooding frown. In seconds he became unaware of the people around him, and all that existed was the meticulous balancing of factors, the weighing and judging of promise and prospect.

His face had long since lost its cherubic aspect. While snapping questions at Trask, it had been the face of the Inquisitor: hard, unyielding, the only expression a faint veil of irritability. Now, in thought, George Roode was almost monolithic. A very far cry from the jovial Father Christmas.

Throughout the entire questioning session, Trask had not been permitted time enough to think ahead, or prepare an answer. It was enough simply to keep up with the flat, fast precision of Roode's voice. He had not even had time to put down the armload of presents he held; and which seemed to keep him always slightly off balance. As he had been, in truth, since Roode first opened the door and greeted Hannah with such heroic courtesy. Now he unloaded the presents to the table, and began to realize what had happened.

Charley Kehwa sat apart, watching Roode. Alone of them all, Charley had seemed to resist the glittering, hypnotic web the fat man had spun in the house. Now he waited.

The conviction grew on Trask that he had been made a fool of, and a flush of anger rose in his face.

"Wait a minute," he said. "What right do you have—"

"Bridge." It was Charley Kehwa's expressionless voice, cautioning. He did not take his eyes from Roode.

Their voices broke the silence, and seemed to waken Roode from his half-trance. He looked up at Trask, standing across the table, and read the hostility in his face. The heavy man raised himself slowly from the chair and stood erect, meeting Trask's eyes squarely.

"Mr. Trask," he said quietly, "it is possible I owe you an apology."

"Maybe you do," Trask said.

"However," Roode continued, with great dignity, "while I may enjoy playing jolly Santa Claus with my own money, when one considers the investment of corporate funds, it is necessary to be concerned with more than simple good will. Otherwise, said corporate funds have a way of disappearing into bottomless gulfs."

5

Roode shrugged and sat down, folding his hands on the table. "One more thing I would like to know, Mr. Trask. What is your interest in Murderer's Harbor, and why do you expect me to finance it?"

"I want to look at the land," Trask said. "That's all. As far as you paying for it—"

Charley Kehwa interrupted. "That was my notion, Mr. Roode," he said quietly. "I did not count on a man like yourself. It was a very interesting thing to see."

Roode nodded. "You are uncommonly frank. I wish it were more frequent."

Charley smiled slightly. "There seems to be little choice. You have much experience in these things, we have little."

Roode shrugged again. "It is my profession, Mr. Kehwa, and I take a certain pride in practicing it effectively. Now,"—he turned to Trask—"I can tell you some things concerning this land without ever seeing it."

"All right."

"If you try to settle this country to the south, you will have endless trouble, regardless of the land itself. I am not theorizing, Mr. Trask, I'm speaking from bitter experience. You will have great difficulty, and you may, in fact, fail completely."

Trask frowned. "I don't see how you can know that."

"Then listen to me. There are two things of vital importance to the future of the Oregon country. One,"—he ticked the point off on his little finger—"is obviously the question of territoriality. It may not be as easy as you think. Now, it's obvious that the settling of the boundary dispute did not dispose of the Hudson's Bay Company. In fact, specific points of the treaty are for the purpose of protecting the Honourable Company's holdings here, isn't that true?"

"Yes, but England recognizes our claim—"

"That's all very well for the future, Mr. Trask. But please. Let us recognize facts. And the fact is that the Hudson's Bay Company is still in economic control of this country. They are the Titans.

"Why, look here! What happened when Hudson's Bay quit buying Oregon wheat a couple of years ago? Disaster, Trask, financial disaster, and you haven't recovered from it yet. No, Hudson's Bay is still a force to be reckoned with, regardless of any paper agreements. And frankly, I don't believe I would care to go up against that kind of competition. If Oregon were officially a territory—perhaps. But not as it stands now.

"Very well. The second point—and this is the key to all problems of settlement—is transportation.

"We are not living in the seventeenth century, Mr. Trask. We have almost reached the middle of the nineteenth, and colonization is not what it was in the early days of this country. It has become increasingly difficult, and increasingly unrewarding, to establish very small settlements that are completely self-sustaining. Our problem is much more complex, these days. In order, for example, to settle an area like Murderer's Harbor with success, you *must* have adequate communication with the interior. Transportation: Just that.

"Where is your land route to the Willamette Valley? Through the coastal mountains? An enormous undertaking, Trask, enormous. Not for many years yet, I fear. And by sea? Your sand bars are so treacherous no captain with his wits about him would try to take a large vessel across regularly."

"The Columbia bar is about as bad," Trask objected. "But it's crossed time and again."

"Ah, but there is a very great difference. Crossing the bar at the mouth of the Columbia gives access to the interior of an entire continent. It is well worth the risk. But what of crossing the bar at Murderer's Harbor? What have you then, to compensate for risking your vessel and crew? Hemmed in by the mountains, Trask, a virtual prison, no matter how beautiful."

"This may be true." Trask frowned. "I hadn't really—"

"Now don't misunderstand me, Trask," Roode said. "I'm not attempting to influence *you* in any way. I am pointing out the difficulties of a commercial and practical nature. These factors will not change your own mind."

"You can't survive in a country like this without being practical," Trask said defensively.

"You misunderstand me. Men like you are incomprehensibly impractical from my point of view. Everything you do, you do the hard way. *I*, on the other hand, could not live for a week in this country, because I wholly lack *your* brand of practicality. We are different, you and I.

"I deal with men of your stamp often, Trask. You wander off into the mountains for no discernible reason. You undergo a kind of life I would find unbearable. Then you come back, by God, and manage to find others like you to *settle* the wilderness! And when the land is tamed, you get restless once more. I can respect this, but it is frankly quite beyond my understanding."

"Somebody has to do it," Trask muttered.

"Quite true. The point is, you take it for granted *you* are that somebody. We are all of us born into an ambiguous world, Trask. It neither loves us nor hates us, but it is inflexible. We must learn the rules of the game, or we are not permitted to play, and rightly so. And eventually, I think, we drift into that segment of the game whose rules we understand best. You can understand the rules of the mountain and the forest and the beasts that walk them; you can live in harmony with these things. Now I, for my part, better understand the rules of commerce and civilization; this is *my* part of the great game, and I play it to the best of my ability. Between the two of us, much is done."

Hannah had been silent through the entire questioning, and the conversation between her husband and Roode. Watching the play of forces between the two men, so different from each other but with an elusive bond of likeness between them. Now she spoke quietly. "You've thought a good deal about this, haven't you?"

Roode's manner had gradually increased in intensity while he was speaking, until he was leaning across the table toward Trask. Now he relaxed and sat back in the chair. He sighed.

"Mrs. Trask," he said sadly, "I am a man who finds it absolutely necessary to comprehend his own position in the world. I believe it is a kind of disease."

Hannah glanced at Trask, who was frowning and absently rubbing his knuckles on his beard. "I think you may have spread it."

"I hope not," Roode said. "It is seldom fatal, but generally quite painful."

Chapter Six

I

I t rained gently in the night, and a cool wind came in from the sea. The rain fell fitfully, pocking the dune sands with tiny craters; and the grasses whispered restlessly along the ridges. Toward midnight the sky cleared and the high-riding moon, this night still full, made silver and gray shadows across Clatsop Plains.

Hannah Trask wakened to some sound in the night, and drowsily realized the bed beside her was empty. She sat up, and saw Trask putting a few more sticks in the fireplace. It had been the sound of the wood crackling that had wakened her.

Trask turned a chair to the fire, and took his pipe down from the mantelpiece. Hannah watched him silently for a moment before she spoke.

"Is anything wrong, Bridge?" she asked softly. There was no sound from the sleeping-loft above, where Roode, Wakila, and Charley had retired.

"I wake you up? Sorry. No, nothing wrong. I just couldn't sleep is all."

Hannah swung her legs over the edge of the bed and walked to stand beside him. "Mind if I keep you company?"

"Course not." Trask looked up at her.

Hannah shrugged, and turned another chair beside his. "I don't know," she said. "Sometimes you'd rather be alone."

"It's all right," Trask said. He filled his pipe with Roode's tobacco and lit it with a twig from the fire. The smoke rolled up, colored red and orange by the fire's warm light.

"Strange, that one," Trask mused after a while.

"Roode? Yes. Not exactly what we expected."

"Or Charley either," Trask said.

Hannah sighed. "Well, I guess it was too much to hope for. It's never that easy, somebody else pays your way."

"Nice idea, though," Trask said.

"That's what happens when you think about people as types," Hannah reflected. "They don't very often come like that."

Trask nodded slowly. "I guess."

"What now? I mean, if Roode isn't going to pay, who is?"

"I expect I am," Trask said.

"How?"

"Hannah, I don't know that any better than you. Charley said he'd wait, and I guess Wakila will, too."

"Wakila doesn't even want to be paid."

"He'll get paid," Trask said stubbornly.

Roode's final decision had been negative. The trip was too long to undertake on such a tenuous basis. "I'm sorry," he'd said finally. "I can sympathize with what you want to do, but you can understand I can't invest money in it that doesn't even belong to me. Stopping off here was just a gamble, anyway. When the territorial thing is decided, I may be back, but until then I'm afraid I couldn't commit myself. I can't, you see. I merely represent my partners, make inspections and advise as best I can."

"He's a strange one, that Roode," Trask said again, thinking about it.

"You think he was right? About the transportation and all that?"

"No idea. He seemed to know what he was talking about."

"He likes you pretty well," Hannah said.

Trask raised his eyebrows at her.

"Well, he does," she said. "He tried awful hard to tell you things that were important to him. I don't think he'd've done that if he didn't like you."

"Doesn't make much difference."

"Not much. Did you understand what he was talking about? About different men playing according to different rules?"

"I don't know," Trask said dubiously. "Little bit, maybe. I never did study too much on that kind of thing."

"If he was right about there not being much prospects at Murderer's Harbor, would you still want to go ahead?"

"There's nothing to go ahead with," Trask said, with a trace of impatience. "I just want to take a look is all."

He was silent for a moment, then added, "Anyway, sometimes you have to do things you know maybe *won't* work out just perfect. You can't figure everything fifty years ahead, least I can't. I got to do what seems good to me at the time. That's the only thing I know."

"I'm not objecting, Bridge."

"No, I know it," Trask said. "But I'm just saying. If a man was to sit down and figure about the chances, he wouldn't ever do anything. If you want to look at it that way, the chances are against about everything, even breathing, maybe. You just do what you think you have to do, and if it turns out you were wrong—well—it's too bad, that's all."

Hannah nodded. "Rules of the game, again."

"Sort of like that. You hunt trail the best you can, and if you miss it you go back to the last mark and start again. Or maybe you have to cut new trail. But you don't stop to figure out what your chances are of finding it."

Outside, from a distance, came the high, petulant yapping of a coyote. It stopped; silence. Then two more short barks.

"Talipas is walking," Hannah said.

Trask laughed shortly. "For a god, Talipas isn't very smart. He just cheated himself out of a meal, 'cause he couldn't keep his mouth shut."

Hannah laughed too. "It's the moon."

Trask nodded. "Yes, the moon. Sits up there and he wants to eat it so bad it drives him crazy thinking about it. Let the rabbits go hang and take a snap at a world."

"Foolishness, foolishness," Hannah observed. "Foolish for a god, Coyote."

"I don't know," Trask said. "You can believe him easier than some. We'd all of us like to bite the moon. We'd all of us be world-eaters if we could."

"Maybe, maybe," Hannah said softly. Then she shook her head sharply and said, "Well, if you're going to have a bite at it in the morning, you better get some sleep."

Trask nodded absently. "You go on. I'll be there in a minute."

"All right." Hannah stood and stretched herself in the firelight. She went back to bed, smoothing out the covers carefully and fluffing up her pillow. Before she closed her eyes, she looked long at the firelit

face of Trask; his hawklike nose and granite forehead stained orange
by the sputtering flames. The short black beard was a shadow on his
face, darker than the fire-cast shadows.

See if I can trim his beard in the morning, Hannah thought sleepily,
as she put her head down. Damn fool Bridge, go out to eat a world
with his beard all scraggly.

2

Roode left for Astoria just after breakfast, declining Trask's offer to
take him up.

"No, no. Good God, man. You got your own work to do, I got mine.
You go about your business."

"Morrison's is about two miles up the ridge from here," Trask said.
"You might could get a horse from Bill Morrison."

"All right," Roode said. "Fine. I'll stop by and see."

"And—ah, thanks very much," Trask said.

"Sorry I couldn't do it," Roode said. "I really am. I hope I'll see you
again. I don't mind telling you it was a very rewarding evening."

"Good-by, Mr. Roode," Hannah said.

"Mrs. Trask." He took her hand. "It's been a great pleasure. I hope
you'll remember me as well as I'll remember you."

Hannah smiled.

"Trask," Roode said, "I wish you luck. I sincerely do. And I hope I
get word that some damn fool has gone down and settled Murderer's
Harbor without knowing where the profit was coming from at all. It
would please me much."

"Well, I'll have a look anyway."

"Good."

Roode turned abruptly and began to walk north.

"Take the beach," Hannah called after him. "Easier walking. Turn
in at a tall spruce for Morrison's."

Roode nodded and waved back at them. He turned and began to cut
across the ridge toward the murmuring sound of the breakers.

"Well, let's get moving," Trask said.

Trask and Charley Kehwa together lashed the wooden panniers on
Doctor McLoughlin's bony sides while Wakila held him. Doctor rolled

his eyes mournfully, but held still for it, and for the tarpaulin-draped pack that rode his back.

The pack Hannah had prepared for Roode was divided between the other three. Charley Kehwa's pack was the biggest, and the lightest, containing mostly bread.

"You take care with the tent, now," Hannah said.

"All right. You put in a file? We'll need to keep things sharp."

Hannah nodded, pursed her lips at him reprovingly.

"All right, I was just asking. You forgot once."

"Yes"—Hannah sighed—"and I'll never live it down either."

"Wakila got Doctor started," Charley said, pointing. In back of the house the boy was leading Doctor around in circles, speaking soothingly in his ear. Doctor ogled him reproachfully; but plodded steadily around just the same. Wakila looked up and grinned broadly at Trask, having made a good start of the trip, even if it was circular.

"All right, well, let's go then," Trask said nervously.

"Calm down, Bridge. You always get so excited. You got time."

She helped him into his pack and adjusted the straps over his shoulders; then they both helped Charley Kehwa. Charley's pack, inflated with the light bread, loomed monstrously on his back like a mushroom gone wild.

Wakila did not want to let Doctor stop walking just at first, so Charley went over to lead him while Wakila got his pack.

"He be fine, that horse, when we get on the trail," Wakila assured them.

"You use a tarpaulin at night," Hannah said. "Even in the tent. "

"Oh, for God's sake, Hannah. We will."

Trask carried a rifle, at which Wakila glanced enviously, but he made no comment.

"All right, let's go," Trask said, frowning.

"Will you quit saying that?" Hannah said.

"Well, damn it, I'd quit if we ever got moving."

"All right, well, you let me think a minute." Hannah put her hand to her forehead and ran over the contents of the packs in her mind. Trask stood silent, absently knuckling his beard and shuffling his feet restlessly.

"Well, go on then!" Hannah said finally. "If you're missing something it's not my fault."

"All right," Trask said. He turned and shouted to Charley. "*Hya!* Get that bag of bones down to the beach!" Charley nodded and began to ease Doctor out of his circle. Wakila ran awkwardly over to take the lead rein from Charley and continue the good work.

"Good luck, Bridge," Hannah said.

"All right," Trask said, watching Doctor's progress up the ridge suspiciously. "If that damn horse gives us any trouble I'm going to kill Solomon."

"Solomon wouldn't've give him to you."

"Better not. All right, well, good-by Hannah."

"Take care, Bridge. I don't want to lose you."

"We will. Back in ten days, maybe not. Depends on what we find." He kissed her perfunctorily on the forehead and moved off. He met Charley where he was waiting and the two began to follow quickly after Wakila and Doctor McLoughlin.

"Take care," Hannah whispered. "Please take care."

She watched until they had disappeared over the ridge without looking back. She touched her forehead absently, turned, and walked back into the empty house.

3

On reaching the beach, the party swung south for over a mile to the thin, triangular spit that marked the northern edge of the Neahcoxie tide flats. They cut across the base of the triangle to the sheltered beach called *tenas-nauits*, little beach. The tide was nearly full in by the time they reached the half-moon bay, and the flats were covered with shallow water. A low morning fog hung in the pocket formed by the bay, its tenuous, wispy edges standing in thin fingers a little distance onto the land. For the most part, the fog remained on their right, and they skirted it. Occasionally a long tendril would sneak across the land, pointing up into one of the dune-depressions, and then they would pass into a landscape of grayness where the light of the sun was veiled and obscure.

They came this far in silence, broken only by Wakila's low and steady encouragement of Doctor McLoughlin. Gradually, as it seemed Doctor would be willing to move alone, even this diminished.

The line of the beach began a gentle, flattening curve, and soon they were moving along parallel to the ocean again. The bay was almost unruffled; the breakers were a quarter of a mile out from here, on the bar.

"We'd better turn inland," Charley said. "We'll have to cross the rivers a little upstream."

Trask nodded. He was feeling calmer now, glad to be on the way. Getting off was always unpleasant for him, and made him nervous.

Wakila turned Doctor. There were two major streams, the Neahcoxie and the Necanicum, to cross before they began the first difficult stage, and several smaller ones. The mouths of both were too wide to ford with the high tide forcing the sea upward into the fresh water. A little way back from the beach they could be crossed with relative ease.

Beyond the Necanicum lay several miles of brush country, tight-packed salal and manzanita and briar, ten and twelve feet high. This scrub was relieved by birch groves; scattered clumps of hemlock and spruce; occasional firs.

"We'll go back down to the beach on the other side of Necanicum," Charley said. "By Latty's place. We double back some to do it that way, but it'll be easier."

Trask nodded. There were well-marked trails through the brush— the route was frequently taken by Clatsops going south—but there was little doubt Charley was right; the beach road was almost always faster in the long run, even if it meant backtracking.

"We going to tackle Neahseu'su today?" Trask asked.

Charley shook his head. "No. That may be hard going, Neahseu'su. We'll get close to the base and make camp. There's a creek right at the bottom."

Going inland to avoid the river's mouth took them along the seaward edge of Neahcoxie village. Trask was vaguely pleased—and Wakila almost ecstatic—to see the greater portion of the Neahcoxie Clatsops gathered at the edge of the village. There must have been nearly forty of them lined up silently, watching the party pass a few hundred yards away. Many of the men still held their tools; women, strands of flax from the net-making. No greetings were exchanged; the gathering was a gesture of both curiosity and respect. Only the dogs yapped excitedly, and this was normal. Their pitch was a little higher than usual—and they obviously could not discover in their dog-experience any sane reason for the people to be lined up silently at the edge of the village—but none of them ventured out to inspect the passing men.

Wakila walked with dignity until they were out of sight of the villagers, then quietly handed the lead rein to Charley Kehwa.

"I must check the trail ahead," he said.

Charley nodded and accepted charge of Doctor McLoughlin.

Wakila ran ahead as fast as his legs would carry him, leaping puddles, small logs, and even low bushes he might easily have stepped around. His exuberance was so full even Trask smiled, watching the rapidly retreating back.

"*Ikt youtl Clatsop*," Charley said with a smile. "He is a proud Clatsop."

"He is," Trask agreed thoughtfully.

"In my memory," Charley continued quietly, this is the first time the people have looked on Wakila with this respect. It is a bad thing when a boy is not respected by his people."

"He's a good boy," Trask said absently.

"Not often can he show it. The people think well of you for taking Wakila. It will show him a thing in himself that is stronger than the wiskey, and the itlokum."

"*Kloshe kahkwa*," Trask said. "It is good so."

Wakila returned, having gained a more fitting composure, and, shortly after, they crossed the Necanicum. When they passed Latty's house, William Latty called out, "Good luck, Bridge. Hope you find something to please you." His Clatsop wife called out, "Klahowya," and Trask nodded his thanks to both.

"Seems like everybody on the Plains knows about this trip," Trask said. There was no reason they should not, but Trask tended to feel that his doings were his own business. The attitude was exaggerated, and he tried to control it, in general. Still . . . There was always the lurking sensation that other people should not be interested in what he was doing, even in a friendly way.

That comes from living alone in the mountains so long, he thought. Ruefully he reflected that, after all, he knew damned little about people and what made them act or think in the way they did. Least of all himself.

"Hard to keep a thing like this secret," Charley observed.

"I don't mean to keep it secret, exactly," Trask said. "But—I don't know. Seems like a man ought to have better things to do than study about what his neighbors are doing."

Charley shrugged.

Soon they reached the beach again, on the southern side of the bay. Ahead of them was Neahseu'su, the two-humped bulk jutting out against the ocean and silhouetted darkly against the sky. They would reach the lower summit first. Then there was a short crescent beach, and the main point began. The beach was a trap; a beautiful and inviting stretch of white sand, sheltered from the winds that raked the cliff faces, easily accessible—at low tide—around the first point. But at high tide the point was lashed by breakers, completely impassable. The inviting crescent of beach became a swirling mass of cross-swells and rip currents that beat against the background cliff; completely submerged. When the tide began to rise, there was no way out but straight up, and that was a route few men had ever taken successfully.

If they camped at the base for the night, their timing was such that they would surmount the first point about noon on the next day; almost the peak of the tide. They could then wait for the tide to ebb so they could cross on the beach, or take the inland trail.

Charley led the way with a bush knife; Trask followed with an ax for whatever obstacles might be too large for Charley's knife. Wakila came last, leading Doctor. When they moved into the brush, Trask tied his rifle to Doctor's pack, freeing his hands for the laborious job of hacking through the thickly tangled undergrowth.

As the late afternoon came on, Trask estimated they would reach the proposed campsite shortly before dusk.

"You figured pretty good," he told Charley.

"I've been here before," Charley said, smiling.

"You been a lot farther south than this," Trask said.

Charley nodded. "But after a certain point, it matters little whether you've been there or not. It is still difficult."

"What point?"

"Just about where we camp tonight." Charley shrugged. "It is all very difficult," he said, as if thinking of something else.

It was nearly five o'clock when Charley finally said, "Well, that was our last crossing. We can take the beach from here to the campsite."

"Good," Trask said. "What do you guess for tomorrow?"

"It may even take us the whole day to cross Neahseu'su. Maybe not so much."

"How far is it across?"

"Maybe ten miles."

"The whole day?"

"Maybe. If not, we have the next ten miles of good walking; beach trail all the way, with luck. Even without luck—if the tide is against us—we will have to climb over only one small point."

"This is not such hard walking," Wakila said.

"It comes," Charley told him. "It comes."

Chapter Seven

They made camp for the night in the shadow of Neahseu'su, by the bank of a small creek. At a place where the stream made a sharp bend, the point thus formed was relatively clear, and would catch the morning sun early. There they dropped their packs.

Wakila unpacked Doctor McLoughlin and led him into the woods a little way, where good grass was growing beneath the ever-present blanket of ferns. He hitched the horse for the night, and wrapped the clapper of the cowbell strung on Doctor's neck; flicked it with his finger and it belled satisfactorily.

"Good horse, Doctor," Wakila told him. "Very fine horse today. Better tomorrow. Eat. Much food." He scratched Doctor behind the ears and soothed him with a steady, affectionate murmur. Nearby he could hear the rhythmic chik-chik-chik of the ax as Trask cut wood. He talked to Doctor quietly for a few more moments, then walked toward the sound of the ax.

When Wakila reached him, Trask had felled a cedar about twelve inches in diameter, and was cutting two logs from it, perhaps four feet long.

"I take these," Wakila said, when the two logs were finished. He dragged them back to the point, one under each arm, while Trask gathered the smaller wood.

While the other two were gone, Charley Kehwa had cut a pole and run it between two trees at head height. From the pole he suspended the small packs; they dangled awkwardly, like bats hanging head down from a limb.

"Cook only coffee tonight," Charley said. "*Tenas muckamuck*, small food."

Wakila nodded. He put the two short logs down at a slight angle to each other; six inches separated the butts, while the small ends were a little over a foot apart. Across the bed logs he laid a small platform of green sticks. Trask returned then with an armload of dry cedar branches and Wakila set to shaving kindling sticks. Picking half a dozen of the better sticks, he shaved them almost through for half their length, leaving the curled shavings attached to the stick at midpoint.

He built a small cone of these kindling sticks on the green twig platform, shaved ends down. Around this kindling tripod he carefully placed another layer of twigs, forming a second cone, this time of slightly larger wood.

Trask, while Wakila laid their fire, had driven a forked branch into the ground on the windward side of the bed logs. He supported a green pole on this, with a notch cut in the end to hold the bail of the coffee pot. Where the pole rested on the ground, he weighted it with a heavy rock from the bank of the stream.

Wakila took the pot to fill while Trask lit the fire with a locofoco match. The whole cone structure Wakila had built was not much larger than a man's hat. It would provide a fast-burning, hot fire; all that was necessary for the boiling of their coffee. As it was needed, Wakila would replenish with other wood. As the sticks burned, the hot coals would drop through the spaces in the little platform, down between the bed logs, catching their inner surfaces on fire. This would provide an adequate campfire for the night, and a bed of hot coals for the cooking of breakfast in the morning.

When the coffee was brewing, Wakila began to make up their bed rolls, and Trask went to help Charley Kehwa set up the tent and spread the groundcloth.

Trask's groundcloth was a double-thickness tarpaulin; one of the rare items of extra weight he permitted in his pack. "Man can't do a damn lick if he don't get a night's sleep," he'd insist. "Don't lose heat into the air half as fast as you do into the ground. Man's better off sleeping bare on a good groundcloth than with all the blankets in the world piled on top."

Charley smiled faintly, the echo of Hannah's advice sounding familiar in his ears. He busied himself with setting up his cooking gear for the morning. Wakila scurried about animatedly, securing the camp for the night. He made a square of crossed sticks, to keep the horse-pack off the ground, and placed it beneath the other packs dangling from their pole. From Charley's pack he took a loaf of bread; from his own, several packages of dried salmon for their dinner.

He then covered the whole with another tarpaulin to keep rain and dew off, and returned to the fire.

Everything he did without being asked or told; and after each small item had been ticked off the list he carried in his head, he glanced shyly at Trask. He was powerless to stop this—he wanted Trask to know that he, Wakila, was not only the finest carrier among the Clatsops, but a fine man in camp, too.

Trask gave no sign of having seen Wakila's efficient set-up work; took it seemingly as a matter of course. But he had seen, and was pleased. The first night was the night for testing. No word of direction had been spoken since they stopped at the point, but now the camp was set; Wakila had just folded the last of the blanket rolls inside the tent.

To himself, Trask nodded. He had never packed with either of these two before, and it was good that nothing had to be said. The duties had been distributed and accepted automatically and without confusion, almost instinctively. They would vary, from time to time—perhaps Wakila would cook and Charley set up tent—but Trask knew now each necessary thing would be done effectively, and he was pleased.

Night was flooding swiftly over the eastern mountains as they squatted before the fire to eat; almost as though the sea of darkness had been held back by the mountain dam until its depth had finally overwhelmed the solid stone. The sun was hesitating over the ocean's rim, hidden from their view by the forest between them and the sea. The sky in the west was still rosily light.

The three tore off pieces of bread, and chewed the tough, smoky-flavored salmon with relish; knowing full well they would be sick of it by the time the trip was finished, but enjoying it while they could.

None spoke. They ate, and watched the fire burning down inside the bed logs, and listened to the gradual shift from the daytime sounds of the woods to the night. A ground squirrel mounted a rock at the edge of the clear point and chittered madly at them; scolding, reprimanding, wild with some obscure rage at their intrusion. Then—having satisfied its need to tell these featherless birds what it thought of them—darted down behind its rock and disappeared into the darkness of the forest.

The three men had listened attentively to what the squirrel had to tell them, all eyes watching it. But it was no more than the usual, and their eyes were drawn back to the immediacy of the fire.

The fire itself grew brighter and stronger as the daylight dimmed; asserted its power to bring light where there was dark. The western sky grew abruptly darker as the sun finally dipped completely behind the horizon clouds. Soon, everything beyond the fire-circle had become invisible, insubstantial. The front of the tent was clearly seen facing the fire; the back had ceased to exist except as part of the hood of darkness that surrounded them.

Trask started to stand, but Wakila stopped him by nudging a small package with his toe. It was Trask's tobacco wallet. Wakila also produced Trask's Norwegian meerschaum, and a plain clay pipe with a long wooden stem for himself and Charley Kehwa. They stuffed the bowls with care, spilling none of the tobacco on the ground, and lit. Charley took a few deep puffs and seemed to enter a kind of reverie. He handed the pipe to Wakila, who did the same.

Trask fondled the meerschaum for a moment before lighting it, a kind of ritual inspection of which he was not aware. He lit, and let the smoke roll in his mouth, mingling with the strong flavors of the salmon and the coffee, and in some strange way completing them. The taste of the smoke was like the last drowsy moment of wakefulness, when you know something has been finished, and then you sink into the richness of sleep.

Branches creaked and sighed around them, and needles and leaves whispered together. The faint smell of salt came to them from the seaward side as a light breeze came up from the west.

Charley Kehwa raised his head and looked at the sky, where stars were sharp and distinct. He closed his eyes and his nostrils spread slightly.

"Rain maybe, tonight," he said.

Trask nodded.

After a while, Wakila stood. He smiled shyly at the other two. "*Hyas ticky moosum,*" he said, almost apologetically. "Very sleepy."

Trask nodded his approval solemnly. "*Mika mamook hyas skookum, hyas kloshe*. You worked very hard, very well." He nodded again emphatically.

Wakila's shy smile broadened to a happy grin, and he turned abruptly lest Trask see too much of his pleasure. He went into the tent and the other two could hear the shuffle and rustle as he settled himself in his blanket roll for the night.

2

The night was silent and the air grew chill; Trask rose and fed the fire from the stack of night-wood beside the bed logs. He came back and squatted on his heels beside Charley, watching the flame take the new sticks.

"If it rains we'll have hard going," he said, after a moment.

"Yes," Charley agreed. "It will be worse."

Both men were silent for several minutes, watching the fire grow.

"What's down there, Charley?" Trask said at last.

"Five rivers and a bay."

"That all?"

Charley turned his head and scrutinized Trask before he answered. "I can't tell you what you want to know," he said quietly.

"What do I want to know?" Trask asked curiously.

"If there's anything there for *you*."

Trask hesitated, unsure. "Charley, you pokin' at me?"

Charley shook his head seriously. "No."

Trask thought about it; finally sighed. "Sometimes I don't understand one word out of ten you say, Charley. You do that a-purpose?"

"No," Charley said. "The way I talk, maybe."

"Maybe," Trask said. After a moment he added, "Maybe it's the tamanawis."

Charley glanced at him briefly, but did not seem offended. "You shouldn't worry about the tamanawis," he said quietly.

"I don't," Trask said. His voice was expressionless, and he looked straight ahead into the fire.

Charley understood it as a declaration that had to be made at some time during the trip, and was vaguely pleased it had happened so soon.

He was acutely aware of the possibility that a destructive tension might have grown between the two of them, if Trask had not chosen to put his resentment into words. Such a tension would be a bad thing on a trip like this, a dangerous thing.

"Bridge," he said at last, "you listen to me a minute?"

"Sure," Trask said.

Charley considered his words carefully. "A people's religion," he said, "is their own thing. It belongs to them, and to no one else. We have not tried to force Kahnie and Talipas and Tsiatko on you or any of the Boston men. But Loveman Anders and the priests and the Jesus-men, they come and tell us we are wrong, that we must worship the Saghalie Tyee and Jesus and all that. This is not a good thing they do, because it confuses the people. They tell us we should not flatten our babies' heads. Why do they care? It is not their concern. We have always been flatheads, and we always will be. It is our pride."

"Why?" Trask said. "Why should you flatten your heads?"

"It makes no difference why, is what I'm saying, Bridge. If we choose to flatten our heads, that is not the concern of God and Jesus and Anders. It is *our* concern. They have no right to interfere. They have no right to laugh at Talipas, because he is sometimes foolish in the tales. This is our land, and these are our gods. The gods and the land are the same, and the people are part of both."

"But you understand we don't all feel like that," Trask said, uneasy at being called on to defend the missionary spirits. "You were educated in a white school, Charley. You can understand these things better than most of the people."

Charley shook his head sadly. "Knowing more, I understand even less," he said. "Because the Saghalie Tyee and his son Jesus *do* nothing. Your machines and guns and sawmills do something, but your gods are useless. They do nothing at all. What kind of gods are they, Bridge? That they do nothing for their people until after they are dead? What good are they, even to their own people? They are no good to anybody.

"But—the tamanawis is not just a thing of death, it is a thing of living. We do not get down on our knees and fold our hands, and then jump up and say words, and then get down again. This seems to us foolishness. But we say nothing, for we cannot know how it is with the whites. But they think they can know how it is with the Clatsops."

"You go up on a mountain and fast for four, five days," Trask said. "Then you come down and tell the people a lot of things you saw."

"Have you ever gone without food for four days, or five?"

"I been on awful short rations for longer than that."

Charley laughed. "It is not the same thing, Bridge, not the same at all. Even a little food makes a great difference."

Trask did not answer.

"Something happens to a man, Bridge. When a man makes strong tamanawis he changes inside. He is not the same man he was before. His wits are sharpened by the hunger; as a file cleans away the dead metal on a knife, hunger cleans away the dead stuff of a man's brain."

"His imagination is sharpened, maybe."

"Maybe. But it makes no difference. Because a man with a strong tamanawis can understand. He can understand this world, and he can become one thing with it. This is all the tamanawis means, Bridge. To become one thing with the world. And then you can know it as you know your own body."

Trask sighed. "I don't understand it, Charley. Sorry."

"Not in words, maybe. Nobody understands the tamanawis in words. This is the difference between it and your gods. Your gods are mostly words.

"You whites, you are always wishing to fight the world, and you ask your gods for help to do this thing, which they never give. You are always trying to overcome something, and you do not see that you fight nothing but your own minds. The world does not wish to fight you. It does not wish to be friends with you, either. The world wishes nothing at all; only men wish, and they make up their dreams and tell themselves they are talking about the world, when they are talking about the ground fog that lies on their minds."

"Maybe, maybe," Trask said. "What are you saying with all this?"

Charley shifted his position a little, hesitated a moment before replying. "I am saying the tamanawis does not hurt you, is all. I am saying you are not threatened by it."

Charley regarded Trask's brooding countenance carefully, his face impassive. Then he turned to look at the fire again, and spoke quietly, his voice flat.

"You say you do not understand the tamanawis, Bridge. Who has asked that you should? No one has asked this of you. But I will say one thing more, and then I will stop.

"If you had been born a Clatsop, you would have been a tamanawis man. I, Charley Kehwa, say this."

Trask looked up, startled, only to see Charley turn on his heel and stride toward the tent. At the flap, Charley turned, and Trask thought he saw the twinkling reflection of the fire in Charley's dark eyes.

"And you would have been a good one, too," Charley said.

He entered the tent and disappeared. A little distance away, Doctor McLoughlin's bell tinkled softly in the night.

3

Some time later, Trask sighed and shook his head. He fed the fire, moved the bed logs a little closer together to hold the heat for morning; then went to the tent.

Wakila was on the far right, a shapeless, immobile mass, with only the top of his head showing above the blanket. Charley was far left; they had left the center place—farthest from the side walls—for him. Trask climbed under the blanket and lifted his legs stiffly to tuck the edges beneath him. Charley Kehwa lay with his head thrown back and his mouth open, looking like a drowned man. In contrast with Wakila's inertness, Charley's hands were moving on top of his blanket, rustling very faintly in the darkness.

Dreaming, Trask thought. If he was a dog, we'd say he was chasing rabbits.

Trask lay back and looked at the ridge above. The flickering fire made dark shadows dance into the tent, and he found he could easily lose his sense of perspective at will; he could see the ridge as just above his face, or an endless distance away, depending on how he wanted to look at it. Finally it became too difficult to focus his eyes, and he gave up the game.

What's he dreaming about? Trask wondered vaguely. What kind of dreams does a tamanawis man have?

Charley was walking. Down a long and narrow stretch of beach, with the ocean on his right and the forest on his left. Just behind him came Trask and Wakila. Trask was impassive, walking behind like a machine, while Wakila struggled along under a tremendous load. His body was bent almost double, and Charley realized the boy was carrying his own pack and the horse-pack, too.

He stopped to help, but Trask put his hand on Charley's arm. "You can't do that," Trask said. "You can't help him." Trask seemed very sad.

Charley walked around behind Wakila and began to tug at a strap. It did not come loose easily, and finally tore off. One flap of the huge pack came open, and Charley saw it was filled with people. They were all naked, and all were whites. They were tumbling over each other confusedly, and the inside of the pack was like a piece of meat after the maggots had gotten to it.

Charley was suddenly afraid they might get out. He didn't know what would happen then; but he knew he did not want it. He closed the flap hastily, and to cover his fear said to Wakila, "I guess it's all right, then."

Wakila nodded and smiled. Charley knew the small pack held the Clatsop tribe, so he did not open it. There were enough people now. Let the others stay in the pack, he thought.

Trask had gotten far ahead of them on the beach. His way was blocked by a huge stone, and he was pummeling at it with his fists. He had his head down low and his eyes closed, and was driving his fists against the stone with a frantic rhythm when Charley came up.

Vaguely Charley thought, If this was real, he would break his hands.

The beach on either side of the stone was completely clear, and Charley said, "You don't have to do that. You can walk around."

"No," Trask said stubbornly. "I got to get him out." He continued to pound at the stone.

Charley shrugged, and walked around the stone. Suddenly he felt very guilty, and decided he should help. From the opposite side he began to hit at the stone. After a few moments, the monolith split down the center and crumbled away. Inside was a tiny baby. Trask appeared delighted, and ran forward to pick the child up.

Charley walked closer, and saw the baby was well formed, except that it had no face.

"He isn't finished," he said to Trask. He was abruptly conscious of a sensation of panic. "We should have left him in there longer."

"No," Trask said. "He would have died. He had to come out now. He's hungry."

"He can't eat without a face," Charley objected.

"Well . . . we'll do something," Trask said vaguely.

Charley turned and ran down the beach, conscious of a great urgency. He was soon breathless from running and with a sharp pain in his chest, but he could not stop. Trask and Wakila were far ahead of him, and he had to catch up to them and tell them something. The beach was very long, and it seemed he ran for an eternity, with the sharpness in his chest and his breath coming in short, ragged gasps.

Abruptly, his way was blocked by a man. He was a canoe-Indian, with the short, bandy legs and tremendous musculature of the upper body. Charley thought at first it was the baby grown up; then grew uncertain. Charley was afraid of him, but would not show his fear. He pretended he was still running, but stood in one place before the man, pumping his legs and arms in the semblance of running. The other man was standing on a flat stone imbedded in the beach sand.

"You shouldn't have come here, Charley," said the other. "Now we must wrestle, and I don't want to kill you. But you have broken the rule, and we must wrestle. I wish you no harm."

Charley was desperately afraid, and he choked back a sob. He knew it would be worse if the other knew he was afraid, and suddenly thought to himself, I shouldn't have helped him get out of the rock.

He ran forward at the reaching arms, and ducked at the last instant. He tripped on the edge of the stone, but did not fall. Instead, the stone raised up at a slant from the ground, and Charley had to climb it to keep from slipping back.

The stone grew and grew until it extended endlessly into the sky. Charley scrambled up the side, and soon came to heavy underbrush. The stone dropped away into a deep chasm on either side, and he recognized one of the canyons on Neahkahnie, as he had seen it when a boy. Then he knew the Indian that had wanted to wrestle was both the baby grown, and Kahnie himself, and this was his place, Neah-Kahnie.

The urgency to catch up with Trask and Wakila was still in him, and he climbed the slope of the mountain until he could no longer feel his fingers and toes. Finally he came to the crest, and the desperation and fear reached their peak. Perched insecurely on the top of the mountain was a burial canoe . . .

The god Kahnie stood beside it sadly, and beckoned Charley to come look. Almost paralyzed with fear, Charley hesitantly made his way to stand beside the god.

"You had better look," Kahnie said, gesturing to the canoe.

Charley turned, slowly; brought his eyes down to look into the hollowed interior of the canoe . . . and screamed . . .

Kahnie grabbed his shoulder and said, "Charley, Charley . . ."

"Charley, Charley."

Charley whimpered; suddenly came full awake in the tent. His body under the blanket was wet with sweat, and there was a hollow, cool feeling in his chest.

Trask's heavy grip on his shoulder relaxed. "For God's sake, Charley, what's the matter?"

Charley shook his head, returning slowly to the reality of the tent. Trask was kneeling beside him, and just beyond, Wakila was sitting up, half out of his blankets, with a worried expression.

"Bad dream," Charley murmured. "Nothing, bad dream is all."

Trask watched the flat face and dark eyes, still fretted around with lines of strain. He searched Charley's face for a long time, trying to read it, read something.

"Let's get some sleep now," he said quietly. He went back to his own blanket and crawled under. Wakila nodded apprehensively, then lay back down himself.

Charley lay shaking for a few moments, until the fear and anxiety had drained out of him. Then he closed his eyes, and sleep came eventually.

4

It did not rain that night; but the morning sky was dull and gray. When the first faint light outlined the mountains, Charley Kehwa was up and out of the tent. He built up the fire, boiled coffee, and Trask woke to the sound of bacon sputtering. He fumbled out of his blanket roll and to the fire; poured himself a cup of coffee and squatted on his heels beside Charley to drink it, staring blearily at the frying pan that lay atop the bed logs.

The hot coffee scalded his throat, and he squeezed his eyes shut, but it helped waken him. "Some people wake up faster than others," he explained defensively.

Charley nodded. "We should go fast today," he said, with a glance at the ominous sky.

"May hold off till tomorrow," Trask said, squinting up.

"Best we're over Neahseu'su when it comes," Charley said.

Trask nodded his agreement, gulped the rest of the coffee and went to take down the tent. He met Wakila on the way, who smiled his apology for late sleeping, looking embarrassed. Trask spoke to him briefly, and the boy went off to get Doctor McLoughlin.

By the time they finished breakfast, the packs were ready and the camp broken except for the utensils in their hands. These Wakila snatched, cleaned, and packed away as they finished. Charley soaked down the fire and began to scoop dirt on it.

Trask knelt beside him to help. "Say, Charley," he said casually.

"Yes."

"Who was it? In the dream last night."

Charley stopped abruptly, turned to meet Trask's steady, impassive gaze. He held his own face equally expressionless, and the two men looked squarely at each other for a long moment. Charley turned away and threw another handful of dirt on the smoking log.

"I could not see the face," he said quietly.

"All right," Trask said blandly. "But it was death again, wasn't it?"

Charley nodded slowly.

"All right," Trask said again.

They finished burying the fire, helped each other into their packs and set off into the brush.

Within an hour they were beginning to feel the rise of ground beneath their feet.

Chapter Eight

The first slopes of the mountain were thick with growth, salal and briar, the undergrowth in some places reaching a height of twelve feet. The trail through was well marked, and the going was not exceptionally hard. The only major delays were for Doctor McLoughlin.

There were many deadfalls over the trail from the spring storms; and streams were full. It was not possible to avoid all the logs by going around, and those the good Doctor could not leap had to be removed from the trail with the ax. The day was cool, the sun's heat screened away by the low-hanging overcast. The briar was in bloom, and the smell of spruce and hemlock thick and clean in the air. To the party's right the throaty growl of the surf could be heard, but they would not see it again until they reached the lower of the two summits, Clark's Point of View.

By midmorning they were well up the slope. A large fir across the trail blocked them, and had to be cut out. This they did, swinging the ax in turn, and then stopped there for a brief rest.

Trask was pleased. He guessed they were making almost two miles an hour, far beyond his original estimate.

"This is better than I thought," Charley said. "The trail is very good here."

Trask nodded. "How far you figure it'll stay good?"

Charley shook his head. "I don't know. I think across the whole cape. No reason for a trail to be cut only halfway."

"Well, if it stays good, we should make the other side by the middle of the afternoon," Trask said.

Charley nodded. "There is a stream there, on the other side, where the elk come. By the stream is a little hut. We could make camp there." He looked up at the gray sky. Considered it; and finally shook his head.

"I don't know," he said. "The hut would be good protection if we get the rain tonight, but we would waste much time, if we reach it in the afternoon."

"Where'd that hut come from?" Trask asked.

"Killamooks," Charley said.

Wakila looked up apprehensively, and Charley explained rapidly in the Jargon that Killamooks had built the *tenas house* at Elk Creek. Wakila nodded, but the mention of the Killamooks seemed to depress him. He leaned back against the log and drew pictures in the dirt at his feet.

"That's still Clatsop country over there," Trask said, puzzled.

"Yes. All the way to Neahkahnie is Clatsop land."

"What were the Killamooks doing up here?"

Charley shrugged. "They came, built the hut and stayed for about a year. Then they went away."

"What were they doing?"

"Waiting for a whale, I think," Charley said. "But nobody asked them. There were four, five of them. Whales come ashore on the long beach fairly often."

Trask shook his head. "Very brave men, to come into the middle of enemy country to wait for a whale."

"Killamooks," Charley said, as if the simple fact explained all things.

"Did your people—wasn't there any—"

"They bothered nobody," Charley said. "They did no harm. They gave us klahowya and were polite." He shrugged.

"Still seems like a hell of a risk to take for a little whale oil."

"They were Killamooks," Charley repeated patiently.

"You know anything about their tyee, Kilchis?"

"No," Charley said.

Trask waited briefly for amplification, but none came.

Well, we'll be finding out soon enough, Trask thought, and did not find the thought comforting.

"Let's be moving," he said.

They reached the top shortly after noon. From the crest they could see the whole stretch of Clatsop Plains to the north, or as far north as the overcast permitted. Nearly a mile and a half out in the ocean from the head, they could see a jagged island. It was small, a sharp, abrupt pinnacle jutting out of the gray water and standing alone. Breakers surged around it, throwing white water far up the wet black faces of the rock. Trask moved gingerly to the edge of the cliff, and stretched out on his belly, looking at the sea below.

Two hundred feet below him the sea pounded and thundered against the cliffs. The tide was high now, and the crescent beach between the two points completely submerged. The sea came in ponderous, swelling rollers that surged toward the land with unreal slowness. With a heavy majesty they swept the last quarter-mile of their own domain and exploded against the rock in foam-lashed fury that shot white water a hundred feet in the air.

Trask watched in fascination, finally inched back from the edge. "Hell of a drop," he said.

"The cliffs at Neahkahnie are twice as high," Charley said. "More than twice." He watched Trask with amusement in his dark eyes. "And we will have to go along the edge."

Trask glanced at him, trying to see if the tamanawis man were joking; and decided not. He shrugged.

"Well, if we have to, we have to," he said. He turned away from the cliff and walked back to where Wakila was holding Doctor McLoughlin. When he left the edge, the sound of the breakers diminished sharply; became again a steady rumbling background.

Wakila was holding the lead rein well up by Doctor's mouth. The horse was nervous at being so close to the edge, and Trask wondered momentarily how he would be able to take the Neahkahnie passage. It was, he decided, a problem that would have to be met when he came to it. But the notion made him uneasy.

They moved on, back into the woods, where Charley again found the trail. A short distance down from the summit there was a small stream running directly toward the ocean. They stopped here, and ate. As he chewed the smoky salmon, Trask mused idly on the notion that the stream simply drifted to the edge of the cliff and toppled over.

For some obscure reason, the image amused him. It seemed so much more direct than the probable reality; a long, winding course down to sea level and an unspectacular entry into the ocean.

He decided if *he* was a stream he'd just go straight for the edge, by God, and the hell with all this witless wandering around.

He laughed aloud.

"What are you laughing at?" Charley asked.

Trask told him, but the idea was somehow not funny in the retelling, and he was disappointed in it.

2

The south side of the cape was even easier going, so far as the trail was concerned, because there were fewer deadfalls. The forest around them was very pleasant in this season, the season of growth. The evergreen boughs were all tipped with the bright green tassels of the year's growth tips, giving them a ridiculously decorated look.

Trask was jubilant by the time they reached the Killamook hut at Elk Creek. So far, they had made better than good time, and he began to view the trip as less formidable than he had thought.

"No point stopping here," he said to Charley. "Day's young yet."

Charley agreed. "It will take another hour to the beach. Four o'clock, maybe."

"What do we have on the beach?"

"Good walking for ten miles except for one point." He glanced back at Wakila and Doctor McLoughlin. Wakila smiled at him. Doctor rolled his eyes in horrible anticipation.

"What point?"

"Woman-in-Bed, they call it."

"That what it looks like?" Trask asked, unable to visualize it.

"No," Charley said seriously. "Only way to get around it is like this." He spread-eagled himself against the air, made squirming motions with his pelvis and upper body as he inched along. It could have represented a man hugging a cliff face, but it seemed to Trask too graphic for that.

Wakila laughed, not having understood the English conversation between Trask and Charley. "*Hyas kloshe, hyas kloshe!*" he shouted, stomping his feet and frightening Doctor McLoughlin. "Do it again, Charley, do it again!"

"I'll break your legs if you do," Trask assured Charley. "That's the dirtiest thing I ever saw in my life."

Charley shrugged. "What can you expect?" he asked reasonably. "All the Boston men make love to their women in the dark. Is that not true? Maybe all white men, even Dutchmen. How do you see anything at all?"

"Let's get down to the beach," Trask muttered.

They made the beach in a little under an hour. Ahead of them was a long stretch of light sand, disappearing into mist far in the south. Trask walked out on the sand and looked back at Neahseu'su with satisfaction.

Charley stepped up beside him, turned to follow the direction of Trask's eyes. "But it gets worse," he said, guessing Trask's thought. "Neahseu'su is the easiest of the points to climb."

"I think you make too much of it," Trask said. "When I was trapping up by Yellowstone we'd make a point like that before breakfast."

"*Wawa delate kahkwa Killamook,*" Charley commented dryly. "You talk just like a Killamook."

"Fact, though," Trask said complacently.

Charley was unmoved. "We will see how our mountain man likes walking the Cape of the Falcons, and Neahkahnie."

Wakila came up with Doctor McLoughlin, and the party started down the beach.

"*Huloima nauits,*" Wakila said after a few minutes' walking. "A strange beach."

"Yes," Charley said. "It is this way all the way to the point, the sand is different."

"Why is that?" Trask wondered. He scuffed his feet and listened to the strange squeak of the sand, trying to grasp the difference between it and the sand of the Clatsop Plains beach.

Charley shrugged. "One of Kahnie's whims, maybe. He had many."

The tide was out when they came to the point Charley had called Woman-in-Bed, but the water still surged against the rocky base. Some few feet above the breakers, there was adequate foothold for a man—but there was no way for Doctor to get around.

"How deep is the water at the base?" Trask asked.

"Not deep, between breakers. You can see bottom. We could probably make it between two waves."

"How about Doctor?"

"I don't know," Charley admitted. "I don't think so."

Trask looked up at the top of the point, where the scrub pine began to grow, swept back in a flat plane by the sea wind. The point was neither high nor broad, but to go around it on the land side would doubtless take an extra hour, possibly more. He glanced at the sun. It was coming down faster now, and he guessed night would catch them in the woods if they went inland.

"There is a small waterfall on the other side," Charley offered unhelpfully. "Good water, good place to camp for the night. Also many mussels for dinner."

Trask watched a roller come in and break on the point. "Damn it," he said, frowning.

"What do you want to do?"

Trask watched another roller. It did not seem too large, but the power of the sea was often deceptive. He reached back and shrugged off the shoulder straps of his pack. "You and Wakila go ahead," he said. "Take my pack."

"What are you going to do?"

"I'm going to bring Doctor between breakers."

"I don't think you can make it," Charley said.

"If we can stay on our feet through one of them, we can," Trask said.

"You are taking a great chance with the horse."

"What about *me*?" Trask said indignantly.

"Doctor has our gear," Charley said.

Wakila was told of Trask's plan, and obviously disapproved. He began to say something, but Charley cut him off with a gesture.

"How do you intend to keep your feet when the breaker hits?"

"I can do it if Doctor doesn't panic. You'll see."

Trask stripped off his shirt and pants and gave them to Charley. Wakila lashed Trask's pack on top of his own, and the two Clatsops began to inch their way around the point, several yards above the water's high point.

Watching them, Trask was startled by the aptness of Charley's pantomime demonstration; the two lay flat against the point with their arms outstretched to the sides, squirming along with a kind of body wriggle. They seemed to hug the point with every inch of their bodies. Finally they inched out of sight around a large rock, and Trask returned his attention to the timing of the breakers. He counted under his breath.

He began to speak gently to Doctor McLoughlin, soothing him, with his hand tightening gradually on the lead rein.

In a few seconds he heard Charley shout, indicating they had made the beach on the other side.

"All right, Doctor, now come on," Trask said. "You just trust me and we'll be all right, you just take it easy and do what I say and don't get scared. Good hoss, Doctor, come on now, we'll make it all right."

Doctor shifted his feet uneasily, but did not seem frightened of the water as he had been of the height.

Trask watched the roller; it came surging up, broke against the point, started to recede . . .

Just as it began to drag almost slowly away from the rock, he moved.

"*Hya! Hya!*" he shouted, and jerked the lead rein.

He ran forward into the water with his fist clenched tightly on the rein. Doctor came after him, hoofs churning up sand and water into a brown mass. Trask was in to his knees, his hips—and then he was moving too slowly, and the water stopped him.

He reached around with both hands, pulled Doctor toward the rock; and stopped him. Trask's teeth were bared with the effort. He got Doctor close to the rock, with himself between horse and stone; glanced over Doctor's rump and saw the next breaker sweeping in.

"Now *hold*, dammit!" he shouted at Doctor. The horse rolled his eyes at the coming wave and spread his feet apart, bracing for the impact.

Trask got his feet against the rock, his back against Doctor's side, like a mountain climber in a chimney. He heard the rush of the water coming, and then a terrible shock on his back. His knees bent, cushioning the strain, and a great cascade of water drenched him. Doctor whinnied, high and shrill; threw his head far back, but held.

The wave, as Trask had hoped, had been mostly white water; he had not been caught in the too deep green water. The cascade poured off him. With the pressure released, Doctor moved out slightly, and Trask fell from between the horse and the cliff into chest-deep water.

He came up spluttering, righted himself against the strong rip current that threatened to pull them both out to sea, and began half leading, half dragging the horse the rest of the way around the point. By the time the next breaker came in the rock was empty.

Charley and Wakila dashed down the beach to help pull Doctor up, but Trask and the horse were doing fine. Trask, stark naked, was almost dancing with exhilaration.

"That's a great horse!" he shouted to no one in particular. "That's a great horse! You see how he held? You see how he stood when the wave hit? You see it? God *damn* that's a good horse!"

Wakila was wide-eyed with astonishment, not so much at the feat performed as at Trask's reaction. Even Charley was startled; it was one of the few times he had ever seen the mountain man's stony shell crack.

"Bridge . . ."

"We made it, God damn your siwash soul, Charley! We made it!"

Eventually Trask's exuberance wore off slightly. He dried himself, put on his clothes, and set about the more prosaic job of setting up camp for the night. He was still very happy, and certainly in a better mood than Charley had ever seen him before.

Charley and Wakila went out to knock mussels off the rocks exposed by the low tide. Before long they had enough for dinner.

"For breakfast, too," Wakila suggested. "Save the bacon."

Charley nodded.

"That Trask, he is very happy now," Wakila said.

"Yes."

"He likes to do a thing like that. The thing he did with Doctor."

"It was foolish. It saves us maybe two hours, and risks both the horse and the man." Charley shook his head.

"Maybe," Wakila said. "Foolish maybe, but a very brave thing."

"Oh, yes," Charley admitted. "A man cannot doubt it was a brave thing."

"It makes him happy to do a thing like that," Wakila mused. "Well, that is the thing he likes, who is to say no? Not me. Not you."

Charley glanced up at Wakila's thoughtful face. Then he turned back and pried a mussel from the rock.

"Yes, that is what Trask likes," he said quietly. "We have enough now." He stood, dropped the mussel into the bag Wakila held.

He met Wakila's eyes for a moment in the gathering darkness, then glanced up at the edge of the wood, where Trask was setting up the tent in the lee of a bank.

Then he turned and walked up to the tent and began to lay the fire.

3

Charley cut and drove two stakes in the ground before the tent; some distance away, and leaning back. Against these he stacked small log sections, until he had a short wall, facing the tent, to act as a reflector for the roasting of the mussels. He built his fire at the base of the wall. Two forked sticks, in front of the fire and on either side, supported the green spruce limb used as a spit. Wakila and Trask shelled and spitted the mussels, and soon they had four sticks waiting to go before the fire.

Wakila unpacked Doctor McLoughlin and led him up to browse. Trask knelt to inspect the pack for water damage. The pack cloth had been soaked by the wave, being on top, but it was heavy tarpaulin, and little had gotten through to the pack beneath. The panniers were dry.

He nodded with satisfaction. Wakila came back, and Trask could hear Doctor's bell tinkling as he grazed just off the beach.

There was plenty of water; the waterfall was a perfect miniature, cascading over the edge of the bank perhaps ten feet to make a tiny pool before it seeped out into the sea. Later in the summer, Charley told them, it would dry to practically nothing, but now it was spring-full.

Coffee was ready long before the mussels were roasted, and each man took a cup, loading it heavily with sugar. Trask had always wondered why that was; at home he drank his coffee black, but on a trip it tasted somehow shallow to him without sugar, no matter how strong.

They stuffed themselves pleasantly; secured the camp against the night's possibility of rain and wind; smoked for a little while and went to bed. Though the going had been easier than anticipated, they had met a fast pace all day, and the three were tired.

Trask's last thought, just as he drifted off into sleep, was to wonder what Charley would dream about tonight. He scratched his chest and surrendered to the blackness.

Drowsily, he half heard Wakila rise in the night.

Feed the fire, he thought sleepily.

Wakila did put wood on the fire, much wood. The driftwood picked up from the beach crackled and sputtered as it caught, and then blazed brightly.

Trask came awake, and looked out the bright triangle of the tent opening to where Wakila squatted in front of the fire. Wakila was intent on examining his own body, occasionally making an indistinct gesture toward the blazing stack of wood.

With full waking, Trask became suddenly aware of an intolerable crawling sensation all over him. He jerked abruptly as the awareness came to him, then leaned back on his elbows and said softly, under his breath, "Oh, sweet Jesus . . ."

Resignedly he threw back the blanket and went out to the fire, brushing at his belly.

Wakila looked up as Trask came. "*Inapoos*," he said shyly, as if he were personally responsible.

"Yeah, *inapoos*," Trask said disgustedly. "*Inapoos* out the ass."

"*Ikta wawa?*" Wakila asked pleasantly.

"Never mind," Trask said. "*Hiyu inapoos*, many, many."

Wakila nodded, and returned his attention to picking the fleas off his body as they scurried from one hiding place to another.

"I could not sleep," Wakila apologized. "The *inapoos*, they eat me up."

Trask nodded, looking down at himself. His hand darted out; picked off a flea just before it reached the sanctuary of his pubic hair; flung it in the fire.

"*Inapoos*, they like me," Wakila confided, with just a shade of pride. "They eat me to death. I am very juicy."

After a moment, Charley Kehwa appeared suddenly in the tent opening. He looked accusingly at Trask, who scowled back at him and threw another flea on the fire. Charley joined the intent little circle.

"Good God," Trask said after a few minutes' picking and flinging. "We'll never get 'em this way. There must be a billion of 'em."

"My blankets are crawling away," Charley told them honestly.

The fleas were, in fact, a kind of louse. And there were, Trask thought, probably quite enough of them to carry away the whole goddam camp if they decided they wanted it.

"If we don't get the blankets cleaned out, we'll never get any sleep," Trask said. "Got you, you little sonofabitch." He flung the presumably mangled body in the fire. "Where'd we get them?"

"They were hiding, maybe," Wakila offered.

"Another of Kahnie's whims," Charley said.

Trask sighed. "Well, get the blankets out here."

Wakila shrugged and went back into the tent. He brought the blanket rolls out, spread them before the fire. He picked one up and shook it at the fire. Enough of the swarming creatures were thrown off to make an audible sizzle as they hit the red coals.

"Oh, Christ," Trask said.

"You can never get them all," Charley observed philosophically.

"The hell I can't," Trask said. He stood, gathering the blankets under his arm.

"What are you going to do?" Charley asked.

"The little bastards can't swim," Trask said grimly.

"We can't sleep with wet blankets," Charley objected.

"We can't sleep with these goddam bloodsuckers either."

Trask carried the blankets over to the waterfall pool; threw them in, and threw rocks on top to hold them down. A steady, monotonous river of profanity flowed back to the two Indians.

Charley winced. He turned to Wakila. "We had best get more wood for the fire. It will be a long, cold night."

Wakila nodded, watching Trask's barely visible figure with fascination. Never before had he seen a man so intent on defeating the ever-present *inapoo*. It must be that the white skin is thinner, he decided.

He shrugged, and got to his feet. In a philosophical tone he said, "Well, no sleep tonight, maybe tomorrow."

Charley nodded, but dubiously. "Maybe," he said. He himself had never known any man to kill *all* the *inapoos*. It might be that Trask could do it, though.

The rest of the night was spent huddled morosely in front of the fire, with the blankets spread on improvised drying racks behind and around them. When the first faint light touched the hills inland, the blankets were still far from dry. Clothing, too, had been found swarming, and, piece by piece, drowned and dried.

Blearily, Trask took the coffee pot over to the waterfall and filled it.

"We will be late starting," Charley said. "And we are tired."

Trask nodded.

"We will need rest before Neahkahnie," Charley said. "We will not try it today, or we would be caught. We will go over the Cape of the Falcons; Neahkahnie is just beyond. Then camp on the lower slope."

"All right," Trask agreed. He was thinking they would now lose all the time they had gained on Neahseu'su, and it made him angry to be balked in such a way.

Particularly by the numerous *inapoo* tribe.

Chapter Nine

It was midmorning by the time all the blankets were dry enough to repack. The dull gray overcast had lowered, and a restless, surging movement was seen in the rolling ceiling above.

"We will have the rain today," Charley said, glancing at the sky. "We could have waited; Kahnie would have drowned the *inapoos.*"

"Just enough to make 'em mad," Trask observed. "Is that Neahkahnie?" Ahead of them a few miles was a great headland, jutting sharply out into the sea. The cliffs were sheer on the face, dropping into the water as though the point had been cleaved neatly with an ax. Behind the cliff, the cape rose to a forest-blanketed summit that looked almost gentle.

"No," Charley said. "Only the Cape of the Falcons. Neahkahnie is beyond."

They left the smooth beach-trail after about a mile's walking from Woman-in-Bed, and headed directly inland.

"This is the last of the beach road until we are over Neahkahnie," Charley said. "Some very short stretches; not enough to go back down for."

"Is there a trail here?"

Charley shrugged. "Something maybe. The people say the Killamooks have a trail around back of Neahkahnie, but no one knows where it is. We will stay on the seaward side."

The rain came about noon; not hard, but a steady drizzle that wet all the brush in a matter of minutes. The party, at Charley's direction, turned more south and began to climb. The timber was thicker as they moved up, the underbrush shorter—still enough to make every step add its own freight of water swept from the brush.

"You stop here," Charley said. "I will go ahead and see if I can pick up a trail."

Trask nodded. Wakila hitched Doctor McLoughlin to a tree, and the two set up a tarpaulin as a half-shelter. From his pack, Trask took the tobacco wallet and pipe; Wakila produced his own pipe. They sat beneath the tarpaulin and smoked.

Already the sleepless night before was beginning to make itself felt. They had managed to doze a little before the fire, but not enough, and their legs felt more quickly the fatigue of the climb. Trask's eyelids burned slightly.

Goddam bugs, he thought bitterly. They smoked with only the sound of rain dropping through the trees above.

The picnic was over.

Charley came back in about an hour. In answer to Trask's question he shook his head. "No. Many elk trails, nothing we can trust."

Trask shrugged. It was what he had expected. "We better get closer to the beach," he said.

Charley agreed. They woke Wakila, who had fallen asleep beneath the tarpaulin. He threw the rough shelter over Doctor's pack and they set off again, angling slightly back toward the sea. Shortly after, they reached the bald crest of a point that rose above the beach. Ahead was a long, heavily timbered slope that ran down nearly to sea-level, then abruptly up again, making a small washboard. On their right ahead was a short, straight beach of a mile or so. On the other side of the valley the slope ran even higher, up to the skyline of the Cape of Falcons.

From where they stood the cape projected far out to sea beyond them, trending south and west.

"Down into the valley," Charley said, pointing. "At the bottom we must go more toward the sea. Possibly we can catch a trail that will go along the edge of the cliffs."

"Do we have to get out there with the horse? He doesn't like it."

"If we stay inland we must cut every foot of the way." Charley shrugged.

Trask thought about it; sighed. "All right, let's go."

In a few seconds they had lost their comfortable vantage point of sight, and had to rely on their own directional reckoning. The sound of the surf was almost hidden under the steady splatter of water in the forest. The timber was thick and gloomy, and the rain dripped steadily down. There were bare, treeless patches where rock came to the surface, and these were black with the pervading wetness; treacherous and slippery.

As they neared the bottom of their downward leg, they crossed long stretches of inexplicable dirt, now turned to heavy mud. Doctor McLoughlin plodded sturdily through the mud, but slipped badly on the wet rock. Twice Wakila was jerked off his feet when Doctor slipped. Trask took the lead rein for a while.

All three had settled into a kind of automatic indifference. In that frame of mind a man can walk for many hours, no matter what the inconvenience, and the difficulty does not reach his emotions.

They stopped when it seemed they had reached the bottom of the valley. Trask stripped off the inner bark of a deadfall fir and built a small fire. They chewed tough jerky elk, ate bread, and had strong coffee.

"How far over this cape?" Trask said.

"Not far, I would think. Maybe five miles."

"Don't you know?"

"No."

"After that?"

"Neahkahnie," Charley said.

2

Twice they were forced to stop on the way up the slope. They came to an area that had been burned sometime in the past, and the deadfalls blocked them in every direction. Charley went out again to scout, and found a relatively clear path. They detoured around the main body of the burn, but the ax was kept in constant use. The undergrowth was not so high in the burned strip, and they were occasionally under clear sky. The advantage was dubious, since the rain could hit them directly then, but it was a change.

The second time they stopped at the base of a steep rock slope. There had been a slide not too long ago, and the talus was loose and shifting under their feet.

"Doctor can't get across that," Trask said.

"I will go see," Charley said.

"You stay here. You walked miles farther already."

Trask skirted the edge of the talus until he caught the timber again. He tracked into it far enough to be reasonably sure they could get through, then returned to where Wakila and Charley waited.

"Quarter of a mile west," he said.

"Much rock here," Wakila observed.

"The Cape of the Falcons is all rock," Charley said. "Close to the surface in many places."

They reached the cliff edge in the afternoon, not yet out on the point of the cape, but at the northern end of its base. A hundred feet below them was a tiny gravel beach. The surf came in, all the way to the base of the cliff, and when it receded the gravel rattled in a steady whir like a rattlesnake's warning. Doctor McLoughlin shied nervously away from the edge.

Wakila talked soothingly to him, drew him back to safer-appearing ground, where he would not be able to see the long drop and the breakers below.

The cliff where they stood followed the small curve of the beach below, then shot out to sea, forming the northern wall of the Cape of the Falcons.

"Follow the edge as far as we can," Charley said. "Out on the sea face we may have trouble."

"Why not cut across the point from here?" Trask said. "It probably isn't more than a couple of miles, that way."

"The timber is too heavy. More cutting, all the time cutting. Around the point is farther, but I think it is easier."

The sea face of the cape was all rock; shale that slipped under their feet. Halfway down a steep, grass-covered bank, there was a broad rock ledge, like a hip on the cape. Walking here was easy, for a short time. Then they came to a four-foot vertical step directly in their path. There was no going around it; one end of the miniature cliff ended in the sea, the other end against a cliff at their left.

Trask vaulted up on top of the step and looked around. The ledge was apparently the same on the other side, and led around the westward face of the cape. It still looked like a better route than going back, but Doctor McLoughlin . . .

Wakila urged the good Doctor forward until he was directly in front of the step. The horse glanced at him reproachfully, then reared with amazing suddenness, getting his forefeet on the ledge.

Charley Kehwa jumped back; when Doctor reared, it seemed certain he would come down backward on the two Indians. Paralyzed with the abruptness of Doctor's decision, Wakila stood stock still, his eyes wide. Doctor lunged hugely, scrabbling frantically with his hind feet, and made the top.

"Hya!" Trask shouted, taken as much by surprise as the Indians. "There's a *horse!*"

Wakila and Charley scrambled up and joined Trask in congratulating Doctor. He snorted wildly once, then permitted his ears to be scratched. He quickly resumed his attitude of complete dejection, implying with every bone of his body that it was entirely impossible to go another step.

By now Trask ignored Doctor's outward appearance. After the session going around Woman-in-Bed, he had great faith in the old bag of bones' ability to negotiate anything, if he took a notion to it. The successful assault on the high step merely confirmed an opinion that was growing steadily stronger: Solomon's choice of Doctor McLoughlin had not, after all, been on the basis of the horse's worthlessness. It pleased Trask a good deal. He had trailed in the mountains with many horses beside which Doctor McLoughlin would have looked three weeks dead; but none of them had given as good account of themselves.

Shortly after this they came to the outermost face of the cape. Here a cove cut into the ledge on which they walked, reducing it to about three feet. The walls of the cove were perfectly vertical, and well over a hundred feet down. It was not wide; the whole length of narrow path was only about thirty feet, and no trouble for the men at all; but the sheer drop was certain to panic Doctor.

There was, thought Trask, a limit to what could reasonably be expected, even of the most willing animal.

Charley took Wakila's pack from him, and he and Trask carried the small packs to the other side while Wakila held Doctor steady. Then the two returned, unpacked the horse and carried panniers and pack over on foot.

Trask blindfolded Doctor, and Wakila began to ease him out over the drop. From the other side, Charley watched Wakila's footing, calling out when the boy was about to step on a loose stone, or other hazard. Wakila moved across backward, his right hand touching the cliff wall for guidance, his left on the lead rein. He coaxed Doctor along gently, while Trask came behind.

They made the narrow ledge, and Trask noted with absent surprise that he had been sweating. They repacked the horse, and moved on.

A steep and tiny ravine came down to their ledge from above. It formed an almost perfect V, and the sides were covered with grasses and brush. They turned up this, climbing up again to the top level of the cliffs from their lower ledge-trail. The climb was steep, but short, and not otherwise difficult. When they emerged at the top, they found themselves at the summit of the cape, facing south.

As if in acknowledgment the overcast broke suddenly, and a brilliant shaft of sunlight lanced out of the sky. Far at sea, the sky began to clear.

Trask had reached the height of land first, and stopped suddenly. Ahead of him lay a beach of incredible beauty. The shaft of sunlight from the west made the breakers sparkle as they rolled gently up the white sand shore. From the point of the cape, Trask was looking at it from the seaward side and an elevation of several hundred feet; the eye of a wheeling gull would have seen it so. The white lines of breakers were tiny as they marched slowly in, and along their humped green backs ran the quicksilver reflections of the sun.

Sheltered in the southern lee of the Cape of Falcons, this cove of perfect grace was peaceful and detached from the wilder grayness of the sea. Directly behind the short crescent of a beach began the forest, thickly packed firs and cedars, the depth of green catching the echoes of the rolling surf; and distinctly outlined in the dark masses were the brilliant islands of blue spruce. Even the sand sparkled in the isolated streams of sun that rolled off the curling back of surf and scattered itself along the beach.

The sand was short, not more than a mile long, and perfectly formed in a gentle curve. Almost at the far end, a stream tumbled over a low bank and into the sea, and just beyond the stream was a jumble of rock that was washed by the deep green waves, and nets of foam slid down to join the swirl below.

Trask was stunned by the miniature perfection of the cove, and it was a long moment before he raised his eyes and saw the mountain that formed the south horn of the crescent. The humpback ridge loomed a thousand feet above him, and he could not even be certain he saw the skyline at all. A streamer of cloud began at the very meeting of land and sea, and cut off the mountain's top as with a knife. As the cloud swept inland, it almost seemed to Trask the massive seaward face of the mountain moved, slowly plowing out into the gray sea like the prow of a great ship. He guessed the cliffs themselves to be five hundred feet, straight down into the turbulent boil of white water.

He was not aware the others had come up to him until he heard Charley's voice.

"Neahkahnie," Charley said quietly. "Where the god walks."

3

They camped that night by the stream at the far end of the beach. While Wakila was laying the fire, Charley Kehwa spoke briefly to Trask, by the tent. Trask glanced at Wakila, then nodded to Charley.

Charley walked over; spoke to Wakila in the Jargon. "Here, let me do this."

Wakila, hurt, said, "I can make the fire all right, Charley."

"You don't know what we are eating; how can you make the fire?"

"What?"

"Crabs," Charley said. He was now digging a hole in the sand.

"Crabs? We have no crabs," said Wakila.

Charley looked up from the hole and gazed placidly at the boy. "That is true," he said, and continued to stare in a speculative way.

"Charley . . ." Wakila hesitated. Then he noted that Trask was watching him, too. He looked back at Charley apprehensively. Finally he sighed, with great discouragement.

He shrugged, and took off his moccasins and pants. As he folded the pants neatly with his moccasins on top he said reprovingly, "It is not fair, Charley."

Trask had come up and now asked, "What isn't fair?"

Wakila knotted the tails of his muslin shirt tightly around his waist, leaving him bare from the belly down. "Charley knows," he said accusingly.

Then he started down the beach toward the tiny rocky point, trotting, his bare buttocks jogging up and down and looking much too big for the bandy legs below.

Charley stifled a laugh, and bent again to the hole in the sand.

"What's going on?" Trask asked. "You said he'd go catch some crabs, what's so funny? What's bothering him?"

"It is nothing," Charley said, but his voice was strained with the effort to keep from laughing out loud. "It is merely a thing between us."

"All right, Charley," Trask said firmly. "You tell me what's going on here or I call him back and we'll eat smoked salmon."

Charley stood up and looked down the beach, a wide grin on his face. Wakila was a hundred yards south, by the point of rocks. He had waded out just above his knees and was bent down peering intently in the water, watching for the characteristic lightness, the fluttery movement of a crab.

"Wakila has—a fear of the crabs," Charley said. "He has told me in confidence he is much too juicy for that line of work."

Trask looked down the beach at Wakila. The boy had moved out a little deeper now. His left hand was poised under the water, waiting to dart down at a crab. With his right he firmly cupped his genitals.

"He believes they wish to nibble on his persons," Charley explained pleasantly. "He has heard them speaking about it, the crabs."

Trask grinned. "Why the hell would he go, if he thought that?"

"He would not wish you to think him a coward."

"Coward be damned," Trask said, laughing. "If I thought they wanted to nibble on *my* person you couldn't *drag* me in the water."

"Me too," Charley admitted freely.

"He's right, though, Charley," Trask said. "It wasn't fair to use me to shame him into it. You ought to be ashamed."

Wakila shouted; thrust his left, or catching, hand deep into the water. His right, or protecting, hand he kept resolutely and firmly in place. He came up with a crab and held it triumphantly above his head, where the legs squirmed and the claws waved and clacked desperately.

"Good," Trask shouted to him. "Good work!"

Wakila ran out of the water, lifting his feet high and causing a terrible commotion on the surface that would doubtless frighten away whatever crabs remained in the vicinity.

He put the crab carefully down on its back, well away from any object it could use to right itself. He stood, looked dubiously at the water, then back up the beach at Trask.

"You go ahead!" Trask called encouragingly. "Get some more, don't be afraid!"

Wakila shouted back, but all Trask could catch was the Chinook for "juicy."

"Never mind!" Trask shouted to him. "You get more!"

"Not if he loses the ones he has," Charley observed.

"I meant crabs," Trask scowled at him.

"I thought I wasn't to use you to shame him," Charley said quizzically.

Trask smiled with childlike innocence. "Not without I know about it," he said.

Charley finished digging the hole by the fire and filled it with large stones from high on the beach where the winter tides had swept them. He built a fire on the stones, and in time they were heated nearly red through.

By this time, Wakila had returned with five crabs of varying sizes. Charley covered the rocks with a thin layer of seaweed and put the crabs, still alive, on top. He blanketed the crabs with a heavier layer of weed and dirt, leaving a small opening at the top of the shallow "cone." Into this opening he poured water, and a billow of steam hissed up. He covered the hole with a blanket to keep the steam in, and sat back to wait for the steaming to finish. From time to time he added more water to the mixture, each time producing a new hiss of steam.

Wakila was in high good spirits—natural to a man who has recently triumphed over great peril—and chattered enough to put the ground squirrels to shame. He modestly pointed out the tender succulence of the crabs, and the great difficulty in being able to choose the very finest under such extreme conditions. When Charley implied the cooking was in part responsible, Wakila favored him with the hurt look of a man who has been misunderstood all his life, and did not expect things would change very soon.

Charley's underhanded attempt to steal his credit did not depress him for long, however, and he soon regained verbal speed. When he returned to the village, it was entirely possible he would hire out as a guide. There were not many of the people willing to guide down into this country. A man like Wakila could probably make a good living doing such a thing, since he was a very strong carrier and food-provider. (Neither Trask nor Charley felt obliged to point out the scarcity of people who *wanted* to be guided into this country.)

Oh, there was little doubt a good man was in demand everywhere. He thought perhaps he was wasting his natural abilities restricting himself to wood-chopping for the whites; there was more than a strong possibility of this. No offense to Trask, of course, for whom he had the greatest respect as an employer, but still . . .

Trask and Charley said little during the monologue. It was neither expected, nor feasible. In his mind, Trask silently contrasted the boy who sat chattering by the fire, full of himself, with the Wakila he knew on the Plains; and he liked the change. Here Wakila was not beset by doubts; in this country he knew himself and his strengths. In a vague way it made Trask ashamed to be a white. He wished fervently he could simply send the boy off into the woods to lead the life his fathers and grandfathers had led, without the complexities and confusions brought by the whites. In this, he thought, Wakila could be happy as he was happy now. With the companionship of a few men; but living in the more durable society of the sea and mountain and forest.

Wakila had a full wind of brag up now, and was expounding his purely fictional exploits with great vigor and a steady guttural patter of the Chinook Jargon. After he had brought down his third elk under unbelievably difficult conditions, he turned and smiled softly at Trask.

Very formally, Trask said, "I am proud such a man is with us here."

Charley glanced at the white man, then turned away quickly.

They had not been bedded down over an hour when Trask was wakened by a faint sound. Looking up, he could see Wakila sitting upright, his body leaning slightly forward.

"Wassit?" Trask asked sleepily.

Wakila quieted him with a sharp gesture and the suddenness of it wakened Trask completely. He sat up; strained to hear.

"Wolf," Wakila whispered.

Trask could hear the faint pad of paws; the rustle of the tarpaulin as the animal nosed it. He reached for his rifle; remembered it had not been reprimed after the rain. He cursed silently, and for the first time wished he had switched to percussion guns.

Wakila leaned far over to whisper, "He must be very hungry to come so near a fire." Trask nodded. He knew he could not get primed and loaded silently in the confines of the tent.

The rustling of the tarpaulin was louder now; the wolf was trying to get inside. Trask was preternaturally aware of sounds, his ears at a high point of sensitivity where sound was almost pain. The slight murmur of the surf, the creaking of evergreen boughs in the woods behind, and—the faint but distinct sounds of the animal outside.

There was no way to tell whether it was alone or not. Sometimes the wolves would run in small packs of five or seven. The animal outside might be one of the bitches that usually were bolder than the rest of the pack. He wondered why Doctor hadn't raised an alarm. Perhaps the wolves had ripped out his throat before he could make a sound.

He lay in indecision, trying to decide what to do. Then he saw Wakila silently slip his knife out of the sheath. The boy crouched for a moment in the darkness of the tent, then slipped through the flap without a sound. There was a flash of the fire's red light on the blade; then— nothing. No sound. The rustling of the tarpaulin stopped suddenly.

Trask could hear the beating of his own heart, the rush of blood in his ears. He rolled over to get his own knife. Wakila had been a fool to go out there, and now he would have to go with him.

Suddenly he heard a whimper—and could not at first tell whether it came from a throat that was human or animal.

A second later he knew, as the whimper became a scream, and Trask recognized it as Wakila. He could hear the sand under the boy's feet as he turned and ran.

Cursing, he threw off the blankets, grabbed the unloaded rifle from beside him and lunged through the tent flap. Outside he raised the rifle like a club, his lips drawn back in a snarl, ready to beat off any of the prowlers bold enough to charge into the fire circle.

He stopped suddenly, his eyes growing wide. Slowly his arms lowered, the rifle came to his side, and he began to back carefully toward the tent, feeling behind him with his feet. He could hear Wakila's voice shouting somewhere, but could not make out the words. He fumbled for the flap of the tent behind him.

Even as he watched, the spotted skunk came down off its forelegs, where it had been poised to spray. The bright little eyes surveyed Trask haughtily. Then, with slow majesty—and tail still raised—the skunk meandered back into the woods. If that was the way they felt about their bacon, it was just too much trouble.

Suddenly Trask relaxed, and his knees felt shaky. From the ocean Wakila was still shouting, and now Trask could hear him.

"Is he gone? Is he gone? *Yaka klatawa?*"

"He's gone, mighty hunter!" Trask shouted. "You can come back now."

Slowly, warily, Wakila came up the beach, looking all around him. He was completely soaked, not having stopped at the water's edge.

Trask started to laugh, and Wakila smiled self-consciously, brushing wet hair away from his forehead.

"I believed it to be a wolf," he explained seriously. "Wolves I have a great suspicion of."

Between gasps of laughter Trask said, "Like—like crabs? What would you do if he'd come—come after you?"

"I would swim," Wakila said.

"Oh greatest of hunters! Oh killer of wolves!" Trask sat down, holding his stomach. Tears were running down his face, release of tension swept through him like a warm wind.

"I am a very strong swimmer," Wakila replied with dignity. He went back into the tent, and Trask could hear him explaining to Charley.

Finally Trask recovered himself, wiped the tears from his cheeks. They had run down into his beard and wetted it, and his belly ached.

He started for the tent flap, then stopped and looked up. Against the glow of the night sky, the great bulk of Neahkahnie reared sharp and distinct. He stood there for a long moment, watching the still, impassive cliffs. Shadowed there in the night it seemed almost unreal; too big, too impersonal; the massive body of some ancient behemoth. Trask was suddenly aware of his tiny position in the shadow of the great mass looming over him like a canopy of stone.

Where the god walks, he thought, remembering Charley's words. It looked it, standing massive in the night and still. The mountain was sleeping.

He turned and went back into the tent.

Chapter Ten

The moon rose bright, lonely as an owl, turning the beach sands silver and gray. The dark water rolled murmurously in against the shore; curled up and broke growling on the sands, leaving lines and pools of foam that glowed with a ghostly luminescence in the lunatic night.

Trask, despite his fatigue, was restless, and rose several times to feed the fire unnecessarily. At intervals he watched the stately swing of the Great Bear behind the Cape of the Falcons.

Listened to the measured roll of the surf and told himself he was a fool on a fool's errand. Returned to his blankets thinking, Well, I guess we all know that. And in any case, what other kind of errand should a fool be on?

That's twisty, he thought as he drowsed, meaning his own reasoning. And the thought gave him a vague satisfaction he could not have explained.

The first cold light before dawn found him awake, and he rose resignedly and began breakfast before Wakila or Charley Kehwa was up. Charley came out a little later, stretching the sleep out of his body and yawning. Trask poured him coffee and went back into the tent to waken Wakila.

"Come on, killer of wolves. Breakfast." He reached down at the shapeless pile of blanket and grabbed what he took to be a shoulder-lump. Wakila muttered something, and his tousled black head appeared from beneath the blankets.

"Come on," Trask repeated. "Get something to eat. We may run into a whole pack of wolves today."

Wakila brushed the sleep from his eyes and blinked. His nostrils worked back and forth as he sniffed the odors of the cooking food.

"It is thanks to me we have any bacon left," he replied with hurt dignity.

"Thanks to you we almost had to throw the whole works in the ocean," Trask said. "What do you want to go and make a skunk mad for?"

"I was protecting our goods," Wakila said. "As was my duty."

"Well, if he'd done *his* duty, I'd've thrown you in the ocean too," Trask said. "Come on and get some breakfast."

"All right," Wakila said, scrambling out of his blankets. "It was a mistake any man might make."

Trask didn't answer directly, remembering his own charge through the tent flap with rifle clubbed and ready. Possibly Wakila remembered it, too.

"Maybe so," he said ambiguously, "maybe so."

They had breakfast and made up their packs again. Trask shoveled sand over the fire, and Charley told Wakila to pack Doctor McLoughlin lightly.

"It is easier for men than horses over Neahkahnie," he said. "Sometimes we may have to unpack Doctor altogether."

Wakila nodded. "It will not take more than one day to do this?"

"No," Charley said easily. "Tonight we will be many miles down the beach."

The first part of the morning took them slightly inland again, out of sight of the ocean. They went down into a heavily timbered ravine, where the ferns were matted waist high, and the duff beneath was thick and springy.

There was much spruce in this sheltered ravine, thick and dark, giving the wood a gloomy air; an aura of deep blueness that was somehow depressing.

"The sun never comes here," Wakila said morosely. "Always the darkness."

The descent was steep and difficult. The ferns and brush impeded them, making the going slow and tedious. Nevertheless, they reached the base by midmorning. The stream in the bottom of the ravine looked too wide to cross at that point, almost a river. Charley looked up the steep slope opposite, which was the next climb. "We come out of the woods shortly," he said. "A little way up. Then it will be easier, I think."

"We got to get across the creek first," Trask said. "You go inland, I'll go toward the ocean, see if we can find a place for Doctor to cross."

Charley nodded and set off along the bank, picking his way around fallen trees and rotting logs. Shortly both men were out of sight along the stream banks, though Wakila could hear the sounds of their progress.

He tied Doctor McLoughlin to a tree and, seeing little reason to stay awake when he wasn't doing anything, lay down for a nap.

Charley and Trask were back in an hour. As far as they had gone on either side, the crossing would be no better.

"We can carry the packs across one of the logs," Trask said, pointing to a deadfall fir that spanned the stream. "You think you could get Doctor across all right?" His tone was dubious.

"Oh, yes," Wakila said cheerfully. "There is no doubt."

Trask frowned and looked back at the stream; of indeterminate depth and running fast; then at the bony horse grazing contentedly the inedible duff. Finally he shrugged.

"Well, unpack him," he said. "Again."

"It will not be the last time today," Charley assured him.

"I suppose," Trask said ruefully. "Goddam nuisance, though."

Wakila unstrapped the big pack and removed the wooden panniers from Doctor's sides. Trask and Charley deposited their own packs on the other side of the stream and came back. Each took one of the panniers and shinnied across the log awkwardly. The panniers were not extremely heavy—perhaps sixty-five pounds apiece—but they were shaped to fit the sides of a horse, not a man's back. Ferrying them across the log was a problem of balance; hitching forward, avoiding limbs, stopping to secure the grip; then hitching forward again. But it was done, and the packsaddle taken across and all the gear piled on the opposite side. Trask and Charley waited there on the low bank while Wakila gently led Doctor down to the water's edge, murmuring steadily in his ear.

"No doubt about one thing, anyway," Trask said admiringly. "He can handle that horse."

Charley nodded. "They understand each other."

Doctor had his forefeet in the water now, and didn't like it. He looked around reproachfully at Wakila, who promptly and loudly berated him for his cowardice. Trask and Charley could catch only a few words of the intimate conversation, just enough to get the general tone of Wakila's remarks.

"Afraid of the water! Hya, what a horse! Your mother was a mongrel bitch and your father an elk!"

Doctor maintained a scornful silence. The assertion was too ridiculous to notice; quite beneath him.

Wakila mounted and leaned over Doctor's neck. He repeated the performance Trask had first seen, of whispering into the horse's ear and drumming monstrously with his heels on the rib cage. After a moment of this unnatural treatment, Doctor snorted loudly and lurched into the water. He stopped immediately as the coldness of it washed his belly.

Wakila increased the tempo of the heel pounding and began to shout. He grew very excited and began to pant with the exertion of pounding on Doctor's ribs. His eyes were alternately wide and clamped shut. "Hya! Hya! Hya! Move! Move!"

Doctor stepped tentatively forward, peering into the water; the slowness of his movement strangely out of keeping with the hysteria gradually being worked up by Wakila.

"Hya! Hya! Hya!" The boy's fury mounted, and Doctor was pressed forward by the sheer violence of his rider's crazy desire to go into that water. Wakila was by now worked into a good frenzy. It seemed to Trask the boy was enjoying it for its own sake, that it was somehow unrelated to the problem of getting Doctor through the water. He sat atop the rack of bones and pounded and screamed and pummeled wildly.

Doctor moved forward another couple of steps and sat down.

Wakila slid off the rump, still shouting and kicking savagely, and the sound of his voice was suddenly a sputtering gurgle as the water closed over his head.

Doctor turned around and looked. When Wakila's head reappeared above the surface Doctor regarded the apparition with a fine disinterest; then bared a mouthful of huge teeth at it and whinnied. He stood and walked casually into the deep water where he began to swim methodically. He reached the other shore and climbed up the bank without breaking stride, walked past Charley and Trask and stuck his nose below the ferns.

Wakila swam across to them, his face split by a huge smile, and scrambled up the bank to gaze affectionately at Doctor McLoughlin. Doctor looked up indifferently; returned to his profitless browsing.

"You see?" Wakila said to Trask, spreading his arms wide in a gesture of total explanation. "You see? He is across, that Doctor."

2

As Charley had said, they came abruptly out of the thick woods a little way up the slope. They stopped at the edge; looked silently up toward Neahkahnie's skyline. Ahead of them was a long, steep meadow; a V-shaped ravine parallel to the ocean and covered with brush and grasses. The right-hand slope of the meadow ran up to a razor-back ridge; on the other side of the ridge were cliffs dropping directly into the sea. The left slope led into the main bulk of the mountain. High on the left slope, perhaps a half-mile above them, timber began again.

"Strange little meadow," Trask said.

"The Meadow of the Ocean Waves," Charley said.

"Waves? This high? Good God!" The razor-back ridge that bounded the meadow on the seaward side was several hundred feet above the surf.

"No." Charley laughed. "Not this high, not even on Neahkahnie. This is where the ocean waves were made, here in the meadow."

"Another of Kahnie's whims, I suppose," Trask said.

"Approximately," Charley said. "The people say Kahnie was sitting here one day, just doing nothing. He did that often, Kahnie, sat here on the mountain and looked around him to see what needed doing. On the other side of the point—you can't see it from here—is a long beach, ten miles long, maybe, a very long beach where people have always lived. In those days the ocean had no waves, no breakers. It was just flat, a flat water."

Gradually Charley fell into the almost-chant of the Chinook story-teller; the ritual telling of the history that slipped into his voice even though he was speaking English.

"It was a flat water, and it had always been all right that way, the sea. On the beach, the people say, there were children playing; they ran into the water easily then, and they ran out again because there were no breakers to stop them.

"The people say: Kahnie saw this and he said to himself, 'This is not good any more, that the sea is a flat water like a lake. The sea must be different. We should have some breakers.' This is what the people say.

"Kahnie said to himself, 'It will be more fun for the children to play in if we have some breakers.' At that time the meadow here was full up like the rest of the mountain with large stones. Thus Kahnie decided to make the breakers with the large stones. This is what the people say.

"Kahnie built a fire here in this meadow on top of the stones. Some people saw him, and that is how we learned to heat stone for cooking the crabs, but that is not why Kahnie heated the stones. Kahnie heated the stones to red hot, because he wanted to make some breakers for the sea. This is what the people say.

"When the stones were heated to red hot here in this meadow, Kahnie picked them all up and threw them into the sea. Some of them you can still see out there. Pretty soon the sea began to boil because of the hotness of the stones. It began to bubble and froth up like the whipped soapberry, and pretty soon the sea was not a flat water any more, because of the boiling. The sea had waves, and when the waves came in to the shore, well, that was the breakers. This is what the people say.

"At first the children were afraid of the breakers, but pretty soon they got to like them all right and played in them. The men of the village were angry because the breakers made it hard to get the canoes out, but the children liked it. Then Kahnie said, 'This is much better, now we have some breakers for the children to play in.' And that is why there is the little valley on the mountain and why the trees do not grow until higher up in this place and why the ocean has breakers. This is what the people say."

Trask looked up the valley, and was startled slightly. It looked very much as if the ravine had been scooped out of the mountainside suddenly; not as if it had been a long time in the making.

"What's on the other side?" Trask asked.

"The south sea-face. The western face runs about even with the beach where we camped, runs up to about three or four hundred feet at the top of the ridge. The south face dips back in a long ways. Very high, many cliffs."

"So where do we go from here?"

Charley shrugged. "Up the meadow. We have to find a way."

The meadow was not as easy going as it had appeared from the edge of the woods. The relatively even surface gave the impression of low brush and grass, but soon they were head deep in heavy growth of manzanita and salal. It would have been virtually impossible to move had it not been for the elk trails. The slopes were crisscrossed with trails, and small open spots where an animal had lain, crushing grass and fern and salal beneath it. But frequently there was no trail in the direction they wanted to go, and then the way had to be cut laboriously, foot by foot.

Trask, in the lead, was panting with exertion after the first few minutes of toiling up the meadow.

"God, this stuff is thick," he said, stopping to rest.

"It is not so bad for the elk," Charley said placidly.

Trask scowled at him and started off again.

He moved forward by sheer momentum, leaning against the solid wall of growth ahead; half falling, and bending it down beneath his weight. When it was bent back, he chopped at the bases of the stems with the bush knife, clearing a path just wide enough for Doctor McLoughlin to scrape through.

"I will break trail for a while," Charley said.

Trask relinquished the bush knife without regret, and took the last position, carrying the ax. The brush was light enough in the stem to be cut with the knife, and there was in any case not room enough to swing the ax. Charley shouldered his way ahead, the knife swinging in short rhythmic arcs, swishing and chikking through foliage and stems. Behind them their trail began to lengthen, a dark streak trending up the meadow slope like the trail of a sea-snail in the sand.

Wakila and Doctor McLoughlin plodded patiently along in the slow wake of the leader. Frequently it was impossible to see where they were, or where they were going. The brush grew well over head height, and the only view was a few inches ahead and to the sides; a matted wall of growth. When this went on too long, Wakila would hoist Charley to his shoulders, so the tamanawis man could find their direction.

As best they could, they maintained a course directly up the bottom of the V toward the south skyline.

"Can we go along the edge there?" Trask asked.

"I don't know," Charley said. "We may have to go higher up." He pointed to the left slope of the meadow, rising up into the ponderous bulk of the mountain's body. "We will have to move farther up when we reach the south face," he said. "It is all cliff."

Ahead of them the skyline was shaped roughly like a step. Going directly upward in the ravine, they were headed toward the lower tread. To the left the mountain rose sharply, its slope as great as a highly pitched roof. At the right, the lower step dropped off into the sea.

According to Charley, the steplike structure did not continue around the south face. It stopped abruptly in a vertical drop, as though the south face had been cut by a great knife.

Trask scanned the slope to their left, considering the choice. If they moved up the ravine to the edge, they would have to climb along the skyline—a sheer drop on the other side—directly up the mountain in order to reach a high enough point to cross the southern cliffs. If they slanted up the slope now, to intersect the top of the cliffs, it would be prolonging the distance they had to cut through the heavy brush.

"Can we get Doctor along the edge of the cliffs?" he asked.

"I don't know," Charley said thoughtfully. "I don't remember it that well."

"Mm. Well, it's for damn sure we can't go straight up the side. We'll have to take it at a slant, so we might as well start now."

Charley nodded. He peered up at the slope, shading his eyes against the brightness of the sky. "See, up there," he said, pointing about halfway up the slope at a point still well below timber.

"I don't see anything."

"Looks like a small ledge. It is hard to tell."

"I don't see it," Trask repeated. "If it's there, we'll intersect it anyway. Let's get moving. It must be near noon."

"Let me cut," Wakila said. "I am bored holding to the rein."

Charley took over the care of Doctor, and Wakila led off. They changed course slightly to their left, climbing up the side of the mountain on a long slant, leaving the bottom of the V behind. Going up the slant was a little faster than Trask had expected. Wakila seemed to have better luck than either of the others in finding elk trails going in their general direction; they were invisible until one stumbled directly on one. Where he had to cut, he did so rapidly, with an energy Trask was afraid he could not maintain. But Wakila showed no sign of slowing, and Trask settled down, trying to resign himself to the slow tedium.

Gradually the brush began to thin, became no more than waist high, and much of it was fern. Then they moved ahead more rapidly, Wakila following animal trails that were much plainer in the thinning growth.

Once he stopped, pointed far up the side of the mountain. "*Mooluk*," he said quietly.

Trask followed the direction of Wakila's pointing finger. Far above them, almost where the timber began to crown the mountain, he saw movement. Suddenly it resolved itself as his eyes caught the perspective.

Browsing near the edge of the timber was a herd of elk. It was a large herd, Trask estimated sixty or seventy adults. The bulls stood tall, raising their heads at intervals, showing the sweeping antlers that towered nearly five feet above their heads. Head and neck were so dark as to be nearly black; the bodies were buff. Judging from the distance and the size of the timber, the larger bulls would stand nearly seven feet at the shoulder.

The herd drifted slowly northward along the race of the mountain, moving easily through brush that would have been impassable for the men. The new spring calves were traveling with the herd, only occasionally visible when the brush thinned, being nosed and prodded by the dun-colored cows. They traveled in amiable companionship; a stark contrast to the mating season in the fall, when the bulls would be trumpeting their wild challenges and fighting for harems.

The herd was aware of the men below. Several bulls came a short way down the slope, rearing their thick necks and surveying the little group impersonally. Then they would turn, move back up the slope and rejoin the main group. In a period of minutes, nearly every bull in the herd had made his own journey of curiosity; satisfied whatever vague impulse bothered him; and returned.

Casually they browsed just below the edge of the timber, the band drawn out into a long buff patch against the green of the brush; moved behind an isolated grove of blue spruce and disappeared from sight. The men could hear the faint sounds of cows calling to their calves, a sharp, barking sound almost like that of a dog.

"Brush sure don't bother them much," Trask observed, when the herd had trailed out of sight.

"They belong here," Charley said. "They are the fleas on Kahnie's body."

"Fifteen hundred pounds of *inapoo*," Trask mused. "What's that make us?"

Charley shrugged. "Fleas of the fleas, maybe."

3

The brush thickened and thinned at intervals. The lead changed hands several times during the long ascent; arms were quickly tired with the constant swinging of the bush knife. It was little better to be behind; moving a few small steps at a time, waiting for the next length of trail to be cleared, moving ahead a little; waiting again.

The lead man was always drenched with sweat now, and his breath came fast and hard. Soon he did not try to carry his pack while cutting trail, but gave it back to one of the others, who balanced it on Doctor's back. Doctor plodded along philosophically, not seeming to mind the slowness of the pace, not becoming restless as did the men.

After another hour and a half they stopped, chewed some dried salmon and washed it down with now warm water. They squatted silent in a small crushed area where one of the huge elk had rolled, with the thick brush all around them like the walls of a low room.

The higher they climbed on the slope, the rockier the ground became. Soon the terrain underfoot was made up of stones the size of a man's fist or larger. Strangely, the change in soil did not appreciably thin the undergrowth; it thrived as surely and well on the stony slope as it had in the richer soil of the little meadow.

When they had finished their lunch Trask stood and surveyed the slope ahead. The sharp profile of the mountain against the sky indicated an angular point, around which they would have to pass to reach the southern slopes. He thought he could see a slightly darker trace across the brush above, which might or might not be the ledge Charley thought he had seen. He looked back down at the valley, and the long, dark trail slanting up the steep incline. It was broken intermittently where they had come upon an elk trail going their way; the animal trails were almost invisible on the meadow, while their own was dark and distinct.

"Not too bad," Trask said. He glanced at the position of the sun. "We're doing all right," he decided.

They were high enough on the slope now to see over the edge of the south precipice, into the distance down the long beach. The sand swept around from the southern base of the cape in a wide curve, then turned directly south. The beach was broad and the far end of it was lost from sight in a thin haze. From this height the breakers were mere threads of white, moving with minuscule slowness into the land. Trask could see a large bay, apparently the entrance of a river, seeming not more than a few miles from the base of Neahkahnie. Near the meeting of the river and ocean, a thin trail of blue smoke rose into the air; was quickly blown away inland by the offshore breeze.

"Is that Murderer's Harbor?" Trask said.

"No," Charley said. "Still maybe twenty miles down the beach from here. The bay is very large, very wide."

"What river is that?"

"Just a river." Charley shrugged. "This is the country of the Nehalem. That is one band of Killamooks. The Killamook band is farther south."

"How many Killamook bands are there?"

"Just the two along here. There are other Salishan-speakers on the other side of the mountains, but not Killamooks."

The razor-back ridge that rose from the seaward side of the meadow was below their level now. Trask could look over the top, crested with scrubby, wind-flattened trees, out to sea. The thin point of Neahkahnie projected about a mile out on the southern side, at a guess, and the southern cliff face ran almost due east and west before it curved smoothly into the beach. They would have to cross around the angular profile high up on the mountain. Then, he hoped, they would begin another slant, this time downward to the broad beach.

"Let's move," he said.

Not long after, Charley's hope of a ledge was realized. It was not much; only a few feet wide and still steeply slanted, but it was better than the ascending course they had had. The ledge ran fairly straight to the profile they could see, then disappeared around the other side. The general course was only slightly upward.

By now, the ground was entirely of loose rock that slipped and rattled from under their feet. Here there was no danger; if one slipped his fall would be stopped before he had reached the ground by the heavy brush on the slope below.

The elk had followed the ledge around the point, to judge from the relative absence of brush. It was almost a trail, though no man in his right mind would have cut a trail that slanted so steeply off to the side. Their legs soon felt the strain of walking on the slant, but progress was generally faster, from the thinness of the undergrowth.

The loose, large rock offered no sure footing for Doctor, and the horse was having as hard a time of it as the men, scrabbling to regain his balance when the trail scattered out from under his feet.

Trask was leading, and gradually the edge-profile of the point came nearer and nearer, until they were only a few hundred yards from it. There they passed with difficulty behind a boat-shaped clump of firs growing isolated directly on the "trail." Beyond the trees they stopped.

A short distance ahead, the growth of salal and manzanita ended abruptly and there was a sheer face of stone, almost vertical, rising perhaps eighty feet above them. The ledge seemed to continue around this face, and Trask offered a silent prayer that they would not have to backtrack.

"I'll go on ahead," he said, "see if we can get around here."

Charley nodded. Wakila immediately sat down on the trail and began to massage his left calf, strained from keeping his balance on the gravelly slant and trying to help Doctor maintain his.

Trask walked to the edge of the stone face and found himself suddenly over the ocean.

Five hundred feet below, the surf crashed against the base of the cliffs with a thunderous roar, throwing white water slowly up the side, as if reaching for him. The ponderous rollers drew back, gathering their strength; revealed a boulder-strewn beach. The face of the cliff down which he looked was so nearly vertical he had to lean out a little to see the bottom. Jagged spires of rock pointed up at him from various points on the face, and the base of the sheer slab was a jumble of sharp and angular pinnacles around which the surf surged and churned.

He stared down the precipice with fascination while two rows of breakers dashed themselves to foam against the rocks. Unconsciously he reached out with his left hand and caught hold of a rock on the side of the face.

He leaned back away from the edge and found himself slightly dizzy. He shook his head sharply, and turned his attention to the path on which he was standing. Tentatively he moved forward along it, starting around the point. It narrowed here until it was something under two feet wide. Like the rest of the ledge they had just come over, its surface was loose, sliding stone, and the slope was quite as steep. The difference was that the low side of this ledge ended not in thick underbrush, but in a vertical drop of half a thousand feet to the churning white water and the rocks.

Holding to the side of the cliff on his left, Trask moved slowly around the point. Here the face was only a hundred yards wide; beyond it the brush began again, and a long downward slope off the mountain.

He found he had to test each handhold, for the cliff was crumbling, and more than once the projection he seized came away in his hand. One he threw off the side, and listened to the faint chink! as it struck the face once on the way down. He could not see it hit the water, both from distance and the foam that boiled around the base of the rocks.

From the other side of the face he could see the whole length of the lowland on the south side of the mountain, extending as far as he could see into the haze. It was very far below him, and he had a sudden, irrational thought that he might be able to glide all the way down, if he just knew how.

Most of the sea birds were below his level, wheeling and gliding off the cliff face, circling in the updraft from the ocean, their pointed white wings rocking slowly as they caught the current. It gave him an odd sensation to be looking down on the backs of the birds; so far below him the huge gulls appeared small as sparrows.

On his left was the sheer face of the cliff, extending up and back until it was lost from his sight; beneath his feet the narrow, loose path with its terrible slope; to his right—nothing. Only the clear blue sky and the endless downward plunge of the cliff his mind almost refused to credit.

Slowly he worked his way back around the point to where Charley and Wakila and Doctor McLoughlin waited. Wakila had kept Doctor well back from the edge, lest he become nervous too soon. Trask noted absently that his toes had a faint tingle, a kind of falling-thrill, when he stepped back into the reassuring brush.

"How is it?" Charley asked.

Trask cleared his throat. "Well, I think we can make it all right."

"Does the ledge go around?"

"Yes. It narrows quite a bit."

Charley searched Trask's face intently, his own expression impassive, his eyes slightly narrowed. Able to read nothing there, he shrugged, as if in answer to some unspoken question.

"We will have to unpack Doctor, then," he said.

"Yes."

Charley relayed the information to Wakila in Chinook and the boy rapidly loosened the diamond hitch and removed the top pack. He dismounted the panniers and pack saddle and piled them in back of the Doctor.

"Get the horse across first and we'll come back for the gear," Trask said.

Wakila nodded.

"You can't go backward on this trail," Trask said. "We'll have to blindfold Doctor and lead him, but you keep your eyes on your own path."

Wakila nodded again, and moved forward to the edge. He looked down at the sea churning below, then back up at Trask again. He saw that Trask was watching him closely, and smiled faintly.

"Listen," Trask said. "Are you afraid?"

Wakila swallowed and nodded, unable to trust his voice.

"You go across, then," Trask said. "I'll bring Doctor.'"

Wakila shook his head sharply. He cleared his throat and said, "No. No, I will take the Doctor. I am in charge of this horse, we will go together, him and me. Like always."

"You sure?" Trask said.

"Yes."

"All right. I'll go first. When I get to the other side, you start. Hang on where I do. Don't look down."

"I must look down to see the path."

"You can feel it with your feet. *Don't look down*," Trask repeated emphatically. "Lead Doctor behind. If you feel a tug on the rein, for God's sake let go! You understand that?"

"Yes."

"I don't care what it is, if you feel anything funny, drop the rein right now," Trask pressed.

"I will do that. We will come across all right, Doctor and me."

Trask glanced over Wakila's shoulder, saw Charley Kehwa regarding him without expression, his dark eyes half closed.

"You come around last, Charley."

Charley nodded. "Be careful," he said quietly.

Trask grinned at him. "Have any dreams last night?"

Charley shook his head slowly, seriously, keeping his eyes on Trask's face. Then, suddenly, he smiled too, and looked at Wakila.

"I had a very strange dream about a skunk," he said. "Very odd. But he was vanquished by a brave Clatsop warrior. I do not know what it means."

Trask laughed, and even Wakila grinned sheepishly.

"All right," Trask said. He moved out on the ledge again, kicking loose stone off ahead of him. It scattered down the face of the cliff and was lost from sight and hearing long before it reached the rocks below.

The sound of the breakers was enormous as soon as he was over the clear drop. He watched the cliff at his left, feeling carefully with his feet, kicking the stones away, hanging on with his hands. The slope of the path seemed suddenly twice as steep, and he cursed silently at the tricks a man's mind will play.

He reached the other side and looked back across the face at Wakila. Doctor was blindfolded, and the boy was waiting for Trask's signal to begin.

Suddenly Trask had a sensation of great relief, and his knees felt shaky, and there was a cool, light sensation in his chest. He was sweating profusely. He took a deep breath, and was startled at how shaky it sounded.

But over all the physical manifestations of fear and relief was a sensation of elation and exuberance.

I beat you, Charley, he thought. You and your dreams and the mountain, I beat you all.

"Hya!" he shouted. He waved at Wakila, and the boy started out, leading the horse.

Trask pinned his eyes on Wakila's feet in their tentative feeling ahead for solid path. The boy came out over the drop, with nothing but space on his right. Doctor followed patiently behind, unable to see, but walking with a strange assurance. His left side brushed against the cliff, but he made no movement outward away from it. They passed the center point, which Trask had found the worst. The white man let out his breath in a long sigh.

"That's coming," he called happily. "You got the worst behind you."

Wakila looked across the remaining space and smiled. Doctor's feet slid out from under him and he fell, whinnying shrilly. Wakila's body was snapped around and off the cliff, and the tiny dark figures crashed once against the cliff and fell five hundred feet to the rocks below. Trask saw the larger bulk of the horse outlined against the waves for a brief second, and then it was gone.

And there was only the sound of the surf and the relentless sweeping in of the rollers to break against the cliff.

Chapter Eleven

For a long moment both men stood immobile, paralyzed by the suddenness of the thing; staring blankly into the air off the cliff face as though searching for some insubstantial image hanging there. A trickle of loosened gravel flowed over the edge; rattled briefly on the face; disappeared into the void and was silent, lost in the roar of the surf.

Suddenly Trask sat down and put his face in his hands. Charley Kehwa glanced up the mountain, almost without volition, as though expecting to see Kahnie standing there. Then he too sat, moving stiffly. Squatted on his heels at the other side of the ledge and stared out to sea, his hands resting limply on his knees and his mouth slightly open.

Death was not a new thing to either of these men. They had seen it come in many forms: violence, accident, the slow and relentless wasting death of disease and decay. But whatever the way in which it comes, one thing the death of a man brings to those who remain; the sudden, instinctive cutting-off of understanding.

There was this thing that existed; now it exists no more. Where it was, there is nothing. The body may remain, tangible, subject to rot and stink, something to be disposed of in one way or another. But of this other thing there is no trace. It has vanished abruptly, between the beats of a heart it has suddenly gone. And having no eyes to see this thing, this life, you could not see it go, and you cannot describe or justify its passage. Nor can a mind comprehend the disappearance of the invisible, the silencing of a thing that made no sound, the stopping short of a thing that did not move.

In time it is necessary to consider what there is to do next; you are not permitted to ponder too long on the imponderable, to grope with your fingers after the final intangible; but in that immediate moment of confrontation a man's mind and body are imbedded in the cold rock prison of absolute refusal. He can neither think nor act.

The absolute negative, the ultimate saying of no to the world, when it is just too late. And always the subtle conviction that if you had said No a moment earlier, it would none of it have happened. But the saying of no comes too late by a little. You are always a little too late in saying it.

Gradually Trask became able to think again; the initial numbness of shock gave way to sickening weakness, and it was hard to breathe. The rising and falling of his chest were erratic, shallow, gasping, like the breathing of a man about to vomit. He tried to swallow and could not. He wondered if he were going to be sick.

His mind fluttered and flickered through the maze of questions that must be answered, the evaluations that had to be made. Who is at fault? Why did it happen? Is it a good thing or bad? And worst of all, What now?

A picture of the thing must be seen before anything else can go on. It was my doing. I am guilty of it.

No.

I could have stopped it.

No.

I am glad of it, glad it was not me.

No.

A black bird of guilt hovers over the death of a man, waiting to perch where it may find room in the minds that remain. It is an easy thing to be deceived by the happenings of the world into believing you are responsible for them. It is part of a man's great conceit that he can believe himself responsible for the universe and its actions. It is a part of his conceit that he can believe himself guilty of the death of every other man, and take the guilt of the world on himself.

But there is no guilt to be taken. It is not necessary that the responsibility be assigned. It is not the concern of those who remain, but a thing between the world and the one who is dead. That which was, is not. It is a simple thing.

Trask stood finally, and steadied the shaking of his legs. He looked across the space at Charley Kehwa. The tamanawis man was still squatted, his posture relaxed, gazing out to sea. He looked like a man who sits down to rest on the trail; stares absently across the horizon and thinks of something else, neither pleasant nor unpleasant.

"Charley—" Trask said. He stopped and cleared his throat.

The broad flat face turned to him without expression.

"We got to get the packs across," Trask said.

Charley nodded silently. He glanced once again at the horizon, as though unwilling to let go of some image; then stood. Mechanically he strapped his own pack on, hoisted one of the panniers, and moved slowly and carefully across the ledge to Trask. The white man helped him unload and followed him back across. Neither of them was conscious of crossing the point where Doctor's feet had slid from under him.

It took three more trips to bring the rest of the gear across, the last trip being the large horse-pack, divided between them.

They spread all the packs out along the trail and opened them, preparing to repack.

"It will be necessary to leave much here," Charley said.

Trask nodded. "There should be game below," he said. "We can leave some of the food."

"The packs will be heavier."

"Yes. We'll make tumplines. Then we can carry more."

Charley cut the headbands from a piece of buckskin, and attached the long binding thongs. The weight of the packs would be distributed between shoulders and head, making it possible to carry a greater load without shoulder-strain.

Trask made an exploratory trip along the ledge, which again was walled by undergrowth. He returned by the time Charley had finished making up the tumplines.

"It looks all right down to the beach," he said. "We follow this for a while, then cut down."

Charley nodded. After dividing the bedding from the horse-pack, they made up two rolls and lashed them with the ends of the tumplines. These would be carried fairly low, acting as shelves on which part of the weight of their back packs would rest. They experimented with the lines until they had established the proper length to distribute the weight; too high and the weight would all be carried by the head, with consequent strain on the neck; too low, and the back packs—now heavier—would be entirely supported by the shoulders.

Their total loads were now about twenty pounds heavier.

"Haven't packed like this since I was trapping," Trask said dryly.

As they gained time from the death, they were able to move more easily, speak more freely. The paralysis wore off gradually, and both shut off their emotions from what had happened. It was enough to be able to understand the two of them were alone now. The rest would have to wait.

Finally the packs had been made to their satisfaction. As they were ready to load, Charley glanced back at the bare rock face behind them uneasily. He turned back to Trask, meeting his eyes for only a flickering second, then squatted on his heels, looking at the ground.

"Bridge—" he started. His voice was hesitant, almost embarrassed.

"What is it?"

"Bridge—we believe—we don't have the same beliefs, you and me. Our people . . ."

Trask hoisted one pack, not looking at Charley, testing the load absently. "What is it, Charley?" he asked quietly.

"We will not be back to our people for many days," Charley said, struggling with a difficult proposition. "No one will know of him-who-died for a long time. His mother, his father, they will not know."

"What are you getting at?"

Charley stood straight, met Trask's eyes without defiance, but with pride. "I wish to ask you this thing," Charley said formally. "I, Charley Kehwa, ask it of you. There is no one to cut hair for him-who-died. Will you cut hair for him?"

Trask looked at Charley for a long moment, scanning the dark, impassive face, the black almond eyes. Slowly he said, "He-who-died was *sikhs* to me, Charley. I will cut hair for him."

Charley searched the white man's face, then turned away. He slipped his knife from its sheath. Trask bent over to the shorter man. Charley took his forelock and chopped it off; then grasped his own and did the same. He took the locks of hair and wrapped them up in a small piece of buckskin left from making the tumplines. He tied it with a thong and carried it back to the rocky ledge, where he threw it off into the sea.

When he came back, Trask helped him into his pack, and Charley did the same for him. They piled the remaining gear beneath the low

limbs of a small hemlock and covered it with boughs, in case they should
get a chance to return for it.

"Bridge," Charley said, when they had finished.

"Yes."

"Thank you."

Trask turned and started down the trail, which had now begun a
slight slope downward toward the beach.

2

The natural ledge they followed grew erratic, sometimes disappearing
completely into the side of the mountain, to be picked up again a few
hundred yards farther on. Finally it could not be found at all.

"It is all right," Charley said. "We do not need it any more."

The ledge had brought them back inland from the point and slightly
lower in level. The beach was now below and to their right. They were
almost directly opposite the long beginning curve of the sand away
from the southern base of the mountain.

Charley pointed down at the broad white expanse. "We should make
the beach in another hour," he said.

Trask glanced at the position of the sun, and estimated it was between
two and three o'clock. "Good," he said. "Three, maybe four hours on
the beach, then."

Charley nodded. "We will make camp tonight by the mouth of the
river and cross in the morning. We should reach Murderer's Harbor
by tomorrow afternoon."

They set off down the steep slope, following the animal trails
wherever they could. The ground was rocky still, and slipped beneath
their feet, but trail was plentiful on this side of the mountain and they
made good time. Once on the long slope they stopped to rest for a few
minutes and Trask dug in his pack for tobacco and pipe. He lit, puffed
a cloud of blue smoke into the air and passed the pipe to Charley.

"Thank god for Kahnie's fleas," he said, looking at the matted wall
of salal that hemmed them in.

Charley nodded, his head veiled in smoke from the pipe. "It is easier
to go where they have gone," he acknowledged.

No more was said until the pipe had gone dead and was put back. Trask threw his head back and replaced the tumpline, juggling the headband across his forehead so it would not chafe.

"Now we are in the Killamook country," Charley said matter-of-factly. "We must walk softly." He stood and refixed his own headband, stretching his neck forward to test the pull.

"Worried?" Trask asked.

Charley shrugged. "It is not a matter for worrying or not worrying. But we are on Killamook land, and it would not be wise to forget this."

"Think they'll give us any trouble?"

"There is no way to know what they will do. Sometimes they are an unfriendly people."

"Well, I guess we'll find out," Trask said.

"Doubtless," Charley replied, without any discernible emphasis.

They started out again, following a rough course that would bring them to the beach some distance from the base of the mountain. As they came farther down the slope, Trask could see the piled driftwood logs, close up against the abrupt dunes on the inland edge of the beach. The winter tides had made a jackstraw pile of huge logs, now weathered silver-gray and smooth. They formed a tangled mass against the dunes as far down the beach as he could see. Then he lost sight of the beach entirely, as they left the main slope of the mountain and descended into a short series of small ridges and valleys that completed the descent of the land into sea. There was timber in these lower reaches of the mountain, long rambling islands of fir, dotted with clumps of blue spruce. As far as possible they avoided the trees and stayed with the elk trails through the brush.

By now both men had fallen into the mechanical rhythm of walking that produces a sense of placid detachment. Their legs moved automatically, almost without sensation.

Trask felt an odd sense of—balance, a state of neutralness. He reverted to the habit of many years, methodically detaching himself, falling into a kind of reverie in which he was only vaguely aware of his progress and the steady pumping of his legs. Through his mind there flowed a slow, somnolent stream of thought, gray and featureless, continuous and without pattern or importance. He could not have said at any time what he was thinking about. He was not thinking; the patterns that flowed before his mind were a vague mental counterpart of the rhythm of walking. He was barely conscious of the passage of time, and slightly surprised when they came to the top of the last row of dune and stood looking down at the beach.

As they picked their way through the jumble of driftwood, Trask noticed absently that the beach high up was not covered with sand, but with large stones washed up by the same tides that had brought the logs.

They walked down near the water's edge where the sand was harder-packed, and turned directly south. The tide was going out now, leaving large flat pools on the lower beach. Gulls wheeled overhead screaming and flights of sandpipers strutted jerkily at the edges of the pools.

When the men came near, the long-beaked birds took off in a body, simultaneously, whirred down the beach a few hundred yards, and settled again. At their feet, uncounted myriads of sand fleas hopped away, and an occasional startled crab scuttled crazily for the protective water. The smell of salt was strong in the air and steady breeze came from the seaward side. After a while Trask's right ear hurt from the steady blowing of the wind; a pain like that of being too cold, though the air was warm.

The jellyfish tides were beginning, and the beach was littered with the featureless, transparent bodies of the creatures, washed up on the sand to rot gradually in the sun, adding their fetid smell to that of the salt.

Ahead of him now he could see only beach; but he knew from the view he had taken from the mountain that they should reach the mouth of the river in a matter of a couple of hours at most. They would still have one, possibly two hours of daylight, and he wondered if there were any chance of getting across tonight and making camp on the opposite side. The mouth had looked quite wide; it might be better to follow the north bank inland until they found a place narrow enough to ford. Otherwise they would be faced with the necessity of building a raft . . .

His reverie was interrupted by Charley's quiet voice.

"What? Sorry, Charley, mind was wandering."

"I said, we have company," Charley repeated.

"Company?" Trask looked around but saw nothing.

"You can't see them," Charley said. He gestured with his left hand at the dunes. "No, don't stop, keep on walking."

"Killamooks?"

"Yes."

"How many?"

"I don't know. They've been following us for the last ten minutes."

3

Trask had walked a dozen more paces, trying to think through the implications of the thing, when he caught movement out of the tail of his eye. A hundred yards ahead of him, an Indian appeared at the top of the dunes. He had come up from the inland side, and was alone; standing straight and silent, regarding the two men who came up the beach toward him. Trask estimated they would pass within a hundred feet of him.

Charley drew up alongside. "Don't break pace," he said quietly.

The lone figure stood silent and immobile, silhouetted against the sky in plain view. Gradually Trask drew near enough to make out his features, but he could read no expression in the rigid, dark face. The man was completely naked, and his long black hair was unbound. His hands were held slightly away from his thighs, somehow giving an impression of alertness. Trask could not settle in his mind what the purpose of the gesture was. Defiance? Bravado, perhaps? Showing his bravery for his companions behind the dunes? It was impossible to tell.

They drew abreast of the solitary figure, keeping the same steady pace.

Without breaking stride, Charley had taken the inside position, between Trask and the dunes. Now, as they reached the Indian, Charley said, "Klahowya," loud enough to carry to the other.

The Indian gave no sign that he had heard; turning only enough to be always facing the two on the beach. He said nothing, and showed no intention of paralleling their course. Watched silently as they passed.

"What was that all about?" Trask said.

"I don't know."

"He didn't give you back klahowya," Trask observed.

"No."

Some yards beyond, with an almost imperceptible shift of his head, Charley glanced back. The skyline of the dunes was empty.

"Are they still with us?" Trask said.

"I think so. In the depression behind the dunes."

For the next half-hour there was nothing to disturb their steady plodding down the beach. Then Trask saw a thin tendril of blue smoke rising from somewhere on their inland side.

"Lodge smoke," he said.

Charley nodded. "We should be reaching the edge of the bay soon."

In the next few minutes they drew nearer the smoke, until finally Charley stopped. Straight ahead, still some distance away, there was a break in the beach; the northern point of the river bay.

"No use going all the way around the point," Charley said. "Let's see where we are."

They turned to their left and scrambled up the steep, sandy face of the dunes. They reached the crest, covered with scrubby beach grass, and stopped to survey the ground ahead from the slightly higher vantage point.

The depression behind the first row of dunes was empty; wind-waves of sand rippled evenly down the slope to the bottom. Silently Charley pointed to the very base of the depression, where the even pattern of the sand was churned and broken by a trail that led back north, parallel to the way they had come. It extended ahead of them a little way, then broke off inland, rising up the opposite slope. On the second row of dunes, undergrowth began; low, shrubby masses of growth leading back into first timber over a series of hummocks and valleys in the sand. The trail seemed to lead directly toward the tendril of smoke. They still could not see where the smoke came from, their view blocked by a long, ragged clump of wind-swept pines a short distance inland; a gnarled and twisted mat of trees, their foliage flattened back by the wind as if planed with an adz. The smoke came from somewhere beyond.

The northern point of the bay was a long finger pointing south; behind it the river came down from a northerly slant. If they went directly inland now, they would reach the shore of the bay by cutting across the base of the finger; following the beach they would have to go around the point and double back again.

"Let's go," Charley said. He started down the lee slope of the dunes, half walking, half sliding in the loose sand, his arms outstretched for balance. Trask followed him, and the billows of sand they dislodged slid ahead of them down the slope, white against the darker color of the surface.

At the base, Charley turned right and began to follow the disturbed track in the sand.

"You taking their trail?" Trask said.

Charley shrugged. "Fastest way to get to the lodge." He pointed toward the faint smoke pattern against the sky.

Trask frowned. It might well give them some little advantage to come boldly up to the lodge. On the other hand, it could make the Nehalems angry that they should presume to make first contact. There was something to be said for both alternatives. He sighed, following close behind Charley's squat figure.

"These are Nehalems, you said?"

"Yes," Charley answered, without turning.

"They slavers?"

"Of course."

"Don't believe I'd care too much for that," Trask mused.

Charley smiled. "They never take a white man for a slave."

"That's good," Trask said. "What about you?"

Charley shook his head. "Grown men are poor slaves, hard to handle. Most people don't bother too much with them."

"What do we have to worry about, then?" Trask asked.

"They would not want us for slaves," Charley said. "But they wouldn't mind killing us."

"Oh."

Unaccountably, Charley turned and smiled at him.

✟✟✟

A few minutes later they topped a rise and Charley stopped short. Trask came up beside him, and together they looked down at the bay below. It was quite narrow here, becoming the river mouth proper. On a bank overlooking the river, but still below their present level, were two cedar-plank lodges, and it was from these the smoke came. Both were about the same size, and placed parallel to each other, facing the river. They were roughly fifty feet long and twenty wide, the walls of cedar planks stuck vertically in the ground. The roofs were steeply gabled, of overlapping planks two feet or more wide, lashed on the outside to vine maple poles that extended from eaves to ridge.

As they watched, there was movement at the edge of the forest behind the lodges, and they could see figures of people melting silently into the darkness.

"They deserting the village?" Trask asked, puzzled.

"There will be some left to meet us," Charley said.

There was a door visible in the gable end of the nearest house, an oval opening a little way above ground, and even as Charley spoke, a man stooped through and stood at the entrance looking up at them.

Trask knew they were silhouetted against the skyline with the sinking sun behind them, and had a moment's uneasiness. If anyone should decide to take a shot at them, they would be perfect targets.

There was more movement at the lodge "door," and a woman stepped out beside the man. The two of them stood motionless, their eyes fixed on Trask and Charley. The man, like the one that had watched them on the beach, was naked. The woman wore a short, knee-length skirt of shredded cedar bark, but she too was naked from the waist up. At the distance she seemed young, but it was hard to tell.

"Hadn't we better get off this ridge?" Trask said nervously.

"It doesn't matter," Charley said. "If they want us, they have us. But they aren't sure yet. That's why the rest went into the woods. It isn't a friendly gesture." He stared for a long moment down at the lodge, and the two figures standing before it. Then he started down the slope, moving slowly. Trask followed.

"Now listen to me," Charley said, speaking quickly and low.

"There are at least eight families in these two lodges. They're four-fire size. They act as if we were enemies—"

"How do you get that?"

"No canoes on the beach; they're hidden. The way the people went in the woods. Now listen. This is a fairly wealthy village. You can tell by the planks. These people are strong, and they know it. You don't want to make any mistakes with them. Let me do the talking when we get there. Also—" Charley glanced quickly at Trask, seeming to debate his next sentence.

"Go ahead."

Charley shrugged. "Also they don't like whites, and they're letting us know it."

"How?"

"The man's naked; the woman's wearing a bark skirt. They don't have to do that, they've traded. They've got cloth and pants and all the rest of it. You'll see metal tools in that house. It was built with iron blades, not the old way. The planks are too good, too smooth. But they're making out they don't want any of the white man."

Trask nodded, his eyes narrowing slightly, watching. The first thing the Indian took from the white man was tools; the second, clothing. He had seldom seen an Indian dressed—or undressed—in the old way. They got white clothes as soon as they could, if only because they quickly learned it was easier to trade if they were dressed "properly." The cedar-bark skirt—simply a rectangle of shredded bark wrapped around and tied at one side—had an unsettling effect on white men, and the native women soon covered themselves more completely or stayed away from whites entirely. The nudity of the man and woman at the lodge was a direct challenge. Without changing the speed of his stride, Charley walked directly up to the two, Trask only a few steps behind.

The man's hair was parted in the middle, and the part streaked with bright vermilion. The hair was long, and glossy with some kind of grease, hanging loosely to his shoulders. The woman's was the same, except for a fur headband that held the hair off her forehead.

"Klahowya," Charley said, his voice expressionless.

The man only continued to regard him indifferently. Trask was momentarily startled by the incredible intensity of the Killamook's eyes, set deep in a face that might have been carven of the same cedar that built the house. He glanced at the woman and saw she was young, as had been his initial impression. She met his eyes, and he turned away quickly.

After a moment of brooding silence, the Killamook stepped slightly to the side, leaving the doorway to the lodge unblocked ahead of them. He still had not spoken.

Without hesitation, Charley unslung his pack and shoved it ahead of him through the opening, pushing aside the elkskin curtain that formed the door.

It seemed a perfectly natural gesture, but it occurred to Trask fleetingly that the pack would look like a man, with the curtain draped over it. And, should there be anyone beside the opening with an ax . . .

But nothing happened and Trask followed Charley into the lodge.

It was, as Charley had said, a four-fire building, one near each corner. The smoke from the fires rose up under the ridge, where it was let out through one of the planks that had been slightly raised.

The room itself was large, roughly partitioned by cattail mats hung from beams into four compartments, one for each family. Around the edge was the sleeping-platform, a continuous ledge built out from the wall about four feet wide, and as high from the ground. In front of this was a lower shelf for sitting. The step-platform ran around three sides of the building, excluding the single wall through which they had come. The lodge was empty of people, though all the fires were still lit. It seemed very large, like a dance-hall without dancers, and was pervaded with the strong smell of the salmon drying on racks beneath the roof.

The two Killamooks followed them into the lodge. The man gestured to the fire nearest them, and Charley sat, putting his pack close beside him. The man sat on the opposite side of the fire, and the young woman brought sticks and placed them on the glowing coals. Shortly they burst into flame, and lighted the faces of the men brightly. Trask saw that the natural intensity of the man's deep-set eyes had been heightened by a red pigment rubbed in under his eyes. He wanted to look at the girl again—she was remarkably attractive for a squaw, her breasts firm and young, her face finely chiseled—but he had noted that Charley studiously avoided even a glance in her direction, and felt himself wiser to follow suit.

After a moment Charley said, "*Mika kumtux Chinook wawa?*"

The man did not answer. He continued to regard Charley incuriously, as he would absently watch a spider on the wall while thinking of something important.

In Chinook, Charley said to Trask, "This is a very strong man, of a strong people. He is almost worthy to be your friend." In English he added, "Say 'Maybe.'"

"*Klonas, klonas,*" Trask said indifferently, meeting the Killamook's eyes.

The man listened, then turned his eyes back to Charley. His expression did not change; he might have heard nothing at all.

By now the girl had taken her seat next to the man, and Trask was able to look at her without seeming to, out of the corners of his eyes. She was not a flathead. The man was, his forehead sloping sharply back from the brow almost to a point leaving a distinct ridge at the top. The woman, then, was either low-born or a captured slave.

Charley was saying, still in the Jargon, "Of all the Boston men, he, Trask, is the strongest, *elip skookum kopa konaway.*"

"Go slow," Trask said in English. "I'm not studying to fight anybody."

"You won't have to," Charley answered. "He hasn't even admitted he speaks Chinook yet. Until he does, he can ignore anything I say, officially."

Still the Killamook did not reply, but Trask thought he caught a quickening interest in his eyes.

"He, Trask, is *hyas tyee*, great chief, among the Boston men."

Suddenly the Killamook spoke. "The Boston men are few," he said in a formal tone. "Killamooks many." He spoke the Jargon with an odd inflection which Trask could not place, but supposed to be a holdover from his native Salishan.

"No," Charley said. "The Boston men are many as the sands of the beach."

"Killamooks many as summer stars," the man said.

"For each Killamook are ten Boston men," Charley said. "All great warriors, all great trees in the forest."

"*Killamook mamook memaloose Boston men.*"

Involuntarily Trask shivered. Tenses were hard to place in the Jargon, it was not a language of much subtlety. The Killamook could have meant they *could* kill the Boston men—in general—or were going to kill this Boston man in particular.

For the first time, Charley permitted the trace of an emotion to cross his face; the faintest of smiles, highly disdainful.

"*Hiyu wawa*," he said wryly. "Much talk. The Boston men come from the land, they come from the sea, with guns to kill. Should a great chief like him, Trask, be insulted, the Boston men would come to kill all the peoples of the Nehalem band, all the people of the Killamook band."

The Killamook regarded Charley intently. Abruptly he leaned back, apparently willing to consider the ritual brag ended. "You come here for trade?"

"No."

"What is carried in the packs?"

"Things," Charley said casually. "Things belonging to us ourselves. And a little more, maybe."

The Killamook thought this over. He picked up a stick, rapped sharply against the wall next to him. Suddenly the elkskin flap was thrown open and a dozen young men swarmed in to stand in a semicircle behind him. Some were naked, some wore simple buckskin clouts. All were armed. There were two rifles among them; each carried knives of metal. Those without rifles carried the short hunting bows, strung with barbed-bone arrows. They stood behind the leader, staring impassively at the two intruders.

The seated man waited until the foreigners fully appreciated the number and arms of the men behind him before he spoke.

"We will take those things, maybe."

Chapter Twelve

Trask had stiffened at the first movement of the flap, reaching for his knife. He was stopped by a quick, almost imperceptible gesture from Charley. Making a rigid effort to control his expression, he relaxed and watched the young bucks file in, keeping his face a mask of indifference.

In a casual tone, as if dismissing the importance of the new arrivals, he remarked to Charley, "Tell me when."

Charley looked up at the figures of the men, weirdly lighted by the flickering fire. He smiled a bit, then yawned, as if watching a children's game that had begun to bore him. Deliberately he reached over to Trask's pack; untied the tump strings with steady hands. He took out Trask's Norwegian pipe and handed it to him, together with the tobacco sack. He got his own pipe out. Trask handed him the tobacco after filling his own pipe. Methodically, as if alone in his own home, Charley filled the bowl and tamped it down. He reached into the fire and extracted a stick that was burning on one end. As he removed it, he gave it a little flick. It might have been accidental, but it scattered a tiny shower of sparks across at the seated Killamook. Startled, he jerked back.

Charley looked over interestedly, and the man's jaw muscles hardened with anger. Charley smiled at him. He leaned over to light Trask's pipe.

"That one," he said in Chinook, "he is afraid of the fire, as the timid doe is afraid. Maybe he is not worthy to be your friend after all."

"So it would seem," Trask said calmly. He puffed deeply on his pipe and blew a long streamer of smoke at the rafters. He thought he could see several of the young men lean forward slightly to smell the smoke.

"That one," Charley said, "he smokes the kinnikinnick. He is too poor to have tobacco." Contemptuously he tossed the small pouch of tobacco across the fire to land before the Killamook.

"Trask potlatch you that tobacco," he said disdainfully. "To ease the misery of your great poverty."

Trask thought he heard the beginning of a snicker from one of the young men, but when he glanced casually up, their faces were all rigidly set in expressions of impersonal menace. Apparently the seated Killamook thought he heard it too, because he looked up angrily.

He glared at Charley, his jaws working, his eyes seeming even wilder than before. Suddenly he stood, and snatched a knife from the clout of one of the bow-carrying braves.

Now it comes, Trask thought suddenly.

But before he could move, the naked Indian had thrown the knife. Not at him—but in front of him, where it stuck into the packed earth floor of the lodge.

"Potlatch Tlask that knife," he said savagely.

Charley looked a little pained. "He, Trask, has more knives than the whole Nehalem band together. But he accepts your potlatch." In English he said, "Pick it up."

Trask examined the knife.

"Do you find the potlatch good?" Charley inquired interestedly.

"What am I supposed to say?" Trask asked in English.

Charley looked greatly surprised. He turned to the Killamook with wonder in his eyes and said in Chinook, "He, Trask, finds the potlatch good. He, Trask, says the man of Nehalem is a strong man, and worthy to be his friend." He seemed quite amazed at this turn. The Killamook smiled maliciously at Charley, all reserve now forgotten in his triumph over the Clatsop.

He looked around him, snatched a bow from one of his men and threw it at Trask's feet. "Potlatch Tlask—that!" he said, glaring triumphantly at Charley.

Trask picked up the bow, nodded approvingly. "The potlatch is good," he said. The bow was a fine one, rawhide-backed to give it additional springiness. In this damp country it was highly impractical, since it was virtually impossible to keep the bow dry enough for the rawhide to be effective. But for some indeterminate reason, the coastal peoples had picked the idea up from inland traders and considered rawhide backing to be the very finest kind of bow-making. When the gift-giver got around to reimbursing his brave, he would find it expensive going.

"He's going to break himself at this rate," Trask said to Charley.

"He's mad, now," Charley said. "He'll give away everything in the village to prove he's a better man than you."

"Can't you stop it?"

"We could make a nice profit," Charley said thoughtfully.

"That isn't playing the potlatch fair," Trask said.

Charley shrugged. He stood and faced the Killamook formally. "Trask wishes to end the potlatch."

The Killamook, taking this as admission Trask had been outdone, smiled. "We agree," he said.

"But," Charley said dramatically, "he wishes to make one last potlatch. Not to his friend"—he nodded to the man—"but to the Nehalem band of the Killamooks."

The naked man looked slightly confused. It was not the usual thing. This kind of potlatching was strictly a contest of prestige between individuals. Did Trask wish to lay his prestige against that of the whole band? He obviously did not understand what was being proposed.

"This," said Charley, "for the use of the entire band. Trask's good friend shall have the keeping of it."

With a dramatic gesture, Charley reached into his pack and brought out a file.

This time there was no doubt; there had been a gasp from the young men. The leader looked completely broken. A file was worth two slaves in trade. The magical ability to restore keenness to a blade was almost beyond price. With a file a man could do in minutes what endless hours of careful stroking on rock and sharkskin would only approximate.

The naked leader accepted utter defeat. Charley had left him no choice. The gift could not possibly be refused. It would be impossible under the rules governing the potlatch, and a terrible loss to the band. The Killamook dared not risk the anger of his village, and could not hope to outdo the gift of the file.

He sat again, and stared bleakly into the fire. After a moment he snapped something at the young girl in Salish. Quietly she rose and moved behind him to the flap. Trask noted that, though her face was expressionless, her eyes never left Charley Kehwa's face.

"Pretty girl," Trask said.

"Want her?" Charley asked. "I can get her for you easy enough."

"Good God, no!" Trask said, shocked. "Hannah'd kill me!"

"We will eat," the Killamook said. He raised his hands in a gesture intended to convey his rich generosity, but which communicated only the utter despair of his humiliation.

2

A short time after, the women of the village began to bring in the food; steamed clams and crabs, camas root, wapato, some dried elk that had been pounded together with fat, and the inevitable smoked salmon. They set the broad serving platters before the men and retired. Other members of the village began to drift into the lodge, several seating themselves around the front fire, others gathering into little groups around the lodge in other places; but all watching the circle around the front fire.

The interval of waiting was painful. The Killamook obviously found it an additional humiliation to play host to the two strangers, after the terrible loss of face he had suffered at Charley's hands.

The food, however, was plentiful and well prepared. Trask—through Charley—commented at length on the quality of the feast, and some of the tension was eased. By the end of the meal, the Killamook had regained his composure, though both men knew it would be a long struggle for him before he regained the respect of the band. As with all potlatching Indians, the loss of prestige was worse than a defeat in battle. It put the humiliated one in a servile position, little better than a slave, and there was not even the saving grace of a noble death. The Killamook would be an object of sly ridicule for some time to come, until he could somehow prove himself again.

Trask knew they had made an enemy. There was nothing that could be done about it. Except to walk carefully and look behind often. By the time they had finished eating, the man had regained his initial belligerence, and was obviously probing for some advantage over the strangers.

"If you do not come to trade, then why?" he asked abruptly.

"We pass through the Nehalem land on our way to the south," Charley said.

The Killamook considered this. In his mind's eye, Trask could almost picture the Indian's thoughts; a quick survey of possible ambush spots on the way south.

"South to where?" the man said.

"To the bay of five rivers," Charley said.

"Ah. To trade there?"

"He, Trask, wishes to see that land, and pay his respects to the tyee."

"Ah. Kilchis, then."

"Yes."

After a moment the Killamook pointed to Charley's forehead.

"There was one with us who died," Charley explained.

"And why have you cut hair for that one?"

"He-who-died had no wife to cut hair for him. The women of his family were far away, and there was no one. That one fell from the mountain."

"Ah. And also the Boston man cut hair for him."

"He, Trask, is a friend to many of the Clatsop people."

The Killamook grimaced slightly, a faint, disdainful smile played across his lips. "And is the Boston man then a woman? The cutting of hair is for women."

"It was I who asked him to do this thing," Charley said calmly.

The Killamook was openly contemptuous now. He gestured with his fingers; spoke to the several young men who still stood at the edge of the fire's glow. "Among the Clatsops," he said deliberately, keeping his eyes on Charley, "even the men are as women. Here, you see where this one has cut hair for one-who-died. More, he castrates the Boston man, that he shall have woman-company."

Charley said nothing. He picked up a strip of salmon and chewed it reflectively. The Killamook pressed his advantage, making the most of his chance to humiliate the men who had degraded him. He beckoned to the girl to bring more food, and waited until she was within earshot before he spoke again. There was now a small group gathered around the fire, sensing the quickening activity.

"And how did this misfortune happen?" he said sympathetically. "Did your father bite off your testicles when you were born, like the squirrel?" He shook his head sadly. "Too bad, too bad."

The young men were smiling now, watching, and a flicker of amusement passed over the girl's face.

"Here," said the Killamook, with an expansive gesture. "We give our food to these men. With neither testicles nor penis. The women of the Clatsops have strange desires, maybe, for men without any organs."

One of the young men snickered, and was stopped by a sudden gesture of the seated man. Taking his own penis in his open palm, the man stared down at it ruefully, and shook his head. "I would miss you, little friend, should you be gone. And my wives would miss you much." He looked around him at the circle of faces, pleased with his own wit. The girl laughed aloud, and the Killamook smiled blandly.

Charley put down the salmon with a slow, deliberate movement and wiped his fingers on his trouser leg. Finally he spoke, and his voice was as slow as his movement.

"Someday soon you will lose it, maybe," he said.

The smile disappeared from the other man's face. His eyes were bright with hatred. He snatched a knife from the clout of one of the other braves and stabbed it into the dirt in front of him. The circle shifted restlessly, the men uneasy, and Trask could hear a rapid, whispered conversation in Salish. Several of the men drifted casually around behind the two strangers.

The firelight flickered erratically, casting long, dancing shadows. The Killamook fingered the hilt of the half-buried knife in front of him. He leaned forward, and his voice was tensely controlled.

"The Clatsop talks very much, very big talk, like an old woman."

Charley shrugged indifferently.

Trask could feel a prickling sensation along the back of his neck. Almost involuntarily his legs tensed to rise. Alternately he watched Charley and the Killamook, for whichever would give him the first sign to move. His hand crept slowly to his own knife. His mouth was dry, and there was a tension at the edges of his eyes, a flickering, spasmodic tightening.

The Killamook withdrew the buried knife and ran the back across his open palm in a slicing motion. "You cut hair for the dead like women," he said. "Maybe you sleep tonight like women, with a hole between your legs. Maybe you sleep with your mouth full of your own flesh." His voice was flat and controlled.

Charley shrugged again. "It does not matter. I have another one maybe."

The Killamook laughed, a short bark like a coyote.

Calmly Charley reached into his pack and took out a stick, roughly a foot long. It was pointed at one end, and the opposite end was carved into figures Trask could only dimly see, and did not recognize. Charley thrust it into the ground, as the Killamook had stabbed the knife.

In the same quiet tone Charley continued. "This is my penis, maybe."

In the sudden silence that followed, the crackling of the fire seemed loud. The restless shuffle of the circle around them stopped. Outside the wind could be heard sighing through the firs.

There was a low, resentful mutter from behind Trask, out of which he caught only the words "tamanawis stick." The men behind the Killamook leader stepped back slightly. Angrily, one of them snapped something at him in Salish.

The leader stared at the upright stick and bit his lower lip. After a moment he turned his head aside.

"*This* is my penis," Charley repeated insistently, forcing the Killamook's attention. "You will cut it off, maybe? You will make me eat it, maybe?"

Charley threw back his head, and from his throat poured the shriek of an owl, a blood-curdling scream like a woman's shrill cry in the night, but full of triumph and disdain. The sound was so shrill and sudden Trask jerked, and saw others equally startled. The weird, ululating cry made him shiver involuntarily, as if a cold wind had come in from the sea.

The Killamooks seemed momentarily paralyzed. Finally the silence was broken by the shuffle of bare feet on the dirt floor. The circle parted to admit a man to the side of the fire. He was very old, and wore only a string around his waist, from which dangled many small buckskin bags that swayed and jiggled as he came up to peer into Charley's face. He looked down at the tamanawis stick and nodded slowly.

He turned to the silent Killamook and said in a reedy, whispery voice, "You go now."

Slowly, as though pulled to his feet by force, the man stood and made his way away from the fire. The young men surrounding him did not make way for him to pass. It was as if they did not see him at all, and he had to press his way through the group.

The old man turned to Charley. "That one, he is *sullic*," he said. "Crazy with the hate in him."

Charley nodded. "That one's hate may cause all the men of the Nehalem band to lose their penises," he said quietly. "They will turn black and fall off, maybe."

The circle stepped back still farther from the fire, and Trask could see the fright in the eyes of the young men. The old man did not seem moved.

Carefully he said in his papery voice, "It would not be fair to the band to do such a thing."

"The people of the band should not let themselves be led by one like him," Charley said.

"You understand," the old man said, "he is crazy with himself. Sick tum-tum." He pointed to his temple. "But he makes big talk, the young men listen to him, maybe."

"That one has shamed the band," Charley said. "He has angered me and Trask. He has defiled the potlatch with hate."

"And yet," the old man said speculatively, "he did not know you were tamanawis. And it is not right that the band should die for the hatred of one man. This is a thing between you and him only."

Charley nodded slowly, as though being reluctantly convinced. "Then let the band choose its leaders better."

The old man bobbed his head quickly. "It will be done," he said. "We will bring his penis and testicles to put in a little bag." He jiggled one of the small pouches he wore.

"No," Charley said. "My anger is gone in the wisdom of your words, old man. The men of the Nehalem shall be left whole, and next time they will listen to your words, maybe."

Charley turned his head slowly, to fix each of the men around the fire with his eyes. "Know this," he said. "When the band follows a trail of hate and anger, each man's penis will turn black and fall off. Listen to the tamanawis man, what he says to you, and they will stand straight like the cedar tree, and you will have much money besides."

There were quick murmurs of assent, and the nervous shuffling of feet began again.

"You all go out of the lodge, now," the old man said. There was a quick movement to the flap, and in a moment Charley and Trask were alone by the fire with the old man. At the other end of the lodge were still a few people, women and older men, but immediately around the fire were only the three.

Charley picked the tamanawis stick out of the ground and carefully replaced it in his pack. Trask realized that in all the packing and unpacking during the trip he had never seen it before, and yet he had not been aware of any effort by Charley to conceal it.

The old man sat down abruptly, in the place the other Killamook had left. He leaned forward and peered intently across the fire.

"I know you," he said finally. "You are Charley Kehwa of the Clatsops."

Chapter Thirteen

I

Charley nodded without apparent surprise. The old man regarded him quizzically for a long moment, his eyes pinching into tiny, thoughtful slits. Finally he drew himself straight again and said, "I am called Tupshin. I wish to speak with you of certain matters, Charley Kehwa."

His manner was full of dignity, and he gave the impression of having come to some decision humbling to himself, yet necessary. He shot a quick glance in Trask's direction; then averted his eyes.

"The matters of which I would speak," Tupshin said, staring absently into the fire, "would be like the murmur of the waves to the ears of the Boston man, of no meaning."

Charley hesitated. Then he said slowly, "This one, Trask, comes with me."

Tupshin frowned and twisted his fingers, still watching the fire. At last he shrugged. "This thing I do not understand," he said. "How it is that Charley Kehwa of the Clatsops guides the Boston down the coast, like a common hunter." He looked up, watching Charley's face.

The Clatsop said nothing. He sat quietly, and the silence was prolonged until at last Tupshin looked away with an apologetic nod of his head.

"It is not my affair," the old man said.

"No."

Tupshin sighed. "*Kloshe kahkwa*," he said. "I will speak, then. Last year, it was. Two of the boys did not return from the Searching."

"There is always danger when men seek a Power," Charley said quietly.

Tupshin snorted. "This we know. I myself have seen men eaten up by the Powers. But the Searching of these boys was in Astoria. They work there for the Boston, carrying things from the great ships. They are lost."

Trask realized dimly there was more involved in this than the desertion of two young men. The Searching of a youth was loaded with meanings of which he was only partially aware. It was a ritual journey of some kind; not secret, but not freely discussed. Glancing at Charley he saw a ridge of muscle tense along the Indian's jaw, then relax.

Charley leaned forward. "And what of the past, old man? Have you never lost men before? Have you never seen the great pirate canoes of the Tlingit pulled up on your beach? Have you never run into the woods like rabbits when the Nootka raiders came prowling?"

"Yes," Tupshin answered calmly. "All this I have seen, and also the fat Chinook traders. But never have I seen this other thing, that a boy refuses the Searching. It is the way of things that slaves should be taken, there have always been slaves. The Nootka come in their long canoes like hungry wolves, a thousand miles up and down the coast, great raiding parties. Well, they are Nootka; it has always been so. Shall they be as the Clatsops? Or the Quinault? No. They are Nootka, and this is the way of the Nootka.

"But they make their Searching like the rest of us; how else should they have the power to raid? And slaves are taken in war, they do not say to their people, 'I go on my Searching,' and go to Astoria instead."

"But they are gone, old man. The band loses them."

"As *men* they are gone, or boys who will be men when they have made the Searching. And maybe we can buy them back. But a man cannot live and work without his spirit helper, without his Power. These are men-who-are-not-men."

Charley shook his head mutely.

"You live among the whites, Charley Kehwa. You can understand these things. What is their Power? What is this that our boys trade for their spirit helper?"

"The whites do not believe in such things," Charley said.

"Believe?" Tupshin was bewildered. "What is this talk of belief? Do they not believe in the sea, then? Or the mountains? There is a thing which *is*, it is not for believing or not believing."

Charley shook his head again. Tupshin stared at him incredulously. Finally the old man put his forehead in his hand and considered his words carefully before speaking.

"Then tell me this thing, Charley Kehwa. A Boston does not go on the Searching as a young man. How does he discover what is inside himself? How does he have the Vision that tells him what is in his own belly, what his Power is?"

"Among the whites," Charley said slowly, "there are few who can hear the spirit voices. They do not have the Vision."

"No," Tupshin said flatly, "no, this cannot be. A man who has not had the Vision is no better than a dead man. You know this, Charley Kehwa. A man who has not had his Vision does not know what his place in the world is to be. How can he live, then?"

Charley leaned back, trying to think of some way to explain to the old man. Explain? As well try to explain how a man could live without breathing, or eating. It would be easier for old Tupshin to understand these things. But to live without a spirit helper . . .

Charley knew what was passing through the old man's mind; the memories of anguish and anxiety, the painful days of the Searching and the uncertain times after. The boy setting out on his lonely journey to find his spirit partner, the partner that would give him his direction in life, that would give him the power to do strong works, that would be the companion and core of his being for the rest of his life . . . Explain to Tupshin that the white men did not need it?

No, the old man would not understand it, not ever. Not when a man's whole life depended on the Vision. Charley remembered the Clatsop tamanawis man who had trained him for his Searching. "You are the arrow," he said. "Straighten your body as the shaft is straight; sharpen your mind as the point is sharp . . ." And above all, the discipline, the endless control of thought and emotion; the feathers that make the shaft fly true. Without the discipline, no man could receive the Power; it was too strong . . .

And after the days of fasting and scrubbing with cedar branches and plunging into the cold waters, maybe you will be clean enough for the Power to visit you; for the spirits hate the smell of food and camps and many people all together. They come in solitude, if they come at all, bringing the Vision, bringing the Power. And then, even after the Vision, the terrifying uncertainty; hiding in the lodge, painting the symbol of your spirit helper on a board, or carving it—and never knowing if your Vision was a true one. For if the spirits promised the power to carve strong canoes, and in later life you were a gouger of splinters—then the Vision was not true, but something made up in your own mind, something springing from the hungry-head. You were cheated; a man whose center was emptiness, a man who did not know his own strength, a man without a Power. But when it was a true thing . . .

Ever after, your life would be given strength by the Vision as the arrow is driven by the bow. Without it—merely dead wood, a stick. A nothingness.

Charley shook his head helplessly. How explain to Tupshin that the Boston men saw no more than the surface of the world? Could a tamanawis man understand that? Could he understand that a tree was to them only wood? A mountain only rock? That these things had no meeting with the man at all? It was against all reason, all experience, and Charley could find no way to make sense of it.

He himself could not understand, though he accepted that it was true. The Boston men did live without the Vision. But he also saw the terrible world they lived in, a cloudy world of anxieties and vagueness. He knew what it was for a man to live without contact; never knowing what Powers hid in his own belly, never knowing what he shared with the mountains and the sea. It frightened him, as the thought of living without arms or legs would frighten him.

He was suddenly aware that both Tupshin and the white man were watching him intently, waiting for his answer.

"Old one," he said regretfully, "this is the way of the Boston men: they do not go on the Searching, they do not have the Vision. There is no more I can say than this." After a moment he added gently, "It is not an easy thing to understand."

"No," Tupshin said dazedly. He looked over at Trask. "No, there is much I cannot understand. Then—then the boys who refuse the Searching, they trade for—nothing?"

"For wealth, maybe," Charley said.

"Wealth? The little pieces of metal? No canoes, no blankets, no slaves—the little pieces of metal?"

Charley nodded unhappily.

Tupshin blinked. He started to say something, then turned his face away from Charley and looked into the fire again. When he spoke the words came hard. "Charley Kehwa," he said, "I am old."

"I respect your years," Charley said formally.

Tupshin dismissed the comment with an impatient shake of his head. "I am old," he repeated, "and I will be traveling to the dead country soon. I think this is a good thing for me. For if I stay in the country of the Nehalem, I will see the people become men-who-are-not-men. This I do not wish to see."

He rose suddenly and looked down at Charley and Trask. "You will be welcome in this lodge," he said.

He stooped and went through the skin flap. As Tupshin turned away, Trask thought he saw the firelight glint from tears in the old man's eyes. Charley watched the skin swing back to cover the entrance, then turned to Trask, his face impassive. The white man did not meet his eyes.

After a moment Trask cleared his throat and said, "Well—" He turned his palms up in a mute gesture of helplessness.

Charley stood and went to the sleeping-platform. Silently he began to roll out his blanket.

2

Trask was profoundly and unaccountably moved by the old man Tupshin. As he sat by the fire stuffing his pipe, he was deeply aware of his own ignorance. He did not even understand the simplest of things: why the failure of two unknown boys to undertake the Searching brought tears to the eyes of a tough old horse like Tupshin.

On the Plains Trask was counted close to the Clatsops, but he realized with a chilling certainty that the gulf between them had not even begun to be bridged; his "understanding" was a kind of condescension no better than that of Loveman Anders and the other moralists.

He—like Anders—judged entirely by white standards. The only difference was that Trask thought the Clatsops measured up pretty well and Anders didn't. His friendships with the Indians were based on a kind of mystical change that took place in his own mind, the change from brown to white. Charley Kehwa was accepted not simply as Charley

Kehwa, but as Charley-who-is-smarter-than-most-whites. And Celiast, not as herself, but as Celiast-who-is-equal-to-any- white-woman. Always the standards were those of white men; the Indian values he could not even begin to comprehend. Trask felt suddenly like a man caught in the middle of a wild, self-aggrandizing lie, and was acutely embarrassed at his own pretensions.

What *did* happen on the Searching? What was this thing, so completely alien to his understanding?

When he rolled out his own blanket that night, it was with an unreal sense of floundering directionless in a world of which he knew nothing.

The morning began in thunder, a huge drumming that jerked Trask upright, reaching for his knife instinctively.

A huge slave woman was standing at the front of the lodge, pounding a club against the wall with all her strength. Shortly she began to shout in addition, "GET UP! GET UP! GET UP!"

Gradually, brown bodies began to slide off the sleeping-platform all around, some cheerfully, some muttering darkly to themselves. Soon the twenty-odd inhabitants of the lodge had gone out through the elkskin flap and separated into two groups. The women and girls went upstream a short distance, on the other side of a grove of birch, to their bathing place. The men and boys took to the river directly in front of the lodge.

Trask, not knowing what was expected of him, waited to take his cue from Charley.

"You going to take a bath?" Charley said.

"Sure, if it's all right."

"It's all right."

The two of them went down to the river and plunged in. The rest of the village males were already there, splashing around in the shallows, rubbing themselves with some kind of crushed leaves and cedar bark. Trask's presence drew cautious side glances.

"They're surprised," Charley told him.

"What, the white skin?"

"Oh, no. But in some tribes they call the whites *humm tillicums*."

"Stinky people? Why?"

"They never bathe," Charley said with obvious amusement. "Just rinse off hands and face and cover up the rest with clothes."

Trask scowled at him, but there wasn't any ready answer. It was quite true that white habits were pretty slovenly compared with the twice-daily baths of the coastal peoples. On the other hand, whites didn't find it necessary to smear themselves with fish-oil, either. He cleared his throat and scrubbed vigorously at his chest, glaring at Charley, who paid no attention at all.

The morning air was split with howls, some laughter, some pain. More than one man, bending to scoop up water in his hands, found himself enthusiastically swatted with a cedar switch, which seemed to be a high form of humor. Trask winced.

The general atmosphere of the bath was highly playful, and the whole band cavorted and splashed in the water for nearly an hour before turning to the more serious business of the day.

When Trask and Charley returned to the lodge they found Tupshin already there, seated before the front fire. The young slave girl was pounding jerky deer meat in a mortar, gradually mixing in fat from a wooden bowl beside her. This breakfast was apparently a gesture of hospitality toward Trask, for the Indians did not customarily eat until they had been four or five hours at work.

When the slave girl had gone, Tupshin spoke without preamble. "It is not a good thing that you take the Boston to the bay of five rivers."

"We have agreed," Charley said slowly, "that this was not your affair."

"The good of my people is my affair," Tupshin said, unruffled. "A bad thing will come of this."

"You have had a dream of this thing, then."

"No," Tupshin admitted. "Two men of the Killamook band came here a little time ago. They wished to go up this river for hunting, and several of our men went with them. They have said the Killamook band does not wish to have white men in their place."

"The Killamook band also has traded," Charley said. "They take the sharp tools and the warm blankets. Now they say they do not want the whites?"

Tupshin shrugged. "This is Kilchis' word."

"Does Kilchis then wish to take the good things without return, like stealing in the night?"

"Trading is not stealing," Tupshin said quietly. "Kilchis does not wish to have the whites bring their strange ways into his country."

"Strange ways are learned from every tribe. This is part of trading. It has always been this way."

"This is true," Tupshin admitted. "But—trading among the people is a different thing from trading with the whites. Kilchis does not want them in his country."

"What will this Kilchis do, then?"

Tupshin shrugged. "Who can speak the mind of Kilchis? He will do what he will do."

Charley leaned back on his elbows and regarded Tupshin across the fire. "We hear much big talk about this Kilchis; all the time hiyu wawa kopa Kilchis. Is he not a man, like the rest of us?"

Tupshin frowned. "It is in my mind that he is not, maybe."

Charley smiled at him. "He is a man, this one. Only a man."

Tupshin nodded thoughtfully. "I myself have never seen a spirit take on a body," he admitted. "But—who can say what it is to be a man as Kilchis is a man? Then the rest of us are half-men, maybe." He shrugged.

"This is one I wish to see," Charley said.

"*Kloshe kahkwa*." Tupshin nodded. "But it is in my mind there will be great trouble if the Boston is killed in Kilchis' country."

Charley laughed. "Yes."

"And great trouble if he is not killed also," Tupshin mused, speaking as though Trask were not present. "Who can say which way makes more trouble for the people? This is something I, Tupshin, cannot say."

"Well that you do not, maybe," said Charley.

"It would be better, I think, if he were killed," Tupshin said thoughtfully. "The blood price would doubtless be very high, but better the band should be poor from paying the blood price than to lose everything."

Charley shook his head. "The whites do not accept the blood payment, old one. As many Boston would come as salmon come into the rivers, and they would kill the Killamook people with guns."

"Even if we paid the price they asked for him?" Tupshin said

"Even so."

Tupshin shook his head. "Are they animals?" he demanded. "Have they no law?"

Charley shrugged. "It is their way."

Trask realized that the old man was not at all concerned about discussing the possible murder in front of him; thought no more of it than he would have thought of discussing hunting before a hobbled deer. It was an impersonal thing, and Trask found the cool weighing of factors more chilling than the violence of the younger man the previous night.

"I have told you what is in my mind," Tupshin said.

"For this you have our thanks, old one," Charley said.

"You will not turn back."

"This one," Charley said, gesturing to Trask, "means no trouble to the Killamook people. Let them receive him in peace, and there will be no trouble."

Tupshin shrugged again. "This is for Kilchis to say," he said.

"Will one of your people take us across the bay?" Charley asked.

The old man stood. He nodded, and his regret was apparent. "There will be a canoe," he said. "Klahowya."

"Klahowya, old one," Charley answered softly.

3

The sun was well into the sky now, and the air was warm. The beach held only the freight canoe in which they were to cross the bay, and a few of the women's shovel-nosed canoes, turned over on the sand and covered with cattail mats. Their freight canoe was somewhat larger than the ordinary hunter's craft. It was built with a sharp prow, but without the high "sitting-pieces" fore and aft that gave the war canoes the appearance of dragons on the water; and it was broader of beam than these. The outside was black, from either charring or paint, Trask could not tell which, and the inside painted a reddish ocher.

Charley made some kind of farewell to Tupshin and the boatman shoved off into the bay. The tide was not running, and the bay was smooth. They glided swiftly across the flat, unruffled water with their wake gurgling softly under the stern and stretching in a long straight line behind.

Trask could discern no evidence of malice on the part of their Killamook; he seemed, in fact, to be of remarkably cheerful disposition. The stroking of his paddle was short and hard, like that of a man more accustomed to rowing with others than alone. Possibly, Trask thought, he had worked the long war canoes more than the one-man hunters' rigs. Trask glanced back at him and the boatman smiled, almost shyly. He seemed on the verge of saying something, but apparently thought better of it.

"*Mika wawa Chinook?*" Trask asked.

The rower nodded emphatically. "*Nowitka, nowitka!*" he said. Suddenly he grinned broadly. "*Chinook, kunamokst Chinook pe—Ingleesh.*"

"English? Speak English too?" Trask said, surprised.

"*Kah mika kumtux* English?" Charley asked curiously. "Where'd you learn English?"

"Astoria," the Killamook said with a certain pride. "*Nika mamook huy-huy kopa* Astoria." He had traded in Astoria.

"Say something," Trask urged, since this was apparently a point of pride with the Killamook. "Say something in English."

The Killamook smiled at him uncertainly, and nodded.

"*Mamook* English *wawa*," Charley said.

"Ah!" the Killamook said, with sudden comprehension. He thought deeply for a moment. "Summabitch," he said. "Durdy red bassahd. Ingleesh? Summabitch. Blan-ket. Low-see siwash. Ingleesh?"

Charley glanced at Trask, who cleared his throat and looked down at the packs in the center of the canoe. The Killamook was smiling pleasantly, with an expectant expression.

Finally Trask said, "*Wawa* English *hyas kloshe.*"

The Killamook nodded with pleasure, grinning happily. They slid over the smooth waters of the bay with the boatman softly chanting his little store of knowledge to himself. "Summabitch. Durdy red bassahd."

The short trip, though it would have taken hours to go inland and ford the river where it was narrower, was over soon. The Killamook, inspired by his new friendship, insisted on unloading the packs for them while Trask and Charley stood idle on the shore.

He assured them they would reach the bay of five rivers by nightfall, the rest of the journey being along the beach, and easy walking.

Trask gave the Killamook a half-dollar—"For spending next time you trade in Astoria"—which pleased him much. He turned it over in his hands happily, repeating, "*Hyas kloshe, hyas kloshe,*" and nodding rapidly.

Charley shoved the canoe off and watched while it started back for the lodges, the paddle flashing brightly in the morning sun.

"Klahowya!" Trask called, cupping his hands to his mouth.

The Killamook raised his paddle in salute and a cheerful "Summabitch!" came ringing over the water.

Trask winced, and bent over to pick up his pack, grimacing with distaste. To his relief Charley made no comment. They wriggled into the shoulder straps and adjusted their tumplines. Trask found the muscles of his neck a little stiff from the unaccustomed strain of tump-packing, but knew they would work out after the first hour or so. He twisted his head under the band.

"Sore?" Charley said.

"A little."

"Me too," Charley admitted.

"Getting soft," Trask said ruefully. "Used to carry beaver pack, a hundred, hundred twenty-five pounds without any trouble."

"Well, you're not a trapper any more," Charley said. "You're a settler. Uses different muscles."

"I guess that's right," Trask said, with some surprise in his voice. "I never really gave it any thought."

"What, muscles?"

"No, I mean—I don't know, I mean I used to be one thing and now I'm something else. I never noticed."

Charley laughed. "Tamanawis," he said solemnly. "One morning you wake up and you're somebody new. You know somebody's put the spirit doctor on you."

"What do you do then?" Trask asked him.

"Got to hire another one to protect you," Charley told him seriously.

Trask laughed. "Makes business for the whole trade. Want a job?"

"Already got one," Charley said.

Trask turned to look at him, but the flat brown face held no expression. Charley turned and started down the beach to the south.

Trask caught him easily within a few strides and they walked side by side down the broad expanse of light sand.

"Say, Charley," he said quizzically. "Could you really do what you said last night?"

"About what?"

"Make 'em all turn black and fall off."

Charley glanced at him out of the corner of his eye. "Worried?" he asked slyly.

"Just curious," Trask said. "Could you do it?"

"Well, Charley said thoughtfully, "I could try."

"That's no answer."

Charley smiled at him with good humor. "Not to you, maybe."

Chapter Fourteen

Their course for the remainder of the day was almost due south, directly down the beach. In the late afternoon, with the sun swinging down on their right, the beach began to slant slightly east. Shortly, the general direction of the coast had changed from due south to a definite southeasterly direction. As they walked along the beach, Trask was conscious of a vague sensation that something was wrong; not important; but—different. In some small way the atmosphere had changed.

"The breakers," he said suddenly.

"What about them?" Charley asked.

"They're not so loud." Trask stopped and looked back toward the sound of the sea. The breakers were crashing some distance away now, instead of immediately at their right hand. He could see the long, turbulent cords of white water at a distance. Then his view was blocked and at first, so closely did the obstruction hug the surface of the water, he could not make out what it was. Then he determined it was a long, low sandspit running directly north and south, and the rollers were breaking on a shoal directly in line with it.

"We're here," Charley said with amusement. "Those breakers are the entrance to Murderer's Harbor."

"Good God!" Trask said. "How'd Gray ever get his ship in over that sand bar?"

Charley shrugged. "Probably isn't so bad when the tide's higher."

The point where they had left their due-south course had been the northern extremity of Murderer's Harbor. But so wide was the expanse of water it was nearly indistinguishable from the sea. Looking more closely, Trask could see that the sandspit swelled up at its southern base; a long, low wall, sheltering the harbor from the pounding of the sea. The harbor itself trended along a southeast axis. In the far distance, almost obscured by the coming evening haze, Trask could see a slightly darker shadow lying on the surface of the bay, which he took to be the opposite end. It was still miles away.

"This is bigger than I figured," Trask said.

"It's pretty big," Charley agreed noncommittally.

"Where's Kilchis' village?" Trask asked.

"I don't know. At the mouth of one of the rivers, but I can't see where they come into the bay."

Trask nodded. As the Clatsop villages were built at the mouths of the Neahcoxie and Necanicum rivers, so it was most likely to find the Killamooks concentrated around the meeting of fresh water and salt; the most convenient place for the summer salmon runs. And when the salmon were not running, the rivers would provide easy access for the hunting canoes, going inland.

The land all around the southeastern end of the bay was flat, a wide plain that ran back—as nearly as he could guess from this distance— almost ten miles. Then the coastal mountains began, almost without transition from the plain. There were no gentle foothills, gradually climbing, that he could see. The plain stretched away from the edge of the bay; then the mountains, sudden and harsh. They humped on the horizon in contorted, sharp shapes; not symmetrical, but lumpy and lopsided like the peaks behind the Cape of the Falcons and Neahkahnie.

Whereas Clatsop Plains was a long, narrow strip along the sea, ending a few short miles from the ocean, the plains here were like a thick quarter-moon crescent around the bay. His first guess was that there would be twice the tillable land; perhaps more.

"We'd better get moving," Charley said. "We won't make it to the other end by dark." He glanced at the sun, now nearing the edge of the sea.

"I'll tell you," Trask said, "I'd just as soon make camp next good place we find. I got a notion I'd rather meet this Kilchis in broad daylight."

Charley shrugged. "That's all right," he said.

They made camp finally a few hundred yards back from the water's edge, in the lee of a low bank. Not being familiar with the beach, Charley had rejected the obvious expedient of settling down for the night on the broad, flat expanse of sand that was so inviting. Too frequently along this coast the tides swept over the whole exposed area of beach, and neither had a mind to be wakened by the ocean's cold caress.

Charley made a small fire, chiefly for the cheer it provided, while Trask strung up the tent a little distance away. As they had for this camp only the water they carried, they made dry-camp. Charley made a short trip in the quickly fading light to see if he could find some berries nearby. He returned empty-handed and they sat to a dry meal of bread and venison jerky given to them by Tupshin.

Though the day's hike had been easy—the easiest stretch of terrain they had met so far—both men were tired. There was little conversation as they turned in.

Trask wondered drowsily why he felt so tired after the easy walk down the beach; decided it was probably the tension of the last couple of days. Anxiety tired you faster than working, he thought philosophically. And he hadn't slept in the Nehalem lodge as well as he might have wished; being somewhat conscious through the night of the possibility of a knife's appearing suddenly through a raised plank in the wall.

He yawned and rolled over. "'Night," he said to Charley. His answer was an indistinguishable murmur from the shapeless lump on the other side of the tent.

Trask smiled slightly, on the edge of sleep, remembering how hard Charley was to wake. No, wait . . .

It wasn't Charley, he thought fuzzily, it was—

The thought of him-who-died startled him into wakefulness, as he realized he had forced memory of the death far back into the dark corners of his mind. Even in thought he shied away from the name instinctively, and was obscurely annoyed with himself for doing so. What the hell was the matter with him? *He* didn't believe in ghosts hovering around after death. *He* wasn't afraid to summon the spirit by calling his name. Hell, if—if he-who-died wanted company going to the dead country he would've come before this. But maybe not.

Trask realized he was too sleepy to be thinking clearly. He was going to need a good night's rest tonight. He twisted around in his blankets and wondered if thinking the name of a dead one would have the same effect as speaking it. Probably not; that would make life intolerable.

It was hard enough for the people as it was, particularly when one-who-died had a name in common use. If Red-Painted-Bear died, then Bear-Coming-Back had to change his name to Deer-Coming-Back, or some such. Red would be referred to as "that color." The men would have to speak of going out to hunt "the shambling one." Trask remembered clearly the death of a Clatsop woman named Betsy. The women of the village had stopped calling cats "pussy," just because it *sounded* a little like Betsy. It was ridiculous.

Just as he dropped over the brink of sleep, Trask had a moment of bitter, clear awareness when he realized again his skill at self-deception; that he could muse idly on convention in order to block out the lightning-sharp picture of a small, top-heavy little Clatsop toppling with a smile still on his lips . . .

2

Once in the night Trask rolled over and blearily saw a dark silhouette between him and the fire, poking up the dying glow and feeding fresh wood. Charley keep it going, he thought. Should do it myself. Hell with it . . .

In the early hours of the night a low overcast came scudding in from the sea, and a wind rose erratically in the northwest. The moon was drowned and blotted out; became a vague splotch of luminescence somewhere deep in the grayness of the sky. The variable wind whispered and lashed across the sea, blowing traceries of spume from the whitecaps in gusts; then slid up the shore and into the trees, making them rustle and sway and shake themselves fitfully under the gray sky.

A stray gust of wind swept up the rear tent flap and slipped inside, blowing coolly across the dark shapes of the sleepers. Trask was vaguely conscious of the coolness and a gentle tugging at his beard. Automatically he tucked the edges of his blanket under him and wriggled securely in the wool cocoon.

The wind rose and fell and picked up in force, bringing the promise of rain. Outside the fire flickered wildly, sending the long shadows of trees leaping frightened for the dark recesses of the wood. The wind began to come more regularly into the tent in sudden, cool gusts, flapping the sides against their lashings like the wings of a great land-pinned bird attempting flight.

Of this Trask was half aware, and the warm snugness of his blankets took on new pleasure. The coolness of the wind on his face was not unpleasant, and the erratic tugging of the breeze at his beard and hair was gentle and caressing.

In time the sliding clouds thickened and the position of the moon was no longer clear except in rare thin moments; and there was rain.

Pattering in sporadic lines across the beach and among the trees; blown restlessly by the inconstant wind like squalls in miniature; thin sheets of rain that found their way rattlingly down through the masses of growth to tap in faint unrhythmic staccato against the walls of the tent . . .

Trask slept half conscious of the play of wind and rain beyond the dark canvas walls, aware of the flickering and dancing of the fire and the tangible presence of air within the tent; the soft and tentative pressure of his blankets, the ruffling of his beard that was there and gone gently between heartbeats.

He slept in that rarest of man's states: perfect comfort and the perfect, sweet awareness of comfort.

Along the dark and solitary beach a single figure came trudging. The overcast kept the night warm, but the gusts of wind and rain were chill, and it was with pleasure the striding man lifted his eyes to see the glow of a fire set back a little from the beach. He smiled faintly in the darkness and decided he would not go all the way home tonight after all. It had been a pleasant, if somewhat trying evening, crouched uncomfortably by the wall of a lodge, whispering through the cracks between planks. The girl returned his whispers only occasionally, just enough to let him know she was still there, while the rest of the family ignored his courtship in stolid indifference.

Of course, he had to keep himself reasonably inconspicuous, or the girl's father would be forced to notice him, maybe, and then he would get himself a beating for his trouble. Tomorrow, he thought.

Tomorrow, maybe, he and his father would go pay a formal call on the family. Maybe not, though. He hadn't, in honesty, decided quite how he wanted to handle the proposal. A formal visit was all right, but there was no denying the dramatic aspect of a sudden, unannounced appearance before the lodge with his canoe and blankets.

This girl, he figured, would be worth one canoe and ten, maybe twelve good blankets. Maybe six, though, would do it. In reality, of course, she was beyond any price he could ever hope to raise. But one canoe and half a dozen blankets was about all he thought he could raise, and even that would put him in debt. If he could, he'd have given fifty blankets and three canoes and two slaves. But he didn't have any slaves.

He sighed. Life was complicated when you weren't rich. He'd hoped to find a spirit helper that would make him rich, but it hadn't worked out that way. His Vision told him of the strength to be a good maker of canoes and carvings, and he had in truth found much satisfaction in it. But it wasn't like being rich. Nothing was like being rich.

He turned off the beach and made his way over the dark and obscure ground toward the welcoming glow of the fire in the woods. It was funny there were no canoes drawn up on the beach. And anyway, it didn't seem quite right that a hunting party would stop so close to home. Perhaps they were men of the Nehalem, come down to see the Killamook girls or talk to Kilchis or race a few horses or something. If they had horses, it would explain the absence of canoes.

As he made his way through the trees, he wondered idly how far his father would back him up in this thing. If the girl's family threw his gifts out the door, would his own father be willing to go back for more? Hard to say, hard to say. A formal visit might be the thing after all. You could tell a lot by the reception you got. If there was no chance at all the girl's family would simply be off in canoes before you got there. He had the notion he was not unwelcome, or he would have received a few whacks across the back before now. He'd been whispering at the crack for more than ten days now, every night, and it was beginning to wear on him.

He sighed. There was also that wrinkled old woodpecker of an uncle, constantly making his nasty comments, pretending he didn't know anybody at all was whispering at the wall . . .

He came out into the little clearing where the fire was laid and strode directly across to it. He squatted on his heels and warmed his hands and looked around him for the fire-makers. At first, because of the flickering shadows, he did not see the tent stretched between two trees at the edge of the clearing; the open front faced him, and no broad expanse met his eye.

When he saw it, he stood up by the fire uncertainly. A little cloth house. Strange.

He padded tentatively over to the opening with a strange sensation growing between his shoulder blades. He looked in, but the darkness was too much at first for his fire-widened eyes. He could only make out the bundles on either side.

He stood in the opening, irresolute. Then the fire flared behind him, catching a pocket of pitch, and cast a bright yellow glow into the tent. His hackles rose and a shiver ran down his spine and his breath caught in his throat.

For one terrifying, soul-destroying moment he thought he had stumbled on a little cloth house of night-monsters! One of the sleeping men seemed at first to have his head on upside down!

He sucked in his breath sharply, and then the panic passed. It was not that—but one of them had the bottom of his face covered with hair.

He blinked and went back to the fire, around on the other side this time. He squatted again, and regarded the tent across the flickering flames. It was a white man in there, he knew that. He had heard about them before, with hair on their faces they didn't even pluck. And so much!

The fire sputtered, and automatically he fed it a few sticks from the neat stack nearby; returned to squat and hold out his hands.

He remained there for several minutes, trying to organize the flood of impressions that trickled through his mind. He couldn't decide what to do. It doubtless wasn't the right thing to stay by the fire. He had heard the old men talking with Kilchis about the whites, but he had never paid much attention. Some of the hunters would get very excited about it, but he had always had the suspicion it was just so they could work up a brag. He himself had never put his mind to the thing. It had never occurred to him as something he might have to meet someday. Things were, he thought, complicated enough, what with learning a trade and trying to raise a bride-price and everything else that was a part of real life.

One of the figures in the tent sighed, shifted a little under his blankets, and the boy felt a cold river of fear trickle down his back.

He wished he could remember what the men were saying about the whites. He retained only the vague impression they were ominous things that were said. He could not remember whether they ate the people or not.

The chill of fear that had passed over him decided him. He had better go home. Once he had decided this, it seemed to him he should have done it long ago.

Cautiously he stepped back, away from the fire and the tent with its sudden air of malignant threat. Reaching the edge of the clearing, he turned and moved silently into the woods. He walked quietly, without haste. For the first time in years he had to call on the stringent mental discipline of his youth, when he was training to go on the Searching. He put fear surely beyond the reach of his mind, walking with dignity and not looking behind.

I am a man entire, he repeated softly to himself, singing the war song silently in his mind. I am a man entire.

When he reached the beach he moved along it rapidly, but wholly without fear, gliding along the dark sand toward the distant river mouth and Kilchis' lodge. He could not disturb Kilchis, but he could tell one of the warriors, and they would know what to do. They would know whether or not this thing was important.

As he walked, it gradually came to him that—if this thing of the white were actually important to the people, why, then there would be a good deal of prestige attached to him for his activity this night. To sit by the fire—even feed it!—stand alone in the night without fear, looking down on the sleeping forms . . .

Ayah! That's a good thing!

The girl's father could not help but be impressed. Then, his thoughts back where he wanted them to be, he picked up his pace and well before the eastern horizon lightened he had reached the village.

3

The sky next morning was still leaden and gray, but the light rain had passed inland. The pale dawn spread into the tent later, because of the overcast. Charley was up first, and made coffee with water from their canteens. Trask joined him sleepily a few minutes later, squatted by the fire and sipped the hot coffee, blinking at the burn as it slid down his throat.

He glanced up at the overcast sky. "Glad we didn't have any worse weather," he commented.

"Mm. We'll get it going back, maybe," Charley observed cheerfully.

"Agh. Parts of that trail I don't think I'd care to run, with bad weather."

They breakfasted, broke camp and were ready to start out by the time the pale brightness of the sun topped the eastern peaks. Trask scooped the last few handfuls of dirt on the fire and stamped it down.

He squirmed into his pack and followed Charley, who had started for the beach. Trask came up with him just as Charley came out of the forest edge and stopped abruptly.

They stood on a slight rise overlooking the beach. A miniature sand cliff dropped a man's height to a jumble of large rocks. The rocks thinned out toward the bay, and became a broad strip of sand beach.

Four Killamook canoes were drawn up on the beach.

The canoes were slim, sharp-prowed hunting craft, graceful as the salmon. They lay empty, their sterns washed by the ripple of the bay, razor-edged bows pointing directly at the two like so many arrow points.

Even as they stood motionless, absorbing the unexpected presence of the canoes, Trask became aware they were not alone. From the woods on either side, silent shapes appeared like black ghosts.

Trask wheeled, and found the swiftly moving figures on all sides. His motion was stopped by a gesture from Charley. The Clatsop watched silently until they were enclosed in a half-circle. His eyes flitted over the impassive faces before him; finally stopped at one Trask found indistinguishable from the rest.

"Klahowya," Charley said. "*Mika wawa Chinook?*"

There was no answer. The man addressed regarded the two in silence. There were six of the Killamooks. Three of them carried short hunting bows held loosely in one hand, with an arrow notched in each string. The arrows were as long as a man's arm, with six-inch points of bone, slim and barbed. The other three carried only metal knives. All six had strips of deerskin wrapped around their legs to protect them from the underbrush; and short elkskin kilts. Their upper bodies were daubed with some kind of black paint, in no discernible pattern.

Finally, still without speaking, the Killamook gestured to the canoes. Charley shrugged. "Let's go," he said to Trask.

He led the way, sliding down the bank with Trask immediately after. The Killamooks maintained a half-circle behind them, but made no effort either to help or to hinder their progress. When he came even with the canoes, Charley stopped. The Killamook gestured, indicating two of the boats. Charley climbed into one and Trask into the other.

Two of the knife-armed men shoved off and climbed in behind the prisoners. They set off diagonally across the bay toward the southeast end, paddling swiftly. Behind them and slightly to either side, the other two canoes ranged. In the prow of each sat one of the bowmen, while the remaining two paddled. They were, Trask thought wryly, remarkably well covered. His rifle had been deftly removed and put in one of the accompanying canoes.

The placid surface of the water was broken in several spots by sandbanks swelling, and in others by white water from shoals not uncovered. These the canoemen skirted easily, with little variance from their course. The canoes were able to float in all but the very shallowest of water, and the paddlers took full advantage of their shallow draft.

There was complete silence, except for the swift dipping of paddles and the gurgle of water past the bow. Far away across the bay a flight of gulls whirled and called. Trask saw Charley turn his head to speak to his paddler. Simultaneously one of the bows in the escort canoes came up and the string was drawn taut. Charley glanced at it, shrugged, and turned back to face forward.

As they drew near the opposite shore, Trask could see the village. It was large as Indian villages went. Two rows of plank houses stood at the mouth of an entering river, on a point that projected into the bay like a thumb. Before the houses on the bay side were drawn up ranks of canoes of all types; more hunting canoes, the larger and wider freight canoes, the tiny, blunt-nosed work canoes of the women. It was bath time, and on the river side of the point the water was full of men splashing around and scrubbing themselves and playing in the water. As the four returning canoes skimmed closer, the jumbled noise of the bathing stopped. Men stood straight to turn and watch. Most of them got out of the water and came around to the bay side. When Trask's and Charley's boats slid up on the sand, they faced an almost solid wall of Killamook men who stared at them curiously. Trask in particular was watched as though they expected him to change shape before their eyes.

The other two canoes beached alongside. The two prisoners were motioned to get out, still under the watchful eyes of the bow-armed guards.

The crowd in front remained closed until Charley was almost touching them. He did not slow or break stride, but kept walking as though he did not see his path was blocked.

As he reached the first of the men, the crowd parted slightly and let him through, followed by two of his captors. There was a faint murmur, quickly hushed. The village was eerily silent. The usual morning jumble of sounds, the shouts of bathing people, and the children playing; all seemed to have been mysteriously damped out. Even the dogs were not raising their usual frantic howl.

There were, Trask noted, no women to be seen. Then he remembered it was bathing time, and they were probably at the women's bathing place.

There was one lodge, no larger than the others, set separate from the rest. Toward this they were guided. At the entrance, Charley stopped. He turned to look at his guard. The Killamook motioned him to remove his pack, which Charley did, laying it beside the door. He stooped and entered the lodge.

Trask followed, after having been relieved of his own pack in the same way.

The lodge was empty. There was only one fire burning, though it was large enough to be a four-fire house. It was built along the same lines as the Nehalem house in which they had met Tupshin; but this lodge belonged to a wealthier man. The walls were hung with mats and the floor was white with a smooth layer of beach sand. The fire-pit was quite deep and lined with stones. The back end was partially screened off by hanging mats, but they could see it was deserted.

Outside sounds began again, gradually. Many feet shuffled around the outside of the lodge at first, but sharp words were spoken in Salish, and soon the shuffling diminished. Through cracks in the planks, Trask could barely trace the passage around the lodge of several men, apparently their guards.

There was a rustling of cloth, and some conversation he could not understand. He heard a pack being opened, whether his or Charley's or both at once he could not tell.

Voices were by turns curious, scornful, and amused. Someone laughed loudly and was hushed.

Trask glanced at Charley, who sat down abruptly on the sleeping-platform. He leaned back and put his hands behind his head, staring at the roof.

"What now?" Trask said.

"We wait."

"What about the packs?"

Charley shrugged. After a moment he added in a placid voice, "Welcome to Murderer's Harbor."

Trask scowled.

Chapter Fifteen

The lodge in which they were quartered was comparatively luxurious. The sleeping-platform was covered with cattail mats, as were the walls. Board shelves were hung along the length of the rafters, and Trask could see they were well stocked; lines of baskets and even wooden boxes were visible from below. The space beneath the sleeping-platform was packed almost solid with one sort of container or another. At the far end of the lodge, behind the mat screens, there was a stack of spare mats almost two feet high, and beside it another neat pile, of blankets. The drying-racks in the rafters still had plenty of fish and meat on them, in spite of the fact that winter was nearly over, and the new season about to begin.

Trask commented on this.

"The salmon don't come into the bay down here until late summer," Charley said. "Not spring, like the Columbia."

"Why is that?" Trask asked. "There's only eighty miles' difference, why should the salmon come months later down here?"

"Why?" Charley said, with a trace of irritation. "That's just the way it is."

Trask shrugged and continued his examination of the lodge. Charley lay back on the sleeping-platform and seemed to lose interest in his surroundings.

At the back end of the lodge, Trask found a long pit dug under the platform. It went well below ground level, and was filled with small, neatly wrapped packages of food being kept at constant temperature. The area directly around this cooling pit was packed earth, without the freshly swept sand carpet of the rest of the lodge. The entire house was immaculately neat; in spite of the absence of any storage containers other than baskets, there was no loose article to be found anywhere. The only element detracting from the atmosphere of cleanliness was the ever-present smell of smoke and fish.

Trask returned to the fire and sat on one of the mats that surrounded it. He noted absently that the stones of the fireplace pit were apparently unworked, and had been selected with great care. They fitted well enough together to make an almost solid wall, as if mortared.

"I wish I had a smoke," he muttered. He stood nervously and went to the skin flap over the entrance. Lifting it slightly, he peered out, trying to remain unseen.

Two of the black-daubed warriors were standing guard. One of them sat cross-legged facing the entrance, while another stood immediately beside it. Trask was looking past the edge of the elk-skin kilt. As he watched, another man came around the corner carrying a strung bow; then another. The last two were apparently making regular rounds of the lodge.

To the left of the entrance were their packs. Trask's was laid open and all the contents spread out on the tarpaulin. He could not see if anything had been taken. One of the walking patrol stopped and squatted abruptly by the open pack. He picked up articles one by one and examined them, turning them over and over curiously, even if their nature and use were obvious.

Trask started to call an objection, but at that moment the guard facing the entrance saw him peeking through the lifted flap.

He made a swift gesture to the entrance-guard, and Trask found himself staring at the long, barbed point of an arrow, inches from his face. He dropped the flap.

"They only opened one pack," he said.

"Yours," Charley said.

"Yes," Trask answered, though Charley's tone had not been one of question.

Charley nodded slowly, as if in confirmation of something, but made no comment.

Trask rubbed the knuckles of one hand on the palm of the other. He sat down by the fire again briefly, then stood and walked back to the other end of the lodge.

Without looking around at him Charley said, "Don't touch anything."

"Hell with that!" Trask said irritably. "What about my pack?"

Charley didn't answer. Trask didn't touch anything. He came back and sat on the lower step of the platform. He leaned forward with his forearms on his thighs and long bony hands dangling between his knees.

Charley continued to lie staring at the roof-planks silently. He had lapsed into a state of suspension that Trask, nervous, found slightly annoying.

"You think the old man sent word we were coming?" he said.

"No," Charley said.

"They knew some way," Trask said. He got up and went back to the flap. Trying to be still more inconspicuous, he raised the edge only a trifle, but this time the guard was waiting for him. The arrow point swung down even with his face immediately, and the guard spoke sharply. Trask jerked back.

"*Ticky* smoke," he said loudly. "Smoke, tobacco! *Mika kumtux* smoke?"

"Try *kimoolth*," Charley said.

"*Nika ticky kimoolth*," Trask said to the flap. "*Hyas ticky.*"

There was a muttered conversation outside, then the rustling of a tarpaulin.

"If those bastards steal my pipe—" Trask began bitterly.

"*Klatawa siah kopa lapote*," a voice said heavily. Trask stepped away from the entrance. After a second the flap was lifted, and the guard who had been standing came in. Except for his initial order to stand back from the door, he did not seem particularly worried about his charges. In his hand he held the package of tobacco from Trask's pack, and a long Indian pipe. It was simply a slimly tapered tube of stone, fitted with a hollow reed. These he put by the fire and, with a glance at Charley lying motionless on the sleeping-platform, turned to leave.

"Wait a minute," Trask said. "I want my pipe. *Mika lapeep.*"

Charley swung his legs down from the sleeping-platform and leaned forward.

"From the pack. The white man's pipe, from the pack." Charley made describing motions with his hand in the air, showing the curve of Trask's meerschaum, and the thickness of the bowl.

The Killamook watched and listened indifferently. He shrugged and turned to the entrance again.

"Do the people steal, then?" Charley asked quietly.

The Killamook faced Charley, expressionless and silent for a long moment. Finally he said, "*Halo kumtux lapeep.* I do not know of this pipe."

"It was in the pack that was opened," Charley said.

"I do not know of this pipe," the man repeated.

"It was stolen, then, from the pack."

The Killamook seemed about to say something, but thought better of it.

"I wish to speak with the tyee about this thing," Charley demanded. "It is not good for the Boston to be stolen from."

"The tyee Kilchis is not in the village."

"Why then are we held in this place?"

"Kilchis will come back today, maybe. He is in the south."

"With the Nestucca? Yaquina?" Charley asked.

"With the Nestucca."

"Does the tyee Kilchis speak to the Nestucca of war?"

The Killamook frowned, and hesitated before answering. He was obviously uncertain about the amount of talking he was doing. "No," be said finally. "The Nestucca have asked him to settle a dispute among their people."

"Is he such a great judge then, that the Nestucca send for him from the north?"

"Yes," the Killamook said, and there was an overtone of surprise that such a question should be asked.

"Ah," said Charley. He swung his feet back up on the sleeping-platform and resumed his air of indifference, staring at the roof. "It is well," he said slowly. "Such a man will be angry that his people have stolen this pipe. The thief will be punished. This is only right."

"I do not know of this pipe," the man said stolidly.

"You had better find out, maybe," Charley said in an absent tone. Without looking at the other man he added, "Go now."

The Killamook bit his lower lip, and with an angry jerk of his head, turned. He swept aside the flap and left the lodge. Outside they could hear his angry voice raised, but the only words distinguishable were "Boston man."

Morosely Trask stuffed tobacco in the Indian pipe and lit it with a burning twig from the fire. Charley lay in silence, considering the roof.

Suddenly he said, "They don't know what they're doing."

"Who?"

"The men who took us. They aren't sure they did the right thing. If they had direct orders from Kilchis, they wouldn't take that kind of talk from me."

Trask puffed thoughtfully on the long-stemmed pipe. "Well," he said, "maybe I'll get my meerschaum back after all. Hate like hell to lose that pipe."

Charley turned his head to look at the white man; turned back to stare at the roof. "We do well if we lose no more than this pipe."

Trask held the stone pipe up and looked at the glowing red coal in the tube. "Charley," he said softly, "I think you may be right."

2

Toward midmorning a light rain began to patter against the lodge. The roof boards were overlapped and tight against the rain, except where the two ridge boards were pushed apart as a smoke vent. Through this crack occasional droplets fell, making tiny craters in the sand-covered floor along the length of the ridge.

Shortly after the rain began, the flap was pushed aside again. An old woman came in, bringing food. She was bandy-legged and fat, and walked with a half-waddle. She wore the usual cedar-bark skirt, but her upper body was covered with a sort of poncho against the rain, finely woven of vertical strips of the same bark. She smelled strongly of fish and grease.

Without looking at either of the two prisoners she scuttled about the fire, laying out eating mats. From a buckskin package she took dried fish and placed it on a wooden tray. In a corner of each mat she put a bowl of whale oil, and opposite this another tray, full of salmonberries. A clean clamshell and a wooden ladle completed the meal setting, and she left the lodge again.

Trask thought she moved as if on eccentric wheels rather than legs.

"We have company for breakfast," Charley observed. For the first time Trask noticed the woman had laid three places around the fire.

When the flap was lifted again, a young man stooped through. He stood erect just inside, letting his eyes become accustomed to the darkness. Trask, sitting on the low ledge, had a chance to observe him.

He was short, as were all the people, but did not give the impression of squatness. His body was slim and his legs straight; he had almost the proportions of a tall white man. Over his shoulders was draped a supple bearskin cape made, as nearly as Trask could tell, of the whole skin, without cutting or sewing. It dwarfed the Indian, and its bulk seemed out of keeping with the man's delicacy. It was belted around his middle with a light fur Trask could not immediately identify.

The man was young—at first he appeared little more than a boy—and his features were finely chiseled. His face was pointed, almost girlish, and this added to the impression of youth. His skin was light in color; his lips curved and sensuous. He was perhaps in his middle twenties, though it was difficult to be certain.

Without preliminary he seated himself before one of the mats, moving with feminine grace. With a gesture of his long fingers he motioned Trask and Charley to join him.

The old woman returned carrying a tightly woven basket of water and a long rectangle of shredded cedar-bark. Silently she knelt by the young man.

He wiped his fingers fastidiously on the bark, dipped them in the water and shook off the loose droplets. He dried again on the bark towel. Then he sat with primly tented fingers while the woman moved around to Charley and Trask.

When the washing had been completed, the old woman stolidly surveyed the setting and, apparently satisfied, waddled out.

With a faint nod and a half-smile, the young man picked up the clamshell spoon. He took up a few of the salmonberries and dipped them in the bowl of whale oil. He ate through almost closed lips, never showing his teeth, sipping delicately from the point of the shell.

Charley and Trask joined in, and found themselves hungry despite the fact they had breakfasted before breaking camp. Charley dipped into the whale oil freely, but Trask had never been able to stomach the habit of soaking everything in oil. It was, he supposed, not much different from butter. But salmonberries drowned in oil . . . He took just enough not to seem unappreciative.

The three ate in silence, covertly and politely observing one another as the meal progressed. The young man's presence made Trask uncomfortable; his diffident and precise gestures were those of a high-born woman, rather than a brave.

By the time the meal was finished, Trask found himself almost preferring the frank hatred and ferocity of the Nehalem warrior to the polite delicacy of this youth.

Charley spoke once; "We are the persons who come," he said, making formal acknowledgment of the gift of food.

The man politely put his eating utensils down and inclined his head to Charley's words. He nodded, and an expression of pleasure flitted across his small-featured face. "It is so," he said. "I am the one who is doing this." His voice, even on the guttural syllables of the Chinook, had an edge to it, an almost whining quality.

When the meal had been finished, the old woman appeared again as if on signal. There had been nothing to drink with the food, and she brought water with which to rinse their mouths. When they had cleaned their hands again, she cleared away the mats and food and left them alone.

The young man smiled primly. "I regret," he said in his high voice, "that you are made to feel unwelcome among my people."

"Is it well that we know your name?" Charley asked politely.

"I am Illga," the young man said with dignity. "Tyee of the Killamook people."

Charley considered this soberly. Slowly he said, "It has come to our ears that the tyee here is him, Kilchis. We are mistaken, maybe."

Illga made a petulant gesture of dismissal. "He, Kilchis, walks as the bear," he said ambiguously. "My father was tyee here; and his father before. Am I not then tyee also?" He smiled ingratiatingly.

"It would seem right," Charley said noncommittally. Trask, while Illga's attention was drawn elsewhere, risked a quick glance at Charley and could read no emotion in the flat face.

Charley introduced himself and Trask.

"Ah, ah!" Illga exclaimed delightedly. "I have a Clatsop wife, also. We are then brothers, you and me."

Charley said nothing, and Trask sensed a strong reluctance in him.

"You understand," Illga said, leaning forward with a slight frown disturbing his forehead, "it is not through me you are brought here without honor."

"It is in my mind this is Kilchis' saying," Charley said.

"Ah, that one!" Illga said despairingly. "Yes, that is so. He is no friend to the whites, Kilchis. Not," he added, fixing Trask with his eyes, "like me, Illga."

"You are a friend to the whites, then," Charley said.

"A great friend. Indeed," Illga added modestly, "I have been many times to Astoria, trading. I am a great *canim-man* as well as a great hunter."

"It is well that the whites have such a friend," Charley said politely.

"Yes," Illga said thoughtfully. "Yes, yes. He, Kilchis, has not ever been to Astoria. Yet he is very rich also. As rich, almost, as I myself. It is difficult to understand." He shrugged resignedly.

The delicate young man seemed to lose himself in contemplation of this calumny, and did not speak again until Charley prodded. "It is well that the whites have such a friend as you among the Killamook people. Else bad things might happen."

"Yes, yes," Illga agreed quickly, looking up. "That is so. It is my wish that the Boston men and the Killamook people should be as brothers." He glanced covertly at Trask.

"That is a good wish," Charley said.

"Yes," Illga said. He smiled quickly. "You, of course, understand these things, being tamanawis. All on this coast have heard tales of Charley Kehwa of the Clatsops."

Charley said nothing.

Illga continued in an injured tone, not looking directly at the others. "It happens that the people will not always listen to the words of their tyee. He, Kilchis, who calls himself tyee, speaks with the roarings of the bear, and the people are deafened, maybe." He looked inquiringly at Charley.

"Such things happen," Charley said. "It is unfortunate," he added casually, "when a man becomes rich whose father was not rich, nor his father before."

"Yes, yes." Illga nodded rapidly.

"But"—Charley shrugged—"in such a case, what can one do?"

"It is in my mind," Illga said intently, "that it would be well for the whites to have as sole tyee of the Killamooks one who has been to Astoria many times."

"One who is a friend to them," Charley added obligingly.

"That is exactly so. *Delate kahkwa.*"

Charley looked at the roof. The sound of rain was a steady tapping now, and through the smoke vent the sky was dark. He seemed to consider the prospect of the sky. In the silence, Trask reached forward and put another chunk of bark on the fire. It caught quickly, and the fire-circle became lighter and wider.

"How might such a thing happen?" Charley said, still looking at the roof.

"In Astoria I saw very many guns of all kinds," Illga said naïvely. "If the Boston wished a tyee other than Kilchis . . . Such a thing could be done."

"Ah. This would require many friends among the Killamook people."

"There are those," Illga said quickly, fluttering his hands in his lap in a gesture Trask could not interpret.

"Strong men as friends," Charley mused. "Men as those who have brought us to this place."

"Those men exactly," Illga said eagerly. He called something in Salish in his high voice, and the flap was thrown back. One of the black-painted warriors thrust his head in.

"Who is tyee of the Killamook people?" Illga asked, keeping his eyes on Charley.

"Illga," the man said without hesitation. Trask noted with some confusion the man was the same who had answered, "Kilchis is not here," when Charley had asked to see the tyee.

Illga nodded with pleasure. "Good so," he said. He dismissed the man with a gesture. Trask thought he saw the man shrug almost imperceptibly as he turned away.

"You see," Illga, said. "Such men as brought you to this place."

Illga seemed to find no contradiction between his disavowal of responsibility in the capture and the implication that the warriors involved were personally loyal to him. Trask turned this around in his mind uneasily; finally decided be didn't understand the situation at all.

"Of course," Charley said contemplatively, "the Boston have not yet said they have any wish to share the Killamook lands."

"Around this bay is the finest land for many miles," Illga said eagerly. "Everyone says so."

"This may be," Charley said. He shrugged.

"This one here," Illga said, gesturing at Trask, "he has come to this country . . ."

"Only to see," Charley said casually. "He sees little from the inside of a lodge."

Illga stood. "He shall see this land," he promised. "I will see that a canoe is made ready. I myself shall paddle for him."

"The honor is great," Charley said.

"I am a great canim-man," Illga said modestly. "Everyone says so."

Charley nodded. "Klahowya," he said. "We will await your coming back."

Illga stooped through the entrance, holding the skirt of his bearskin cape delicately in one hand. When the youth had gone, Charley sat silent before the fire for half a minute, staring blankly at the coals. Finally he sighed. He stood and stretched widely. "Well," he said. "You'll see the bay now."

3

"I don't care overmuch for our friend," Trask said thoughtfully.

"He may be the only friend you've got here," Charley said, glancing sharply at the white man.

Trask shrugged, and toyed with a piece of firewood. "I didn't say anything about that," he said. "I just don't care for him much."

"Well, he doesn't care much for you either."

"He seems awfully anxious to show me the country."

"To him you're just a strong possibility of guns," Charley said. He snorted softly. "There is a sad thing. A weak man with a strong ambition."

"Is he really tyee?" Trask asked.

"You do not understand about this thing," Charley said, a little impatiently. "To you, 'tyee' means a chief. But we are not like whites, you have to understand this. It does not matter who your father was. Naturally a rich man is likely to have had a rich father. But nobody has claim to be tyee just for that. If this man Kilchis is as we have heard—why, then he will have a certain authority in the natural course of things. But you must understand that a tyee is all right while he can do the things the tyee must do. The people will follow a strong man as long as they respect his strength and wealth. If he does not seem to do the people any good with his money, they will follow somebody else.

"Anyway, we all know when the salmon come in. We all know how to do what we have to do. We do not need someone to tell us how to live, and this is what white men mean when they say 'chief.'"

"What's a tyee do, then? If he isn't a chief, what is he?"

Charley shrugged. "Somebody has to give money to the old people that cannot work any more. Somebody has to decide who is right and who is wrong when there is disagreement. If there is trouble between bands, somebody must negotiate so there will be no war. And if the negotiation does not go well, maybe there will be war. Then he will lead the people if he can. But if he is not a warlike man, somebody else will do that.

"There must also be a tyee to pay for the feasting that is done, because the *tillicums*, the people, could not afford to have nice feasts otherwise. But he is not a 'chief,' who can speak for everyone.

"Coboway is," Trask objected. "And in the Clatsop, Concomly was before him."

Charley squatted beside Trask and peered at him intently. Finally he turned away. "Do you know why that is? Because of the whites. It was not that way before, that a tyee could take goods from his people without return, as the one-eyed Concomly did. But Concomly saw this thing when the whites began to come: that the people must learn to act as one person. That the tribe must all think alike about things, and act alike. If they did not, they would be helpless before the whites, for this is how the whites act. The Clatsops needed a 'chief.' They had to join together, what *you* call a tribe. It was not like this before. There were the villages: Neahcoxie, and Neahkeluk and Neahkowin and Necotat—but nobody ever thought all the villages should *think* the same way. This is not natural. This is a white man's way of living, not ours."

Trask considered this thoughtfully. Finally he said, "Then why's this Illga so eager to knock down Kilchis?"

Charley shrugged. "To be tyee is still a fine thing. He fishes in the best place, sometimes the hunters give him a share of the kill. There is much respect for the tyee, and this is what that Illga wants, I think. That one is ambitious, yes, but he is foolish. In Astoria they call him by the name Yes-Yes-No. He is very changeable."

"You think he could do what he says?"

Charley hesitated. "I do not know," he said finally. "He must have some support among the people." He stood up and looked around the lodge, as if he could see Illga's strength somehow massed invisibly before his eyes.

"I do not know," he repeated.

Trask pulled thoughtfully at the ends of his beard; tucked them under his chin. "You think it would be good to have him on our side?"

"It is not good to anger anyone. We are not in our own place. But I think we must meet Kilchis before anything could be said about that."

Trask nodded slowly.

"I will say this," Charley said abruptly. "It is not good to anger anyone, because we do not know what happens here. But it would also not be good to make any kind of agreements. You understand this?"

"I guess I don't have to ask for more trouble than I got."

"No. This is a thing you should not become involved in."

Trask sighed. "He's right, though. It would be easier with somebody like him leading the Killamooks."

Charley laughed. "You know Kilchis so well, then?"

Surprised, Trask looked up. "Well, what we hear—"

"Me," Charley said, "I will meet him for myself. *Then* I will say about that Kilchis. We have nothing but other men's words."

"All right, all right," Trask grumbled. "You and your goddam Siwash wisdom. Sometimes you make me sick, Charley."

Charley grinned broadly.

"We'll wait and see, then," Trask said.

"Listen," Charley said seriously. "I will tell you this. So far—so far I have been able to talk with the people. You understand it is easier this way."

"Yes," Trask said. "I know it, Charley. You—"

"But," Charley interrupted, "it is not me who comes to see this land here. It is you. I am a Clatsop. I risk no more than any Clatsop among Killamooks. Less, because I am tamanawis."

"It's enough," Trask said.

"A time is coming when you must speak your own mind. This will happen with Kilchis. I have done nothing but find out things, but it is you who must use what I have found out."

"What are you getting at, Charley?"

Charley appeared reluctant. "I mean—when you speak your own mind—"

"What you mean is, you can't be responsible if I say the wrong thing."

Charley lifted his hands in a gesture of helplessness. "This thing will be between you and Kilchis. I cannot interfere."

Trask nodded. "I hired you to guide me, Charley. Not to do my fighting for me," he said.

Charley was silent for a long moment. When he spoke again it was slowly, as though he found an unaccustomed difficulty in putting his thoughts into words. His voice was low, and he looked in the fire. "I would do that if I could."

Trask, startled, looked around quickly. Charley's face was blank, and he squatted before the fire as though carved from wood, with the warm light flickering fitfully over his face. Suddenly he stood and went over to the sleeping-platform, with Trask's eyes following him.

There seemed to Trask nothing he could say. The declaration of loyalty was as unexpected as it was obviously sincere, and the white man found himself embarrassed. With him-who-died it had been one thing, the respect of a boy for a man. But Trask had a notion Charley's loyalty was not so easily come by, and was greatly pleased. He turned back to the fire.

"He should be back with that canoe soon," he said.

Chapter Sixteen

The hunger for land is not a simple thing; not so simple a thing as wishing it to produce under your hand. The hunger is a vast and complex mixture, a compounding of dreams and desire and visions with the solider masses of soil and mountains. A river of water, flowing swift or slow out of the mountains, can become more real and necessary to a man than the river of blood that flows in his body; a black soil more tangible than flesh itself.

The taking possession of land is the first—and the final—grasping of a man toward permanence; toward what he has occasionally called immortality for want of a word that means more. As a child clutches blindly at his mother's breast, so a man will strain to land; without understanding, without even volition, but moved by a necessity beyond his comprehension. And as a child cannot distinguish between himself and the object of his possession, so too there are men who can draw no clear line between themselves and the land they walk. They are as much the possessed as possessors.

Neither a simple thing nor a reasonable one. Reasons may come later, and indeed they must; a fine fertility of soil, an excellent prospect on clear days, perhaps. There is an embarrassment about these things, these apologies, these wistful longings for reasonableness in our passions. The reasons count for no more than thin varnishes of logic, ill concealing and perhaps defacing the twisted grain of the wood beneath.

That thing which possesses a man to open a land is simple lust, and we are obscurely ashamed of our lusts; unable to forge them into comprehensible patterns, and thus both ashamed and fearful. Hidden lusts are a seething caldron, a witch's kettle terribly boiling and glimpsed fearfully in unexpected moments. And when the writhing foam spills over we must scuttle about putting all in neat order, never looking squarely at the black and ominous shape or the fire beneath it. And this putting in order, this housewifery of the emotions, we dignify by calling logic; and in the mere naming of it we justify the existence of the unspeakable and grudgingly recognize the invisible.

There are places of desert; sand and rock and whipping wind, incapable of sustaining the life of a blade of grass. And yet to some dumb creature this will seem the finest land of any; the final form that land should take; the very end of all creation, beside which all other prospects are bumbling, gross attempts. To the man who holds this patch of arid rock all other land is somehow unreal, without clarity, without substance; the amateurish apprenticeship of a god that hasn't got the hang of the creation business. He finds it quite incredible that every man on earth is not clamoring to steal away his hunk of desert. And the only reason he can give for his passion is a vague conviction that the air in the morning makes him feel better; probably it's good for him. The apology of his life, delivered with embarrassment and a hasty turning away from the demanding gaze of logic.

It is, in fact, no matter of clods of earth and stands of timber and runs of water. These are reasonable things, and the land-lusts of a man have no more than passing congress with them. What moves a man—and ultimately, the only thing that moves him deeply—is the finding of his own image, the solid configuration of himself, worked in materials of better staying quality than bone and blood.

If he listens to the river and hears the coursing of blood through his temples; if he looks at a mountain and sees the strength of his own arm; if he is lost in the forest as in the darkest wells of his own mind—then that land is his, and he has lost the faculty of choice concerning it. He is chosen, and from that moment the land and he work each other, not always with gentleness, but relentlessly. A molding and carving and forging takes place between them, bitterly, happily, angrily, exultantly . . . And in time there is no more telling which is which between them, no sharp distinction, no clear edge of difference where it can be said that here the land ends and here the man begins.

The moment of recognition, the moment when a man rounds some corner and sees clearly his own face before him, begins in suddenness and ends in obscurity. It begins like the fall of a fir in the woods; a thunderous, stately crash, sweeping all things inevitably before it. It ends like the tide, imperceptibly, obscurely, and no man can say with certainty the ebbing is done and the flow begun. But the knowledge of that moment remains with him from them; relentless as the falling tree and inevitable as the tide.

It can happen at any time a man looks on new land. It happened to Elbridge Trask under a sullen gray sky, cramped uncomfortably on the thwart of a Killamook hunting canoe with droplets of cold rain running down his neck and caught hanging in his beard.

Charley Kehwa, kneeling behind Trask on a cattail mat amidships of the canoe, watched the set of the white man's back more intently than the banks of the river. Watched the restless, alert swinging of his head from side to side, the cant of his body from one view to another, the growing eagerness as they approached each new bend, reflected in the perceptible tension of his body forward.

The banks of the river slid slowly past to the faint sound of water rippling under the bows of the canoe and gurgling along the sides. Overhanging boughs of trees sometimes formed a near-complete canopy over them, and the canoe glided quickly beneath them like a fish into the shadow of a rock.

Illga himself was unobtrusive, seeming content to let the land speak for itself. His canoemanship, slightly to Charley's surprise, came up to his own estimate; he was in truth a "great *canim-man.*" Perhaps, Charley mused, that accounted for his unexpected silence, for a man engaged with pleasure in his skill seldom has any necessity to talk.

They passed through a narrow strait, where the river ran swiftly, and the tempo of Illga's paddle increased. On either side were dense walls of timber, mostly the dark spruce with its air of mystery and gloom, its aura of perpetual night. The trunks moved past in a stately procession, almost obscured in the gloom, like dark ghosts moving slowly down to the sea.

Sounds were muted in the gray light, and the water beneath them was dark and opaque, seeming so heavy it was wonderful it could flow at all. The noises of the wood were muffled, as though the low-hanging blanket of cloud absorbed and dissipated them in its bulk. The sudden chittering of a graydigger on the bank was startling; too shrill, too sharp. The animal sat on its haunches with its brush curled up behind its back and scolded them nervously as they passed.

They came suddenly out of the thick forest, and the river turned sharply to the right. A glimpse of the dark and misty shapes of the mountains hovered just over the bank.

"Stop here," Trask said suddenly

Without comment, Illga paused; then shot the canoe for the left bank. He held it steady against the shore while Trask and Charley got out and climbed the dirt face, clinging to exposed roots.

Reaching the top, Trask turned slowly to look. In the distance the blue shadow of the mountains that ringed the bay was indistinct, a dreamy barrier between this land and the outside world. Before them stretched a long plain, dipping slightly at first, then rising on an almost level slope straight away into the obscurity at the mountains' base. There was no direct light; the faint drizzle fell gently, and the landscape under it seemed almost luminous, as though lit from within. Nearby it gleamed with an unearthly distinctness, each lifted tip of fern separate and distinct, shaking faintly in the light breeze.

The plain itself was covered thickly with fern, deep as the height of a man and stretching in a richly textured plane off toward the mountain edge. Beneath the fern, grass grew. Trask shouldered his way a little distance through the wet growth; pulled up a clump of grass and rubbed it reflectively between his palms. He dropped it and wiped his hands absently on his trouser leg, his eyes still roving out over the plain, stopping briefly to survey a clump of trees that rose like an island halfway between them and the mountains.

When he turned to come back, it was without comment. He passed Charley and scrambled down the bank. Their eyes met only briefly, but in that flash Charley saw a strange, fierce exultation mirrored on Trask's face. In his eyes the lust burned, unveiled, clear and bright. An intensity emanated from the white man that was almost a physical blow; something with the strength of maniacal anger, but was not anger. As though a freshening wind had blown a fog away, Charley saw clearly in Trask's face the reflection of a consuming flame, a flame that swept through him as a fire sweeps through dry forest, relentlessly driving all things before it in swift, flashing fury.

Charley was only briefly shocked by the apparition of something akin to insanity in Trask's face. In it were challenge and triumph and the hot intensity that intervenes between these two, mingled in one moment as though the process of birth and life and death had been distilled into a single instant of power.

When Charley reached the canoe, the decent mantle of composure had fallen over the white man. Of the moment of raw intensity there was no trace. The brutal nakedness of his soul had been discreetly clothed again, and it was bearable once more to look on his face, without fearing to be overwhelmed and destroyed by the godlike exultation there.

"Could run cows on that grass," Trask remarked.

"Yes," Charley agreed seriously. "Probably could."

Illga shoved off again, speculating vaguely on why the Clatsop shook his head as if in profound wonder.

2

They were returned to the lodge near noon, as closely as they could estimate from the gray sky. Though they had been unaccompanied on the canoe trip except for Illga, Trask noted that their guard took up his position at the door. Illga, ingratiatingly friendly, came in with them and Trask wished he would go away.

"There is no finer land in any place," he said eagerly.

"It seems all right," Trask said, not looking at him.

"The hunting upriver is very fine," Illga said. "The salmon come into the bay so thick you can walk across on their backs."

"The Boston men have no interest in hunting or in the salmon," Charley said indifferently.

Illga was momentarily taken aback, but decided to ignore the comment. "It would be well for the Boston men to have a friend such as me in this place. If a man such as me were to be the only tyee of the Killamooks, it would be a much easier thing for the Boston men to come to this place."

Trask did not trust himself to answer. He was faintly disgusted by
Illga's entreaties, and resented the intrusion of something so trivial and
distasteful on his contemplation of what he had seen. Inside, he was
conscious of a seething turmoil, and he desperately wanted this foolish
child to quit talking and go away.

Finally Illga shrugged, delicately, and rose to go.

"You will find others," he said, "not so easy to trade with, others
without friendliness to the whites like mine. It would be well for you
to remember this." Illga's voice was suddenly cool. "I will speak to you
again of this thing," he said.

He stooped through the door hole, and Trask could hear him
speaking, to the guard outside in low tones.

"He's sure anxious to get me down here," he reflected.

Charley shrugged. "He is a weak and greedy man," he said. "He
could have no strength at all without help."

"From outside guns," Trask said.

Charley nodded.

Trask stirred up the coals of the fire. He sat for several minutes, lost
in silent thought. Charley watched the faint play of emotions across
his face, wondering what turmoil was going on behind the deep-set
eyes. Finally Trask sighed. He stood and went to the neat stack of
firewood, which had been replenished in their absence. Taking a
stick, he juggled it from hand to hand thoughtfully, before returning
it to the fire.

"I want to come down here, Charley," he said, methodically shoving
the end of the wood into the brightest spot of the coals. "Matter of
fact," he continued, "I want to come down pretty bad."

Charley waited.

As though changing the subject, Trask said suddenly, "You think if
this Illga got the help he wants, he could come through?"

Charley hesitated a moment before replying. "I told you," he said
finally. "It would be a mistake to become involved in this thing between
him and Kilchis."

"But do you think he *could* do it?" Trask pressed.

"Bridge, listen—"

"I'm just asking, is all."

"You should not interfere in this thing within the tribe," Charley said flatly. "You do not understand it."

"Charley," Trask said patiently, "if I didn't fool with anything I didn't understand, I wouldn't do a damn thing."

"You know what I'm telling you," Charley said doggedly. "This Illga means trouble, even if he could help you now."

"It might be easier," Trask said stubbornly.

Charley said nothing for a long while. He leaned back against the sitting-ledge and stared across the lodge at the opposite wall. Beside him Trask toyed with the end of a piece of firewood, stirring up the coals, prodding the flames. There was a stiffness about his movements, as though all the muscles in his body were being held in a state of high-keyed tension.

When Charley spoke again, his voice was low and flat, deliberately emotionless. "I tell you this, Bridge," he said. "If you do this thing you will carry it in your belly for the rest of your life."

Trask turned to fix the little Clatsop with his eyes. "All right Charley," he said. "You told me. Now I'll tell you. I hired you for a guide, not a conscience. If I have to play along with Illga to get what I want, I'll do it."

"You don't know what you're doing."

"I know," Trask said.

"So," Charley said slowly. "It is like this. You are no different from the rest of the Boston. A liar and a thief and a murderer. Whatever you break, it is all right if you get what you want."

Trask wheeled, and the back of his hand caught Charley across the mouth. His head snapped back with the impact. For a moment the sound of the blow seemed to hang in the air; all movement was stopped, as if time itself had frozen at the instant. Charley's body stiffened sharply, then a rigid mask of control slipped across his features, and he relaxed again.

He wiped his mouth calmly with the back of his hand, examined it indifferently for blood. He met Trask's eyes, his face bleak.

Trask was momentarily numb with the sick realization of what he had done. The tension in him snapped abruptly, and his belly felt empty, his legs weak. He put his hand out tentatively, as if to call back the blow. "Charley—"

"An Indian," Charley said, accenting the word softly, "does not like to be touched." His voice was cold, and he turned away from Trask.

"Charley listen, I didn't mean—"

"I do not wish to speak of this thing," Charley said quietly.

The muscles along Trask's jaw worked with anger at himself, and indecision. "Listen—" he started again.

"No. You know what is in your mind. I do not wish to know." Charley stood, touching his mouth in a thoughtful gesture. He walked over to the sleeping-platform and lay down with his hands behind his head.

Cursing silently, Trask shoved the stick of firewood entirely into the flames with a vicious gesture, and watched the bright yellow feathers of the fire climb up its sides.

3

A breach of faith is the more serious when that faith is implicit, unspoken. Trask's regret for his unconsidered action of violence was genuine—it was an unforgivable thing he had done. He had not been aware he was tautened to such hair-trigger responses. And yet he bitterly resented Charley's disappointment in him over the affair with Illga. He resented being condemned for a betrayal when he had betrayed nothing.

He had made no assurances, no promises, no commitments. What the hell did Charley want? What did he expect? He assumes too much, Trask thought angrily.

He had made no promises. He had hired a guide, that was all. The only promise he had made was to pay the man, and he would not break that.

Though gradually, as the sense of injustice and anger diminished, Trask realized the pettiness of his response. And he was aware that he had done a fair bit of assuming, too. It had occurred to him only briefly to wonder why a man in Charley Kehwa's position had hired out as a guide, no matter what the fee. Yet it had been one of the first things old Tupshin of the Nehalems had asked. Why was Charley Kehwa of the Clatsops guiding a white man down the coast?

With some surprise, Trask found he could not even recall what
Charley had answered. It had seemed an adequate answer at the time;
at any rate the subject had been dropped, but he could not bring the
sound of Charley's voice to his mind. Something vague, ambiguous. A
reason that was no reason at all.

He glanced quickly at the sleeping-platform where Charley lay. The
Clatsop was apparently napping.

Uneasily, Trask began to feel the growing conviction that things
were going on that were not known to him. He could not in honesty
conceive of Charley's being involved in some kind of devious scheme,
but still . . .

It seemed to him suddenly there was much hidden behind that
apparently simple question.

Why was Charley Kehwa guiding a white man down the coast?

They were left alone in the lodge for the remainder of the afternoon.
Illga did not return, though Trask expected him any moment. He had
decided not to commit himself to any course of action with the delicate
young man until he had seen Kilchis, and could better estimate the
nature of his opposition. It was small comfort that Charley had advised
this course beforehand.

Trask alternately paced the length of the lodge, stirred up the fire,
and dozed fitfully. The waiting made him more nervous, though it
seemingly affected Charley not at all. That one lapsed into a kind of
impassive detachment, expressing no particular interest in what awaited
them; relaxed, uncommunicative.

Outside the lodge, the midday sounds of the village went on, heard
only faintly. Most of the men were gone, probably up the river, and
there were not many dogs left. Their lodge was slightly isolated from
the others, and the voices of the women that remained in camp were
muted and distant. Occasionally Trask could hear them chattering as
they worked, either in front of their own houses or down at the river's
edge, pounding dried meat with water to soften it, mending seines,

weaving baskets, grinding fern-root flour; the dozens of activities necessary to keep a village going. In the distance he could hear the flat chipping of an adz, probably a carpenter working on a canoe.

Shortly before sunset, the volume of sound increased, and new voices began to be added. The yapping of gods was heard as hunters came back from upriver, high shouts of greeting from the village women to others coming back from the gathering of berries and roots.

Little Chinook was spoken, except for the ubiquitous "Klahowya," which seemed to have replaced whatever greeting was normal to the Salishan tongue. Some few words Trask could make out—*skookum, kwelth, elip*—native Salishan words that had been absorbed into the Jargon, but for the most part he could not understand.

The one guard who had been left at the door seemed to consider his duties more or less perfunctory. Illga, in taking the two of them in his canoe, had expressed no concern for their possible escape, and this seemed generally to have determined the attitude of the other Killamooks. This was a trifle disturbing to Trask, as it seemed to indicate there was no place to escape to if they tried. They would be picked up without difficulty in the strange woods the Killamooks themselves knew as well as their lodges.

Shortly after the noises of the village had raised to a stable din, there was a muttered conversation outside the lodge, and their guard thrust his head in and peered around dubiously in the dark. Trask noticed he had, sometime during the day, cleaned off the black war-decorations that had been daubed on his upper body.

The guard said something querulously in Salish and appeared to wait for an answer.

"*Halo kumtux*," Trask said. "I don't understand." The guard glared at him for a moment, then disappeared behind the flap. He shouted and after a moment Trask heard him talking to someone in angry tones. The flap lifted again, and the blank-faced slave woman came through. She waddled over to Charley, ignoring Trask, and peered into his face.

"*Chuck!*" she shouted. "*Mamook chuck!*" She appeared to think volume might prevail where vocabulary was weak. She made vigorous scrubbing motions around her upper body.

"*Nowitka, nowitka,*" Charley said calmly. He swung his legs off the sleeping-platform. "You want another bath?" he asked, looking at Trask without expression.

"I suppose. How many times a day does this go on?"

Charley shrugged. "Two, three times, depending." He showed no anger, though it would have been impossible for an Indian to have forgotten the incident at noon.

They filed through the entrance under the disgruntled eye of their guard, who seemed to disapprove heartily. Trask wondered briefly whose notion it was that they be allowed to bathe, and asked Charley.

"Almost anybody's," Charley said. "Except for our friend here"—he gestured at the guard—"we're being treated like guests. They'd no more deprive us of our bath than they'd starve us to death. It would have to be pretty bad before they'd keep a man out of the water, even a white."

As they walked down to the river, the slave woman scuttled up beside Charley and pushed a little bundle of mock-orange leaves into his hand.

"What's that?" Trask asked.

"Soap," Charley said. "You crush 'em up, they make a kind of lather. It's for when you aren't too dirty, otherwise you should scrub with cedar bark or sand."

"These people are fanatics," Trask said. "Are the Clatsops like this?"

"They were until the white men came," Charley said. "They like to be clean, if that's what you mean by fanatic."

They stripped down and plunged into the cold water. Trask came up sputtering, and a chill breeze made him shiver. As before, they were slightly apart from the main group of bathing men, on the upriver side. Near the horizon, the sun came briefly below the overcast, red and huge, shining in a long, ruffled track across the broad waters of the bay, casting the bodies of the Killamook men into half-silhouette as they cavorted in the water.

Trask watched the horseplay with amusement. Half playing, half bathing, the men of the village had the exuberance of a wild and unruly pack of children. The children themselves, in fact, were more subdued—the privilege of irresponsible gaiety being reserved for those who had already passed through the rigid disciplines of training that characterized the youth of the people.

The illusion of children playing was heightened, Trask realized, by their short stature. Standing five-ten, Trask was taller than the tallest of them by several inches. He realized, not for the first time, the tendency of a tall man to underestimate a short one; the almost instinctive feeling of superiority—however unconscious—those additional few inches gave him. It was, he knew, a wholly illusory impression, and one he would not entertain deliberately for a minute. But still—it was there . . .

A canoe came slowly into view around the point, sliding smoothly across the orange sun-track. It had a high, raised prow, slightly resembling the head of an animal, and gave the momentary impression of a serpent slipping smoothly along below the surface with its neck raised.

Immediately the loud sounds of the men splashing and bathing were cut off, as though by a knife, and all eyes turned to watch the canoe. There was still a danger of raiding parties from the north, in spite of the presence of the established white settlements at Astoria and Clatsop Plains.

There was a faint hail from the canoe, and the paddler lifted his paddle high in the air in salute. He carried one passenger, sitting forward.

The hail was returned by the bathing men and they went back to the immediate task of getting clean and enjoying themselves, apparently satisfied as to the identity of the canoemen.

Gradually the canoe glided around the point and headed for the actual river mouth, where the village was situated. It grounded silently on the opposite side of the bathing group from Trask. Four men detached themselves from the group and ran down the shore; among them Trask thought he recognized the slightly built form of Illga. They pulled the canoe well up on the beach and stood in a half-circle while the passenger debarked.

At first glance Trask thought the man was standing in the canoe, so far above the others did he tower. Then the figure moved, and Trask saw he was walking along the beach in their direction.

With the sun behind the group, Trask could see only the silhouettes of the men. The figure in the center was gigantic; the four accompanying men barely reached his shoulder, giving the impression of four dogs prancing around a huge, shaggy bear. They were speaking rapidly, to judge from the babble of sound that drifted down, turning half sideways to the giant and moving their hands in explanation. They had to scamper to keep up with the rapid, stately progress of the other.

When they came abreast of the main group of men, the giant made a slight motion with his hand, and the four Killamooks stopped. They stood together in a tight group with the bathing men, watching while the massive bearlike figure moved up the beach toward Trask and Charley Kehwa.

With one corner of his mind, Trask noticed the noise had stopped again. The assembled men of the village stood silent and straight in the water, shadows against the sunset.

As the giant came closer, Trask could see that the bearlike appearance was partly due to the great, shaggy robe the man wore, belted around his waist and hanging only to his knees.

So silent had the village become that Trask could hear the measured shuffle of the man's feet on the sand as he drew near. Charley stood by Trask's side silently, watching.

As if in a dream, Trask suddenly found himself looking well up into a massive black face, implacable as the face of Neahkahnie and seeming carved of the same black stone; listening to the voice that was like the rumble of thunder on the horizon.

"I am Kilchis."

Chapter Seventeen

For a long moment after he had spoken the giant Kilchis studied Trask's face silently. Then his eyes flicked quickly to Charley Kehwa, standing quietly beside the white man. Finally he nodded almost imperceptibly, as if to himself. He turned without any further word and strode up the river beach toward the lodge the two prisoners had occupied; stooped and entered.

Trask turned to watch him go, knowing with a stunned clarity the image of that searching face would remain with him the rest of his life. Kilchis stood several inches over six feet, topping Trask himself by four or five inches; the Killamooks by nearly a foot. Trask guessed his weight at 230, more or less; a mountain beside the generally small Indians. While he was studying the white man's face, Kilchis' own expression had been unreadable, his face an ebony mask carved in lines and planes of a mountainous scowl that seemed to carry no particular malice. Rather it was as if his repose had been shaped by an angry rock-carver whose own anger had been subtly transferred to the stone he worked.

In that endless moment of scrutiny Trask was aware of an aura of power from the tyee, so strong as to be almost tangible. His massive form exuded an air of strength as shocking and certain as the sudden wind from the sea. And strangely, this overwhelming sense of power did not seem threatening to Trask, any more than the scowl in which the shining black features were fixed. This giant of a black man seemed almost to transcend such petty notions as malice and dislike; he was full of an unsuppressed world-exuberance; an animal authority in his bearing that swept all other considerations aside as trivial.

By his side, Trask heard Charley clear his throat. He turned to the Clatsop and raised his hands loosely; let them drop again.

"Well . . ." he said helplessly. "He's big, all right."

Charley laughed, a short, sharp bark. "Yes, big."

"What do we do now?"

Charley looked back at the Killamook men, still standing silent down the beach, watching. None of them moved toward the two. Illga made a motion as though he were about to, then apparently decided against it. He stood with the other three men of the group that had run to the canoe, waiting silently.

"Put on your clothes," Charley said quietly.

While they dressed, Trask tried to sort out and evaluate his impressions of Kilchis; and found he could not. The personal impact of the man had been too much, too unexpected. He found in his mind a strong conviction that the intelligence behind those searching eyes was quick and alert; though he could not say where the idea had come from.

"Let's go," Charley said, when they had dressed.

"After him?"

"Yes. Have to face him some time."

"He's black, all right," Trask mused. "Like they said. I wonder how that happened?"

"I don't know," Charley said. "I never put much trust in the stories before. Killamooks being pretty light, I figured he was just a darker skin than most."

"No, he's *klale man* all right, nigger. *Jesus*, how can that be?"

Charley shrugged. "I don't know," he repeated. "Why don't you ask him?" They were now nearly to the lodge entrance. Trask scowled bleakly at Charley, who essayed a feeble smile in return. It was little comfort to Trask to note that Charley had been as unexpectedly disturbed by Kilchis as himself. It meant that even Charley might have underestimated the caliber of opposition they were likely to meet.

As they had come up the beach from the river, the trees on the point had suddenly cut them off from the warmth of the setting sun. The air was abruptly chill, and the shadows were long and thick before the lodge. On their left, the glaring red ball of the sun could be seen between the trees, but no heat came through; it gave them no warmth. In minutes it would dip into the sea and be gone, and the night would be with them.

As they reached the lodge, the flap was thrown up from inside, and the fat slave woman came out. Behind her they caught a glimpse of the fire freshly kindled and burning bright yellow; then the flap lowered behind her.

Seeing Trask and Charley, she hesitated briefly; then came over and peered into Charley's face. "Kilchis *yukwa alta!*" she shouted.

"We understand that, old woman," Charley said. "We have seen him arrive. We wish to speak with the tyee."

The old woman nodded rapidly. "Yes, yes! You go in! You go in that place now!" She pointed to the oval entrance.

Charley covered his ears with his hands and winced. "We understand you, old woman. We will go in."

The slave nodded again contentedly and scuttled off down the beach toward the waiting men.

"She going to get the others?" Trask asked.

"Probably. Some kind of council. Listen. Try not to say too much with the whole band here. Try to see Kilchis alone."

"If I get the chance," Trask said.

"Make the chance," Charley told him. "Better to deal with him first alone. He can handle the band, all right."

Trask nodded. He lifted up the flap and went in with Charley just behind. For a moment the two were blinded by the brightness of the newly laid fire, and could see nothing but dim, deep shadows behind it. Then they made out the gigantic form of Kilchis on the sleeping-platform to their right, propped negligently up on one elbow while he chewed reflectively on a tough strip of dried salmon.

2

After motioning them casually to sit by the fire, Kilchis said, "You have eaten this day?" Receiving their affirmative answer, he grunted and lapsed back into silence. He surveyed them across the fire intently, and Trask was reminded of the eyes of a wolf just beyond the fire's range. Even when the other men began to file in through the small opening, Kilchis did not let his eyes waver from the two strangers, nor did he speak any word of greeting to the newcomers.

These numbered about ten in all, and included Illga. Most of them came directly from bathing, and were either naked or had thin strips around their waists from which hung small pouches of leather and an occasional knife. Otherwise they seemed to be unarmed. Most of the men were young—there were a few exceptions—apparently the most vigorous hunters and warriors, the tribe's spine. Trask recognized two of the men who had taken them, and assumed the others were present also. He had not seen them without the black painted war-markings, and could not immediately recognize them.

They took their places around the fire and on the sitting-ledge without apparent pattern, lounging casually in postures of unconcern. When they had settled themselves, and the last shuffling had died away, Kilchis lifted himself to a sitting position, keeping his eyes fixed on Trask. The slave woman appeared beside the tyee as if by magic, with a length of shredded cedar bark on which he wiped his fingers without taking his eyes away. He swung his feet down and leaned forward on the palms of his hands.

"How do these people come to this place?" he said slowly.

There was a brief, muttered conversation between several of the seated Killamooks. Finally one stood and began a rapid, singsong chatter in Salishan, apparently explaining the coming of Trask and Charley. Trask caught only a few words, including "Charley Kehwa" and "Clatsops," which the man pronounced in the Indian way, as "Tschlashlopsch."

The Killamook finished suddenly and sat down. After a moment Kilchis said in a thoughtful tone, "The boy shall have three blankets for his bravery and wisdom." Trask, not knowing of the youth's visit to their tent the night before, did not understand this. He waited, noting with some optimism that Kilchis had been speaking Chinook before them. It seemed to him a hopeful sign, a welcome gesture of courtesy.

"You have come through the Nehalem *illahee*," Kilchis said finally.

Trask nodded. "Yes. That is so."

"In peace."

"Not entirely so," Trask said.

"And how is that? Has the Nehalem band then gone to war?"

Charley leaned forward. "We met there—"

He was silenced by an abrupt gesture from Kilchis. "I would speak with the Boston man, Charley Kehwa. I would know his mind."

"Know his mind from my words, tyee Kilchis," Charley said persuasively. "Lest there be misunderstanding."

"He speaks the Chinook," Kilchis said with puzzlement.

"But sometimes the Boston man's Chinook wawa may seem to mean something different from what he holds in his mind. It is difficult."

For the first time Kilchis smiled, very faintly. The whole massive aspect of his face was changed by the small gesture; from perpetual scowl to a gargantuan amusement.

"Yes," he agreed tolerantly. "Yes, it is difficult. But it is more difficult, maybe, to know what is in the Boston man's mind if Charley Kehwa is his tongue."

"I know what is in his—"

"No," Kilchis interrupted impatiently. "No man can speak what is in another man's mind. No more talk about this. I will speak with the Boston man."

Charley subsided, with a rueful glance at Trask.

The smile faded from Kilchis' broad face. "Now. How did it happen that you did not pass the Nehalem country in peace?"

"There was one there who had angry words," Trask said quietly. "One who made sport of one-who-died."

There was a sharp intake of breath around the fire, and several of the lounging figures sat up suddenly with new alertness.

"And how did this thing happen?" Kilchis asked without expression.

Trask explained the ridicule to which they had been subjected for the cutting-of-hair ceremony they had performed on Neahkahnie.

"Ah." Kilchis said quickly. "This one made sport of you, then. Not one-who-died."

"It is the same," Trask said. "We cut hair for him-who-died, and to make sport of us for this is to dishonor his ghost."

Kilchis moved his hand sharply in a gesture of irritation. "You make slippery talk. It is *not* the same. You know this. I know this. You do not speak to children or fools, but to me, Kilchis. No more slippery talk, then, but exact words. *Delate wawa.*"

"Good so," Trask said. "But we who mourned have been insulted in our mourning, and made light of."

Kilchis considered this aspect. "That is true," he said. "Is it your wish that this one of the Nehalem band should pay you the fine?"

Trask thought about it. "No," he said finally. "There was one other there, Tupshin, who gave us food and a canoe to cross the river mouth. This will be the fine on the Nehalem for disturbing the mourning."

Kilchis nodded. "Good, good," he muttered under his breath. "This is fair for all men," he said formally, and looked around. There was muttered agreement among the young men in the lodge. Those who had come to sudden watchfulness with Trask's accusation against the Nehalem had relaxed again.

One of the older men stood and said, "This is fair for all men."

Outside, darkness had come fully now. Through the raised plank in the roof, the gray of dusk had deepened to a velvet black. The fire cast long, eerie shadows of the rafters into the deep recesses of the ridge. The shadow figures of misshapen men fluttered and waved on the cattail mats. The grotesque and massive shade of Kilchis dominated them all, wavering hugely like the figure of a great bear seen through flowing water. The firelight shone from his face and arms as though the flesh were highly polished wood.

Trask held his eyes on the tyee; waiting for his questions with a preternatural sense of alertness; holding himself with tense awareness. A rapid, whispered conversation had started between two of the men out of Trask's seeing, but he heard it only vaguely. With night a light wind had risen and added a faint susurration to the occasional sharp crackling of the fire.

Kilchis had drawn his legs up under him, and now sat cross-legged on the sleeping-platform with his huge hands resting lightly on his knees. He stared into the fire in a brooding silence, motionless. The light, coming from beneath his level, distorted his face and gave it a wild and diabolic look. Still looking at the fire, Kilchis spoke again, and it took Trask a moment to realize the words were addressed to him.

"It is not the custom among the Boston men to cut hair for one-who-dies."

"No," Trask said.

"Why did you do this thing?"

Trask hesitated. "It was Charley Kehwa that asked me to do this."

Kilchis frowned, as though the explanation was not adequate.

From beside Trask, Charley said suddenly, "Let me speak now, tyee."

Kilchis raised his eyes and regarded Charley for a long moment. Then he nodded slowly. "Yes. You speak now, Charley Kehwa."

"He, Trask, was a friend to him-who-died on the mountain," Charley said, using the personal *sikhs*. "To me also. That is why I asked this of him."

Kilchis made an impatient gesture with one hand. "It is clear enough why you asked it," he said, still frowning. "But this thing is not clear to me: why did the Boston man do as you asked him? You cannot tell me this, I think."

"He was *sikhs* to him-who-died," Charley repeated stubbornly.

Kilchis sighed deeply, and Trask had the distinct impression of patient resignation, as though Kilchis was accustomed to dealing with people incapable of understanding subtle distinctions, and this was more of the same.

"All people," Kilchis said patiently, "have their own way of respecting the dead. The Boston must do this too, I think. But their way is not our way. Why, then, does the Boston man cut hair like our people, instead of doing whatever the Boston do in such things?"

Now Charley was impatient. "Will he-who-died wish to have words read out of a little book? No! He will wish to have hair cut for him, as it has always been done. The way of the Boston means nothing to him-who-died."

"I understand the wishes of him-who-died," Kilchis said dryly. "But does the Boston man? The people say whites believe their way in such things is the only true way."

"Ah," Charley said. "The people have misled the tyee, maybe."

"Some of my people have been to Astoria," Kilchis said, unoffended.

"Among the whites," Charley said slowly, "there are those who say, 'You must worship the Saghalie Tyee and his son Jesus and no other.'"

"This is what the people say," Kilchis nodded.

"But," Charley continued, "there are those who say, 'Let the people live with the beliefs that are theirs from old times.'"

"I have not heard of these."

"One sits in this lodge."

Kilchis shifted his implacable gaze to Trask. After a long consideration he said, "You have talked enough now, Charley Kehwa. I will speak with the Boston man again."

To Trask he said, "Is this true, what Charley Kehwa has said?"

Kilchis leaned forward intently, and Trask was struck by the black tyee's insistence. The man seemed driven by a relentless passion to comprehend precisely whatever was said; to examine minutely the implications of every statement until he was satisfied with his understanding of it. This was one who would not act until he had adequate and persuasive information. But Trask could not speak loosely; Kilchis too readily pounced on ambiguity and inconsistency. He considered his answer with care, trying to shape the jumble of attitudes in his mind into some kind of exact statement. It was not possible. He was acutely aware of Kilchis' eyes on him as he struggled with his own notions. When he finally spoke, it was hesitatingly.

"You understand this, tyee. Words cannot always shape themselves exactly like what is in the mind."

Kilchis nodded slowly, and seemed pleased. "If words opened a man's mind, where would he go to be alone? We understand this."

"*Kloshe kahkwa*," Trask said. "Then I will say this, and you will understand it is not all that is in my mind: It is true, there are men among my people who would have your people worship none but the Saghalie Tyee. But they are not many. They get their living in this way, as a fisher gets his living from the salmon. But there are others who are not sure this is a good thing."

"These others are very quiet," Kilchis remarked.

Trask carefully refused to be nettled. "That is true," he said. "Because they are not certain, they cannot talk in a loud voice about what is right and what is not right."

"All people have their own way," Kilchis said abruptly.

"That also is true. But it is not necessary to share another man's belief to respect it."

Kilchis nodded again thoughtfully. "We have lived in our way for a long time," he said finally. "We are a rich people here. We have no wish to change."

Trask said nothing.

"When the white man comes, he brings great change. He brings us metal for tools, good cloth, many such things. But also he brings sickness and wiskey and the Saghalie Tyee." The giant lost himself in thought for a long moment; finally shook his head sharply and sat erect. "I must think more on this. Otherwise my words will have no mind behind them, and be like rattling stones. We will speak of this thing later, maybe."

Trask nodded. Several of the young men started to rise, whispering among themselves. Trask glanced at Charley and read approval in his face. He had scored significantly with Kilchis. Trask smiled.

One of the warriors—Trask recognized their guard of the morning—whispered something in Kilchis' ear, glancing at Trask. Kilchis stiffened.

"Wait!" he said suddenly. The whispered conversations stopped in mid-sentence, and all eyes turned to the black man. He leaned forward and studied Trask's face.

"Is there no more you wish to say?"

Puzzled, Trask shook his head.

"Do you not wish to call the Killamook band thieves?" Kilchis inquired mildly. "Do you not wish to say they have stolen that which belongs to you?"

3

Trask heard Charley's sharp intake of breath beside him. He cursed silently that the good impression he had made was now wasted. He was regretting this when he heard his own voice say calmly, "Not the band, Kilchis. But I say there is a thief among the Killamook people."

There was a long moment of silence in the lodge. Trask could feel his hackles rise against the wave of chill hostility that passed over the group. The men who had begun to rise seated themselves again. Kilchis' face was stony, the thoughtful expression of a moment before now completely gone, replaced by the scowling ebony mask.

"What do you wish to say against the Killamook people?" he asked coldly.

"Nothing," Trask said, keeping his voice rigidly calm. "Nothing against the people. But I say that *one* among them has stolen the tobacco pipe that belonged to me. It was taken from my pack, which was opened."

"You say a serious thing."

"It is true."

Kilchis gestured with his hand. "Bring me this pack."

The guard who had whispered in his ear glanced first at Kilchis, then at Illga. Illga made an almost imperceptible gesture, and the man left the tent. While he was gone no word was spoken. Kilchis sat stiffly erect, staring at Trask as if trying to read the white man's intentions and honesty. Trask met his eyes.

After what seemed a long wait, the guard returned with both packs, walking awkwardly under the burden. Trask's had been tied up again. They were put beside Kilchis on the sleeping-platform.

"Which is the pack that was opened?"

"This one," Trask said. "That is not my tying."

Kilchis hesitated momentarily. "You wish me to see that right is done in this thing?"

"Yes," Trask said.

"Then this is my word," Kilchis said. "One who accuses falsely shall be punished as if he himself had done the wrong thing. In this way there will be no slippery talking."

Trask nodded, abruptly aware of how tenuous his accusation was. His forehead felt cool.

"Open the pack," Kilchis said.

With fingers that suddenly seemed awkward Trask fumbled at the thongs around the pack. He loosened them and unfolded the tarpaulin flat on the sand floor with the contents still holding roughly to their packed shape. In the center, its warm bowl and curved stem distinct against the pile of objects, was his meerschaum pipe.

There was silence around the fire. Trask was not surprised to find the pipe there; he had been forced to overextend himself, and was suffering the inevitable result. He stared blankly at the pipe, wondering what to do next. A light breeze whispered along the ridge, and the fire wavered. The faint, hesitant tapping of rain was heard on the roof.

"This is the pipe that was stolen?" Kilchis said.

"Yes."

"Then it was not stolen at all."

Trask raised his eyes to meet Kilchis' expressionless gaze. The other men around the fire were alert, but immobile as stones. All casualness had gone from their posture and they sat tensely, waiting.

"The pipe was stolen," Trask insisted quietly. "That it was returned later does not change the stealing."

At the edge of his vision Trask saw one of the seated figures rise, but he did not take his eyes from Kilchis.

Illga came forward gracefully, moving around the seated men. He smiled warmly at Trask and made a faint salute with his fingers. Turning to Kilchis, his face assumed a concerned expression.

"This is a bad thing," he said in worried tones. "There is a mistake here, maybe."

"What is this mistake, then?" Kilchis asked quietly.

"With the coming of the white, naturally my men were concerned for the welfare of our people."

"Your men? Your men?" Kilchis said sardonically. "Ah."

"In their concern," Illga continued smoothly, "they opened the pack of the Boston man. He speaks the truth in this," he added solemnly. He turned again to Trask and favored him with an ingratiating smile. "This one might have carried wiskey, or weapons. Now, this is what the Boston man is talking about, this opening of the pack. It seemed to him as if this thing were being stolen. A misunderstanding, Kilchis. He is not to blame for believing the pipe was stolen. It is a misunderstanding only, and no punishment is necessary."

Even in the midst of his growing anger Trask appreciated Illga's deft handling. Concerned by the relation that seemed to be developing between Trask and Kilchis, Illga had adroitly forced the issue of the thievery, knowing Trask could not back down. There was little doubt that Kilchis was angered by it. And now, Illga had let Trask know where he would find friends in the band.

Kilchis had now turned to him. A wall of indifference had descended between him and the scene before him, and his mind seemed far away, as though he were bored with the whole proceeding.

"Is this your word also?" he asked without inflection.

For a moment Trask balanced precariously on the edge of decision. To agree would set everything right, and simply. No punishment, no theft, Illga had assured himself of Trask's gratitude . . . It was clearly what Kilchis expected, and would put an end to the unpleasant situation developing.

But in Trask, the sense of having been manipulated rankled, and thinking of it he felt the anger rise again in him.

"No," he said slowly. "No, this is not my word. The pipe was stolen, and the thief should be punished."

Illga turned to him slowly and blinked with surprise. Then his body stiffened and his finely molded features twisted into an expression of such malevolent hatred that Trask was momentarily shocked. Not even the viciousness of the Nehalem Killamook had carried such a sharp weight of loathing. Suddenly he turned and swept across to the entrance, his bare feet whispering on the white sand floor. A gust of cold air when the flap was thrown back made the fire flicker erratically and the long shadows leap against the walls.

Kilchis leaned forward, his attention focused sharply again. "Who is accused?"

"Ask that one," Trask said, pointing to the guard. "I spoke to him about this thing, and he said he knew nothing."

"Is this true?"

Nervously the man stood and faced Kilchis, glancing apprehensively at the circle around the fire. "This is true," he admitted. "The Boston wanted tobacco from his pack. I gave it to him, and also a pipe. He said he wanted the pipe that belonged to him. I knew nothing of this pipe. In a little while I spoke of this to him, Yahluk. Yahluk showed me this pipe which he had taken from the Boston man's pack. He smoked it. These are all my words." He sat down abruptly, not looking around him.

"Yahluk." Kilchis' voice was low and expressionless.

From the shadows another man appeared, and Trask recognized him as the guard who had sat cross-legged at a little distance from the lodge.

"Is this true?"

"I smoked that pipe," Yahluk admitted unhappily. "I had not seen a pipe like that, and I took it to smoke. It was returned to him."

"When was it returned?" Kilchis pressed.

Yahluk hesitated. "Today."

"When today?"

"Not long ago." Yahluk's voice stumbled. "No harm was done. The pipe was returned."

Kilchis grunted. "And if Clatsops came and raped your wife and returned her to you, you would say no harm was done, maybe."

Yahluk did not answer.

Kilchis pressed his forehead into his hands and was silent. Finally he looked up again at Yahluk. "When was the pipe returned?"

Yahluk hesitated, glanced around. "I do not know," he admitted miserably.

"You did not return it, then," Kilchis said. "How did that pipe come to be in the pack?"

Silently the first guard stood, his face blank.

"*When?*" Kilchis snapped.

"When I brought the packs to this place," the man said in a low voice.

"You were told to do that," Kilchis said flatly.

"Yes."

Kilchis shook his head angrily. "That one brings shame to the band. Agh!" He lapsed into an angry, sullen silence that endured so long it was broken by a quiet question from one of the older men.

"What is your word in this thing, Kilchis?"

"My word? My word?" Kilchis looked up as though surprised to find the man Yahluk still standing before him. He shook his head again angrily. "You listen to other words until the time comes to decide what is right. *Then* you listen to Kilchis. Then it is too late. Then there must be punishment for those who listen to the words that slide from slippery tongues."

He drew himself erect, standing on the sleeping-platform. He towered over the firelit circle like some gigantic tree about to fall on the tiny creatures below. Trask thought he had never seen a face so full of suppressed anger.

"This is my word," Kilchis said, his voice rolling and echoing from the far end of the lodge. "*Yaka kapswalla*. Yahluk is a thief."

Chapter Eighteen

The light of the early morning came sliding almost imperceptibly up the eastern sky, silhouetting the ringing mountains as if they were the tumbled seas of a great storm that stopped just short of the placid plain. In the lodges of the Killamook, fires were kindled from the embers of the night, and wisps of smoke furtively appeared at ridge peaks; were quickly whipped away into nothingness by a freshening breeze in the northwest. The dew-heavy ferns of the plain nodded and pressed against one another, leaning away from the wind, and wind ripples crossed the open flats like rollers coming to the shore.

Two dogs yapped querulously, scrabbling over something of importance to them; and then were silent. The rustle and papery whisper of the firs formed a roof over the village. Gradually the Killamook people filed out of their lodges and separated, male and female, to go to the river for the morning bath. In all stages of wakefulness, some shuffling sleepily down the beach, some already alert and happy, they straggled to the water's edge; those still clogged with sleep enduring the thousand verbal tortures devised for their harassment by the happy wakers.

Trask and Charley had been given a fire in the far corner of Kilchis' own lodge, the others being all full. Once in the night, wakened by some small sound, Trask had rolled over to see Kilchis at the other end of the lodge, sitting lonely and gigantic before the fire, brooding over the flames. He wondered what was going on behind the black mask, what anguish for the pride of himself and his people. No sign could be read in the firelit face of the tyee; only a vast and oceanic loneliness was there.

Kilchis had pronounced the punishment before the council was dispersed: a fine of one blanket and a beating of ten strokes, administered by the one who had been stolen from.

Charley, before he slept, had only one comment. "Do a good job of it," he advised unhappily.

"I'm not mad at him," Trask said.

"You have to do it right," Charley said.

"I really messed this up."

Charley shrugged. "I don't know what you could have done. But now you're in it, do it right."

As they bathed in the cold water of the river, Trask was faintly surprised to see Yahluk bathing some little distance away. He was not held under any kind of restraint, and had left the lodge with the others. Apparently there was no question of his running away. At one point his eyes met Trask's, and he looked away. There seemed to be more regret than malice in his look.

On this morning of punishment, otherwise no different from any other gray dawn with the smell of rain, the hunters did not take to their canoes. Instead they clustered up the beach in small groups to stand before the lodge of Kilchis. The women and children of the band also gathered there, and there was no work done.

When Charley and Trask returned to the lodge, there was a large and silent crowd in a semicircle around the front, watching them come. More and more were added to the group rapidly, until Trask estimated them at over a hundred. The front rank, nearest the lodge, were all young and sturdy men, to the number of thirty; the band's hard core of strength. All were high-born, and showed pronounced head-shaping. Their black hair was unbound and hung loosely around their shoulders, and their light skin still glistened with droplets of water from the bath. The women of the band formed a rank behind them, some of them holding children. Last were the slaves and the older children and dogs, all of whom scurried around the outskirts of the circle and were unnaturally silent.

As Trask and Charley made their way into the circle it parted before them smoothly and closed behind, like water over a pebble. Glancing at the faces of the young warriors in the front rank, Trask was worried. They seemed to study him intently, and with a cold hostility that made the back of his neck prickle. Keeping his face impassive he walked steadily past the line of faces and stopped before the skin-covered entrance, where Kilchis stood waiting with his arms crossed. The black giant wore the same bearskin robe as he had the day before, but around his neck was a necklace of deer hoofs. A seven-foot pole leaned against the wall of the lodge, and this was strung for several feet at the top with more hoofs. At its base was a cattail mat, on which lay two objects. One was a braided quirt of rawhide, almost four feet in length and the thickness of a gun barrel, with pieces of metal worked into it along its length. The thongs had apparently been woven around some kind of stiffener, for the quirt lay rigid and seemingly inflexible. Beside it was a large carved bowl full of clear liquid.

Kilchis took the long pole and faced the assembled band. He shook it and the deer hoofs rattled against one another, making a rapid, jumbled clacking. He stamped the butt of the stick heavily on the ground several times. When he spoke his voice carried no emotion whatever. It was as low and impersonal as the steady rumble of the surf at the bar.

"There has been thievery going on in the band," he said. "And also lying. These will be punished. This is my word."

As the tyee's eyes scanned the crowd before him, it seemed to Trask they deliberately rested on Illga for a moment before passing on. In the back, out of sight, a woman's voice was heard. In a flat, nasal monotone she began to chant slowly.

"*Ya-ya-ya-ya-ya-ya . . .*"

"Let the fine be paid," Kilchis said. He did not raise his voice, but his words carried over the chanting background easily.

"*Ya-ya-ya-ya-ya . . .*"

The crowd shifted; parted slightly and Yahluk appeared, walking slowly up the aisle they formed, holding before him a blanket draped across both forearms. His face was without expression, but the side of his mouth jerked spasmodically. He put the blanket before Trask. The two looked into each other's eyes.

With a sense of unreality Trask heard Kilchis' voice. "Is the blanket good?"

Wrenching his eyes away from Yahluk's face, Trask knelt to feel the corner of the material. Standing again he said, "*Hyas kloshe.* It is good." In Yahluk's eyes Trask could read nothing; no appeal, no malice, no regret. The slight twitching of his mouth was the only element that made the face seem alive.

"Let the beating be done."

Yahluk held Trask's eyes, as if reluctant to turn away. Several women had joined in the monotonous chant, and the crowd seemed to surge restlessly in time to it.

"*Ya-ya-ya-ya-ya-ya* . . ." The implacable, flat sound made Trask shiver.

The ridgepole of Kilchis' lodge projected beyond the roof by six or seven feet. Over it was thrown a braided cedar-bark rope. Yahluk's hands were tied together with one end and lifted over his head. He was hoisted up until the tips of his toes were just touching the ground. The standing end of the rope was looped around a stake.

Now there were words along with the steady chant:

"*Ya-ya-ya-ya-ya-ya,*
The hands of the thief are tied.
Ya-ya-ya-ya-ya-ya,
The thief is lifted from the ground.
Ya-ya-ya-ya-ya-ya . . ."

The women's flat voices were louder now, though the pitch remained the same. Always over the nasal chant, the song described the lifting of the thief, how he hung like drying meat, the picking up of the whip . . .

As he held the whip in his hand, his eyes fixed with fascination on the muscular back before him, Trask heard Charley's low voice saying, "Everything you've got. Everything. Everything. Everything . . ."

He braced his feet apart and let his arm swing back, holding the barely flexible shaft lightly. He drew a hissing, shallow breath between his clenched teeth and brought his arm forward in a great sweeping arc with all the weight of his body behind it . . .

"YAH!"

And then there was silence.

Trask blinked dazedly. A broken line of red suddenly appeared traced across the brown back, and the whip was hanging loosely from his hand again. The broken line grew brighter and wider and joined itself rapidly. From the lower end droplets of blood ran down into the valley of the spine.

"Again," came Kilchis' flat voice into the stillness.

Trask drew his arm back again.

2

He remembered little of it later, and that unclearly, like the outlines of a dream gone suddenly bad. How he got through the ten strokes he could not have said; or whether he had. A part of him stood detached and watching, caught in a paralysis of horror at his own action. At some time, the shape of the man strung there before him lost its significance, and became a meaningless collection of lines and planes that formed no comprehensible whole; and certainly there was no meaning to the repeated mechanical swinging of his arm and the flat whack! that sent a shock running up to his shoulder. More of the bright red lines appeared magically, standing brutally distinct in the gray light of the morning; but he could not, somehow comprehend them.

Several things remained clear in his memory, scenes still and distinct as the engravings in a much-studied book. Yahluk had fainted twice, and had to be revived. Then Trask had to stop the automatic motion of his arm and wait while someone splashed water over the slumped head. The waiting was an agony, for all time stopped then, and his mind caught up on the number of the stroke. Five, he thought, five. But then the time for six came and passed and his arm had not lowered and he repeated witlessly to himself, Five five five five five . . . until the word lost meaning. Then, slowly, the black shock of hair came upright again, and Trask's arm flew back.

Six! he thought, and was grateful that time had begun again.

During one of these times of waiting he had found himself staring beyond the hanging brown figure at a face that came suddenly distinct from the pale blotches around it; and it was that of Illga.

The face was ugly with hate and the black eyes were narrow with malice as they met Trask's beyond Yahluk's limp form. Trask thought he had never seen such raw, feral malevolence in a human face.

Then Yahluk was revived again and Trask's numb right swung back almost without volition; a machine set irrevocably to stroke ten times and unable to stop before the full ten were given.

When it was over they had given him the carved bowl, which held salt water, and he had sponged the long slashes with it, feeling the back under his hands stiffen with the further pain; but the head did not turn and there was no sound but that of Trask's own breathing.

Then he washed his hands and dried them on the shredded bark that was thrust before him. A hand was on his arm, and he followed it blindly, to find himself back at the remote corner of Kilchis' lodge with Charley sitting silently beside him. The rest of the lodge was empty.

"Was it all right? Did I do it all right?"

"It was fine," Charley said. "It was done strongly and without anger, as punishment should be."

Trask shook his head weakly. "I don't even remember it much."

"You did it all right," Charley said. "You look sick."

"I don't feel so good." His forehead and chest felt cool, and his breathing was shallow and loud in the secluded silence of the lodge. He lay with his cheek pressed into the corrugated surface of a mat on the sleeping-platform, breathing through his open mouth, staring unseeing at the fire.

"Are you going to be sick?" Charley asked.

"No, I'm all right. I never did anything like that before, whipping a man that was tied. I don't like it."

"Done in anger it would be an evil thing. As a punishment it is all right," Charley said. "It is anger that is the destroyer."

"I don't like it. I feel funny inside."

Charley shrugged. "Nobody could like it but one who was mad."

"How is he?"

"Yahluk? You hurt him bad, but he will be all right. He did not cry out once," Charley added with some satisfaction.

"Jesus," Trask whispered, almost to himself. "He must hate my guts."

"Hate?" Charley said, surprised. "No, why should he do that? If your canoe turns over in white water, do you then hate the sea? No. You have done the wrong thing, and been punished for it. This is the way things are. There is no hate in it. It is the way things are."

"Illga hates."

"Ah. That is a different thing. You must watch for that one."

"There's more to him than we figured on, more than just greed. He's no child, by a ways."

"As a friend he would be nothing," Charley said slowly. "But as an enemy . . . You must take care for that one. He would kill you."

"Why the hell? He didn't get the beating." Trask sat up.

"You feel better now?"

"Yes, I'm all right."

"Good. I must talk to you. Kilchis is coming back soon. Illga offered you his protection in the band. You refused it. Why is that?"

Trask, painfully remembering the exchange of the previous morning, thought it odd Charley should have to ask, but did not comment on this. "I don't know," he said. "It seemed better not to."

"It was," Charley agreed. "He could be little help to you in what you want to do. But now he will do everything he can to stop you, even if it means killing you."

"Could he do that?"

"Not in the village, I think. He would not dare go so far against Kilchis. But do not let him get you where it could be an accident or where you could disappear."

Trask nodded slowly.

"If this one moves that way, it will be secretly. You understand this?"

"Yes," Trask said. "I'll watch him."

"You must if you wish to live," Charley said flatly. "Now listen. Kilchis is coming back, and you will have to talk to him. You understand he is not an easy man."

Trask laughed shortly. "No, I wouldn't say so."

"But he is a great man," Charley said without emphasis. "You are going to have to remember this too. I do not think you can persuade him, or threaten him, or fool him. He will judge according to the facts, I think. He will not be moved by emotion. In this he is not as other men, who can be pushed this way and that."

Trask nodded again. "By what, then?"

Charley shrugged. "By talking straight, is the only thing I can say. I do not know what will move such a one. This is up to you."

Charley studied the white man's face as he considered the problem. Suddenly he said, "Do you know how much easier it would have been for Kilchis to decide against you in the matter of the theft?"

Trask nodded. "I thought about it," he said.

"The band would have been spared shame, there would have been no conflict between him and Illga, and he could have had the white man punished in all fairness. It is a question, I think, whether theft was done or not, since the pipe was returned after all. It could have gone either way. I do not know myself what I would have decided."

"What are you saying?"

"I don't know," Charley admitted. "But to judge in your favor was a much more complicated thing. It tells you something about the man Kilchis, maybe."

"Maybe. Maybe he was afraid of other whites coming."

Charley laughed. "It could be. But you have seen this man. Does it seem likely to you?"

"No," Trask admitted reluctantly. "No, I suppose not."

Both were silent for a long while. Finally Charley said, "Well, there is nothing more for me to say. I cannot help much in this. I do not think the tyee will permit it."

Trask shrugged, and stared glumly into the fire.

3

In that Charley was wrong. When Kilchis returned, near the middle of the day, he was insistent that Charley remain with them in the lodge, and seemed to be more interested at first in what Charley had to say than he was in Trask. He pursued his line of questioning with the same dogged insistence as he had the previous night, and as consistently refused to deviate in the least from his own line of thought.

At first he questioned Charley in general about conditions among the Clatsops: How many were in each village, who was tyee, and did the people listen to him? How many had been in each village five years ago? Ten? Who was tyee then?

He snapped questions at the little Clatsop rapidly, and was answered quickly and accurately, which seemed to please him. As the three sat around Kilchis' fire at the front of the lodge, an alert tension grew between them, a fine knife-edge of awareness, heightened by the quick and staccato exchange in Chinook.

How many whites were in Astoria? Where were all the King Chautch men who used to come trading? Why were the Boston men now more numerous?

Charley's explanation of white men's politics and the relations of Great Britain and the United States in the Oregon country made Kilchis frown. It did not satisfy him and did not seem reasonable to him. He did not, however, question the accuracy of Charley's limited information. He had apparently decided Charley could be trusted, and having decided this would accept what was said as truth, as Tupshin had.

Occasionally he asked for an opinion: Did Charley think this United States would protect the Boston men in the Oregon country? To what extent?

But in general the tyee waved opinion aside with an impatient gesture of his hand, and had an uncanny sense of when opinion was being presented as fact.

In the course of an hour and a half Trask spoke only three times, when he as a white man could amplify Charley's comments. For the rest of the time he watched and listened, intrigued by the fleeting play of expressions on Kilchis' face. The stony mask was an illusion, born of near-perfect control. In actuality Trask found the black giant's expression incredibly flexible, responding in small and almost imperceptible ways to each internal shift of feeling.

Watching was itself both exhilarating and exhausting; it seemed to Trask he had never seen so huge a volume of information passed between any two people in conversation. Every superfluous word was gradually weeded out, until raw facts flowed from Charley to Kilchis like a river in flood. The more information Kilchis received, about the activities of whites and Indians, conditions, prospects of religion and economy and politics, the more sharply pointed his questions, the more precise his narrowing of focus. It was altogether a fantastic performance, and Trask was again confronted with the unmistakable certainty that intelligence was not the monopoly of the sophisticated.

Gradually the area of questioning narrowed to the crucial point so far as Trask himself was concerned; the point where this razor-edged intelligence behind a black face would be slanted in his direction and he, rather than Charley Kehwa would be the focus of those darting, relentless eyes.

Kilchis was examining Charley minutely on the subject of the tamanawis among the Clatsops, when he abruptly asked the question that was coming to have an unpleasantly familiar ring in Trask's ears.

"Why is it that a tamanawis man has hired out to guide this man?"

Suddenly Charley relaxed; the alert tension drained away from his body as if a set of invisible wires had been cut. He leaned back against the sitting-ledge and drew in a long, sighing breath.

"Kilchis," he said slowly, "now you are finished with me. I have told you how it is with my people to the north. I have told you what you wished to know of the whites and what they do and how they believe. Now we have come to the question of this one man, who sits in your lodge. Would you have me describe what is before your eyes?"

The suggestion of a smile flickered briefly over Kilchis' face. "I did not ask about the Boston man, but about Charley Kehwa."

Charley glanced at Trask; lowered his eyes to contemplate the sputtering coals at the fire's edge. Finally he said quietly, "This is not a thing to talk about while that one is with us." He raised his eyes to meet Trask's frankly, with a hint of apology.

Kilchis' gaze passed from one to the other, his eyes narrowed, his expression neutral; weighing, evaluating. He studied Charley Kehwa for a long moment without speaking.

Trask got to his feet. "I will go, then."

"No." Kilchis gestured sharply with his hand, still watching Charley's face. "I would speak to you now."

Trask felt a tension along his spine. Suddenly there was something not to be talked about. It was an abrupt contrast with the rapid flow of information, the unconcealed frankness existing before. He tried to read some hint in Charley's expression, but found nothing.

"All right," he said, sitting again. The air set in motion by the movement of his body made the flames wave, and the yellow light played fitfully over the faces of the two Indians, confusing any hint of expression.

Kilchis was silent for a long time, watching Charley. When at last he spoke his voice was low. "Let it be so," he said. "But this other thing . . ."

"You must understand this is a private thing," Charley said quietly.

"No," Kilchis said, with what seemed genuine regret. "When the Boston man comes to my country no thing about his coming can be hidden from me."

Charley nodded slowly. "*Kloshe kahkwa*," he said finally. "We will speak of this some other time, then."

Kilchis gestured with his hand, dismissing the problem temporarily. He turned to Trask with shocking suddenness. "Why have you come here?"

Chapter Nineteen

Trask was startled. The unexpected, flat demand of the tyee allowed him no masking of his answer in acceptable terms, no buffer of ambiguity between thought and word. It was, Trask thought ruefully, almost perfectly designed to prevent him from misleading even himself.

"I wish to bring my woman to this country and settle here," he said simply.

Kilchis jerked his head back, and Trask was again startled; for he had expected the statement to be absorbed without reaction. He saw Kilchis dart a quick glance at Charley and, inexplicably, a slow smile grow on the Clatsop's face. Puzzled, Trask looked back at Kilchis and saw he was frowning.

Charley's voice, full of amusement, said quietly, "There is your straight talk for you, tyee."

Kilchis nodded slowly.

"The tyee has asked for straight talk," Trask said.

"One asks for many things one does not expect," Kilchis muttered. When he looked up at Trask, his eyes glinted, and it was obvious the tyee was perfectly aware of the humor involved in his own reaction. He seemed to look at Trask with new respect—for the first time as a human being, rather than a white man. Trask knew it would make no difference in the long run, but the sensation of having startled the implacable giant was a pleasant one. Then, as suddenly as it had come, the humor was gone from Kilchis' face.

"Why this land?" Kilchis said. "There is much land elsewhere for you to have."

"This is the land I want," Trask said calmly. "The Killamook people do not use the land I would build on, the flat land."

"The land belongs to us."

"You hunt in mountains and fish in the rivers. The flat land is no use to you."

"Where the Boston men go, they take *all* the land," Kilchis said. "It was not so with the King Chautch men, the Hudson's Bay men."

"The men of Hudson's Bay wanted only trading and trapping. The men of the United States wish to root themselves in the land like the cedar tree. And even the men of Hudson's Bay have changed in this. North of the big river called Columbia, they have made farms."

"I have heard of this thing," Kilchis mused.

"But the Hudson's Bay men have no more to do with this country here," Trask said. "They have agreed that it shall belong to the United States."

"How can they give away what does not belong to them?" Kilchis demanded. "This land is not their land to give. It is ours."

Trask frowned. "It is," he said hesitantly, "an agreement between their tyee and ours. In time a man will come from the United States to see that your people suffer no harm."

Kilchis laughed shortly. "And who will see that *he* suffers no harm'?"

"Behind each man stand a thousand more," Trask said.

"*Hiyu wawa!*" Kilchis said. "Big talk."

"Straight talk," Trask said quietly.

Kilchis considered it thoughtfully. "The Cayuse beyond the mountains were not afraid," he said suddenly.

He was referring, Trask knew, to the massacre at the Whitman mission some six months before.

"The Cayuse," Trask said slowly, "were fools. They kill a dozen people, and now are running. By this they have lost everything, and they will run before the whites until they are all dead and the names of the Cayuse have been forgotten."

"This will not happen, maybe," Kilchis suggested. "Maybe the Cayuse will join with the men of Hudson's Bay and drive the Boston men from this land."

"This thing between Hudson's Bay and us, you do not understand," Trask said. "There is no war between us."

Kilchis glanced accusingly at Charley Kehwa. "That one has said there was bad feeling."

"Bad feeling, maybe. But the prisoners of the Cayuse were bought back, those that were not killed. Those goods for the buying-back came from the Hudson's Bay Company."

Kilchis frowned. "How can this be? You drive these men from the land, and yet they buy back your own people for you? This is not according to reason."

"If a flathead finds another flathead in slavery—even if one of a different tribe—will he not buy him out?"

"Sometimes," Kilchis admitted. "But this is among those whose heads are shaped. It is a different thing."

Trask raised his hands. He found himself unable to explain the political situation between England and the United States, the boundary agreement of two years before, the present role of the Hudson's Bay Company in the Oregon country. Kilchis, accustomed to dealing with small, autonomous bands of people, could not comprehend membership in a large nation, and that individual groups did not act independently. It would have been an unnatural thing to him, one not "according to reason."

"It is a mixed-up thing," Trask said helplessly. "You have heard, maybe, of Joe Meek in the valley of the Willamette."

"His name has been spoken by Clackamas people who come here," Kilchis admitted.

"Even now, as we sit in this lodge, Joe Meek is many miles away in the lodge of our tyee Polk. He asks that this land be made a part of the Boston *illahee*, the United States."

"Why does he not ask me, Kilchis? How can the tyee Polk say yes or no to this thing?"

"He will—he gives word that his people go and settle this land."

Kilchis shook his head. "But my people do not wish this, maybe."

Trask raised his hands helplessly. "It will happen, tyee."

Kilchis looked at Charley for denial of the preposterous notion. Charley only nodded his head slowly, with resignation.

Kilchis frowned. "There would be war, maybe."

"That would be an evil thing. Much blood would flow, and the Killamook people would die or be made to run, as the Cayuse run now."

Kilchis did not answer. He lapsed into a brooding thoughtfulness that seemed endless, staring into the fire as if in the glowing coals he could read some obscure sign. It was Charley Kehwa's low voice that broke the uneasy silence.

"Among the Clatsops," he said absently, as if relating some event of no importance, "the white man came long ago, in the time of my father's youth; when he was a young man. These were ships that came over the bar, and the people traded with them all right. They went away again, and the people did not think much about it.

"Then, after a little while there came the white men from inland, the red-haired Captain Clark that the people called 'brother.' These men built a stockade and stayed for a little while and then went away also. Concomly-the-One-Eyed was tyee at this time, and he talked with these men, even though they were uneducated and could not understand the Jargon.

"Then pretty soon many traders came, and also the Hudson's Bay Company, and the people traded with them as Chinooks have always traded with all strange tribes. But many of these men did not trade and then go away. They set up buildings that were to last, and they built houses for themselves."

"All this is known to me," Kilchis said irritably.

"All right," Charley said, unruffled. "I am saying this for a reason. Among the Chinooks, the coming of the white men was over many years, from my father's time to mine. Because of this, no one knew exactly what was happening. My father himself told me this before he died. There was no way the people could know what was going to happen, and many bad things came of this."

"All this you have told me also," Kilchis said. "Wiskey and the Saghalie Tyee and the taking of land. Anger and killing. These things the white man brings. You see in this band, already there is trouble from the one white man who comes. A man has been beaten for stealing; there is shame in the village; there is hatred in the faces of some of my people."

"All right," Charley agreed. "This is true. But I am saying that it does not always have to be so."

Kilchis laughed, a humorless bark. "You yourself have told me this would happen."

"No," Charley said. "I have said the white men will come to this place, and this is true. They will come, sometime. For this is their way, to go everywhere."

"Ayah! This we understand," Kilchis said bitterly.

Trask leaned forward, catching Kilchis' attention. "The tyee must look to the welfare of his people," he said. "In whatever thing, he must see that his people are kept happy and unhurt."

Kilchis looked at the white man sardonically. "You do not have to tell me this. *I* am tyee, not you."

Trask rocked back, looked off to the side with an almost contemptuous expression. "This tyee here," he said deliberately, "is like the fear-blinded buck that runs into the sea."

Kilchis stiffened, and his eyes narrowed. Trask wondered if he had misjudged the length to which he could go with this man, and spoke quickly, but with the same deliberation.

"When the storm comes from the sea, does the tyee shout and throw rocks at it to protect his people? No. He sees that there are houses that are strong, so his people may be kept dry inside. He does not make war against the wind, for the wind will come in spite of his war. He plans; that his people may not stand naked when the wind comes with thunder and lightning."

Kilchis said nothing, but the tension in his body eased. Trask went on.

"The Cayuse make war against the wind; and now they are running before it up the river. Is this according to reason? The Clatsops did not make war, but neither did they think to protect themselves against the wind; they stood shivering on the beach. Is this according to reason?"

"There is no choice," Kilchis said. "If there is war, then the people die. If there is no war, the people die also. Who is to choose between these things? Better to die in war, maybe, than die of the Boston sick like the Clatsops."

"It is not because they were peaceful that my people are dying," Charley said. "It is because they could not see what was happening, and could not plan against it. If one knows the winter is coming, one can build a house against it. If he does not know, then he will be caught. Concomly did not understand this thing until it was too late for house-building."

"What kind of house will stand against this wind of white men?" Kilchis asked.

Trask tapped his temple. "A house built according to reason. A house that is built with understanding. Not fear, or anger; these mean nothing. It is the understanding. There can be friendship between your people and mine, not killing. And it is necessary for the tyee to think about this thing, so his people may be protected."

Kilchis put his forehead in his hands.

Charley said softly, "Not all among the Boston men think this way, maybe. Maybe the next of them that came to this place would not care if there were friendship or not. Maybe the next one would come with many guns, and start to kill everybody. Then there would be war."

Trask leaned forward. "Here is the thing, Kilchis. Whites will come to this place, because this is our way. Many thousands of whites will be coming if our tyee Polk calls this country part of the Boston *illahee*. This is how it is, whether he has the right to do this thing or not. It is in the hands of Kilchis to say what this will mean to his people."

"It is in my mind," Charley said, his voice somehow detached, "that what has happened to my people the Clatsops does not have to happen in every place the white men go. That strong and honest men who see clearly may prevent this bad thing from happening."

Without raising his head from his hands Kilchis spoke, and for the first time his voice was soft; almost inaudible. "This is in the mind of Charley Kehwa. What, then, is in the mind of the Boston man?"

Leaning back, Trask closed his eyes as if withdrawing himself from the fire's circle. Automatically he tucked the ends of his beard under his chin before replying. When at last he spoke, his voice was clear and the words came without hesitation and without betraying the sudden cold thrill of exultation that swept through him.

"It is in my mind to make of this bay one house where we may all live in peace. These are all my words."

2

For a long moment Kilchis did not move; might not have heard. Then he nodded slowly, not in agreement, but as if he confirmed some inner notion.

"Go now," he said finally. "I must think about these matters."

"Will you call the men into council?" Charley asked.

Kilchis hesitated. He passed his hand over his eyes as though brushing something away. "No," he said slowly. "There are things the people cannot well decide for themselves. There are things that must be taken on one man alone." He looked up at Charley almost defiantly, as if expecting the Clatsop to challenge his right.

"*Kloshe kahkwa*," Charley said. "It is my wish that you decide well."

"And mine," Kilchis said. "Go now."

They left him sitting disconsolate before the fire, and Trask once again was struck by the sense of great loneliness that surrounded the massive black figure. His shoulders were bent as though by a great wind, and his face was a mask once more. Trask hesitated briefly at the entrance of the lodge, looking back. He was already forgotten; lost in thought, Kilchis did not look up.

Outside, the freshness of the air was sharp and sweet in their nostrils, dulled by the pervading smell of smoke and dried fish in Kilchis' lodge. The sky was still cloudy, but not evenly overcast now. Layers of gray, darker and lighter, scudded across the bay from the sea; moved swiftly over the plain and into the eastern mountains, cutting off the peaks in flat, level planes. The air itself was almost luminous under the pearl-gray canopy, and small detail stood out with abnormal clarity at a great distance; far to the south, at the extreme southern tip of the bay, a canoe was moving slowly across the water, a distinct black needle on the gray surface.

"What do we do now?" Trask asked.

"Wait," Charley said. His face was bleak, and his voice morose.

"Something wrong?" Trask asked.

"Let's go up the river bank." They walked down to the beach and started inland along the northern bank. The village was nearly deserted, except for the women who remained and the dogs. After the punishment of the thief both men and women had gone about their usual duties, which at this time of the year took them into the woods for the better part of the day. Since the salmon did not come into this bay until late autumn, the rush to prepare nets and canoes would not begin until later.

The two were not hindered in their going, though the women they passed peered at them curiously. No effort was made to restrict them, but Trask had the notion they would be stopped if they moved too far away from the village.

"No, nothing wrong," Charley said after they had started along the river. "It is a terrible weight we place on him."

"It would be better if it could be done peaceably," Trask mused. "Much better. At least there is a decision for Kilchis to make. Concomly didn't even have that."

"This is true," Charley said reflectively. He sat down at a place where the bank dropped abruptly into the water and the current ran fast. The ripples glinted and rolled in the strangely bright light. Charley dropped a stone in the water and watched the circular ripples it formed swept quickly away in the stream. Trask squatted on his heels with his back propped against a fir whose branches overhung the water.

"What do you think he'll decide?" Trask asked.

"I think he'll say yes," Charley said, after a moment's thought. "Otherwise I would never have come."

"Hope so," Trask said thoughtfully. "Hate to make that trip again."

Charley looked over his shoulder with surprise mirrored on his flat face. "Again? Bridge, don't—" He broke off, and laughed faintly. "You don't seem to understand. If Kilchis decides against us, it will mean he's decided to fight. We'll never go back to the Plains."

Trask blinked, then looked away.

"This is not a game we are playing, not for Kilchis, not for us. He would not kill secretly, as that one Illga would do it. But if he thought it necessary for his people it would be done quickly enough."

Thinking about it, Trask decided, was useless. The bets had been made, now it remained to see which hand held the man-stick.

"Where do you think he came from?" he asked.

"Kilchis? Here in the bay, he was born in the Killamook band."

"Charley, that man's a nigger! He's no more Indian than I am!"

Charley shrugged. "Well, the story is that many years ago a ship was wrecked north of here. There have been many ships wrecked on this coast. Long before the white men came to trade there were ships that went aground. The people say that on this ship was a *klale* man, what you call nigger. When the whites came ashore after this wreck, there was this *klale* man with them, a blacksmith. He taught the Killamooks to make tools from the metal they found off wrecked ships."

"What happened to the rest of the crew?"

"Oh, the people say they were all right for a while, but pretty soon they got to be nuisances around the village, so they were killed. All but the *klale* man, because of his skill, and he married into the band. Kilchis would be—his son, maybe. Maybe grandson, I don't know. But part Killamook blood anyway."

"Funny," Trask mused. "Being black, he's as much different from the Killamooks as I am. But he's tyee, and I'm a stranger."

Charley shrugged. "He is a Killamook," Charley said. "What color doesn't matter. He was born a Killamook and lives and will die a Killamook. They say he is the wisest tyee in many years, that one."

"Maybe it's a good time for him to be here."

"A good thing for you, I think," Charley said.

They sat waiting by the bank of the river for more than two hours. Trask had begun to be nervous and was walking idly along the bank throwing small pieces of bark in the water and watching the current whirl them away.

"Listen," Charley said suddenly. "If Kilchis agrees to this thing, you know you will have to walk carefully."

Trask nodded. "I know."

"It is a great thing, to be trusted by a man like that."

"What are you getting at?"

"Nothing." Charley shrugged. "But you should understand that there would be much responsibility on you, as well as on Kilchis."

"I know that," Trask replied with slight irritation.

"That's all right," Charley said. "You would take much on your shoulders. You would not want it, maybe."

"I'll take it," Trask said shortly. "You think I couldn't handle it?"

"Who can say what a man can do, until the time comes? Men can do many things."

Trask walked over to Charley and sat facing him. "Look, Charley. Maybe we should get this straight. From what you told Kilchis, you brought me down here because you thought I could prevent what happened to the Clatsops from happening here."

"This is a part of it," Charley admitted.

"If you didn't think I could handle it, you wouldn't've brought me. Why all this hedging about it? What's so mysterious about it?"

"Nothing," Charley said. "But who can be certain about any man? I will say this: I look into men, because I am tamanawis, because I am Charley Kehwa. But—even the tamanawis spirits can tell a man the wrong thing, maybe. This is a thing I do not wish to make a mistake about. For this reason I worry sometimes."

"And you're not sure of me," Trask said flatly.

Charley looked at him impassively. Slowly he said, "I am not sure of myself, maybe. In the dream that made me come to this place, I saw clearly that you were one who could do this. The dream was strong, and I must trust these things. The man in the dream was not a man who would bargain with this one, Illga."

"I didn't. Did you think I was going to do something like that?"

"It was you who said so, not me."

From the edge of the forest behind them a Killamook hunter appeared silently. Trask caught the movement out of the corner of his eye and turned to face the man.

"Kilchis wants you," the man said. Without waiting for an answer he turned and disappeared back into the shadows of the forest.

Trask stood, watched until the hunter had gone, wondering how long the man had been observing them. It was, he thought, some confirmation of his idea they were not so free to move about as it had appeared.

They began to make their way back along the river bank toward the village, almost reluctantly.

Trask said, "You said this was part of the reason you brought me here. What's the other part?"

Charley glanced at him briefly, then turned his eyes forward to the rocky path. "In this dream," he said, "the Trask I saw had a strength in him. He was—different. Different in the way a young man is different when he has gone on the Searching. He is the same as before, but what was hidden in him—what is his strength—is now uncovered by his spirit helper." He glanced again at the white man, and found no anger in his face.

"The Boston men," he continued slowly, "have no spirit helper to uncover that-which-is-hidden. They do not go on the Searching as young men."

Trask smiled wryly at the little Clatsop. "So you thought you'd be my spirit helper."

Charley laughed. "Maybe that is it after all. It is not how I thought about it."

They walked for a few steps in silence. Then Trask said, "Well, maybe I need one, Charley. Maybe I do."

Chapter Twenty

They found Kilchis as they had left him, brooding before the fire, the bulky robe loose and humped over his shoulders. He did not look up when they came in. Charley sat immediately, opposite the bearlike figure of the tyee. Trask remained standing momentarily, looking down at the man, trying to read in his expression the decision he had made.

Without preliminary, Kilchis spoke; still staring at the fire. "You must not come before the salmon run into the bay twice more."

Trask hesitated, then sat down. A little over a year, perhaps a year and a half. It would take him that long to get a party of settlers; money and equipment.

"Agreed," he said.

"In the two colds after that, no more than ten men and their women and children."

"This is difficult," Trask said. "To settle a land requires men and much work."

Kilchis looked up at him stonily.

"Agreed," Trask said.

"No wiskey can be made in this place. No wiskey can be sold or given to any of my people. A white man who does this will be punished according to my word."

"Agreed."

"The old laws of the band will apply to the Boston men as well as Killamooks, in the matter of wrongdoing. This is fair for all men."

Trask nodded.

"Concerning gods, each of our people have their own. There must be no confusion in this, and my people must not be forced to worship the Saghalie Tyee and Jesus."

Trask frowned. "For my part, this can be promised. But there are those among my people—"

"Then these may not come to this place. It is on you that this agreement may be kept. Otherwise there will be war and killing between us."

Trask leaned back thoughtfully. "It will be done carefully."

"If hurt is done to one of my people, the white man shall pay the fines and be punished as though he were a member of the band. And if one of the Killamook people does hurt to a white man then he shall be punished according to the white man's law."

"This is fair," Trask agreed. "This is a good way. People will be more careful."

Kilchis went on, detailing his requirements of Trask in a flat, emotionless voice. The pattern of his desire was clear enough; the settlement must be gradual, and order must be kept in the bay. Some of his conditions were demanding, difficult. It would be hard to clear much land with a maximum of ten men in the first two years. Others— the division of authority in white-Killamook affairs—struck Trask as sound and fair.

It was impossible to know how much Kilchis had known of the white man before they came and how much he had learned from his rapid exchange with Charley. Wherever the information had come from, Kilchis foresaw many dangers to his people that would have escaped Trask; and accounted for them in his long series of qualifications. Trask found the black tyee's grasp of the situation and its implications somewhat incredible; Kilchis seemed to know instinctively what authority would have to be vested in the whites; how far his demands could go. Behind his words were two driving passions, almost tangible in their power, glowing through his talk like a forest fire seen through trees: the passion to see that his people were cushioned against the shock of transition; and the passion for fairness and exactitude.

Trask was sweating from the strain of following Kilchis' driving, exact mind. The tension in him had grown until he was leaning forward intently, peering at the black man's face, every sense preternaturally alert and receptive. At first he did not grasp the meaning of Kilchis' last statement, so abruptly did it come.

"These are all my words."

The sudden collapse of tension was like the breaking of a spring in his belly. Trask leaned back and closed his eyes, his mind a running cloud of provisions and requirements and qualifications. He tried to sift them out in his mind and succeeded only partially. As far as he could tell, he had missed no important notion; had adequately understood.

"*Kloshe kahkwa*," he said finally.

Kilchis looked up at him, but there was no pleasure in the tyee's face. It mirrored the anguish of the man clearly; for his people, for himself, for his land. Trask saw his agreement as a desperate attempt to salvage as much as he could in the face of the inevitable; and wondered if he himself would do as well if such a condition came to him.

Kilchis stood at the fire, and wrapped the robe about his shoulders. "*Kloshe kahkwa*," he echoed, without inflection.

"Tyee," came Charley's low voice, "when shall the people be told of this thing?"

"The men will meet in council when the sun has gone down," Kilchis said. "I will tell them what my words have been."

"Your words have been worthy of the tyee Kilchis," Trask said.

Kilchis shrugged, as if to indicate this was of no importance at all. "We do not have much time," he said softly, almost to himself. In the same tone he added, "There are those who will think me mad."

He shook his head sharply, clearing away the gray thoughts that threatened to swamp him as a stormy sea swamps a canoe. "You will be in this lodge after the sun has gone down. The council will speak with you then."

Kilchis stooped and went out through the skin flap. Outside the lodge he stood straight and silent. Slowly his head turned to take in the great half-circle of the bay. To his ears came the faint familiar sounds of the trees and the water and the people of his village. The lodges stood out against the forest background as though he had never seen them before; fresh growths come up between the flicker of an eye. Slowly he walked down the beach to the farthest tip of the point, jutting like a tiny finger out into the bay. Resting his back against a boulder there, one that had cradled this same broad back a thousand times, the tyee Kilchis looked out across the broad flatness of the bay to the threadlike line of breakers that separated his country from the sea. The thin white line seemed very far away. He watched it for a long time.

In the lodge, Trask stared at the fire and wondered almost resentfully why there was no exultation in him for this victory. Absently he noticed his hands were shaking.

2

In late afternoon the overcast began to break up over the bay. The heavy masses took on an oily look, hard and thick, and the luminous quality of light under the cloud cover vanished and became dull. The wind shifted a few points into the northwest and lessened, bringing a chill. There was a quietness in the air, and the distant thin screaming of sea birds could be heard clearly. Flights of gulls began to wheel over the flat waters of the bay in long floating arcs.

The sun disappeared behind a line of rapidly banking cumulus piled on the horizon, and the sky was a coppery, pale green when it had gone. Darkness slid quickly across the dome of the sky, leaving a brightly haloed moon poised over the mountains.

The Killamooks did not enter the council in a group, but singly or in pairs. Almost casually they drifted to Kilchis' lodge after the evening meal; straggled in and arranged themselves around the fire and on the sleeping-platform. Some few of them glanced curiously at Trask and Charley, seated close by the fire, but no comment was made. Several— interrupted in their after-dinner smoke and conversation—lit pipes, and soon the characteristic odor of the kinnikinnick mixture mingled with the smells of fish and cedar smoke in the lodge. There were more men assembled than at the previous council.

Illga was one of the last to enter. He stopped briefly inside, accustoming his eyes to the glare of the fire; then swept gracefully past without seeming to notice the presence of either Trask or Charley Kehwa.

Trask glanced at Charley; the Clatsop shrugged almost imperceptibly. Absently Trask took out his tobacco pouch and filled his pipe, realizing too late that many eyes fixed on the bulky, curved shape of the Norwegian meerschaum that had resulted in the beating of one of their men. Pretending not to notice this, Trask methodically tamped the tobacco down into the bowl and passed the pouch to Charley. He leaned forward to pick a coal from the fire with the wooden cooking tongs and light the pipe. Without hesitation, Charley passed the tobacco pouch to the man on his left and indicated he was to pass it around. With some satisfaction Trask noted several of the men who had already lit up hastily knocking the kinnikinnick out of the long tubes, to replace it with tobacco.

There were appreciative smiles when the tobacco was lit, and several approving, if covert, glances in Trask's direction. The pouch was virtually empty when it returned to the white man, and Trask thought he had probably never made such a good investment. Illga was among those who took tobacco, but gave no recognition to its source. It came, so far as he was concerned, from the man on his right. He blew a long stream into the air where it wavered fitfully in the drafty space, and watched it intently.

Kilchis did not come until the rest of the men had gathered. He came in silently and took a position standing on the opposite side of the fire from Trask and Charley, who sat with their backs to the entrance. His face and attitude were perfectly neutral, neither relaxed nor tense. He began to speak without preamble, his voice flat and expressionless.

"This council is called here so the Killamook men may hear the words that have passed between Kilchis and the Boston man. Hear, then: When the salmon have come into the bay two more times, this man will come here with his woman, in peace, to live with the Killamooks as brothers in one house."

He went on to outline briefly the agreement reached that afternoon, with emphasis on Trask's agreement to abide by the tribal laws. The men sat silent and impassive, listening attentively, but—as far as Trask could tell—without great concern. He realized there were few among them, perhaps three or four out of forty, who could interest themselves deeply in what happened after the salmon had run two more times; the main reason Kilchis had been forced to take the burden of decision on himself alone. Scanning their faces as the tyee's voice pervaded the lodge, he could detect no reaction other than respectful interest in his words. Several of them, noticeably the older members of the band—

though they were still active hunters—nodded thoughtfully over their pipes as Kilchis touched on the inevitability of the white man's coming.

Trask relaxed slightly and leaned back, turning his eyes with the others to watch Kilchis as he spoke. The tyee's voice was even, ringing through the lodge with the steady authority of the sound of surf heard at a distance. While it continued all eyes were fixed on him intently. He finished with a formal request that the council verify the words he had spoken. He took a seat on the sleeping-platform and leaned slightly back with his hands placed flat on his knees.

There was a low murmur around the fire, the slow nodding of heads as individuals spoke with one another. Fire-cast shadows tilted and leaned toward one another, and swayed with the swaying of the flames.

Trask glanced at Charley, and the Clatsop nodded with satisfaction.

"*Kloshe kahkwa*," Kilchis said finally, when the murmur of conversation had died. "Are there more words to be heard here?"

"Yes. I would speak."

With a chill at the base of his spine Trask recognized the high-pitched voice of Illga even before the slight figure rose in the shadows.

"Illga will be heard," Kilchis said, his voice reflecting no emotion whatever.

Charley scowled. The eyes of all the assembled men followed Illga as he moved gracefully through the circle to stand at the fire's edge. Illga's glance passed over Trask with a singular lack of interest. He smiled faintly; made a delicate, respectful gesture before Kilchis.

"It is in my mind," he said slowly, "that the tyee takes too much upon himself in this. This is not a thing that can be agreed to by one man alone."

"For this reason the council was called," Kilchis said calmly.

Illga inclined his head. "This was put before the council of men as a thing to be approved; not as a thing for them to decide. This is a thing the council should consider carefully."

Kilchis frowned. "Then let it be considered. You do not have to tell us this."

As each man spoke in turn, the eyes of the group shifted to the speaker, where they remained until he had finished. No comment was made, and Trask had the distinct impression of a deliberate suspension of opinion on the part of the hearers until the last word should be spoken. In the flickering half-light, Charley's mouth distinctly formed the English words "Be ready." Trask nodded and turned his attention back to Illga. Around his slim shoulders Illga wore a sea-otter cape, very smooth and rich, the glossy pelts reflecting the glow of the fire in ripples of light. His finely chiseled features were almost apologetic as he said, "Many of us here are accustomed to follow Kilchis' saying without thinking where it may lead us."

"The words of others also," Kilchis commented dryly. "Yahluk could speak more of this, maybe."

Illga bristled visibly, but his voice was controlled. "This may be," he said coldly. "Kilchis is not the only man who can be followed in this band, maybe."

Charley had moved closer to Trask until he could whisper without being overheard. "What's he doing?" Trask said. Charley shook his head, frowning. "I don't know. He is making you a part of his fight with Kilchis."

"Illga pecks at words like a seagull at a clam," Kilchis said placidly. "If he wishes to speak about this thing, let him do so and not go crying about the lodge."

Illga's apologetic and courteous manner had disappeared entirely under Kilchis' baiting, and now his expression was frankly belligerent as he stared at the tyee. The intent scrutiny of the assembled men was no longer a matter of courtesy, but of profound interest in the battle that began to take shape before them. Aside from the intensity of their gaze, there was no other visible response, no immediate taking of sides.

"For too long," Illga said with suppressed anger giving unaccustomed strength to his voice, "Kilchis has deafened the people with his roaring like the bear. Now other voices will be heard, maybe."

Kilchis made an impatient gesture. "Speak then."

Charley leaned closer to Trask, not taking his eyes from the standing figure before them. "He is very confident," he whispered. "Doesn't worry Kilchis much," Trask said doubtfully. "Yes, it does," Charley said.

". . . if this is a necessary thing," Illga was saying. He turned deliberately away from Kilchis to face Trask.

"The reasons for this have been spoken here," Kilchis said. "Better the band receive the whites in peace than war. For they will come."

"Ah." Illga contemplated Trask thoughtfully. "Ah. This may be. I have been many times to Astoria, which Kilchis has not. Maybe I know these things, too."

"Illga has never been quick to share what is in his mind," Kilchis observed.

Illga tapped his teeth lightly with his forefinger, still gazing at Trask, ignoring Kilchis' comment. "Yes," he said thoughtfully. "The whites will come, this is certain." He blinked and nodded, confirming his own opinion. "And as the great bear Kilchis says," he added condescendingly, "better they come in peace than war."

He narrowed his eyes sleepily, pleasantly, seeming to forget his surroundings—almost to drowse slightly as he stood. "But—" he began sweetly, and his eyes snapped open again, glaring with bright hatred at Trask. His mouth twisted in a contemptuous snarl.

"*Such a one as this?*" Illga spat viciously to the side of Trask's feet.

Trask stiffened involuntarily and his hackles rose. Simultaneously he felt Charley's restraining hand on his arm and heard his soft voice say, "Wait."

Deliberately Illga turned away from them, moving slowly, his head swaying in a gesture that somehow conveyed the greatest contempt. He made a low sound in his throat.

"Agh. This one is not fit to lick up the blood in the women's huts." His nostrils wrinkled with distaste, and his lip curved disdainfully.

There was a sharp intake of breath from somewhere in the circle; then silence, deep and profound; filled with tension like the air after a thunderbolt. All eyes were on Trask, waiting for his reaction.

Charley was frowning, aware that Illga was not insulting merely for the sake of insult. His hand pressed firmly on Trask's arm, restraining the white man until he could discern some pattern in Illga's actions. It was Kilchis' voice that finally broke through the oppressive silence; calm, strangely. Placid and amused.

"Illga speaks strong words," he said. "But—as is his custom—little meaning comes from them. This is an offer to fight, maybe?"

"Fight? Fight?" Illga turned round with his hands spread in mock bewilderment. "Fight what? There is no man here for me to wrestle with; no man to hold a knife against me," he started, accenting the word "man" slightly.

"The Boston man would think differently, maybe," Kilchis suggested.

"Ah!" Illga exclaimed with sudden enlightenment. "The Boston man! Then indeed my meaning is not clear to the wise Kilchis!" He turned back to face Trask, and the mask of malevolence crossed his face like a veil. He examined the seated man interestedly.

"Ah, this one," he said thoughtfully. Then his tone hardened. "This one stands in the sun and casts no shadow. This one walks on the sand and leaves no track."

With a sense of grateful relief Trask felt Charley's restraining hand withdrawn. Slowly he stood to face the slight Killamook, standing over him and looking down into his contemptuous face.

"*Sit!*" Kilchis' voice snapped across the fire like a whip. His eyes were furious and the muscles at the base of his jaw worked. When he spoke again his voice was like the controlled growl of the cougar. "You foul this council with hate. Sit! Sit and speak like men. Illga. Make the meaning of your words clear or be quiet. You cry and call names like an old woman. If there is meaning in them, then let it be understood."

Illga looked long into Trask's carefully blank face; turned on his heel and went to the other side of the fire. He sat cross-legged and tented his fingertips before him, staring into the fire. Silently, Trask sat again.

"This, then," Illga said. "I have said this one is no man, and this is true. What is it makes a man, and makes him strong? His spirit helper. This one has no spirit helper, for never has he made the journey alone."

Kilchis frowned. "To go on the Searching is not the white man's way. How can this be expected?"

"Am *I* responsible for their madness? Must *I* suffer for it?" Illga asked. "I say he has no spirit helper and is not worthy to come to this place."

"It is not the white man's way," Kilchis repeated.

"Did not the great and wise Kilchis himself say the white men would live in accordance with the old laws? Does he now deny this?"

"This is the matter of wrongdoing," Kilchis said angrily. "Thievery and lying, with which Illga is familiar."

"Ah," Illga said, ignoring the insult. "Then we have not heard all the agreement between you, maybe. There are other things the people may not know, maybe. Are the young men not to go on the Searching any more? Is this a part of your agreement that you do not see fit to tell the men in council?"

"You speak into the wind."

"I speak true," Illga said stubbornly. "If this one would live with the old laws, let him begin now. Let him prove himself."

Kilchis leaned forward. "This is foolishness. The Boston man is not a Killamook. They have their own ways."

"A man is a man," Illga insisted angrily. "And he is nothing without his spirit helper. Whites are flesh, like us. Blood, like us. Bone, like us."

"This is wild talk," Kilchis said. "I will listen to no more."

"It is in my mind that Kilchis wishes to hide the white man's cowardice. Kilchis, ask the men in council what they would say. If this is council and not trickery, let the men consider who is right."

"Speak then," Kilchis said sharply. "Who has words?"

"There is this thing," one of the older men said slowly. "A man is a man, Illga is right in this. Kilchis is black, but a man. He has gone on the Searching; because of it he has a strong helper that does not care for the color of his skin. There is something in this that Illga says."

"Let me speak, Kilchis," Charley said, standing. Kilchis nodded and Charley turned to Illga.

"I will tell you where the trickery is in this. In the mind of Illga, who hates the Boston man. From the time a boy can walk, he is training to go on the Searching, all the time. This is what his youth is for, that he may prepare the mind and body for the Vision. Is this not so?

"But Illga, this Illga that makes woman-talk but does not fight, he would send the Boston man on the journey alone without preparation, as he would send him to sea without a canoe! Is this fair?

"More: listen!" Charley pointed upward. In the silence that followed, the wind could be heard racing around the ridge; it had risen steadily since dusk.

"It is too early in the year; the weather is turning bad. Illga knows this. I will tell you the truth in this thing: Illga wishes the Boston man to die and is too womanly to say it in open council!"

Illga looked up at Charley with a confident, disdainful smile, "No," he said calmly. "I wish only that the Boston man prove himself indeed a man, as he claims to be. There is cowardice and lying here, but it does not come from Illga."

Low murmurs of conversation were heard around the circle. There were many sharp glances cast at one or all of the four most immediately involved.

Trask looked at Kilchis and saw him frowning at the fire thoughtfully. One of the low conversations burst into a rattle of angry Salish. There was disagreement, and it seemed to be growing.

When he stood, Trask's chief emotion was annoyance at being forced into such a position by Illga. The victory was such a petty one.

"If it is the wish of the men in council," he said quietly, "I will do this thing. I will go on the Searching." It suddenly seemed inevitable to him, as though it had been coming for a long time, and he had not seen it.

Only silence met him, and even Illga looked slightly surprised.

3

Once made, the decision had a strangely comforting effect on Trask; he felt a sense of placidity and satisfaction he could not explain.

Charley Kehwa, oppositely, spent the better part of the next day either in a bitter rage or sunk in some gloomy depth known best to himself. His anger seemed about equally divided between Illga and Trask; the first for being cunning, the second for being a fool. Trask accepted his spasmodic outbursts with a good-natured tolerance strange to him, and even found a certain amusement in Charley's discomfiture.

"You shouldn't get so excited, Charley," he observed pleasantly.

"Excited? Agh!" Charley sat abruptly and stared at Trask like one unable to believe the incredible folly of what he sees. After an impassioned and angry harangue before the council Charley had been granted a postponement of one day; so he could instruct Trask, he said. In actuality he used the time in a vain attempt to persuade the white man out of his decision. Kilchis had accepted both Trask's offer and Charley's plea for time without apparent emotion, but it had been obvious to Trask he was greatly relieved.

"What else could I do?" Trask said reasonably. "Look at the position Kilchis was in. It looked as if he were betraying the tribe."

"This is not a thing you should die for."

"Well," Trask said, "I don't know how it came up about me dying."

Charley jumped up and began to pace around the fire again, clenching and unclenching his fists. "You don't understand," he muttered. "You don't understand."

"Listen, Charley," Trask said. "I should think you'd be pleased. You're the one always talking about me not having a spirit helper. I'd think you'd be glad I'm going to look for one."

"Look for one! Look for one! Do you think Raven will come to you out there? Or Talipas, or Thunderbird? Or *anything*? Except a knife in the dark!"

"Never can tell."

"You are wrong!" Charley snapped. "I tell you this: No spirit helper will come to you. You think you are playing a children's game."

"Charley, I really don't understand you," Trask said ruefully. "Here all the time you talk about how I don't understand the Searching and what it means to you people, and now I get the chance to find out and you're mad about it. I really don't understand you."

Charley let out his breath in a long, ragged sigh, and closed his eyes tightly. He passed his hand over his forehead helplessly. "It would be nice if a baby should kill a bear; then the baby would have done a brave thing. But a baby does *not* kill bear, no matter how badly he may want it, because he does not know how. Any more than you know how to go about receiving a Vision. You are a baby that can barely crawl going out bear-hunting. A nice thing."

"Well, I don't think it's that bad," Trask said, amused.

"It is! It is!" Charley shouted. "What if the baby crawling *finds* a bear? While he is blinking and drooling around the woods, what if he *finds* a bear?"

"Bear eats 'im, I expect."

"Yes! Yes!" Making an effort to control himself Charley continued, "You will not find a Vision. And if you did find one it would eat you up. *You do not understand.* The Vision would eat you up! Bridge, you do not know about the Visions, and about the Power."

"Tell me, then," Trask said.

"Tell you," Charley repeated dumbly. He turned away, walked two paces and whirled back. "Tell you! If I could tell you, would the boys have to spend the years of their youth training? No! One day their father would say, 'You go get a Power, now.' And they would. It is not that easy, it is not a simple thing. If it were so easy it would not mean anything! Don't you see this? If you could just walk out and fast for a few days, there would be no meaning in it! Nothing!"

Trask shrugged. "Well, we'll see."

"You will see nothing but the dead country," Charley said flatly. "Illga knows this, I know this. Maybe Kilchis too, I can't tell. Don't you understand this? Nobody thinks you will get a spirit helper in this way. You do not have the years of discipline. Without that there is no meaning in it. There will be no Vision."

"Maybe I'll fool 'em," Trask said pleasantly. "I think I will."

"Think!" Charley snorted. "There is only one who is thinking in this thing, and that is Illga. He has fooled you all, even Kilchis who is three men to him. The thing the men of the council did not see, what you did not see, what Kilchis did not see, is this: There is no question of you going to receive a spirit helper. You are not an Indian, and pretending for the rest of your life will not make you one. The only question is, shall you live or die?"

"Maybe."

"No maybe. Illga wishes you to die. And you have helped him to arrange this thing in a beautiful way. There is a loosening of the mind with hunger that you do not know, and with the cleansing ritual, and the cold water. There is loneliness. You will begin to wander, maybe in your mind, maybe in the woods. *This* is why the boys are disciplined; so they may control themselves and be strong when their senses begin to lie to them. You do not know how to do this.

"So maybe you will die up there, and will be lost. Or maybe Illga will send some one of his men to be sure. I think that would be the best. Nobody would be surprised if you did not come back, Bridge, not even me."

"You think he'll try that?"

"I think so, yes. There is no other reason for you to go on the Searching than that; to put you far away and alone, so that you may die, one way or another. This comes of you trying to be an Indian."

Trask frowned. "I thought—well . . ."

"I know," Charley said. "You thought you were doing the right thing. You thought you could be closer to us by doing this thing. It is well that you wish it.

"But I will tell you this, Bridge. If you should somehow come out of the mountains and say you have had the Vision, and begin to carve the symbol of your spirit helper; then you may fool some. But I will know you for a lying Boston, and I think Kilchis also will know. The Searching does not begin with the fasting and end with the carving of the symbol; it is something that happens for many, many years. You cannot do this thing as you would take a long walk."

Trask was silent; then spoke in a low voice. "Charley, I never exactly promised you a damn thing, but I will now. I promise you I won't lie about this. To you or anybody. I promise you that."

"Do not do this thing, Bridge. Please."

"I got to do it, Charley."

"Why? Why do you have to?"

Trask shook his head stubbornly. "I don't know, Charley. Something in me, that's all. I just got to."

Charley sighed. "All right, Bridge. I will not ask you again. "

"It's just the way I am, Charley. You know I can't back out now." And as he spoke, Trask realized there was more to his blind stubbornness than that; for even Charley's words had disturbed only the surface of his mind; in his belly he was still content with his decision.

"Watch for Illga," Charley said unhappily. "He will kill you if he can."

"I will," Trask said. "I'll watch."

Charley shivered. "It's getting cold."

"Can I take a blanket?"

"That would be all right, I think," Charley said. "You could do that."

"It's been a long winter," Trask said after a while.

Charley nodded.

So it happened that in the last week of April, 1848, Elbridge Trask of Clatsop Plains walked out into the ragged mountains behind the bay he knew as Murderer's Harbor. He was alone.

Chapter Twenty-one

He carried a blanket, the clothes he wore, and a torch made of tightly rolled shreds of cedar bark. He was to walk into the mountains until the torch gave out; find the nearest stream in which he could bathe; and this would be his place.

Kilchis lighted his torch without ceremony, and all the men he had seen in council gathered in a silent semicircle to watch him go.

They could not watch him far; for just beyond the limits of the village the tall ferns of the plain closed in, and there was no track. Just as he entered the wall, Trask glanced back at the line of men. Kilchis loomed mountainously in the center, and Charley was by his side. He could not see Illga. He raised the torch to them, turned, and entered the ferns.

The ferns were taller than man-height, and Trask could never see more than a few feet ahead of him. They were still wet and his clothing was soaked before he had gone a quarter of a mile. He was closed in a yielding green envelope, and wherever he looked there was only the endless variation of greens; the complex netted tracings of the delicate fern leaves.

He glanced at the torch, and realized he had not the faintest notion of how long it might be expected to burn, whether two hours or two days. Sometimes, by leaping, be could just see over the flat plane of green before him, and keep his course roughly toward the mountains. When he figured he had made nearly half the distance, the torch had shown no signs of diminishing. The flame it gave was small and steady, except when fluttered by the gusts of wind that were coming more and more frequently out of the northwest.

This day had dawned gray and chill; comfortless, and with the scent of storm in the wind. Trask had felt the air about him dubiously, and Charley had seemed to take the weather as a confirmation of some private conviction. "Illga will be pleased," he said resignedly.

"Well, I've lived through storms before," Trask said.

Charley grunted unhappily, but made no comment.

For the first several hours, his progress was surprisingly rapid through the ferns, and he covered more ground than he had expected. Leaping up above their level, he looked back toward the village. He thought he could see faint streamers of smoke from the lodges, but could not be sure. He chuckled slightly at the mental image of himself popping up above the ferns like a porpoise in the sea, peering around, disappearing. In fact he did feel much as if he were immersed in an ocean; a never-ending sea of green, finely worked and reticulated into patterns of no meaning.

The surface of the ocean, a foot above his head, rolled and swished in the wind, but he was sheltered. Only occasionally an icy rivulet came sliding between the stalks to give him a hint of what the wind was doing.

His blanket was rolled around his shoulders. It too was wet from the constant damp caress of the ferns and, feeling it, he frowned. He crouched down and stuck the base of the torch into the soft, loamy soil. He unstrapped the blanket from his shoulders and put it around his waist like a bulky belt, thinking to protect it from the wet by pushing the ferns before him out of the way with his hands. He would need his blanket dry.

This done, he picked up the torch and started again. Gradually the ground began to rise beneath his feet, and he knew he was approaching the brief foothills of the tangled mountains. The stalks of the fern grew slightly heavier and more woody; other kinds of vegetation began to appear, scattered like small islands in the wide sea. Soon the tops of the ferns were barely clearing his head, and ahead of him he could see clearly the purple shadows of clefts and valleys on the mountains' faces. The ground became rockier, though still not difficult. He glanced again at the torch and dubiously estimated it had shrunk by a little. It was going to last longer than he had thought.

Ahead and to his left a bare hillock rose covered with grass; a tiny convex meadow on which no fern grew, though he could not say why. He turned and made his way to it, climbing the slight slope with a pleasant sensation of change that was a relief from the growing monotony of the ferns.

From the top he had a clear view of the surrounding land, including that he had just passed through. For a short distance he could see a faint dark streak, his own trail; but it disappeared quickly and there was no sign over the broad expanse of green that a man had ever passed there. He could not see the village at all, and thought perhaps his earlier glimpse of smoke had been illusion.

Past the long sweep of green to the west was the gray sliver of the bay, and beyond that, fading into invisibility, the ocean. The air was not clear, and he could not see the horizon; even the jumbled shapes of the clouds far out were indistinct.

He stuck the torch in the ground again and turned to face the mountains. They were close now, and in another hour he would have to start climbing. He wondered briefly if it might not be a good idea to slow down slightly. He estimated the time at a little past noon, and at his present rate he would be well into the mountains by nightfall.

He shrugged at the thought. It didn't, after all, make much difference how far in he went. Automatically he reached for his tobacco pouch before he remembered he had none: the spirits didn't like the smell of tobacco any better than any other human smell.

"God damn it," he muttered.

The Absaroka he'd known around Wind River had believed the gods were fond of tobacco smoke, and used it ceremonially. Maybe—if he was going to do this thing at all—he'd have been better off to do it in the Rockies, where at least the Indians would have let him have his tobacco, even if no food.

Habit, he considered ruefully, was a funny thing. He'd had a good breakfast just before he left the Killamook village, but he was already hungry.

Well, I'll be hungrier than this, he thought ironically. Somewhere he'd heard that after three days you didn't even notice it.

He spread out his blanket to see how far the wetness of the ferns had penetrated. The dark patches lay across it like stripes, but it was not too wet to dry quickly if he got a little sun. He glanced at the sky and decided the chances of that were slim, at least for today. He rolled the blanket up again and tied it around his waist. He stood and yawned widely, squinted up at the mountains before him. Timber started a mile away, but not heavily. Slightly to his right was a dark streak that appeared to be a small ravine leading up into the heavier growth and he decided to take it. He picked up the torch and swung down off the rise into the sea of ferns.

Two hours later he stood at the base of the mountains and peered up into the timber. He was in the open, on rocky ground, and the wind at the back of his neck was gusty and cold. He looked back toward the ocean, and the sky above it was oily and dark. There was no source of light—not even a lighter spot in the clouds—to show the sun's position. It seemed to him the temperature had dropped five degrees in as many minutes. He surveyed the black sky behind him for a long moment; then sniffed angrily.

He looked at the torch and decided it was probably going to last all night. Cursing silently, he moved into the forest.

He was not supposed to stop until the torch gave out, but he was damned if he could see how he was going to plow through the woods in the middle of the night, with nothing but this inadequate bundle of bark to light his way. The hell with it.

Under the trees it was quiet, except for the shaking and swishing of the limbs overhead. The grove he had entered was spruce, and the air had a gloomy, blue cast. It occurred to him he had not seen an animal of any size since he left the village. Scared off, either by the coming storm or himself, he thought. Not that it mattered.

The undergrowth in the forest was not heavy here, and he plodded along in a kind of dull detachment from his surroundings, holding the torch upright mechanically. He kept on a general upward slope, and had a notion he might make camp at the top of the first good ridge he came to, or perhaps on the lee side. He would have to have shelter from the winds and rain he knew were coming. He thought bitterly the weather couldn't have worked out any worse if Illga had put in a special order for it. Which he probably had, Trask reflected.

He was well into the woods when the first wave of cold rain hit, and well sheltered under the trees. As he climbed the slope the spruce had been replaced by taller firs, and the sheets of rain lashed themselves away a hundred feet above his head. The initial effect of the storm was only a sudden, unpleasant heightening of noise.

A few minutes after the rain started, he came suddenly to a broad, rocky slope that reached up the side of the mountain for several hundred yards, ending in a steep cliff. On the rim of the cliff were several trees fallen, and overhanging at odd angles, the roots of one standing upright and distinct. Beyond the edge was forest again, and Trask realized there had been a slide here in some past time. Boulders and stones of various sizes studded the talus, as if it were an oversized gravel pit, and a number had rolled down the slope into the woods. A few dead branches stuck up here and there out of the rock, showing where the trees had been bowled over and buried by the slide.

Coming out into the clear, he was suddenly aware of the sharp force of the rain slapping at the back of his neck. Hurriedly he backed into the shelter of the firs and surveyed the talus slope.

Rain rattled on the rocks like duck-shot; large drops that splatted venomously on the stone and blackened it quickly. Even as he watched, a gust of wind blew a gray sheet across the surface of the slope; the sheltered overhang of a nearby boulder was drenched and the raking grayness dimmed his vision of the cliff edge. From the tops of boulders bright rivulets ran down to collect in pools or disappear in the gravel beneath.

Involuntarily, Trask shivered, from either the coldness of the rain or the prospect of it.

There was little point in crossing the rock-strewn slope, even if the walking might be a little easier; he would only have to scale the cliff on the high side.

He stuck the torch in the ground, well back in the shelter of the trees, and unbelted his blanket. Leaving them where they would stay dry as long as possible, he went back to the edge of the woods and peered out to the sides. On his left, he lost sight of the slide over a ridge; to his right he thought he could see the end of it, perhaps a quarter of a mile away. So it seemed, at any rate, but he could not be sure. The wind whipped sheets of rain spasmodically across his vision like sudden veils pulled between him and the outside world. The outlines of the forest that far away were no more than a dark smudge against the gray of rain and rock. He went back to the torch and tied his blanket on again, wondering if it were worth the trouble to keep it dry. Already it seemed soaked, but he didn't want to pause and unroll it again. He moved off to his right, keeping roughly parallel to the edge of the slide, near enough to it so he could catch frequent glimpses of the rocky slope between tree trunks.

Ten minutes later he came to the southern edge of the tumbled rock. The cliff on the high side dwindled and merged back into the face of the mountain, and the edge of the slide coincided with its final disappearance. The rock ended abruptly, almost in a straight line running down toward him.

He glanced at the torch; it still flickered with a cheerful indifference to the passage of time and weather. Scowling, he struck off upwards again, skirting the edge of the slide-plain.

The rain stopped as suddenly as it had begun, but the day did not clear. It remained bleak and dark, and Trask could take no comfort from the stopping of the rain. The upper branches of the trees had been thoroughly soaked in the flashing shower, and now the woods were filled with the steady drip of water from above. There was no place he could sit down without a trickle of water somewhere on him, so he kept moving.

He passed upward with the slide on his left and a steep rise a half-mile to his right. There, steeper by half than the slope he climbed, the ground slanted sharply up to the first of the small peaks on the ocean side of the range. Even that low peak was capped in cloud, and he could not see the tops of any of the peaks around him. The cloud ceiling was flat and undifferentiated, a smooth, oily layer that flowed like a river above him, moving inland. The air immediately around him seemed clear enough, but his visibility extended no more than a half-mile in any direction, and considerably less than that ahead, where the ground rose into clouds.

He steered away from the rising ground on his right, hoping to penetrate the wall of mountains by the small valley he had seen from his grassy hill; and he was fairly certain he was in it now.

He could hear the gurgle of a stream somewhere ahead, and made for the sound, hoping to follow the banks farther inland. When he reached it, he found the growth at its sides heavier than that he was going through, and regretfully abandoned the notion. He stooped beside the little brook and scooped up some of the cold, clear water in his hands.

Won't die for lack of something to drink, he thought wryly.

He sat back on his heels, deliberately disregarding an obstinate patter of droplets from the fir boughs overhead.

It was a pleasant little stream, he thought absently. Not more than four feet across, it tumbled and spilled over a rocky bottom in a cheerful way, gurgling and spitting over the rocks, churning bubbles and white water to the surface. If it were a little bigger there might be trout in it.

He grimaced, remembering it didn't make any difference whether there were trout in it or not; they would do him no good. He was conscious of the hunger pangs in his belly, and did his best to ignore them. He suspected they would have gone unnoticed under normal circumstances; but the knowledge that no food was to be forthcoming made him abnormally aware of the stirrings inside him.

Hell with it, he thought angrily. Anything an Indian could do, he could do. Worst part was, there wasn't any time limit. You either stayed until the Vision came, or until you couldn't take it any more.

Above him a fir bough bent, and a stream of water splattered against his shoulder. He jerked; then shifted position slightly.

He had not, he realized, given much thought to how he would end it; there was trouble enough beginning it. Charley Kehwa had filled him with cautions up to the time he had left; mostly cautions against Illga.

"Watch out for him," Charley had repeated time and again.

"I *know* that," Trask snapped finally. "You just tell me what I'm supposed to do on this trip and I'll take care of Illga."

"You're too confident," Charley insisted. "You can't afford to be overconfident."

"I can't afford to be afraid, for God's sakes!"

Charley shook his head. "You know what I'm talking about. You've got to be careful."

"All right, Charley, all right. Now, what am I supposed to do?"

"Walk into the mountains until your torch gives out. Then you find a stream. Scrub yourself down morning and night and compose your mind." He shrugged. "This is all I can say that you would understand."

"Can I have a fire?"

Charley frowned dubiously. "I don't know—it is different when a boy goes out . . ."

"Why the hell different? I'm *doing* it, that's all."

"You're going the wrong time of year. The boys don't have a fire, but it is warmer when they go. You would freeze without one if the storm comes."

Well, the storm had come all right, Trask thought, so he'd have to have a fire. At least the torch would give him that; one item of good in it. Thinking, he glanced at it, and the yellow flame still flickered around the top. He wondered how it managed to burn so long, and decided it was probably the tightness of the bound bundle of bark.

Sighing, he stood and looked up. Through the break in the foliage above the little stream, he could see there had been no change in the sky; still dirty gray and threatening. The rain spattering him before had been only the forerunner of the storm. By his estimate the main force should hit the mainland shortly after dark, and it would be well if he were in a sheltered place, at least on the lee side of the first ridge.

He resolved to keep moving until he was certain the main force was on him; then, whether the torch still burned or not, he would stop and take shelter for the night. He could not imagine even the hardiest Killamook trying to make his way up the side of the mountain in the middle of one of the coast storms, torch or no. There was, he thought almost petulantly, a limit to what could be expected.

He was slightly angry, for beneath his easy reasoning he thought he detected the sour smell of self-justification; arguing away his own reluctance, making his unwillingness neat and honorable. There was a suspicion lingering at the edges of his mind that one of the Indian boys would probably be quite willing to do just that, if it seemed necessary.

"Well, the hell with them," he said aloud.

He grabbed up the torch and set off. He had to go slightly south of the stream—which at that point ran nearly east-west—before the undergrowth was thin enough to push his way through. It would have been so much simpler if he had been allowed a bush knife. But no. Everything had to be just as difficult as they could possibly make it.

Suddenly he stopped, in mid-stride. He recognized his own irritability as a sure and certain sign of hunger. It was always the first sign; touchiness, irritation at small things, the feeling of being put upon in petty ways. It brought him up short for a moment, hearing Charley's cautioning words in his mind: "Now listen, Bridge, you will be thinking all strange things when the hunger begins. It is necessary to know them for hunger-thoughts, what is called *olo latate*, the hungry-head. These you must control, you must always control . . ."

He had agreed offhandedly at the time, thinking Charley referred to delusion or delirium or some such thing. Now it occurred to him the changes of mental state that might be important were just such minor things as this abnormal irritability. Not so dramatic as visions and fevers, maybe. But important. An attitude of carelessness, or annoyance, clouded your judgment, and that was not a good thing in the woods.

He nodded slowly to himself and started off again. There was more to this hunger business than met the eye, he thought. He was acutely aware of the hazards of sloppy thinking in wild country. It could kill you faster than anything else. He realized he was going to have to keep a close watch on himself, as well as on the forest around him. Suddenly the ritual disciplines of the young boys made more sense. There might well be something to it, he admitted reluctantly. He had a notion he was going to learn a good deal on this trip.

He topped a small ridge an hour later and stood looking down a sparsely wooded slope into a miniature ravine that stretched parallel to the coast, and across his route inland. The opposite slope reached several hundreds of feet higher than his present vantage point and looked strangely naked and spiky. Years ago a fire had raced down that side, leaving gray spikes where trees had been; slim and silvery fingers that pierced the sky. In the ravine was a stream no bigger than the one he had left, and possibly the same one on a different course. It ran the full length of the tiny valley as far as he could see to either side, bordered by short, heavy growth of salal and the fire-killed trees.

The fire had burned down the ravine, but unaccountably not climbed the seaward side where Trask stood. In the dull gray light beneath the clouds, the gray snags stood clear and distinct against the dark, almost black brush.

Trask glanced upward, and thought the sky was darkening more quickly than the storm would account for. It was quite possible that he had miscalculated the amount of daylight remaining to him.

He hurried down into the ravine and crossed the stream without pausing, anxious to get beyond the burned strip before night caught him. These lightning flash-fires frequently ran along a ridge and then petered out, cutting a narrow swath that might stretch a long distance but was not wide. If he could get across the opposite ridge and into the timber on the other side, he would have more shelter.

At the top of that ridge he stopped. He could see one more top, and that too was spiked with the weathered snags. Beyond it the next slope rose into the low clouds; but the slope itself was the same. As far as he could see to the north and south, the burned gray fingers jutted sharply out of the ground like broken bones.

He turned to go back and the first rain hit. Seconds later it was coming in lashing sharp sheets that drove stingingly against his face, and the visibility had dropped to a flat zero. The rain came like whiplashes, driven out of the low clouds with a startling viciousness. It drummed and whacked against the waxy leaves of the salal with such force it seemed certain to tear them from their stems. The undergrowth shuddered in gusts as the wind lashed across it, and Trask had to squint to see at all.

There was suddenly no question of going back to the live timber two ridges behind; he had to find the nearest shelter he could. He turned inland and scrambled down the slope, hoping the force of the wind would be less on the lee side.

It did abate slightly, but as the front of the storm passed over it ceased to have any definite direction at all; spasmodic bursts whipped at him from all sides, and each gust carried a heavy, chilling freight of cold rain. There was no predicting what direction it would come from next.

Almost halfway down the slope there was a slight overhanging ledge. He came up on it without seeing it for the stinging rain in his face, and stopped just in time to avoid going over the edge. Hurriedly he skirted to one side of it; came back beneath and found some shelter from the main winds. The erratic whipping still brought occasional gusts under the overhang, but at least he was sheltered on the northwest side. He pressed himself back against the dirt wall and drew his feet up to get as much of his body beneath the ledge as possible. The sheltered space was a gash in the slope, a little over three feet deep and possibly fifteen long. It was not high enough to stand up under.

A few inches ahead of his feet was a solid sheet of water, almost as though he were in a cave behind a waterfall. He shook his head and droplets of rain flew out of his hair and beard. With the edge of his shirt he wiped the rivulets off his face. After a moment, he gingerly untied the rolled blanket from around his waist. It was soggy to the touch, and heavy. He grimaced at it, then shrugged. There was nothing he could do about it at this stage, and probably nothing he could have done before.

Coming down the ridge he had sheltered the cedar-bark torch with his body as well as he could, and the yellow flame danced and flickered at its top. Trask examined it ruefully, and shook his head. The torch had managed better than he in the suddenness of the storm.

There was no indication from the shrill whistling of the wind and the lashing patter of rain that the storm would stop any time soon, and Trask put the rolled blanket on the ground with the side that had been next to his body up. It seemed to be slightly less wet than the other, though the difference, he thought, was slight. He pillowed his head on it and lay full length under the ledge with his hands folded on his chest.

Above him was the uninteresting bottom side of the ledge, so he closed his eyes and listened to the rain. Closing his eyes was pleasant, for he could feel the beginnings of a headache lurking behind them.

More hunger, he thought absently. And he hadn't even finished the first day.

Out of the tail of his eye he could see the fluttering yellow feather of the planted torch near his feet.

Chapter Twenty-two

He dozed fitfully for perhaps an hour, and wakened to find the sky darkening rapidly. The cascade of water still poured and dripped off the front of the ledge, drawing a silvery-gray curtain between him and the tiny valley outside. The gusty wind had gone down slightly, and the rain splattered on the wet earth with a constant and steady rattle like the sound of gravel on a rocky beach. At his feet the torch still flickered, and much of its length was unburned.

He woke to find himself shivering uncontrollably, a spasmodic shaking that jerked his breath. Sleepily he unrolled the blanket—awkward under the ledge—and stretched it out flat. It was little dryer than the dirt, but would at least keep some of the seeping cold from him when his body had warmed the wetness. Gingerly he stretched out on it, stiffening involuntarily at the clammy coldness. When the blanket had warmed slightly he wrapped his arms around himself. He could not seem to stop shaking, and his fingers were numb. He tucked them under his arms and drew his knees up, presenting as little surface to the cold as possible. With a last sleepy glance to be certain the torch was lasting, he closed his eyes again and tried to sleep.

At first, each time he was growing drowsy he would begin to shake, and the shaking would waken him. Finally simple fatigue overcame his shivering, and in spite of it he drifted off into a light, uncomfortable sleep, full of flitting dreams and images and the present consciousness of cold and wetness. He still shivered erratically, and was aware of it in a dim way, feeling enveloped in a dismal gray fog.

With this, he eventually became aware of a pressure, and a greater cold on his feet. He dreamed his feet were being crushed between two heavy blocks of ice. He shifted uncomfortably, and found it difficult to move his feet, as though they were lashed together with icy ropes.

He wakened slightly; opened his eyes. He blinked, but the darkness did not go away. In his ears was the same steady background of rain, but he could not see anything. For a moment, he could not grasp the meaning of this sudden blindness. His eyes—felt open—but . . .

With a thick panic in his throat he sat upright, and ran his hand down his leg. The feeling of constriction and pressure was still on his feet, and instead of cloth his fingers found cold, sodden dirt. He jerked his feet violently, bumping the back of his head against the wall of his tiny cave. His feet came free, and he scrambled onto his hands and knees, feeling in the blackness where his feet had been pinned. The end of his blanket disappeared under a pile of the clammy dirt, already half mud.

Feeling above him, he found the place where the far end of the ledge had crumbled and fallen, washed down by the relentless flow of water over the edge. His head was still sheltered, but where his feet had been the patter of rain on the back of his hands told him it was open to the sky. It had been the fall of part of the ledge that had buried his feet.

And, he realized suddenly, now fully awake—put out the torch.

Frantically he began to scrape the dirt away, throwing it behind him like a burrowing dog. His groping fingers touched the bark of the torch and he pulled it out. Hastily he pulled it back under the remaining shelter and tried to brush off the mud with his stiff fingers.

It was still smoldering, a few red sparks glowed on shreds of bark. He blew gently on them and they brightened, eating orange paths down their strands of cedar. While he blew they remained bright, but dimmed to a dull coal-red as soon as he stopped. Even as he watched, the precious sparks burned down to mud-soaked spots and faded slowly away.

With the fading of the last hope of fire, the black cold seemed to grow bolder, more penetrating, and he shivered again, gasping raggedly.

"Oh, God," he whispered.

He set the sodden bundle of bark down gently, as though it might break, and sat back on his haunches, staring into the darkness where he had last seen the faint red glow turn to blackness indistinguishable from the rest of the cold night. A few inches from his shoulder was the unchanged sound of the cataract pouring over the remaining portion of the ledge, spattering to the ground and running in rivulets down the hill and into the valley.

He looked out into total blackness. There was not even the faint reflection of the moon on rain; he might as well have had his eyes closed.

Numbly he drew the bottom end of his blanket out from under the muddy pile and brushed it off as well as he could. Then he curled up on it again, still shivering, to wait for daylight.

When he woke the headache that had been threatening was full on him; a dull, throbbing pain behind his eyes. The hunger pangs in his belly were sharper now, imperiously demanding attention, and he reflected it had been less than twenty-four hours since he had eaten. His nose was clogged, making him breathe through his open mouth, and his whole head felt swollen and heavy, aside from the headache. His mouth and throat were dry from breathing, and his eyes burned.

Fine, he thought. Take cold the first night out. He shook his head, but stopped quickly as a new shaft of pain shot behind his eyes. He grimaced, thinking how pleased Illga would be to see him—without fire, without dry clothes, with inadequate shelter, and taking cold to boot.

He grunted, and looked out over the small valley. The rain was still falling, and the coming of light had not noticeably reduced the cold of the air. It seemed to him the rain was lighter, and he debated waiting until it stopped completely before leaving the scanty comfort of the ledge. But, he thought, there was probably a good chance the steady drizzle would last for days, and he couldn't get much wetter than he was.

His first necessity was fire; and he did not look forward to it. He had, once or twice, gone through the ordeal of making fire from scratch, while trapping. It was not an achievement of which he was particularly proud, for only the damnedest sort of fool would let himself get into a position without adequate provision for fire-making. To make a friction fire was in itself a kind of admission of sheer, unforgivable stupidity.

Well, there was nothing for it; he would have to do it.

He ducked under his miniature waterfall and stood outside the cave. He examined the top of the ledge and found to his satisfaction that what remained seemed to be rock, rather than dirt, and in little danger of washing away under the continuous rain. There was still enough left that he could stretch out under it.

He stumbled down the slope to the bottom of the little gully and found the expected stream. He scrabbled with numb fingers in the rocky bed, picking out a rock the size of two fists, and roughly pointed on one end. Halfway back up the slope to his ledge was a fallen snag, and he crouched in the lee of it. He started the tedious task of picking his way into the sheltered underside with the pointed end of the stone.

Fifteen minutes later he had splintered and hacked away a strip six inches wide and a foot long in the wet, pulpy wood, and he thought the splinters were beginning to be slightly lighter in color. His head resounded with every blow of the dull stone, and he tried scraping for a while, but made so little headway into the log he had to abandon it and go back to pounding.

The exercise warmed him a little, and at least he stopped the uncontrollable shivering that had shaken his body through the night. His hands were still numb and slipped on the stone, and each time he hit, the ends of his fingers throbbed painfully.

It was another thirty minutes before he was reaching wood that seemed dry enough, and then he had to estimate from the color because he could no longer tell by touch. Water was running in streams from his matted hair, down into his beard and under the collar of his homespun shirt. The beard gave some protection in front, at least broke up the steady rivulets that streamed off his face, but in back the streams ran unhindered down his skin.

He began to pry off splinters from the inside of the log, working the point of the stone under the grain and levering it up until a shard broke off. These he gingerly stuck upright beneath the log, trying to keep them dry until he could carry them back under the ledge. When he had a load, he humped over the rows of upright splinters and carefully tucked them in his shirt next to the skin. He carried them back under the ledge and stacked them in the farthest corner; then returned to the log for more.

Four trips he made in this way before he was satisfied there was enough to keep the fire going while he hunted more. His shoulder already ached from the incessant hacking at the log, but he could not afford to think about it. He knew perfectly well both arms would be aching and sore by the time he had finished. With some surprise, he noticed that the skin at the base of his right palm was abraded and raw from the stone. His hands were numb enough that he had not been aware it was badly scraped; feeling only the dull, throbbing pain of the blows.

He paused to rest briefly under the ledge and think—no matter how hard he tried to turn his mind away from it—how much easier it would all be with a couple of locofoco matches, or his gun, with its flint striker, or a fire-steel. Or even an Indian fire-shell, like those taken from camp to camp while moving; a clamshell filled with smoldering punk, and a tiny hole drilled at the lip for the smoke to escape. You could carry fire a full day in a fire-shell with no trouble, and a little of the punk could be fanned into flame in no time.

Well, he *didn't* have matches or a steel or a fire-shell. So he had to do the best he could.

His throat was irritated from breathing through his open mouth, and he coughed, sending a lance of pain through his head. He felt the chill begin to crawl on him again. He pushed himself out from under the ledge and back down to the bank of the stream. The rain was almost freezing now and his clothes felt like a mantle of icy slush.

There were no flaking stones in this country, no stone that would conveniently chip away to form the semblance of a blade, so he would have to content himself with a scraper of sorts for cutting. He broke a round rock the size of his fist by the simple expedient of pounding on it with a larger rock. It broke almost straight across, and the edges of the break would have to serve.

Irregularly spaced in the underbrush were young, green trees; the forest's reseeding after the fire. They were small, the tallest of them no more than six feet, and the average something less than that; perhaps four. With the pointed rock, which he now thought of as "the ax," he pounded off several of the tougher limbs for making fire-bows. Without really springy, resilient wood, he knew he was going to need more than one. But he was not in a position to choose his materials.

He started to cough, and the pain in his head made him hold his stomach muscles tight. The spasm kept on, the cough finally turning into something that was almost retching, and shaking his body. He had to squat on his heels until it had passed; then returned to pounding off the limbs.

He tested one, bending the ends like a bow, and found it had some spring, but not much. He shrugged. They would have to do. He took the bow sticks back to his ledge and, using a flat stone as an anvil, smashed them off to a length of about eighteen inches with the "ax" and cleaned off the small twigs.

For string, he stripped off the fibrous outer bark of a salal stalk, sawing tediously with the edge of his scraping stone. The bark sheet he then placed on the anvil-stone and scored and rescored it with the point of the "ax" until he had long strips. These were tediously braided together for the bowstrings. He made several of them, strung each bow, and set aside spares.

The work of twisting the makeshift strings was not active, and when he had finished he was shaking again from wet and cold. He went outside the ledge and ran in position, beating his hands against his shoulders to warm them. The jogging in place started him coughing again, with the consequent racking ache in his head, but it was better than freezing.

Back under the ledge he picked out his splinters with care—and suddenly remembered he had nothing hard to use for a firestick. He peered blearily out at the landscape, hoping against hope for a nice hardwood nearby, and knowing he would not find one. He saw nothing from where he was, and had to go out into the drizzle again. A quarter of a mile away down the valley, he thought he saw a blow-down of birch.

Tediously he plodded down, along the side of the slope. He found his balance was going bad already, and he wavered, holding sometimes to the young firs he passed. He had to stop and rest once, but the cold came through to him so strongly that he had to stand again almost immediately.

He dropped the "ax" twice, and had to scramble down the slope after it. He could not feel his fingers enough to know how tightly he was holding the stone, and eventually had to grip it with unnecessary tightness in order to keep hold of it at all.

Returning to the ledge with his birch splinters, he selected the widest of the fir for a board, and the thickest for holding piece. He dug away at the wide piece with the point of the "ax" until he had a slight depression. He carefully saved the tiny grains of wood produced by the rubbing of the stone, and made a little pile of them near the depression. The fire-board was almost a foot long, and under two inches in width. He took one of the birch splinters and patiently scraped it into a roughly

rounded shape. With some satisfaction he noted that the shavings—
really closer in size to sawdust—were curling away cleanly. This, at
least, was reasonably dry.

It was now almost four hours since he had started collecting the
materials, and he had enough to keep the fire going for possibly twenty
minutes. If he got it started at all.

He was cold again when he finished shaving the firestick. His fingers
fumbled and were without sensation as he pushed the shavings into
the pile with those from the depression he had gouged. He clamped
his fingers under his armpits and rocked back and forth slowly; trying
to warm up without starting the coughing again. When a little feeling
returned, he ground out a hole in the holding piece to receive the butt
of the firestick, and put the grindings from it with the others.

He split and pounded more of the splinters into matchstick size,
and placed them in a neat pile on the end of the little board. Now he
was ready.

He looped the thin, round stick of birch through the bowstring and
put the small end point down in the depression of the wide board. He
capped the butt end of the stick with the holding piece, which he held
in his left hand. In his right was the bow, and he began a steady sawing
motion with it, making the stick twirl in its loop of salal fiber.

Immediately the butt popped out of the holding piece. He stopped
and patiently dug the hole a little deeper, twisting the point of the "ax"
around and around. When he was satisfied the stick would remain in
the holding piece as it twirled, he took up the bow again, and flexed it
gently. Even the momentary twirling of the stick had left the bowstring
a little slack, and the bow was not springy enough to take it up.

He sighed, and it started him coughing again. His belly hurt now,
from holding the muscles tight when he coughed, and also from the
hunger that was beginning to gnaw importunately at him.

When the coughing fit had passed, he wiped the tears from his eyes
with the back of his hand and tried to think how to stiffen the bow.
At last, unable to think of anything better, he took one of his precious
splinters and pounded a V-shaped nick in each end. These he wedged
against the ends of the green stick on the inside of the curve, pushing
them as far toward the back as he dared go without breaking the splinter.

The splinter would tend to wedge the ends of the bow apart, keeping the string taut. It seemed to work all right.

He twisted the stick again in the bowstring, fumbling a little because of the numbness in his fingers. Into the depression he pushed a little pile of the kindling-shavings, about half of what he had collected in the various cutting and shaving operations connected with making the firebow.

He began to saw back and forth again steadily. This time the stick remained in place and twirled nicely as the looped string spun it. He kept on sawing with a mechanical, even rhythm, keeping a steady light pressure downward on the stick with the holding piece. Too much pressure and the stick was held immobile; too little and not enough friction would be generated.

He had sawed for what seemed a long time when the string broke.

He looked at it blearily and started coughing again. The ends were frayed from twirling the stick, so he knew the salal-bark strings were not going to do the job. He picked up the firestick from where it had flipped when the string broke; felt the tip of it. His fingers were numb again and he warmed his right hand by rubbing it violently on his pants leg. The tip of the firestick was not even warmed.

Patiently he untied the salal strings from all the bows and threw them out in the rain. Then he sat back against the dirt wall and wondered what he was going to use for strings. There was a buckskin lace on his shirt, but it was soaked.

Resignedly he tried it anyway, but it stretched uselessly after a few strokes of the bow, and even if it had remained fairly taut he knew the wet leather would tear from the friction as rapidly as the salal strings.

If I had a fire I could dry 'em, he thought foolishly.

The thought amused him for some reason and he started to laugh. The laugh turned into a cough and he doubled over, hacking. The only thing he could think of was his shirt. He went out to get the flat stone and bring it under the ledge, because the rain had increased again, or so it seemed. When he stood straight outside, he had to hold to the edge of the rock for a moment; rising quickly had made him dizzy. He swallowed, his mouth feeling thick, and went to get the stone.

He brought it back in the shelter, settled it on the blanket and put his shirttail on it. He began to scrape back and forth just above the hem, sawing with the edge of his scraping stone. When he had made a rip in it, he tried to tear it the rest of the way, but the homespun resisted his efforts.

Well, all the better, he thought. Last longer on the bow.

He felt quite cheerful, except for the headache and the packed-full feeling that made his eyes feel as if they were bulging out. Patiently he sawed away at the strip of cloth until he had the hem nearly detached for eighteen inches of its length. As he leaned back to survey it with satisfaction, his eyes caught sight of the blanket on which the stone lay.

Why didn't I use the blanket? he wondered. There was no need to chop up his own clothes, he could have used the edge of the blanket as well. It didn't matter, just the hem of his shirt, but it bothered him that he should have overlooked the blanket completely. He wasn't thinking clearly.

For a moment he couldn't decide whether to abandon the shirt and start on the blanket, or continue with the shirt. Then he realized he would waste all his work so far if he were to go to the blanket.

What the hell's the matter with you? he thought angrily.

He stooped suddenly over the shirt and sawed viciously at it with his stone. Soon he had a long strip, which he twisted into a cord. He had to split the ends for tying to the bow, and this he did with a sense of urgency.

He was suddenly aware of the passage of time; nearly an hour—perhaps even more, he couldn't tell—had been spent fooling with various strings. He was going to have to straighten up and get this thing done if he was going to have any fire at all. He thought it must be past noon already, but he wasn't certain. He couldn't tell from the sun, and he had suddenly lost confidence in his own time sense.

Take it easy, he thought. Easy, easy.

He forced himself to calm down, move methodically in spite of the shivering that shook him from time to time. It seemed to him he was shivering more than the cold would warrant, but in that again, he could not be certain. He was not pleased with the erratic suddenness of his emotions: a surge of anger that quickly passed; the abrupt panic over the passage of time—it wasn't good. He couldn't let himself be carried away by his own emotions. He had outside problems to think about.

He warmed his fingers in his armpits again, rocking back and forth and thinking, Take it easy. Take it easy. Take it easy.

He looped the firestick carefully in the new string and began to saw again. This time the string held, and he was pleased. The stick twirled under the holding piece, and he fell into a steady back-and-forth rhythm that made him lose track of time. Gradually the tension on the string loosened; it grew slack as the green bow bent and refused to spring back enough to keep the string taut. He watched it closely, and found he could make it last longer by pulling the bow slightly out and away from the stick. The string then formed a straight line no longer, but a constantly changing obtuse angle with the loop and stick at its apex. Twice he paused momentarily to push the wedging splinter farther toward the back of the bow, but finally no combination of wedging and position would keep the string taut enough to twirl the stick.

He tried to judge carefully; get the last possible use out of the bow before he discarded it; but at last the loop was so slack it simply slid around the stick without twirling it.

Carefully he fought down the impulse to rush, and untied the string from the bow tips. He threw the old bow out into the gray drizzle, mounted the string on a new bow, and started again. As far as he could tell he had made no mistakes through haste, and had managed the change in faster time than if he had hurried.

That's more like it, he thought. Just take it easy.

He had even remembered to remove the wedging-splinter before he threw the old bow away, though it did not fit the second one as well, being a little short. The tip of the firestick was definitely warm now, and he was well satisfied with his progress.

After what seemed a timeless eternity filled with the incessant back-and-forth stroke of the bow, a faint wisp of white smoke appeared at the base of the stick. He speeded up the stroke, careful not to go so fast he could not maintain it, and crouched close over the depression in the wide splinter. Some of the tiny shavings were blackened and smoking.

His shoulder was aching, but he forced himself to keep up the rhythm, and began to blow gently at the base of the stick. The little wisp of smoke, at first so small it was almost invisible, slowly thickened, making a tiny pool around the whirling stick, with faint streamers that rose and blew away.

A vagrant gust of wind flicked a streamer of smoke into his face and set off another spasm of coughing, which he stifled as rapidly as he could, without pausing in the sawing motion of the bow. This was the critical point, and the job was far from finished. If the tinder shavings caught now, it was fine, but it was also possible simply to char them at this stage, so they would not catch at all. Then he would have to begin all over again, with only the warmth of the board and stick to show for it. So he breathed gently on the smoke, coaxing it into life, praying for the faint glint of red that would mean a spark had finally been created.

Finally he saw it, a miniscule glow buried in the trough of smoke, barely visible through the white. He paused long enough to push more of the shavings—gently, carefully—near the tiny glow. It seemed to take life from his breath, and after a little while he could see it definitely grow brighter when be breathed on it. Gradually it grew larger as adjacent shavings began to smolder from it, and what had begun as a mere pinprick grew to match-head size. Gingerly he withdrew the firestick and fumbled blindly for the smallest of the shredded splinters he had smashed, without taking his eyes or his gentle breath away from the magical red glow. If he lost it now, he would have to make new shavings for tinder, and it suddenly seemed to him he would not be able to repeat a single step of the operation again.

Take it easy, he thought desperately. You got it. Just take it easy and don't spoil it.

Still, his hand was shaking as he pushed the slivers near the glow. He placed several of them, working as meticulously as a surgeon, fanning them out from the glow in a little wheel, and gradually working the sharp tips directly into it. So rapt was his vision of the slivers he would almost have sworn he could see the almost invisible fuzz curl away from the heat of the coal. His eyes burned from the fixation and the muscles of his neck felt locked in position.

The tip of the smallest began to darken; smoke; glow. He moved the next one nearer, and it, too, began to glow. Finally, after a long series of delicate maneuvers with the slivers, more delicate breathing on the red glow, the red turned orange, flickered, and suddenly—there was a wink of yellow, a tiny flame.

It disappeared almost immediately, but he coaxed it back again with a tight throat, and nursed it with more slivers and more gentle breathing until finally in the center of the board stood a wavering, feeble feather of a flame the size of his fingernail. He leaned back, almost unable to believe it had finally happened. The flame fluttered; then grew as if testing its new life and strength.

He reached for more of his wood, bigger this time, without ever taking his eyes away from the flame.

It was the most beautiful thing he had ever seen.

Chapter Twenty-three

He pegged his blanket out flat against the wall to dry, and for a while simply sat warming himself and savoring the sensation of heat; turning his hands back and forth in a kind of drowsy reverie, his eyes half closed. What he would have liked best was to sleep for a couple of hours in front of the fire, but he realized he could not trust his own judgment, and had best do what needed doing before he lay down.

Regretfully he left the warmth under the ledge, and returned to pick at the deadfall with his "ax." He took several armloads back, and was now able to take wood something less than bone-dry. When he had dug far enough into the log he was able to use wedges of flat stone and pound off slabs, which he then broke either by simple smashing with the point of the "ax," or by jumping on them. In a couple of hours the end of the sheltered space was stacked adequately, and he felt free to sit again and warm himself luxuriously.

From the beginning he was obliged to fight down an impulse to make the fire larger than was practical; everything urged him to put more wood on, make it bigger, bigger; more flame, more heat. But experience had taught him that he would be no warmer with a large fire than with a small one, except for the dubious warmth generated from carrying wood.

With his attention freed from the immediate necessity he was once again unpleasantly aware of the puffed-up sensation in his head, and the pain that lanced through it every time he coughed. The smoke from the fire tended to pool under the ledge and, though he could generally clear the air by fanning, it seemed to make the cough worse. His throat was thoroughly dry and irritated now, and the coughing spasms were closer together and seemed to be more intense.

When he fanned the smoke away it rolled out under the ledge like a waterfall in reverse, and was quickly scattered by the northwest wind.

In between times, his eyes watered and burned almost constantly; but he thought this was not entirely due to the smoke.

The rain let up; and stopped entirely toward late afternoon. Trask left the shelter of the ledge to survey the kind of country he was keeping his vigil in. His glimpses of it before had been distorted by anxiety and the desperate attempt to get the fire going; and when the rain had hit, the visibility had been so limited he couldn't have seen anything anyway.

The clouds had lifted, but were still heavy and black—no sign of relief from the storm. They rolled over the plain unceasingly in long thick streamers, hurrying inland. Where there were passes in the tumbled mass of the coast mountains the clouds went through them; where there were none, it was as if they sliced away the height of land in their haste.

To Trask's right was the steep approach to one of the peaks. He could see no more than his first glance had shown him the day before; it was studded and prickled with weather-clean snags from which all the char had long since been scraped by wind and rain. Seen from the tail of his eye, the landscape to either side seemed to flicker with silvery gray. The jutting fingers were everywhere around him, marching in stiff disorder down to the valley's base and up the other side, stretching off to the mist in desolate, lonely ranks.

Several snags were by the ledge on the downhill side, and more above. Seen close, the wood was checked and scarred, scraped smooth and battered and scraped again; sun and rain and wind; freezing and sleet; snow. The surfaces were traced with tangled trails of long-dead borers that had once woven and chewed an aimless skein beneath the living bark. Now they too were gray and like the trails of sand snails on the beach, wandering witlessly, shallow furrows, gray on gray.

The underbrush was relatively heavy, and runty, as though nature in her desperate effort to replant the burned area had squandered her energy on thickness, and gotten no height out of it. Salal and even a little manzanita; fragile young firs with needles that looked too big for their branches. A few pines, too—in a hundred years it would be forest again.

In this place the dead stood taller than the living, and the thick squalor of green underbrush was no more than background for the lonely gray majesty of the dead snags that lifted high above.

The sight depressed him, and Trask thought he could have gone in almost any direction and found a more pleasant place. Then he shrugged, to minimize its importance to himself.

He went back under the ledge and lay down, suddenly feeling a great, aching fatigue in him, barely distinguishable from the hunger pangs in his belly except that the tiredness flowed down into the smallest reaches of his body, and even his fingers and toes protested.

He fell asleep almost at once; wakened once to peer through bleary, burning eyes at the rain outside and feed the fire a little.

When he wakened in the morning his throat was raw from coughing in the night, and he could hardly open his eyes. He was hot and sweating under the blanket, and when he raised himself up on his elbows a wave of dizziness swept over him and he closed his eyes to let it settle out. He stumbled out from under the ledge, and when he stood to full height the dizziness took him again. He leaned against a snag, breathing heavily and peering down the slope, trying to study out where the valley had gone to. A few yards below him was a white blanket that stretched flat across the valley to the same height on the opposite slope. It filled the depression to either side of him, leaving the ridge where he was—and the opposite one—lean strips of dark against the white. The dead gray ends of snags stuck up through it on the slope below.

At first he thought it was snow; but he had never heard of such a snow; and then the ledge would be covered, too.

Fog, he thought foolishly. Just *fog.*

What was wrong with him, he couldn't tell simple fog when he saw it? What?

When he had regained his balance he started down the slope to the level mist that stretched there. It was so sharply divided from the clear air that he could stand in it up to his knees, or to his waist, whichever seemed better to him; like standing in a thick and turgid white pool.

That was pretty good. He laughed, and retreated back up the slope a little. The fog drew away. A coughing fit hit him, and he sat down doubled over until it passed, with his arms wrapped tightly around his belly. The edged pangs of hunger had gone, now; but were replaced by a solid stone of pain that kept him doubled over even after the coughing had stopped.

Maybe that's it, he thought fuzzily. Y'aren't hungry after three days, you just hurt like hell.

He hoisted himself to his feet again, intrigued by the fog. He plunged back into it up to his chest; then cautiously let himself slip down until it rose up around his neck and over his face and finally his head was completely under and he was kneeling on the wet ground. He looked up, but he couldn't see anything. It was a little lighter overhead than straight in front, was all.

"Hey!" he shouted, for no particular reason. There was no answer, and he didn't really know what answer he had expected. It had seemed like a good idea, though, at the time. Damnedest fog he ever saw, that had something to do with it.

The ground felt wet and cold on his knees, but he was still sweating, and he couldn't figure it out. He better go down to the stream and take a good cold bath like Charley said. He hadn't been doing that, he realized, and he had promised. He better do that now.

First he stood back up, holding his hands out to the sides for balance. His knees shook, just raising him upright, and he felt very weak all over. Well, a good cold bath would take care of that. He backed up the slope until the layer of fog was again below him, and studied it suspiciously.

A sudden cramp twisted his belly, and he gasped and doubled over. When it had gone, he gingerly tried to straighten up and found he couldn't, not all the way. Or didn't want to, because if he stayed a little bent he discovered it didn't hurt him so bad, this hot ball of pain his belly had become.

Stooped slightly over, his shoulders hunched, he peered down at the floor of fog across the valley. It looked solid enough to skip a stone on, solid enough he could maybe even walk on it. His eyes lost focus, and suddenly two planes of fog appeared, one rising slowly above the other to hang motionless there.

Trask laughed, thinking if you put a little meat in there you could have a fog sandwich. He blinked, and the two layers came back together again. He better get that bath. He wasn't seeing so good.

Slowly he shambled down the slope in the fog to the stream and fell on his knees before it. He scooped up a double handful of water and dashed his face into it. The coldness of it was shocking, and hurt at first, but after that it felt good. He'd washed his face in colder water than that, round up by the Yellowstone Canyon. He remembered. Run from the goddam Blackfoot, too, like a rabbit; and hid in the woods till the war-party had gone on.

Who was he running with then? Russell?

He took off the homespun shirt and threw it behind him. The cold water washed some of the dirt off where sweat had dried. That was good; he doubted the spirits liked all that sweat and dirt, the way they were.

Yes, Russell. Poor old fool Russell wrote up his journal in a book and sent it off to New York, he heard. Just this spring. In the Willamette Valley now, politicking or some such. All the mountain men were gone, now. Him too, even old Elbridge Trask.

He chuckled to himself about it, scrubbing his legs down with the icy water of the stream. The water was making him feel better, he thought. He didn't figure he'd get so damned dizzy next time he stood up. It was that dizziness that bothered him, that and being so weak and shaky all the time.

He put his head in his hands and tried to think. He hadn't been able to stand up worth a damn since he got up this morning, and saw that fog. He lifted his head, and it was all around him, ghostly wisps and vapors, and he couldn't see more than a couple of feet. The stream directly ahead of him was steaming like a pot on the boil, only the steam was heavy and thick, and hung above the surface in layers like smoke.

All the mountain men gone now, every last one of 'em. Where'd they go? Crazy bastards, where'd they go? Some of them settled in the Willamette Valley, and him and Cal Tibbets and Solomon Smith down at Clatsop Plains. But where'd the rest of them go? Didn't seem like you could lose a bunch of men like them that easy, without even a trace.

Though to look at him now you'd never think him for a mountain man. Just a poor old farmer lying with his legs half in an ice-cold stream like a crazy man, and sick.

Sick . . .

With great clarity the word stood before him, and it was somehow a body-shaking relief to recognize it and take stock of it. Sick. He was sicker than just taking on a cold. Fever he had, and bad enough to make him sweat when he should be shivering, by rights. Hastily he grabbed his pants and drew them on. The skin of his legs seemed oversensitive, and the homespun shirt scratched his shoulders.

Sick . . .

He damned himself for a fool not to see it. Jesus God, it sneaked up on him without him knowing it. He was remembering how—how warped everything looked, like seeing the bottom of the ocean through the waves, and that was how his thinking was, too.

Weakly he scrambled to his feet and struck off up the slope through the soft, blinding fog, stumbling occasionally, and holding on to the slippery gray snags for support.

He came out of the fog and kept on moving up. Suddenly he found himself at the top of the ridge, looking down into the adjoining valley; also flat-floored with whiteness. For a moment, so much did it look like his own valley, he couldn't figure out in what direction he was facing. He tried to stand up straight to take his bearings, but the pain in his belly wouldn't let him. Finally he figured out that he had missed his ledge and come up to the top. It wasn't surprising, the whole thing was only ten feet long at the most now. He must have lost his direction in the fog coming up.

Carefully he retraced his steps down the slope, scanning to both sides. Only a few yards to his right he saw a wisp of smoke that seemed to come directly from the hill. He turned to it, and in a second saw it was the smoke of his fire rolling out from under the ledge.

Automatically he put more wood on the fire, the pieces sticking out like spokes so he could shove them farther in with a minimum of effort. He folded his blanket around him with his head to the fire. It wasn't safe, but he had to be where he could keep the fire going without moving too much.

He put his head down, and almost immediately was asleep, as though after a day of hard labor. He didn't think it was noon yet.

Noon of the third day. He knew he was in trouble now.

2

The fog dissipated; as though from the sheer weight of its gray mass it had sunk silently into the wet ground. The oily river of cloud flowed overhead and turned black; lumpy, rocklike masses scudding in from the sea pregnant with rain; and in time the torrents came again, slashing down out of the sullen sky as though driven from a gun.

Trask did not see it, though he lay on his belly with his face turned toward the open valley slope, the breath coming sodden and shallow through his open mouth. The sudden splatter of the rain roused him only slightly, and his eyes opened dully to see that the fog was gone and curtains of rain raked back and forth along the valley. The cold wind whirred and shook the underbrush like a rattle; angrily, erratically. He heard it vaguely and closed his eyes again.

The sweating gave way to the inevitable shivering—spasms ran through his body and shook it as the wind shook the salal. Once, from the stinging splatter on his face, he knew he had rolled somehow beyond his shelter. For a long moment he lay face up, feeling the rain rip across his face and the wind pull at his beard; but too damn tired to move. Finally he rolled to his side and raised himself painfully on his forearms. His head hung down and his legs did not move, but remained crossed as they had fallen when he rolled. Water dripped in a steady stream from his head, and cold needles chittered at the back of his neck and became snakes of ice that crawled beneath his collar and down his back and collected in cold pools at the small of his back.

He could not seem to move more than one set of muscles at once; if he raised his head, there was not energy enough to spare for untangling his legs. His eyes were heavy, and burned as though hot coals were pressed into the sockets. Squinting, he made out the yellow blur that would be his fire. It was only a few feet away, and he crawled back beneath the ledge with his eyes closed, moving through the mud like a wounded animal, without volition; with only necessity.

He fumbled at the blanket with unfeeling fingers, but could not maintain the attention necessary to fix it over himself well, and his hands dropped limply by his sides. There was a terrible metallic flavor in his mouth, and his throat was clogged with phlegm. He coughed, and spat weakly. He shivered violently and drew his knees up to his chest. His eyes were closed again, and he slept.

Night came without his knowing, and the rain continued. Beating its rattly tattoo on the ledge above and splattering wetly on the ground beside him. His dreams were full of terror; strange shifting forms of menace; cold and heat; fire; blood and fever.

Illga was there, his delicately feminine features masked by torrents of blood that streamed out of his hair. Trask crawled on the cold ground, slithered in the mud weakly, trying to evade the fire-eyed figure that walked blindly over him and pressed his face in the mud until he could not breath and the panic was tight in his throat.

"I am your brother," Illga said sweetly, smiling his ingratiating smile. "I have one Clatsop wife." He stretched forth two slimly tapered fingers tipped with glowing coals, almost a gesture of beneficence. They curled smoking around Trask's eyeballs and Illga pulled gently back. Trask could hear the sizzling and feel the sharp fire-agony as his eyeballs were pulled out and dripped down his cheeks, leaving bloody, smoking sockets in which pain danced like sparks above a fire.

Trask gasped and choked.

"No," he said. "No more."

"I am your brother." The gentle, chiding voice; the fine, womanly features.

Illga's face became clouded, mixed, jumbled together with the face of the Killamook at Nehalem and his fiercely hating eyes.

Then it was all gone, and there was only a bloody fog that choked him as he walked through it; great trees loomed up on either side and disappeared above the fog. Beside him was a comforting figure, walking beside him in the fog that swirled hotly into his bloody eyesockets.

"Illga wishes you to die," Charley said pleasantly.

"All right, Charley."

"Watch for him."

"I will."

"You must watch for that one."

"I will, I will."

"He will kill you if he can. He will drink up your blood. Watch out for him. Watch out for him. Watch out, watch out, watch out, watch watch watch . . ."

"Yes."

"I am your brother," Illga said. "I like white men. I have been many times to Astoria. I am a great trader."

"That's all right," Trask said, walking quickly. Illga followed, and somehow Charley was gone. "Wait," Illga said.

Trask began to run, and realized his mistake, for the panic surged up in him irrevocably then. His fear was almost a tangible thing, it filled his chest with flaming irons and choked the breath out of him. There was nothing ahead of him but a thick white bank of fog, and he plunged into it with a sense of huge relief, knowing he would be safe, hidden in the vast grayness.

Charley was walking ahead of him, and Trask hurried to catch up. He was very pleased, and he was sure Charley would be pleased.

"I told you to watch," Charley said reprovingly.

"I did. I did."

"No you didn't. See?" He peeled off his face and threw it to the ground, where it writhed in pain. Illga's was beneath.

Trask wheeled and ran.

From the fog came great voices, "Watch out for him, watch out for him . . ." Endlessly repeated into the wilderness.

Trask put out his hand to grab Charley's shoulder and explain it to him, but the shoulder came away, smoking. It seared his hand, and the pain made him scream.

"I will, I will, I will I will I will . . ."

He woke, still screaming, with the palm of his hand lying flat on the red coals of the fire by his head.

Chapter Twenty-four

I

He jerked his hand away and the faint odor of burning flesh came to his nostrils. Strangely, it did not disturb him; he was suddenly calm. He raised the palm of his hand to his face and sniffed at it tentatively.

With a tongue that felt wooden, he licked at his hand, and found it tasted slightly salty, and gritty. It was hot to his tongue. He wondered if anyone had ever eaten part of himself, and in a detached way regarded his hand for a moment as meat; as something apart from himself. It would not last long, he decided regretfully.

Then the pain came, a shrieking, raw spear of flame that shot up his arm and gripped his throat. He heard a shrill whimper that he knew calmly to be himself. The smell came to him again, and this time he gagged, retching uselessly. His stomach was tightly knotted and had nothing to give up. He jerked in spasms, holding the burned hand clear of the ground as his body knotted up; loosened, knotted again. He drew in a long ragged breath and blinked the tears away. His eyes still burned, and in his mind he could hear the echo of the dry retching, as of something dying in agony.

He crawled from under the ledge and raised himself to his knees, pushing with the flat of his good left hand. His right remained raised before his eyes, limp and dead.

It was still night, and the pitchy darkness lay over the valley and ridges. He stumbled down to the stream, falling twice over unseen traps, and lay full length by the edge, his hand thrust into the water. It was cold only for a moment before his hand grew numb from it, and the pain of the burn lessened. He raised his head and blinked open his eyes. The back of his hand was white, and moved gently in the current like a dead fish nodding, decomposing quietly in the water.

It was stiff and numb now, and there was nothing else he could do. He pillowed his head on his left forearm and went back to sleep, letting the water tug gently at the lump of flesh that seemed so far away.

When he woke it was light again. He got to his knees and looked at the hand. It was a deep, bluish red on the palm. Tendons stood out rigidly along the back as though they were not flesh at all.

The palm had not yet begun to blister badly, so he knew he had not slept long. He stood up and leaned against a snag, trying to think. There was nothing he could do about the burn but bandage it, he had no fat to put on it; so he forgot it. There was something else, something that had nothing to do with his hand . . .

Then he remembered, and nodded to himself. Illga was coming. Charley said, "Watch out." He would have to do something.

Don't come, he thought desperately. Please don't come.

Then he was angry at himself. Trask begging, Trask pleading. He tried to spit, to show his contempt for himself, but only made a sound like a baby. He couldn't remember ever being this drunk before, not even at the rendezvous. Trask begging, that was not right.

Fuck Illga, he thought, clenching his teeth. Fuck him. And all of 'em. I'll kill 'em all the dirty bastards. I'm Trask!

"Trask!" he screamed at the sky. "Trask! I'll kill you dirty whoresons! Kill you!"

He pounded on the snag with his fist, staring at the sky, waiting for an answer, waiting to kill them.

"Fuck 'em," he muttered wearily. He would kill them all right. He was Trask. He could kill them, he was a man.

He stumbled back to the ledge, shambling stooped over from the pain in his belly. Viciously he ripped at the hem of his blanket with the scraping stone until he had torn off a ragged strip four inches wide and the full length of the blanket. He bound his hand, clumsily tying off with his teeth and the leaden fingers of his left hand. The long bandage was bulky, but it would cushion.

He would make a weapon. That was what Charley was telling him, he should make a spear to get ready, because Illga was coming.

He was tamanawis; he had the strength; he would kill them all.

As he bent over the bulky bandage, drawing it tight with his teeth, he was vaguely aware that tears were streaming down his face and soaking into the blanket, and his breathing was almost a sobbing. It didn't matter, it was all outside. Not him at all, outside of him. Inside he was Trask and he knew he could do it. There wasn't anything he couldn't do. He was Trask.

He crawled back out from under the ledge, carrying his cutting stones in the crook of his right arm. He picked out one of the fir saplings, larger than most—as big around the base as his forearm. He sat cross-legged before it and began to saw with the scraping stone. He sawed until a patch of white wood showed; something he could keep his eyes on. Then he took up the "ax" and began to pick away at the white spot. All his attention was fixed on making the point of the stone hit the right place, the little white spot. The only thing that existed was the white spot, and he smashed at it again and again, and pried slivers loose and picked some more and pried.

His burned hand was beginning to hurt again but he could not stop. He didn't know how long he would be able to hold the stone; already the palm of his good hand was bruised and scraped. Finally he had dug into the wood for two inches, a ragged notch. Shakily he stood. Balancing himself with great care he kicked at the sapling, and felt the solid impact of his foot, and the yielding of the tree. He lost his balance and fell backward. He dared not stop himself for fear of hurting his hands more, and he deliberately held both of them in front of him as he fell, gritting his teeth in expectation. He fell slowly, all time waiting, a long and dreamlike slant to the ground he thought would never end.

He fell squarely on his back; a bone-jarring shock racked his body and he gasped for breath.

He lay still for a moment until he could breathe again, and then rolled over, levering himself to his knees with his elbows on the ground.

The sapling bent away from his notch. He leaned against it with his shoulder; finally fell on it with his whole body, bringing the top to the ground and hearing the satisfying crackle of breaking fibers. He had not used his hands at all, and it pleased him.

He took the "ax" up again and began to pick at the bent fibers of wood that held the trunk fastened. After a while, to rest his hand, he sawed at them with the edge of the scraping stone. When he had cut a few away, he stood up and jumped on the trunk near the break. It gave slightly.

He went back to alternate picking and sawing and jumping until finally the wood parted. By this time his burned hand was throbbing again. He kicked off as many of the small limbs as would break easily, and hooked the trunk under his armpit and dragged it down to the stream.

At first he tried to soak the hand and work on the spear with his left at the same time, but he could not find a position where he could do both. At last he ended by soaking the hand only.

When it was numb again, he began to chop off the branches that would not break. It went slowly, because he could not hold on to his stone for more than a few strokes at a time. It would drop from his hand, and patiently he would fumble it up again and strike once more. Before long he had to rest after each stroke, and he was getting sleepy again.

Stroke, rest. Stroke, rest. Stone gone, pick it up, where . . .

Stroke, rest. Stroke, rest . . .

He was endlessly patient, and was not annoyed that he kept dropping the stone. He soaked his hand twice, not hurrying it, before he had finally stripped off the branches.

He broke off the top end where it was about the thickness of his wrist, and he had a shaft about five feet long, white-scarred where the limbs had been ripped away, but smooth enough.

He dragged it back to the ledge, fed the fire and put the small end of the spear just in it. The wet wood sizzled.

He wrapped himself up in the blanket and went to sleep again. It did not seem to him he would ever have enough sleep.

He woke at intervals and took the end of the sapling out of the fire. Patiently he scraped away the charred wood, and after several of these operations the end began to assume a point. It was hard to hold on to the scraping stone, but he could not find a way to tie it on securely. He spent fifteen minutes on one attempt, only to have it fall out of the binding at the first stroke.

Calmly he unwrapped the cloth from his hand, picked up the stone and began scraping again.

By evening he had his spear.

2

The morning of the fifth day came gray, but without rain. The clouds even seemed slightly thinner, and the diffuse light was bright.

Trask felt a little stronger when he woke, and crept out into the light with more confidence than he had felt before. He blinked at the brightness, and looked up at the clouds. It made his eyes water, so he turned back to the ground.

A yellowish substance was oozing out from beneath the blanket-bandage on his right hand, and he thought he had best clean himself while he was feeling strong. He stood slowly outside his little cave, hanging on to the ledge when the dizziness hit him. He took the new spear for a staff and hesitantly made his way down to the stream, where he unwrapped his hand.

It was a raw mess; blisters had formed and broken and the whole palm was puffed and suppurating. He looked at it with detachment, only faintly moved. It did not seem odd to have his hand that way; or even bad. There was no good or bad connected with anything any more. Pain had lost most of its terror; he barely felt it. Consciously he knew the pain of his hand was severe, but somehow it didn't seem to make much difference. It couldn't reach him.

He regretted nothing; wanted nothing. He was simply existing, and the way things were was the way they had always been and always would be. He didn't care any more. He did what had to be done, and endured in a timeless present, without past or future.

He soaked his hand for a long time, because that was what there was to be done. He washed the bandage without any thought of infection or dirt or sticking, but simply automatically. He bandaged again with care, but could not have said why. He did it, simply that.

Only one thing disturbed the perfect peace of his endurance, only one intrusion from the world outside: the knowledge that Illga was coming. That alone was important, and he knew that once he had taken care of this one thing, he could simply exist. It was what he wanted, he wanted only to exist, with peace. He wanted to be alone, away from the world, and bandage his hand. He resolved to get quit of this one final annoyance as soon as he could.

The greater portion of his mind was somnolent; resting deeply, while errant thoughts skittered over the surface like waterbugs on a deep pool. He knew if he could just get rid of the harsh irritation of his conscious thinking, then he would be all right; then he would be at peace.

He sat up, resting back on his heels, and looked around him. He was neither pleased nor displeased. He half remembered being depressed once by the lonely desolation of the burned land, but it no longer affected him that way. It no longer affected him at all. It was there.

He began to look forward to Illga's coming as something to be desired, something to be got done with so he could rest.

Leaning heavily on the spear-staff, he made his hesitant way to the top of his ridge, and peered over the next valley, squinting his eyes.

"You can come now," he said softly, waiting.

Nobody came.

"Hurry up," he said. "Hurry up."

He turned and went back to the ledge and wrapped up in his blanket. He put the spear beside him and smiled, patting it with his good hand.

That's all right, he thought lazily. That's fine.

He dozed.

When he woke he went back up the ridge again to watch but there was nobody coming and he was disappointed.

He lay down again peacefully, holding the spear on his chest. Through his half-closed eyes the spear glowed, a bright warm glow from inside it, all the warmth of the sun, and a soft and lovely light.

He suddenly realized the spear was the one real object left, the one connection he had with the world outside. All the buzzing jumble of things and people and ideas and thinking; pain; pleasure; love and hate and desire; all were gone. Disappeared somewhere over the next ridge. It gave him a warm taste in his mouth.

The spear was the last—a great key; the unlocker of mystery and the solution of all questioning. To drive that staff into Illga—this was the thing. It was greatly important to do this. When it was done, when the key was turned in the lock of flesh, then he would know what it was he wanted to know.

There was a halo of significance about the spear—an aura of huge, immeasurable meaning just beyond his reach. He would understand it all, and soon—the spear was the key.

It was the finest thing he had ever known, this anticipation. He knew with a certainty beyond question that the meaning of the spear would soon be revealed to him. And with it would come perfect knowledge, the understanding of all things perfectly, the measureless merging with the world that would make him and it the same. He would know what it all meant; it meant more than he had ever thought. It was only a little beyond his reach now.

The glow of the spear communicated itself to the whole tiny cave, lighting it up. He could see clods of dirt clearly over his head, and the tiny, threading rootlets that came down from above. Wrinkles in the dirt, an ant crawling beautifully along . . . The ant's body glowed with the same incredible importance as everything else.

It was just out of reach, the meaning of it. It was huge and dimensionless, everything and nothing together, and he realized he was on the verge of perceiving existence raw, the ultimate significance of the billion foolish particles of the world.

He could feel it coming, and it choked him in his throat that he had to wait for it. He wanted to reach out and put it all in his mouth and swallow it, so he could become all the world and all knowledge without waiting for it any longer.

He wondered that he had never before seen the impartial and lovely glow with which all things were lighted. He could not—thinking of some other person he had known named Elbridge Trask—understand how it was this one had missed seeing the beauty and meaning of the spear; that it was the final unlocker.

He clutched it close to his chest and slept, smiling.

3

He slid smoothly from sleep to wakefulness and back to sleep throughout the day, his mind like the back of a whale that appears briefly above the surface and then silently glides back into the depths. There was no distinction between waking or sleeping and he could make the transition without effort or disturbance.

He was saving himself with a kind of tolerant amusement, knowing that for a brief instant he would have to be back in the world again; the instant when he drove the staff into Illga's body. So he rested deeply, waiting for that moment of final release, the final freedom to let his mind settle quietly into calm and depth; the massive and ultimate insight he knew was coming with the thrust of the spear. Even the waiting became a peaceful interlude, a floating just beneath the surface, ready to spring up with energy and thrust deeply . . . and then to go deep down, retreat, lose the surface glare and find the cool deep depths . . . green and dark . . . comforting and lone . . .

The day moved on, neither quickly nor slowly. He was not conscious of the passage of time at all; feeling he could start or stop it at will. He was for the first time in perfect control and possession of all things, and all things would move to his hand.

When darkness came again, still without rain, he greeted it indifferently, with only a faint sense of surprise that dark and light were alternating with such speed. He could not remember how long it had been since he left the village, nor did it seem to matter. He could have figured it out if the desire had been strong enough.

Lazily he patted the glowing spear as if it were an old companion; rolled over and gazed out into the friendly dark. Illga would come soon, he thought, or one of his men. Possibly, even probably, one of his warriors, but it didn't matter. The thing was the thrust of the spear; in that gesture he would release the flood of meaning that hovered all about him, waiting to be made clear in the flow of blood.

He faintly regretted the necessity of resuming such close contact with the world; but there it was; the final remaining thing to do.

But it must, he realized, be done without hurt to himself, or the whole thing would be spoiled. He crawled out from beneath the ledge and lifted his head in the air as if smelling. There was no moonlight to penetrate the perfect blackness, and his eyes were useless for now. But ears, perhaps . . .

He was not surprised when finally he heard the rustling of brush in the west. Still far away it was, very faint. Not to be heard at all, except by one whose hearing was as sharp as his.

He smiled softly to himself, and crouched back under the ledge to put several more large splinters on the fire, making it spurt up brightly. He began to feel the blood flow in him again, and his hand throbbed under the bandage.

He surveyed the fire with satisfaction, then backed away from it, still on his hands and knees. He lifted his head, and between cracklings of the fire heard the rustle of brush again. Just the other side of the next valley, he guessed. Only minutes, now.

Silently, he crept down the slope away from the firelit cave, carrying the spear beside him. Not too far—it had to be just right, or he could not get there properly. In a dim way he realized his legs would not sustain him very far, but that was as it should be.

He pressed himself flat to the ground and felt his chest thump against the solidity of the cold dirt. His right hand throbbed in time with the thumping of his chest, and he could feel a pulsing at his temple no more substantial than the tug of the breeze.

He spread his legs apart, taking a firm grip on the ground with his thighs. The rustling grew louder, and took a more certain direction; still beyond the ridge, but over to his left now.

He glanced up at the fire, orange and warm in the blackness of the night, lighting the cave with a flickering glow. The ledge cut off the light sharply at the top, and the cave was a bright oval that wavered uncertainly, set precisely in the center of total blackness.

Only by straining his eyes could he see the faint silhouette of the ridge, black against black in the night, not vision so much as some other unnamed sense that brought the shape and bulk of it to him.

The rustling stopped.

Now his throat was pounding too, and he was certain the other could hear the dull thudding transmitted through the ground. His breath was shallow and hissing, and he opened his mouth wide to stop the sound.

The rustle began again, louder now. The Killamook—Illga—had crossed the ridge. Far to his left, a hundred yards or more, Trask thought he saw a shadow move away from a shadow and into a shadow; all blackness, all darkness; but there was motion.

He heard the rustling stop once more as the Killamook paused, catching sight of the glow of the fire. Trask moved slightly on the ground, and the shifting of his spear seemed loud in his ears.

Then the papery sound of the brush came nearer—slowly, slowly— and in a flicker of light he saw the leaves of salal move. He smiled again to himself. Illga was moving cautiously along the slope toward the glow, moving carefully.

The sound stopped, the motion stopped.

Come, Trask thought silently. Come, come, come.

The world hung balanced, waiting to fall . . .

He came. Moving with ridiculous care, making too much noise, and Trask was contemptuous. Now he could see the Killamook's body occasionally through the brush, glints of firelight on dark flesh.

Trask dragged himself to his knees, keeping his back hunched over and his head down so the fire would not reflect from his face. Inwardly he gathered himself. Just one, he thought. Just one thrust . . . Illga . . . peace . . .

With a moment of bitter clarity he knew he would have to do it right the first time, for once was all he had strength for.

Everything, he thought desperately. Everything you've got. Everything. Everything. Everything . . .

The Killamook moved across the firelit oval, silhouetted, bending down to reach beneath the ledge . . .

Trask was up, holding the spear before him, running, thrusting, up the few sloping yards. A whine squeezed from his throat.

The Killamook heard him—whirled—tried to dodge . . .

The spear took him in the abdomen, pointed up, with all Trask's weight behind it. He felt a soft giving as the point thrust in and punctured; ripped upward; and the Killamook doubled. He was carried by momentum backward under the ledge, folded around the spear, and Trask felt the rush of warm blood around his hands. He whimpered again, and jerked back on the spear. One of the twig ends caught coming out; brought a small loop of intestine that hung red and dripping below the hole. The man gurgled softly and tried to put his hands where his abdomen had been.

Trask stood over him and stared down blankly.

"Charley?" he said. "What are you doing?"

Chapter Twenty-five

Charley turned his eyes away from the gaping redness of his belly and looked up, with an expression of surprise. His dark, almond-shaped eyes showed white all around, but his flat face was blank.

He said, "Try—" His body convulsed, and he vomited a huge gout of blood that soaked his chest and merged with the blackening flow from his belly.

"Charley . . . Charley, it's a . . . I didn't mean it . . ."

Trask was on his knees, his hands reaching tentatively toward the little Clatsop, his fingers shaking.

"Charley . . ."

Charley's face had lost its woodenness and was twisted in a way that frightened Trask. From his throat came a tiny series of high-pitched yips like the barking of a prowling owl. His body began to twitch convulsively, and with each spasm forced a high "Hnhk! hnhk! hnhk!" from his nose. Frothy red foam ran from his nostrils and over his mouth.

"Try—hnhk!—try—help—hnhk!—hnhk!" His voice was lost in gurgling and the sharp whining grunts as his body contracted against itself. He coughed and another gout of blood came up and Trask wondered that there could be so much.

"Put that back in," Trask said. Shakily he pushed the loose loop of intestine back into the gash with his fingertip. "There—better . . . Charley? . . . I take it back . . ."

The convulsions grew stronger, and Charley's limp legs flew up, writhing like mindless blind snakes. There was one, final stiffening; Charley's fingers flew away from the hole in his belly, scattering droplets of blood on Trask's face. The Indian looked up again wide-eyed, and a steady torrent of blood began to flood over his dropped jaw.

The twitching stopped.

"There, that's better," Trask said. He took Charley's shoulder gently in his hand. "You better take it easy, Charley. I hurt you. I didn't mean to hurt you, I didn't want that . . . Charley? Charley?"

When there was no reply, Trask carefully tipped the body down to lie flat. "That's all right, Charley. You rest a little bit. I got to take you back. We got to get back. All right? You rest first."

He squatted on his heels and the tears fell from his beard and mingled with the blood. His eyes burned, and he realized the tears were streaming down his face only when he saw them spatter in the bright red pools that were rapidly darkening. His body was racked with uncontrollable sobbing that he couldn't understand.

It's tension, he thought. Tension. "I'm just tired, Charley," he explained. "It's all right."

Charley's fingers were like claws and Trask reached over to straighten them out.

Sleeping, he thought. That's good. We got to get back. Soon as he's rested up some we got to get back.

"I'm not going away, he assured Charley. I'm right here." He moved out of Charley's range of vision and fed a few more sticks to the fire.

"You know I wouldn't do somethin' like that on purpose, Charley. That warmer? Charley?"

He moved back and squatted again. There was a wide black stain on the ground all around now, and a faint warm steam curled up from the ragged gap in Charley's abdomen.

"You can't sleep with your eyes open," Trask said softly. He reached over and pushed the eyelids down over Charley's staring eyes; then sat back again. "That's better. Soon as you get rested we got to start. You think you can walk all right?"

Old Charley was really off, he thought. Well, it didn't matter. If he couldn't walk, he could help him. He looked out at the darkness, but had no way of estimating how long it would be until daylight. Suddenly he started sobbing again for no particular reason.

He smiled quickly afterward, and blinked. "*Hyas Kloshe siwash*," he said affectionately, and patted Charley's forehead.

He looked vacantly over the still form at the opposite wall, and sat that way for a long time.

"Y'old hoss," he said gently. "I don't think we better wait for day, do you? I—I don't like the looks of that cut." He stared dubiously down at the blackening raw cavity of Charley's abdomen. Then he turned away, looking at the wall again.

"Charley, I take it back. I didn't mean that, I didn't—you know that. Don't you? You're the best friend I got, Charley, I wouldn't hurt you on purpose."

Wish he'd let me know he didn't blame me, Trask thought. He noted absently he had started the racking sobs again, but no tears were coming now.

Like the dry heaves. Jesus. He wished he could stop this damn crying all the time, but that was just the way it was.

"Charley, I think we better start back. I know you need the rest, but I don't like the looks of that—Can we start now?"

Charley didn't tell him No, so Trask bent down and put his arm under the shoulders.

"All right, old hoss," he coaxed. "Let's go now, let's get up. Come on." He struggled with the inert form, getting it to a sitting position finally, with the head slumped down on the chest.

"All right," he said. "Here we go. Come on, Charley. You got to help a little more. All right? Up we go."

He lurched to his feet, bumping his head on the ledge. "Short fella's lucky in a place like this," he congratulated Charley. "All right, come on."

He dragged Charley out from under the ledge. A little blood was flowing still, but not much.

"That's better, stop that bleeding some," Trask said. "You ready, Charley? You set to go? We got to get back."

He looped the Indian's arm across his shoulders and stumbled a few steps in the darkness. "Can't you help any more than that, Charley? You're feet're just dragging."

Well, I guess not, he thought.

"It's all right, then," he said comfortingly. "It don't matter, we'll get there somehow."

He started to move slowly through the brush toward the top of the ridge, outlined faintly against the black sky.

2

Through that night the going was slow and bad. He couldn't remember it being so bad, ever. The night blinded him, and Charley couldn't help at all. He stumbled through the brush, dragging Charley beside him awkwardly. Charley's feet kept getting tangled in growth and tripping them up.

After what seemed like three hours, Trask looked back and saw they had only made it over the ridge and a little way down the slope.

"We're not movin' too fast," he told Charley dubiously. "We got to pick up a little, old hoss, or we won't make it by Christmas. Can we go a little faster? We got to get back, have somebody look at that cut of yours."

Unaccountably this set him to crying again, and he felt very foolish, standing there in the night with Charley's arm around his shoulder and crying his head off like a baby. But he didn't apologize. Charley'd understand, all right.

He felt kind of dizzy, and the next tug from Charley pulled him over and sent the two of them crashing to the ground.

Trask got to his knees and laughed. "I swear to God, Charley, you're the worst walker ever was. You get your big feet tangled in more damn brush than I got on my face." He laughed again, and crawled back toward Charley's feet. He patted him on the back as he passed, to show him he was just joking him. Patiently he untangled the salal stalks from around Charley's ankle and hoisted him up again.

"Here we go," he said. He leaned forward into the brush. "How'd you like to have that old Doctor McLoughlin here now?" he asked. "There's something, by God! Then you could ride. How'd you like that, Charley?"

But Doctor McLoughlin's dead. Wakila too.

"Well," he said hastily, before Charley could get sad on him, "it's all right anyway. We'll make it somehow. You just don't worry."

But he was not as confident as he made out. He had walked hard for a full day, getting out here, and he was a good walker. The rate they were going, it was going to take a good long while. He had to admit Charley wasn't helping worth a damn, but there wasn't anything that could be done about it.

We'll make it somehow, he thought. Always have. I expect we could do about anything we had to, Charley and me.

"Charley," he said, "I'll tell you what." He was suddenly washed with a warm affection for the little Clatsop, and wanted to show it. "When we get back, suppose I give you that old meerschaum of mine? Would you like that, Charley? That Norwegian pipe? That's a good old pipe, Charley, smokes fine. Hell, I don't give a damn for it, though, if you'd like it. I'll do that, Charley, you don't let me forget."

He stopped to rest a little farther on. The ground seemed to be swinging under him, and he had a hard time keeping his balance. "Charley," he said confidentially, "I'm tired. Honest to God I am, now. I'm just going to have to rest for a little while if that's all right with you."

It seemed to be all right with Charley, so Trask closed his eyes and dropped off. He dozed for only a few minutes, then woke up again, feeling a little refreshed.

"That's better," he said cheerfully. "Here we go again."

He plowed through an endless sea of brush and tangles, falling now and again, but trying to stay cheerful about it. In time the sky behind him began to lighten and dawn spread up through the clouds, gray and cold. By this time they were moving up the slope on the other side of the ravine.

"That's more like it," he said, looking back. "Now we got some light. Now we'll make better time." The thought put new freshness in his legs, but only for a few steps. When the light was high enough, he turned to look at Charley, and quickly looked away again. The Clatsop's face was gray and unpleasant to look at. For some time, Trask had been privately worried about the cold.

"Charley," he said dubiously, "are you pretty cold? You think you'll make it all right? You're stiffening up pretty bad."

He had noticed the stiffness coming on a while before, but hadn't said anything because he knew Charley wasn't doing it on purpose.

"Tell you the truth, it makes it kind of hard, you getting stiff."

He didn't like to say it, because he knew Charley was doing the best he could, but there it was, just the same. It made it harder than hell to get Charley around clumps of bushes and things, when his legs were stiff like that.

"Just like draggin' a board," he said jokingly. "Maybe I better carry you. Would that be better?"

He glanced again at Charley for his reaction, but had to turn away as quickly as before. He stared down at the ground, trying to decide. Unexpectedly he began to whimper and had to control himself.

"That's what we better do," he said. "Then your feet won't drag.

"We'll make it somehow," he muttered.

He lowered Charley gently to the ground and squatted beside him, staring absently over the hills. He lost his balance and fell back; levered himself up again, to sit cross-legged. He hoped Charley hadn't noticed how bad his balance was getting.

With Charley not able to hang on, he would have to be tied on, Trask thought. Like packing a horse. He wished they had Doctor McLoughlin there. Things would've been a hell of a lot simpler if Doctor McLoughlin was there to ride or something. Even old bag of bones.

He stretched Charley out on his side and straightened his arms and legs. They were getting very hard to move. It was a good thing he had decided before he got completely stiffened up and you couldn't move him at all. He bent the little tamanawis man carefully, at the middle, and tied his wrists and ankles together with the thong from his shirt. He sat upright.

"There," he said. "Just like a blanket roll, Charley. How's that? We'll get there yet." He kept his eyes carefully on the knots in the thong, not wanting to look at Charley's face. Seemed like every time he looked at his face, it started him crying.

He crawled around to Charley's back, got his hands under the ribs and lifted. When the Indian's side came off the ground, he quickly thrust his arm under, up to the shoulder. He levered up with that arm, still lifting with his other hand. When there was room enough he ducked his head under. Charley's body came down across the back of his neck, making him grunt.

"All right, we almost got it," he said, panting. "Here we go." He wriggled a little farther under until his head was in the open loop formed by Charley's body, and the Clatsop lay across the middle of his back.

Bracing his forearms on the ground, he hung his head—heaved up.

"Made it!" he said. "We'll get there. You'll see, we'll have a smoke together yet!" He drew his knees up until he was on hands and knees with the body draped across his back.

"All right, Charley, now you just come up around my neck," he said. He lowered his shoulders and jiggled, to make the body slide down around his neck. He grabbed Charley's bound arms as he came forward. Painfully he pushed up with his other hand and staggered to his feet, swaying as he caught his balance.

"Here we go," he said. He hunched around until Charley was bent over his right shoulder, with his legs running diagonally across his back. His arms and upper body hung over Trask's chest like a bandolier, and the bound wrists and ankles dangled by Trask's left thigh. The white man staggered back and forth, getting the balance arranged.

He was panting hard when he finished, and had to stand and rest for a minute. Then he began to trudge toward the next ridge, moving slowly and unsteadily through the underbrush.

His feet felt as though they were buried in tubs of tar; lifting each required a separate, strong effort of will. He concentrated on this alone—first the right, put it down—now up the left, put it down—until the will gave out entirely and he had not the smallest scrap left.

He stood looking down at these feet of his that would no longer move, then up at the sky. The motion of his head threw him off balance and he staggered backward.

"*You sonsabitches*," he muttered. "You can move back, you can damn well move front. Move!"

He started off again.

After a while he found he could forget about the feet and they would take care of themselves. What he had to think about was just—move. And he did move.

"We'll get there, Charley," he said. He was more cheerful, finding he didn't have to pay any attention to his feet. He should have remembered that's how it was: you forgot about everything on a long march except *move*. And then you moved all right, just like a goddam steamboat, by God. Chunk-chunk-chunk-chunk-chunk. It was funny how a man could forget.

"I sure am sorry about what happened," he said remembering. The tightness came up into his throat and he tried to shut it off before he started that idiot caterwauling again.

"It's all right," Charley said. "I don't blame you."

"I knew you wouldn't," Trask said gratefully. "Was an accident, Charley. You know that."

"I know it all right," Charley told him.

It made him feel better, a lot better. Charley's face was bumping against Trask's body, but his voice was just like ever, strong and calm.

"I believe I better take a little rest," Trask said after a while.

"No," Charley told him softly. "You best keep moving. We'll make it somehow. Wait till you get to timber."

"All right, Charley."

Trask looked ahead of him and blinked. The brush wavered, as if through heat waves; blurred and sharpened. The horizon was indistinct and tilted at a funny angle, swinging slowly up to his left.

He caught out with his left hand and grabbed a salal branch just in time to keep himself from falling. He laughed.

"Almost got us that time, Charley." He blinked hard and the horizon tipped down to horizontal again.

"We'll make it somehow," Charley said.

"Goddam right," Trask muttered.

He played a little game with himself, seeing how far he could walk with his eyes closed before he bumped into something, or couldn't feel his way around it. He did pretty well, long as he opened them for direction once in a while.

Time had begun moving again. But it would not hold to a steady progression through the day; it skittered and went off in all directions, like the gusts of wind that were coming up again. Sometimes when

Trask looked back, he could figure maybe a mile—but sometimes only a hundred feet or so. He couldn't figure it out.

Tired as he was, he had to control his movement. He didn't dare stagger, for the weight of Charley across his shoulder threw him off balance, and he was afraid to fall down. He knew how hard it would be to get up again, and he was privately afraid he wouldn't be able to make it. He didn't say anything about it, but Charley knew just the same.

"You got to watch that, Bridge," Charley cautioned.

"All right, Charley."

He took care that when he lurched off balance it was in a forward direction, because he could usually catch himself by putting a foot out. And it also got them another step farther. Kind of a little trickery, pretend you were going to fall down and then take a step instead. That was all walking was anyhow, fall forward and catch yourself. It was working fine.

"We'll fool 'em, Charley," he said confidently.

"We'll make it somehow."

The day was warmer, and by late afternoon Trask was sweating under his load. A few flies had come out and were buzzing around peskily.

Awful damn early for flies, he thought resentfully. He'd damn near froze the night before—or was it the one before that?—and now flies. He couldn't seem to get nights straight in his head. Or days either, as far as that went.

The warmth did not last long, however, only the late part of the day, and when it began to get dark it was already cooler.

They had reached timber, then, though Trask could not remember the transition from the burn. He looked behind him and it was all forest, so he had been in a fair while.

"Charley, I plainly got to rest. That's all," he said. "We can't get through here in the dark anyhow."

"All right, Bridge. But you got to figure something so you can get up again."

"That's right," Trask said, "you're right, there."

He leaned against a tree to think it over.

"Wonder if that strip of blanket would hold you?" he said finally.

"Might try. I don't weigh too much."

"You sure do, old hoss," Trask said. "*Way* too much." He thought Charley laughed too, taking it for a joke the way it was meant.

He was glad now he had used such a long strip on his hand. Carefully he unwound it, and found it didn't begin to stick until the next to the last layer. He didn't like the looks of his hand when he had it open. It was blotchy and puffed and oozing, and the air was like a blow on it. Patches bled red where he had torn the skin getting it off. There was also a bad smell, a rotten smell like decaying meat, but he couldn't be sure it came from his hand. Maybe was something dead lying in the brush around.

He shrugged, and felt Charley's weight heavy and aching on his shoulder. He only began to realize how tired he was.

He threw one end of the strip over a low limb and worked the other under Charley's arms. Then he tied the two ends together, making the loop over the limb as short as he could get it. As he was tying he wondered how in God's name he would ever get up again if he once lay down. He wasn't really sure he should risk it.

Just then Charley said, "We'll make it somehow. We'll make it somehow. We'll make it somehow."

He knew he was all right then.

When he had the loop tied off as securely as he could make it with fumbling fingers, he simply sank down to his knees, letting the loop take the weight of Charley's body. It held.

He crept out backwards. The body slipped around—the blanket strip sliding up the arms until it caught at the sharp angle where the ankles and wrists were tied. There it swung gently, back down like a trussed deer, with the head cocked at a funny angle. The neck had stiffened up good now, so the head didn't lie back like it should.

"All right, Charley?"

"Just fine. You get some rest now." Charley swung solemnly back and forth like a child on a swing running down.

"All right," Trask said. He crumpled in a heap to the ground and slept, dreaming of Hannah's sharp face and gentle hands.

3

"Think we can make it today?"

"Don't know today or not," Charley said. "Can sure try."

Trask nodded. "We'll make it somehow."

He struggled to his feet and blinked at Charley's form, hanging from the limb. When he got closer he knew where the smell was coming from all right, because it was getting pretty strong now; but he didn't say anything. He still didn't like to look at Charley 's face.

He put his head through the loop of Charley's body and found himself staring down in the opening in his belly, where it seemed that most of the rotten smell was from. A little twinkle met his eyes, and after a minute he realized the twinkle was just the white of maggots wriggling. He backed slowly out and looked absently up at the tree towering overhead.

Awful damn early for flies, he thought again.

"Say Charley," he said hesitantly, "them blow flies got to you. You're blowed all to hell. Sure am sorry."

Charley swung quiescently, and turned a little as a breeze whispered under the tree. "It's all right," he said. "Few blow flies don't bother me any. We'll make it somehow."

"That's right," Trask said. "We will."

When he got Charley scrunched around on his shoulders he thought he could feel the maggots crawling on the back of his neck. Probably not, though. They'd go back inside where it was dark. Just his imagination running away. He hoped the flies wouldn't blow him.

He set off through the woods again, stumbling, catching himself, keeping his head turned to the left so the smell wasn't so bad. After a while he couldn't avoid it any more, so he just turned off that part of him that did the smelling. After that it was a lot better.

"Like goin' down white water," he said reflectively. "Don't take you long to get down, but sure is hell going back."

"*Delate kahkwa*," Charley said. "It's a long portage."

"Sure as hell is."

It rained again during the day, but he wasn't conscious of it. There was only the moving ahead, it was all his mind had time for.

Also—at one bad time—the thing he feared most came about: he fell down.

Oh, God, he thought desperately. I'll never make it up.

He lay there with his face in the mud, his body humped on top of Charley, and felt the rain patter gently on his neck. He must have dozed off, because he couldn't remember how he had gotten where he was. There were getting to be large empty spaces in his mind, as if great segments shut off and refused to be opened.

"We better be moving now," Charley suggested.

"Yes."

But he did not move. He tried to, but there wasn't any connection between what was left of his brain and his body. The mud was in his mouth, a thick, tasteless clabber that was choking him.

"I can't move, Charley."

"Sure you can."

"No, honest to God. I tried."

"No you didn't. Get up."

Trask tried again, but all that happened was that one arm slid a little in the ooze.

"I better sleep a little here."

"Everything you've got," Charley said. "Everything. Everything. Everything ..."

So he tried again and got his face out of the mud. He spat the stuff out of his mouth and swallowed what he could not spit out. Charley's weight on his back was unbearable.

"Everything . . . everything . . . everything . . ."

He was on his hands and knees. "That's all," he said.

"Crawl a ways," Charley told him. "Get up speed like a duck. Crawl."

He put his left hand forward; then the opposite knee;

"That's all right. Now the other one."

He put his other hand forward—

—and screamed—

"Just that burn," Charley said quietly. "Try it again."

He tried again.

"... everything ... everything ... everything ..."

It was like a little chant Charley was singing, and pretty soon Trask started to sing it too, panting it in time with his breathing, and he couldn't tell his voice from Charley's, but he was getting forward a little bit at a time while he was singing it in his head and whispering it as he crawled ...

"... everything ... everything ... everything ..."

... and it was funny how he couldn't feel his hand any more at all but he could see the stains he was leaving on the ground ...

"... dragging your back, Charley ..."

"... it's all right ..."

"... no more ... can't ..."

"... make it somehow make it somehow make it somehow ..."

"Grab the tree and pull yourself up."

"Charley, I can't ..."

"Pull."

"... can't ..."

"Pull!"

"... can't ... please, Charley, please don't make me do it, please Charley please please please ..."

"PULL!"

He did. "Wouldn't—wouldn't make it without you, Charley."

"Walk."

"... everything ... everything ... everything ... "

"... *oh God ... oh God ...*

move move move move move move

"darkagain?"

everything ... everything ... everything ... everything ...

Hands and voices, legs water—the sound of current—

"*Leave him* alone!"

Muttering frightened—"Kilchis . . . *kumtux . . . cooley cooley hyas hyak . . .*"

Hands again, darkness, cry like a child . . .

Great black bear ohjesus great black bear reaching reaching paws turning to hands touching God God God then, clearly: "*Mitlite nika house.*"

Lifting now not-black hands—brown—twisting falling—no—canoe, back of a man—back of a giant—black Kahnie paddling . . .

". . . everything . . . everything . . . everything . . ."

"We'll make it somehow." Very clear.

4

The smell of smoke and dried fish was in his nostrils, and his ears throbbed with the steady pounding of his own heart. He opened his eyes and saw drying-racks above him, filled with strips of salmon. The rack network wavered eerily, and he realized dully that they were lit by a fire somewhere.

He turned his head toward the light, and found the throbbing that seemed to fill his head was not his heart after all. At the other end of the lodge was a huge fire, with two lines of men facing each other across it. They were seated, and the line on his right held long poles, reaching up into the shadows of the ridge. The poles moved, thumping rhythmically on the ground. Some of the men in the left line—also seated—beat on small rawhide drums with the same monotonous rhythm of the poles. Several wore headdresses of shredded cedar bark, a head-circling crown with side pieces that fell like hair to the ground. Others had painted faces; the top red and black below. A heavy blue bar ran vertically down the center of the nose, and on either side a slightly narrower strip of blue ran through each eye and down on the cheek.

He lifted himself slightly on one elbow. He was at the back end of a lodge on the sleeping-platform, and with a sense of relief that almost made him weep again, he realized the mats beneath him were dry. As he shifted, his elbow touched something beside him, toward the wall, and he turned to look.

Kilchis lay there, his gigantic body in shadow. His hands were straight down at his sides, and his eyes were open. They did not move. He was as rigid as a fallen tree, and Trask thought he was dead. Then he saw the slow rise and fall of the great black chest and realized the tyee was in some kind of trance. The terrible dread of one-who-died was too strong in Indians to allow the body of a dead man to remain in a lodge anyway, he thought. They would go to any lengths to avoid touching a dead man.

The poles thumped and thumped, rising and falling in the firelight steadily, relentlessly, inevitable as the beating of a heart . . .

He put his head back down and closed his eyes.

Some time later he was wakened by a shrill scream. One of the painted men was standing before the fire, his legs spread wide and his arms straight out to the sides. He was between the fire and Trask, and cast a long, slowly moving shadow the length of the lodge and up on the wall. Dimly Trask could see the man's arms were trembling violently. The two seated rows peered up at him, squinting in the smoky light.

"Ayah! It is coming," the painted man chanted in a high voice.

"Ayah! It is coming." The lines of men repeated his words tonelessly. They watched the standing man intently, as though afraid to miss what he might say.

He ran quickly around the fire twice, hopping in what might have been a dance, leaped in the air.

"*Ya-ya-ya-ya-ya-ya-ya* . . ."

"*Ya-ya-ya-ya-ya-ya-ya* . . ." the chorus echoed. The poles moved, the dull, beating pace was never broken.

"There is a bird in the wind!"

"There is a bird in the wind."

"He makes a noise!"

"He makes a noise."

"Ay-ah-la!"

"Ay-ah-la."

The man sat down again abruptly, and the poles stamped in the dirt. It all seemed very far away.

When he woke again there was gray showing above the lifted plank at the ridge. The lines of men were still in place and the poles still pounded. It seemed to Trask he had lived all his life with the steady slow thumping of long poles against the dirt; it was more a part of him than his heart's rhythm.

He could see the huddled forms of sleeping men now, behind the two lines by the fire. Their figures were distorted by the waving dark shadows that swung and leaped with the fire. Even as he watched, one of the sleepers stirred and shook himself. He sat up and tapped one of the pole-wielders on the shoulder. That one jerked, as if suddenly wakened from a dream.

He handed the pole to the new man, who took up the rhythm without missing a beat. The first then stretched himself out behind the line and ceased to move.

Knowing how long the Indians could do without sleep during the making of ritual, Trask realized it must have been going on for several days or more. There was no sound in the lodge but the terrible beat-beat-beat of the poles. After a few minutes in which Trask watched uncomprehendingly another man staggered to his feet and stood swaying before the fire, barely able to stand. A woman scuttled out of the shadows and held his elbow until he steadied himself. Trask saw the man was ancient. His eyes were wild, and yet strangely blank. He shook off the woman, and she moved back into the shadows. The faces of the lined men turned slowly to watch the old one.

"*Ha-ya-ha-ya-ya!*" The old one's voice was creaky and broken.

"*Ha-ya-ha-ya-ya.*" When the chorus answered, Trask noted they imitated not only the old man's words, but his tone and inflection. From the anxious way in which they watched him, Trask realized they had no better knowledge than he of what the old one would say next.

Suddenly the old man began to dance, at first a slow, angular movement like the browsing of a crane, growing faster. He stamped on the ground and began to move behind the line of poles. He danced with energy that seemed unbelievable in such a feeble person, leaping into the air like a boy, throwing his arms around. He babbled crazily in some language Trask had never heard, and the chorus tried to follow him. The men in cedar-bark headdresses seemed to have no trouble, and Trask realized these were the professional singers, probably hired. The others did the best they could.

The poles pounded incessantly, until Trask thought his heart would be forced into the same beat.

Beside him Kilchis stirred slightly, restlessly. Trask turned, to meet the impersonal gaze of the great black tyee.

"Hya!" Kilchis growled, with a fierce exultation growing on his face. "Never have I searched so far. Come."

The black man sat up on the sleeping-platform, his expression a wild, animal vision of triumph. He reached out to take Trask's arm, and draw him upright.

"Your spirit has wandered very far," Kilchis said. "I sent my own to bring it back, and now—it is come. You must dance your spirit before the people, as the others are dancing."

Weakly, Trask allowed himself to come off the sleeping-ledge, fully expecting his knees to buckle when his feet touched the ground. They did not, and as he stood erect Trask felt more strength in his legs than he could remember.

The old man had finished dancing now, and all faces were turned to the two men at the end of the lodge. Kilchis moved slowly forward leaving Trask to stand by the sleeping-ledge. His mountainous form blotted out the fire from Trask, who stood in deep and somber shadow.

"The spirit has come back," Kilchis said.

"The spirit has come back," the chorus chanted after him. Each phrase of his chant was repeated, as they had repeated those of the dancers.

"This spirit is strong—ya, ya;
This spirit went a long way—ya, ya;
This spirit is one that is great—ya, ya . . ."

The poles pounded on the floor as the chorus echoed Kilchis' song, pounding, pounding, pounding . . .

"This spirit went to the salmon country—ya, ya;
This spirit went to the baby country—ya, ya;

This spirit went to the dead country—ya, ya;
Drawn by one-who-died—ya, ya;
Kilchis' spirit followed there—ya, ya, . . ."

The drums began to beat more strongly now, and the poles rose and fell faster. Kilchis told of the far places the spirit had been and how strong it was. He told of walking through the dead country, chasing the spirit of Trask that leaped like a great buck among the spirits, and finding it almost too strong to bring back.

He told how the spirit was so strong it had no fear of the dead, and the echo faltered a little; eyes turned warily to Trask with something of awe in them.

In time, everything before him blurred and coalesced; the chanting and the flickering of the fire and the pounding of the poles; became a dream through which he walked without volition.

He knew when the time had come for him to dance his spirit for the Killamook band, and he moved forward with the pounding of the poles and drums working in his blood. He did not remember dancing; nor speaking; but remembered the clear voice in the back of his mind just before he began.

Everything you've got. Everything . . . everything . . . everything . . .

He might have laughed then, knowing he could dance or speak or walk or crawl or any other thing he might ever have to do. For the power surged out of his belly and he felt the strength on him to do anything.

And he knew there was no country too rough but he could walk it; no trail too steep; no darkness too profound. As long as he could hear in his mind the voice that told him what he had to do, and what there was in him that he must give:

Everything
everything
everything

Chapter Twenty-six

H e thought he lay in Kilchis' lodge for several days after the dancing; but he could not be certain of the passage of time. The sky above the smoke vent was light and dark in sequence, but Trask did not count the times, nor could he even be certain the darkness was night at all. The storm outside rose and fell with as much—or as little—variation as the change from day to night.

Within the lodge it was always dark. Light and sound alike were strangely muffled; occurring somewhere just beyond his range of sight and hearing. The cedar planks precisely closed a space from which the clamor and confusion was kept out; inside, the air was almost liquid-thick. Time, thought, and movement slowed and gentled, until he might almost have floated between the bottom and the surface of some vast dark sea. For what seemed a long time he was not even able to distinguish clearly between waking and sleeping; caught often in some central cleft between the two where his mind was neither controlled nor uncontrolled, but existed in a neutral state. Perception and dreaming were indistinguishable, and "awake" a word with only a dimly remembered significance.

Kilchis brought him food from time to time, and Trask noted his presence almost indifferently; as the intrusion of a dream character. He neither knew nor cared where the great tyee was at other times. At first Kilchis simply left the bowls beside the sleeping-platform within Trask's easy reach. As time passed, he began to hesitate a little after setting down the food, and finally came to sit on the platform while Trask ate. He said nothing, but watched the white man's face. Trask was not unconscious of this scrutiny, but it did not affect him. He ate, and lay back, and after a time Kilchis left. Trask knew the black tyee would say nothing until he himself spoke; and he did not yet feel the necessity. He existed quietly, without restlessness, content to lie on the cattail mats and watch the beautiful sharp lines of the roof above him. He ate when food was brought and accepted it as a natural thing without disturbance of his passive mind.

From time to time Kilchis would change the dressing on Trask's hand. The poultice he applied was of grease melted with some other substance of a fresh and pungent odor. Trask thought it might be spruce gum. While the dressing was cool and pleasant, he did not feel he needed it; he was able to detach his mind from the pain with ease, and let it slide from him unnoticed as a leaf falls from a tree. It was a kind of control he had not often known. In time he found that all his perceptions were subject to the same easy control; and he came to enjoy it almost for its own sake, as a carpenter enjoys a sharp tool.

As he lay quiescent in the lodge, the focus of his mind drifted without the guidance of his will. As a child explores the reaches of a new-found cave, he worked along the huge dim passages of his mind and body; touching, wondering, watching, exploring. He found without surprise that both had been scoured clean in the ordeal; and tempered in the white heat through which he passed somewhere beyond the limits of his strength. He felt, as he explored, a newness; as he had been in the beginning, a vessel of worth waiting to be filled.

In this time of calm, images came to him with the clarity and unexpected suddenness of silver salmon flashing across dark bottoms. He frequently dreamed—or thought—of one recurring scene. He was haunted by this trivial dream-memory, and when the bright, clear image came he was unable to rid himself of it. He could not understand why it should obsess his sleeping mind as it did.

Returning from the Searching he had found the path blocked by a great fir; and in his desperation to move on had come up dead against it and tried to scratch it out of his way with his bleeding fingers. He could not have said how long he stood against that tree, sobbing deep in his chest and tearing at the bark with his bleeding hands. It had been only the calm, amused voice of Charley that stopped him at last.

"This tree wishes you no harm. Go around it in peace. You are hurting yourself."

Blindly, Trask stumbled off to the side, and had been amazed how easy it was in the end. It seemed very simple then to understand about the tree and himself. The traveling was a little easier after that, knowing it was not necessary to destroy each tree that blocked him. He had torn his hands badly on the fir, and realized dimly he had caused himself pain because he had not understood how it was with the tree. At first it made him angry, and he wanted to blame the tree.

"Turned upside down, Charley," he muttered. "Tree hurt me. Something. I can kill it, Charley. I can do that."

"You kill yourself," Charley told him, and Trask knew then it was true that the tree was himself. It was why his hands were torn.

This insanity of a memory traced an aimless, repetitive pattern across his mind as he lay in the lodge. At first, for no reason he knew, it made his heart beat faster and his breath come short. He could tell when this image was coming because of the sense of excitement he began to feel in his belly. But as he turned it over in his mind, the sense of urgency was gradually replaced by something, calmer and more stable. The alien strangeness diminished, and he made his peace with this crazily remembered tree. By slow degrees he absorbed the dream into himself, and the time came when he could call it up if he wished, or put it from him if he had no desire to see it. It was part of himself by then, and, with the other parts of himself, was responsive.

The image-tree was most pressing, the most insistent, though when it had been taken into him there were others. Sharp, discontinuous presences that flashed across his mind unexpectedly. He dealt with each in the same way. When the dream came, he accepted it; examined it; acknowledged its meaningfulness to him and, in time, absorbed it. He could tell when the process was completed, because the dream would come and go at his direction; before that time he had little control over its coming.

When the last of the dreams had been absorbed, he felt he was ready to come back.

The storm died suddenly in the night. One last clattering slash of rain against the lodge; then silence, like the pause between two breaths. The thick and sullen mass of cloud slid off into the hills and left the clean sky bright with moon and stars. Morning came clear, a hot and yellow sun skimming the mountain ridges and burning away the last of the valley fog.

Through cracks between the cedar planks thin beams of sunlight slid in, barring the opposite side of the floor with brightness. The reflection from the white swept sand was almost painful to Trask's eyes, accustomed so long to the gloomy darkness.

Kilchis came in at midmorning, carrying food. As he stooped through the entrance hole there was a flash of light behind him. Trask raised himself on one elbow to watch the long march of the tyee down the lodge. Raising his head made him slightly dizzy, but he steadied himself without effort.

Kilchis put the bowls down; sat on the step below the sleeping-platform.

"Klahowya, tyee," Trask said.

Kilchis leaned forward suddenly, as though he had been given permission, and studied Trask's face.

"Ah," he said finally. "The dreaming has passed." He straightened and nodded with satisfaction. Trask was only vaguely surprised.

"Yes," he said at last. "It has passed."

After a moment Kilchis asked, "Can you walk now?"

"I think so," Trask said. He swung his legs over the edge of the sleeping-platform and put his feet on the sitting-step. When the dizziness approached again, he put it away from him.

Standing was harder yet, but he did it, and stepped down to the white sand floor. His legs were much shakier than they had been before he danced for the band, but he was able to control them.

He went out through the elk-skin flap, blinking at the sudden sunlight and leaning against the lodge to steady himself. Kilchis followed him out, and the two walked slowly around to the bay side of the building. Trask looked out to sea, watching the breakers on the bar still snarling from the storm; curling green, dropping, bursting into spindrift that was whipped away across the surface by the steady breeze.

"Kah yaka," he said softly. "Where is he?"

Kilchis turned his head to look up the shoreline, and Trask followed his eyes. Perhaps a half-mile north of them was a small rocky point, and behind it an almost black wall of dark spruce. Shining distinctly against the forest was a tiny white sliver; a white-painted canoe, mounted on posts, with the sharp-edged prow pointed out to sea.

Trask began to walk unsteadily toward the beach.

"Not today," Kilchis said. "Tomorrow you will be stronger."

"Now."

Kilchis shrugged, and followed.

It took them a long time to walk up the beach; the best pace Trask could meet was slow. A few hundred yards from the burial canoe Kilchis turned abruptly and walked to the edge of the woods. There he sat, propping his back against a tree and staring out across the bay while Trask moved on. After a decent time, he turned to watch Trask's back as the white man climbed the short, steep bank of the point. Saw him stand for a moment, his body clearly outlined and distinct against the stark white of the slim canoe. Saw him slide slowly to his knees and rest his head against the supporting post.

Kilchis looked away, and put his mind on the sea and sky. He listened to the sobbing cry of gulls and wondered why a bird that flew so sweetly should carry so much pain.

2

The trip to the burial canoe was the longest Trask was able to make for several days. The fever—he thought it was the fever—had left him weak. After this one necessary journey he contented himself with going down to the beach at bathing time. When he first appeared he was welcomed by the men of the band without ostentation; he was simply absorbed into the groups that splashed happily in the water. He saw Illga there, for the first time since he had left on the Searching; but saw him only once. One of the young men went over to the slight figure and said something Trask could not make out. As he spoke the man gestured at Trask where he stood bathing. Illga stiffened angrily and snapped a reply. The other Killamook burst into gales of laughter, and was soon joined by others nearby. Illga, his face contorted with rage, left the beach, and Trask did not see him again at bathing time.

He felt no sense of triumph; he knew the band was in awe of him over a thing that was—in his own mind—nothing. The terrible dread of one-who-died was so strong in the Indians that Trask's return from the Searching was invested with unbelievable power in their eyes. Even Kilchis had mentioned that Trask must have had a strong vision to enable him to walk with one-who-died as brother with brother.

To Trask himself it showed only a hardness; a hardness he had once been proud of, but was no more. All his life had been based on this hostile kind of strength; a strength that viewed the world as a thing to master, to overcome, to fight. As a problem that might be solved by destroying. It seemed faintly ridiculous to him now; and he found it difficult to remember that a life could be based on such fear. There could, he thought, be no impulse to destruction that was not rooted in some terrible fear, and he was no longer afraid. A bitter price had been exacted for his fears, and for his dark compulsion to destroy what frightened him. More bitter for the fact that others had been forced to pay it. He wondered if a tamanawis man could foresee his own death, and then be unable to change it. If so, the tamanawis would be a curse too heavy to bear.

As his strength returned, he spent more of each day walking in the woods around the village. He was coming to be obsessed with the sensation of pure existence; but it was an existence he had not known. A richness, a fullness that were new to him.

At first he thought the fever had not entirely gone; that sickness still roiled his mind as the aftermath of storm could still be seen at sea. His eyes seemed somehow different, seeing with the abnormal clarity of fevered vision. He felt almost light-headed, as though his consciousness had swelled to take in more than his own life.

He remembered lying beneath the rocky shelf with the sharp, clean taste of expectancy in his mouth; watching the minutiae of the world take on a meaning he had not known. This sensation did not dim as the fever left him and he gained in strength; rather it increased, until it became the cardinal fact of his existence. Soon, the once eerie sense of being not separate from the world around him came to be normal and necessary. He could not imagine living without the deep sense of participation in everything he saw or heard or felt; participation in the pulse and breath and heart of the world; in the deepest center of his own existence.

All his senses shared the same bright clarity; the intensity of any simple act of perception was almost unbearable. The sheer brilliance of color was blinding; the sweet, clear tone of every sound came to him almost as a physical shock, making him catch his breath. The swinging glide of a gull came to have an almost-grasped significance that kept his mind hovering on the edge of joy.

Reticulated swells of ferns across the plain; a time-eroded face of weathered wood; the mingling net of needles on the forest floor; a smear of paint across a grained rock; the quick-smooth sliding of a cloud across the fretted surface of the sea; there was to all these things a richness and relation deeply sensed; felt so profoundly in the hidden reaches of his being that each facet of the world thus caught became at once a part of him and he of it.

His senses cast beyond their former scope, and what they caught was carried down more deeply to his center than experience had ever been. The clear precision of his body made the simple act of living so intense his mind had room for nothing more. The ground fog on his mind had burned away; a searing sun caught veils of mist and scorched them out of being.

He saw a world he had not seen before; a world made not for mastery but for living. Once seen it was a very simple thing to understand. The wonder was that he had been so blind.

One thing he knew; in pressing past the limits of endurance man could learn. Out of the scourging fire there came a sure and certain sense of depth; and Trask felt now that more was in this terrible joy than just a sense of self's dimension.

There were long hours when he wondered deeply about this certainty that came upon him; it was a thing he had not known. Restlessness he had known, and an insatiable curiosity, and a ceaseless searching for a thing he could not name. But not the calm and depth he felt now, that grew stronger and more sure each hour. There was enormous pleasure in simple existence, a depth of pleasure he had not believed possible. As he moved he felt his body like cool water flowing; the perfect and unvarying instrument of his mind.

Once before a thing had happened to him that filled him with a kind of wholly inexplicable strength; strength far beyond anything that seemed reasonable for the situation.

He and Russell, it had been. Trapping, wandering far down into Digger country; the territory of that almost subhuman band of Shoshones who sometimes seemed to exist on nothing more substantial than fear. There had been starving times for the trappers, then, down to scraping up roots; sticking their hands into an anthill and licking off the collection; crisping their moccasins and pieces of their shirts just to tantalize the pain in their bellies. Nearly three weeks of this and then Russell had staggered back into camp with news of meat; a dead horse, not yet too badly wolf-eaten. They had gorged themselves that night and in the morning his simple physical exuberance had been almost unbearable.

His body felt—alive, and his mind had been full and rich. The simple movement of his muscles had been incomparable pleasure, and he was more acutely aware of his body than when the hunger racked it.

It was the meat hunger, and it made a man feel shallow and helpless. When the meat came again, it brought a sense of excitement and strength that was wholly irrational. He felt like a god.

This was like that.

He walked at the edge of the forest with the consciousness of great pleasure in the moving of his legs, beautifully aware of the stretching and sliding of muscles under the skin.

The swinging of his arms was immense intrinsic joy; the tensions of his shoulders, the release, the perfect and inevitable sequence that built rhythms on the instrument of his body. He listened to the physical song, and knew it was his own and unique to himself. Each man had his own, compounded of the strength that flowed through him like a clear floodstream and the surging song the world sang around him. To the rhythms of this song each man moved through life, making his way better or worse according to how perfectly he heard; if only he could learn to hear, to sense, to know and understand the song his body sang in moving.

He was immersed in the pure exuberance of perfect and complete perception of his body in its deepest reaches. He moved his shoulders slightly, feeling the roughness of his shirt against the skin, feeling the pull-release of tension on his throat. The wind came off the sea, swinging up the beach and tugging gently at his beard. It seemed no more apart from him than his breath, and he accepted the gentle throbbing pressure with the same knowledge and understanding he had of his own breathing; accepted it without anxiety or approval; as something which existed, a part of the world, a part of his living, a part of himself.

Something surged up inside him, catching at his throat, swelling in his chest. He breathed deeply, feeling in his temples the beating of his heart, the rhythmic swelling of his blood. His body was shaken by a sudden coursing shock.

He steadied himself, reaching out to touch a tree, and suddenly knew with a clear and present knowledge why the Indian feller-of-trees presented his tools to the tree and promised it new life: "Forgive me, Brother," ran the code. "I will make you live again."

An exultation gripped him, bursting out of him with the bright, sudden sharpness of the sun. He turned and began to walk into the forest.

As the village was lost from sight behind him, he began to walk more quickly. Faster and faster until his feet would no longer keep the walking stride. He broke into a run, unable to slow himself, and the trees slipped by on either side like shadows darting from a sudden light.

The sunlight flashed and glittered in patches around him, falling sharply down between the leaves, sprinkling the forest floor with drops of gold. The flashing of the sun and shadow across his eyes was a physical shock.

He ran until the breath came sharp and quick in his throat; until his chest could expand no more; until the muscles of his thighs were tight and hot. Suddenly he broke into a clearing flooded with light. So great was the sudden intensity of light he faltered.

He looked around the clearing, feeling the great gasping breaths rack his chest, feeling the sharp texture of the streaming sun, feeling the richness of the trees and soil, the terrifying exhilaration of the sky and sun; feeling the growth of life itself.

He threw himself headlong and buried his face in the carpet of pine needles, becoming part of the forest floor. The sun warmed him and dizzied him with its beauty.

At the edge of the clearing a startled squirrel leaped sideways; then began to chitter and spit in monstrous indignation. Trask rose to his knees and listened in fascination until a door within him opened and he began to laugh.

The more he laughed the more the fierce and burning joys possessed him; the more the squirrel scolded. The laughter poured out of him like a tide in flood, spreading around him in the clearing, echoing back into the woods, and rising into the sun. He roared with simple delight, bellowed until he gasped for breath and tears poured down his cheeks. He doubled over, recovered, and began again until there was no sound in all the world but clear, clean, godlike exultation.

Trask lifted his face to the sky while tears of joy streamed down his face and wet his beard. He spread his nostrils wide to taste the world; it was sweet with pines and the sea, and the day was fair.